MICHAEL KORYTA

THE CYPRESS HOUSE

Hodder & Stoughton Ltd
338 Euston Road
London NW1 3BH
www.hodder.co.uk

HODDER

First published in Great Britain in 2011 by Hodder & Stoughton
An Hachette UK company

I

Copyright © Michael Koryta 2011

A CIP catalogue record for this title is available from the British Library.

B Format ISBN 978 0 340 99827 4
A Format ISBN 978 1 444 72362 5

Printed and bound in the UK by CPI Mackays, Chatham ME5 8TD

Hodder & Stoughton policy is to use papers that are natural, renewable and
recyclable products and made from wood grown in sustainable forests.
The logging and manufacturing processes are expected to conform
to the environmental regulations of the country of origin.

For David Hale Smith and Michael Pietsch:
It's a team game, and I'm deeply grateful for the wisdom,
encouragement, and, above all else, faith.

Part One

SOJOURNERS

I

THEY'D BEEN ON THE TRAIN for five hours before Arlen
Wagner saw the first of the dead men.

To that point it had been a hell of a nice ride. Hot, sure, and
progressively more humid as they passed out of Alabama and
through southern Georgia and into Florida, but nice enough all
the same. There were thirty-four on board the train who were
bound for the camps in the Keys, all of them veterans with the
exception of the nineteen-year-old who rode at Arlen's side, a boy
from Jersey by the name of Paul Brickhill.

They'd all made a bit of conversation at the outset, exchanges
of names and casual barbs and jabs thrown around in that way
men have when they are getting used to one another, all of them
figuring they'd be together for several months to come, and then
things quieted down. Some slept, a few started card games, others just sat and watched the countryside roll by, fields going misty
with late-summer twilight and then shapeless and dark as the
moon rose like a watchful specter. Arlen, though, Arlen just listened. Wasn't anything else to do, because Paul Brickhill had an
outboard motor where his mouth belonged.

As the miles and minutes passed, Brickhill alternated between explaining things to Arlen and asking him questions. Nine times out of ten, the boy answered his own questions before Arlen could so much as part his lips with a response. Brickhill had been a quiet kid when the two of them first met months earlier in Alabama, and back then Arlen believed him to be shy. What he hadn't counted on was the way the boy took to talk once he felt comfortable with someone. Evidently, he'd grown damn comfortable with Arlen.

As the wheels hammered along the rails of northern Florida, Paul Brickhill was busy telling Arlen all of the reasons this was going to be a hell of a good hitch. Not only was there the bridge waiting to be built, but all that sunshine and blue water and boats that cost more than most homes. They could do some fishing, maybe catch a tarpon. Paul'd seen pictures of tarpon that were near as long as the boats that landed them. And there were famous people in the Keys, celebrities of every sort, and who was to say they wouldn't run into a few, and...

Around them the men talked and laughed, some scratching out letters to loved ones back home. Wasn't anyone waiting on a letter from Arlen, so he just settled for a few nips on his flask and tried to find some sleep despite the cloaking warmth and the stink of sweating men. It was too damn hot.

Brickhill finally fell silent, as if he'd just noticed that Arlen was sitting with his eyes closed and had stopped responding to the conversation. Arlen let out a sigh, grateful for the respite. Paul was a nice enough kid, but Arlen had never been one for a lot of words where a few would do.

The train clattered on, and though night had settled, the heat didn't break. Sweat still trickled along the small of Arlen's back and held his hair to his forehead. He wished he could fall asleep; these hot miles would pass faster then. Maybe another pull on the flask would aid him along.

He opened his eyes, tugged the lids up sleepily, and saw a hand of bone.

He blinked and sat up and stared. Nothing changed. The hand held five playing cards and was attached to a man named Wallace O'Connell, a veteran from Georgia who was far and away the loudest man in this company. He had his back turned, engaged in his game, so Arlen couldn't see his face. Just that hand of bone.

No, Arlen thought, *no, damn it, not another one.*

The sight chilled him but didn't shock him. It was far from the first time.

He's going to die unless I can find a way to stop it, Arlen thought with the sad, sick resignation of a man experienced with such things. *Once we get down to the Keys, old Wallace O'Connell will have a slip and bash his head in on something. Or maybe the poor bastard can't swim, will fall into those waves and sink beneath them and I'll be left with this memory same as I've been left with so many others. I'd warn him if I could, but men don't heed such warnings. They won't let themselves.*

It was then that he looked up, away from Wallace under the flickering lights of the train car, and saw skeletons all around him.

They filled the shadows of the car, some laughing, some grinning, some lost to sleep. All with bone where flesh belonged. The few who sat directly under a light still wore their skin, but their eyes were gone, replaced by whirls of gray smoke.

For a moment, Arlen Wagner forgot to breathe. Went cold and dizzy and then sucked in a gasp of air and straightened in the seat.

They were going to have a wreck. It was the only thing that made a bit of sense. This train was going to derail and they were all going to die. Every last one of them. Because Arlen had seen this before, and knew damn well what it meant, and knew that —

Paul Brickhill said, "Arlen?"

Arlen turned to him. The overhead light was full on the boy's face, keeping him in a circle of brightness, the taut, tanned skin of a young man who spent his days under the sun. Arlen looked into his eyes and saw swirling wisps of smoke. The smoke rose in tendrils and fanned out and framed the boy's head while filling Arlen's with terrible recollections.

"Arlen, you all right?" Paul Brickhill asked.

He wanted to scream. Wanted to scream and grab the boy's arm but was afraid it would be cold slick bone under his touch.

We're going to die. We're going to come off these rails at full speed and pile into those swamp woods, with hot metal tearing and shattering all around us...

The whistle blew out shrill in the dark night, and the train began to slow.

"We got another stop," Paul said. "You look kind of sickly. Maybe you should pour that flask out."

The boy distrusted liquor. Arlen wet his lips and said, "Maybe," and looked around the car at the skeleton crew and felt the train shudder as it slowed. The force of that big locomotive was dropping fast, and now he could see light glimmering outside the windows, a station just ahead. They were arriving in some backwater stop where the train could take on coal and the men would have a chance to get out, stretch their legs, and piss. Then they'd be aboard again and winging south at full speed, death ahead of them.

"Paul," Arlen said, "you got to help me do a bit of convincing here."

"What are you talking about?"

"We aren't getting back on this train. Not a one of us."

6

2

THEY PILED OUT OF THE CARS and onto the station platform, everyone milling around, stretching or lighting cigarettes. It was getting on toward ten in the evening, and though
the sun had long since faded, the wet heat lingered. The boards
of the platform were coated with swamp mud dried and trampled into dust, and out beyond the lights Arlen could see silhou-
etted fronds lying limp in the darkness, untouched by a breeze.
Backwoods Florida. He didn't know the town and didn't care;
regardless of name, it would be his last stop on this train.

He hadn't seen so many apparitions of death at one time since
the war. Maybe leaving the train wouldn't be enough. Could be
there was some sort of virus in the air, a plague spreading unseen
from man to man the way the influenza had in '18, claiming lives
faster than the reaper himself.

"What's the matter?" Paul Brickhill asked, following as Arlen
stepped away from the crowd of men and tugged his flask from
his pocket. Out here the sight was enough to set Arlen's hands to
shaking — men were walking in and out of the shadows as they
moved through the cars and down to the station platform,

7

slipping from flesh to bone and back again in a matter of seconds, all of it a dizzying display that made him want to sit down and close his eyes and drink long and deep on the whiskey.

"Something's about to go wrong," he said.

"What do you mean?" Paul said, but Arlen didn't respond, staring instead at the men disembarking and realizing something — the moment they stepped off the train, their skin slid back across their bones, knitting together as if healed by the wave of some magic wand. The swirls of smoke in their eye sockets vanished into the hazy night air. It was the train. Yes, whatever was going to happen was going to happen to that train.

"Something's about to go wrong," he repeated. "With our train. Something's going to go bad wrong."

"How do you know?"

"I just *do,* damn it!"

Paul looked to the flask, and his eyes said what his words did not.

"I'm not drunk. Haven't had more than a few swallows."

"What do you mean, something's going to go wrong?" Paul asked again.

Arlen held on to the truth, felt the words heavy in his throat but couldn't let them go. It was one thing to see such horrors; it was worse to try and speak of them. Not just because it was a difficult thing to describe but because no one ever believed. And the moment you gave voice to such a thing was the moment you charted a course for your character that you could never alter. Arlen understood this well, had known it since boyhood.

But Paul Brickhill had sat before him with smoke the color of an early-morning storm cloud hanging in his eyes, and Arlen was certain what that meant. He couldn't let him board that train again.

"People are going to die," he said.

Paul Brickhill leaned his head back and stared.

"We get back on that train, people are going to die," Arlen said. "I'm sure of it."

He'd spent many a day trying to imagine this gift away. To fling it from him the way you might a poisonous spider caught crawling up your arm, and long after the chill lingered on your flesh you'd thank the sweet hand of Providence that you'd been given the opportunity to knock the beast away. Only he'd never been given the opportunity. No, the stark sight of death had stalked him, trailed him relentlessly. He knew it when he saw it, and he knew it was no trick of the light, no twist of bad liquor upon the mind. It was prophecy, the gift of foresight granted to a man who'd never wished for it.

He was reluctant to say so much as a word to any of the other men, knowing the response he'd receive, but this was not the sort of thing that could be ignored.

Speak loud and sharp, he thought, *just like you did on the edge of a battle, when you had to get 'em to listen, and listen fast.*

"Boys," he said, getting at least a little of the old muster into his tone, "listen up, now."

The conversations broke off. Two men were standing on the step of the train car, and when they turned, skull faces studied him.

"I think we best wait for the next train through," he said. "There's bad trouble aboard this one. I'm sure of it."

It was Wallace O'Connell who broke the long silence that followed.

"What in the hell you talking about, Wagner?" he said, and immediately there was a chorus of muttered agreement.

"Something's wrong with this train," Arlen said. He stood tall, did his damnedest to hold their eyes.

"You know this for a fact?" O'Connell said.

"I know it."

"How do you know? And what's wrong with it?"

"I can't say what's wrong with it. But something is. I got a . . . sense for these things."

A slow grin crept across O'Connell's face. "I've known some leg-pullers," he said, "but didn't figure you for one of them. Don't got the look."

"Damn it, man, this ain't no joke."

"You got a *sense* something's wrong with our train, and you're telling us it ain't no joke?"

"Knew a widow back home who was the same way," spoke up another man from the rear of the circle. He was a slim, wiry old guy with a nose crooked from many a break. Arlen didn't know his name — hell, he didn't know most of their names, and that was part of the problem. Aside from Paul there wasn't a man in the group who'd known Arlen for any longer than this train ride.

"Yeah?" O'Connell said. "Trains talked to her, too?"

"Naw. She had the sense, just like he's talking about. 'Cept she got her sights from owls and moon reflections and shit like you couldn't even imagine."

This new man was grinning wide, and O'Connell was matching it. He said, "She was right all the time, of course?"

"Of course," the man said, and let out a cackle. "Why, wasn't but nine year ago she predicted the end of days was upon us. Knew it for a fact. Was going to befall us by that winter. I can't imagine she was wrong, I just figured I missed being raptured up and that's how I ended up here with all you sinful sons of bitches."

The crowd was laughing now, and Arlen felt heat creeping into his face, thoughts of his father and the shame that had chased him from his boyhood home threatening his mind now. Behind him Paul Brickhill was standing still and silent, about the only one in the group who wasn't at least chuckling. There was a man near Wallace O'Connell whose smile seemed forced, uneasy, but even he was going along with the rest of them.

"I might ask for a tug on whatever's in that jug of your'n," O'Connell said. "It seems to be a powerful syrup."

"It's not the liquor you're hearing," Arlen said. "It's the truth. Boys, I'm telling you, I seen things in the war just like I am tonight, and every time I did, men died."

"Men died every damn day in the war," O'Connell said. The humor had drained from his voice. "And we all seen it — not just you. Some of us didn't crack straight through from what we seen. Others" — he made a pointed nod at Arlen — "had a mite less fortitude. Now save your stories for somebody fool enough to listen to them. Rest of us don't need the aggravation. There's work at the end of this line, and we all need it."

The men broke up then, drifted back to their own conversations, casting Arlen sidelong stares. Arlen felt a hand on his arm and nearly whirled and threw his fist without looking, shame and fear riding him hard now. It was only Paul, though, tugging him away from the group.

"Arlen, you best ease up."

"Be damned if I will. I'm telling you —"

"I understand what you're telling us, but it just doesn't make sense. Could be you got a touch of fever, or —"

Arlen reached out and grabbed him by his shirt collar. Paul's eyes went wide, but he didn't reach for Arlen's hand, didn't move at all as Arlen spoke to him in a low, harsh voice.

"You had smoke in your eyes, boy. I don't give a damn if you couldn't see it or if none of them could, it was there, and it's the sign of your death. You known me for a time now, and you ask yourself, how often has Arlen Wagner spoken foolish words to me? How often has he seemed addled? You ask yourself that, and then you ask yourself if you want to die tonight."

He released the boy's collar and stepped back. Paul lifted a hand and wiped it over his mouth, staring at Arlen.

"You trust me, Brickhill?" Arlen said.

"You know I do."

"Then listen to me now. If you don't ever listen to another man again for the rest of your life, listen to me now. Don't get back on that train."

The boy swallowed and looked off into the darkness. "Arlen, I wouldn't disrespect you, but what you're saying…there's no way you could know that."

"I can see it," Arlen said. "Don't know how to explain it, but I can *see* it."

Paul didn't answer. He looked away from Arlen, back at the others, who were watching the boy with pity and Arlen with disdain.

"Here's one last question for you to ask of yourself," Arlen said. "Can you afford to be wrong?"

Paul stared at him in silence as the train whistle blew and the men stomped out cigarettes and fell into a boarding line. Arlen watched their flesh melt from their bones as they went up the steps.

"Don't let that fool bastard convince you to stay here, boy," Wallace O'Connell bellowed as he stepped up onto the train car, half of his face a skull, half the face of a strong man who believed he was fit to take on all comers. "Ain't nothing here but alligators, and unless you want to be eating them come dinner tomorrow, or them eating you, you best get aboard."

Paul didn't look in his direction. Just kept staring at Arlen. The locomotive was chugging now, steam building, ready to tug its load south, down to the Keys, down to the place the boy wanted to be.

"You're serious," he said.

Arlen nodded.

"And it's happened before?" Paul said. "This isn't the first time?"

"No," Arlen said. "It is not the first time."

3

THE FIRST TIME Arlen Wagner saw death was in the Belleau Wood. That was the bloodiest battle the Marines had ever encountered, a savage showdown requiring repeated assaults before the parcel of forest and boulders finally fell under American control, and the bodies were piled high by the end. The sight of corpses was not the new experience for Arlen, whose father had served as undertaker in the West Virginia hill town where he was raised, a place where violence, mining accidents, and fever regularly sent men and women Isaac Wagner's way to be fitted into their coffins. No, in the moonlight over the Marne River on a June night in 1918, Arlen saw something far different from a corpse—he saw the dead among the living.

They'd made an assault on the Wood that day, marching through a waist-high wheat field directly into machine-gun fire. For the rest of his life, the sight of tall, windswept wheat would put a shiver through Arlen. Most of the men in the first waves had been slaughtered outright, but Arlen and other survivors had been driven south, into the trees and a tangle of barbwire. The machine guns pounded on, relentless, and those who didn't fall beneath them grappled hand to hand with German soldiers who shouted oaths at them in a foreign tongue while bayonets clashed and knives plunged.

By evening the Marines had sustained the highest casualties in their history, but they also had a hold, however tenuous, in Belleau Wood. Arlen was on his belly beside a boulder as midnight came on, and with it a German counterattack. As the enemy approached he'd felt near certain that this skirmish would be his last; he couldn't continue to survive battles like these, not when so many had fallen all around him throughout the day. That rain of bullets couldn't keep missing him forever.

This was his belief at least, until the Germans appeared as more than shadows, and what he saw then kept him from so much as lifting his rifle.

They were skeleton soldiers.

He could see skulls shining in the pale moonlight where faces belonged, hands of white bone clutching rifle stocks.

He was staring, entranced, when the American gunners opened up. Opened up and mowed them down, sliced the vicious Hun bastards to pieces. All around him men lifted their rifles and fired, and Arlen just lay there without so much as a finger on the trigger, scarcely able to draw a breath.

A trick of the light, he told himself as dawn rose heavy with mist and the smell of cooling and drying blood, the moans of the wounded as steady now as the gunfire had been earlier. What he'd seen was the product of moonlight partnered with the trauma from a day of unspeakable bloodshed. Surely that was enough to wreak havoc on his mind. On anyone's mind.

There were some memories in his head then, of course, some thoughts of his father, but he kept them at bay, and as the sun broke through the mist he'd done a fine job of convincing himself that this was nothing but the most horrifying of hallucinations.

It was midafternoon and the Marines were readying another

assault, seeking to push deeper into the Wood, when he turned to two of the men he'd known best over there, known best and liked best, good boys who fought hard, and saw that their eyes were gone. The flesh remained on their faces but their eyes were gone, the sockets filled with gray smoke that leaked out and formed wreaths around their heads.

Both of them were dead within the hour.

For the rest of the war it was like that—bones showing in the night battles, smoke-filled eye sockets smiling at him during the daylight. That promise of death was all he ever got. Never did a ghost linger with him after the last breath rattled out of tortured lungs, never did a phantom version of one of those lost men return in the night to offer him some sense of the reason behind it all. No voices whispered to him in the dark, no invisible hand guided him in battle or menaced him in sleep.

He spoke of it only once, knew immediately from the looks exchanged around him that if he kept telling the tale he'd soon be hospital-bound with all the other poor shell-shocked bastards who gibbered on about things far from the grasp of reality. Arlen kept his mouth shut and kept seeing the same terrible sights.

As the war went on, he discovered some of them could be saved. They would perish if left to fight alone, but if he could keep them down and out of the fire line, sometimes they made it through. Not often enough, though. Not nearly often enough. And there were so, so many of them.

After the armistice the premonitions ceased, and for a time Arlen thought it was done. Then he'd walked into an Army hospital back in the States to visit a buddy and had seen smoke-eyes everywhere he looked, stumbled back out of the place without ever finding his friend. He'd gone to the first speakeasy he could find and tipped whiskey glasses back until his own vision was too clouded and blurred to see smoke even if someone lit a match right in front of his face.

He'd worked in a railyard for a time, had seen a man with bone hands and a gleaming skull face laughing over a joke just minutes before the chains on a log car snapped and he was crushed beneath one of the timbers. The last time Arlen ventured back into West Virginia — it wasn't a place of warm memories and welcoming embraces — he'd gone hunting with a friend from the war who'd turned into a bitter drunk with a stump where his left hand belonged. One-handed or not he'd wanted to go hunting, and Arlen had agreed, then saw the smoke swirling in the man's eye sockets about thirty seconds before he stepped into a snarl of loose brush and a rattlesnake struck him in the calf, just below the knee. Arlen had shot the snake, whose thick coiled body would've gone every bit of five feet stretched out full, and cut the wound to bleed the venom, but still the smoke wouldn't leave those eyes, grew thicker and darker as Arlen dragged his old friend back to town, and he was dead by noon the next day.

So there were incidents, but in this warless world they were far less common, and he worked hard at burying the memories just the same as they'd buried the men who created them. Drinking helped. Even through Prohibition, Arlen always found a way to keep his flask filled.

Like many of the men back from the war, he'd wandered in the years that followed, taking work when and where he could, unable or unwilling to settle. When the Bonus Marchers had moved on Washington, demanding wages for veterans, only to be driven away with tear gas, he'd watched the papers idly, expecting nothing. But after Roosevelt allowed that some veterans might join his Civilian Conservation Corps, out to save the nation one tree at a time, Arlen had some interest. Dollars were getting scarcer, and the idea of laboring outdoors instead of down in a coal mine or inside a foundry sounded mighty fine.

In the end he'd signed on in Alabama as what they called a

local experienced man. It was CCC labor, same as any else, but he didn't have to join up with one of the veteran companies. Instead, he was tasked with providing instruction to a bunch of boys from New York and Jersey, city kids who'd never swung an ax or handled a saw. Was the sort of thing that could try some men's patience, but Arlen didn't mind teaching, and just about anyone could be shown how to drive a nail or square an edge.

Paul Brickhill, though...he was something special. The closest thing to a mechanical genius Arlen had ever seen. A tall, dark-haired boy with serious eyes and an underfed frame, same as almost all the rest of them, he had not the first bit of experience with carpentry, but what he did have was the mind. The first thing that caught Arlen's attention was how quickly the boy learned. In all those early days of instruction, Arlen never repeated himself to Brickhill. Not once. You said it, he absorbed it and applied it. Still, he'd appeared little more than a reliable boy and a quick study until they got to work building a shelter house. They'd laid masonry from foundation to windowsill and Arlen was checking over the rounded logs they'd set above the stone when he caught Brickhill changing his measurements for the framing of the roof.

He'd been ready to light the boy up—took some first-class ignorance to dare pick up a pencil and fool with Arlen's numbers, make a change that could set them back days—when he looked down and studied the sketch and saw that the boy was right. Arlen had the angle off on the beams. He would've discovered it himself once they got to laying boards, but he hadn't seen it in his measurements.

"How'd you know that?" he asked.

Brickhill opened his mouth and closed it, frowned, then steepled his hands in the shape of a roof and then flattened them out and said, "I just...saw it, that's all."

It wasn't the sort of thing a boy who'd never built a roof should see. Not a fifteen-degree difference without a single board set.

They got to talking a bit after that. Arlen had been in the

habit of telling the juniors only what was needed — cut here, nail there — but Brickhill wanted to know more, and Arlen told him what he could. Didn't take long to see that the boy's innate understanding of building was such that Arlen's experience didn't seem all that impressive. A few months later it was at Brickhill's suggestion that Arlen approached the camp foreman with the idea of constructing a three-hundred-foot-long chute to get concrete down to a dam they were building. The chute worked, and saved them who knew how many days.

It was getting on toward the end of summer and things were winding down at Flagg Mountain when Brickhill's six-month hitch finished up. He intended to reenlist — expected he'd continue to for some time, long as they'd let him, he told Arlen — but he didn't want to stay with his company, which was set for a transfer from Alabama to Nevada.

"I got something else in mind," Brickhill said. "But I figure it's going to take your help to get me there."

The boy proceeded to inform him, in exorbitant detail, of a new CCC project in the Florida Keys. They were building a highway bridge that would conquer the ocean, same grand thing that Henry Flagler had done with the railroad. Labor for the project was being provided by the Veterans Work Program, but the CCC had just taken over the management. As they didn't have a junior camp down there, it was going to take a bit of work for Paul to join up. Considering how Arlen was an ex-Marine, same as the local officer in charge of enlistment, and might have some pull, Paul was looking for help.

Arlen agreed to it, and what he told the enlistment officer had been true enough — the boy needed to be working on such an endeavor, not planting trees and clearing drainage ditches in Nevada.

"What you have here," he'd said, "is the next great engineer this country will see."

It didn't fly. Seems they'd had trouble in the camps down there, and the old Veterans Work Program was becoming something of a black eye thanks to circulating national news reports about the violent and troubled men who populated the camps in the Keys.

"You want to go down there, we could use you, Arlen," the enlistment officer had said. "Matter of fact, I'd appreciate it were you willing. We need some steady men in those camps. But we won't be sending juniors."

Arlen figured that verdict would close the discussion with Brickhill. It didn't. The boy simply said that if Arlen accepted the transfer and went south, he'd tag along and talk his way onto the project. It was, Arlen had discovered, a situation typical of the boy. He had a sort of focused determination you just didn't come across much, and when you did, it tended to be held by men who got things done. Paul Brickhill would surely be such a man.

"Once I'm down there, I bet the tune changes," Paul promised. "They need workers. And if it doesn't sort out, I'll go on to one of the other Florida camps and reenlist."

"Might be so," Arlen said, "but that requires me going as well, and I ain't looking to transfer, son. This is my camp."

"Why?"

Well, because he'd happened to be in the area when he hired on. It was that simple. A local experienced man, that was what they called him, but truth was he was hardly more local than the boys he supervised. Experienced, yes. Local, no. Wasn't any place where Arlen could be considered a local.

"You don't have any reason not to head down there," Paul said. "You're not one with family around here, or..."

He stopped as if fearing he'd said something offensive, but Arlen just shook his head.

"No, I don't have any family here."

Here, or anywhere. The work at Flagg Mountain was nearing

a close—there was a reason these boys were about to be trans-
ferred west—and it might be interesting, as Brickhill suggested,
to work on an ocean bridge...

That was how Arlen Wagner came to be sitting beside a boy
from New Jersey in a muggy train car on the last day of August
1935.

For a time after the train had left, they just stood there in the
glow of the station platform and stared off down the dark rails.
The flat air billowed up one long gust and pushed the trapped
wet heat out of the woods and into their faces, and Arlen
dropped his hand for his flask and then stopped when Paul's eyes
followed the motion. He didn't want the kid to think this was all
due to liquor. Wasn't drinking that caused it, was drinking that
could ease it.

"All right," Paul said at length, "we aren't going to die on that
train tonight. We also aren't going to get anywhere on it. So
unless you intend to spend the night right here..."

"Hold on. We'll find someone to ask."

There was a station attendant, a stooped man with a squint
that seemed permanent, who met all of Arlen's questions with
the same statement: *I don't understand—why didn't you get back
on your train?*

At last he was made to accept the idea, if not understand it,
and informed them that there was a boardinghouse five miles up
the highway.

"Look here," he said, "why go five miles away to spend the
night if you're not looking to stay around here anyhow? Now
that you got off your train, where is it you're bound?"

That was a hell of a question. Paul looked at Arlen, a challenging look.

"Next train to the Keys?" he said.

"If'n you still want to go to the Keys," the attendant said, "why in the hell didn't you stay on your damn train?"

Arlen ran a hand over his face. The next train for the Keys might well be safe, but it might well not. How could he explain that to the boy? All he knew for certain was that those men they'd just left were heading toward death. And if somehow he'd been wrong, then he wasn't real eager to chase after them, set up in a camp down where every man looked at Arlen and chuckled and whispered.

"You said you're with the CCC?" the station attendant said.

"That's right," Paul said.

"Well, there's a camp down in Hillsborough County, out toward Tampa, and I could get you on a train headed that way tomorrow afternoon. Bunch of you boys are down there. Working on a park."

"We aren't heading to a park," Paul said. "We're going to build a bridge. A highway bridge. In the Keys."

"Well, don't know that you can get on another train to the Keys till late tomorrow. If you're still headed that way, then why did you—"

Arlen interrupted him and pulled Paul aside.

"Here's the problem, as I see it," he said, fumbling out a cigarette and lighting it. "It's not just a matter of finding another train. It's a veterans' camp, not juniors, you know that. They didn't want you down there in the first place. Now those fellows are going to show up ahead of us and tell this tale, and we're going to have ourselves a reputation before we arrive. Understand?"

Paul gave him a long look, one that said, *You're going to be the one they've heard tales about, not me,* but he didn't let the look turn into words.

"So there you're going to be," Arlen said, "in a camp where you don't belong, and now they'll see you coming and see a problem. That's my fault, not yours, but it's the fact of the matter, son. I wasn't sure I could get you a hitch down there to begin with. Won't be near as easy now. So could be time we think about a different direction."

All of this sounded like wheedling even to Arlen, and it dropped Paul Brickhill's face into a sullen frown. This was the first time in their short acquaintance that Arlen had actually seen him show displeasure.

"We had it all set and planned," Paul said. "You got a worry with that train, okay. We need to get on another one, though!"

"I don't know," Arlen said. "Let's just hold on a minute here, all right? I'm not sure of what we need to do now."

What Arlen wanted, now that they were off the train, was to head in the opposite direction, try to forget this had ever happened. He'd drifted on his own for so many years and it was so much easier to do that. Now he had Paul with him, and with every word that came out of the boy's mouth Arlen wanted to walk off alone, the way he always had before.

"Not sure?" Paul echoed in disbelief. "Arlen, shoot, there's no question about it! We're due in the Keys, and we better find the next train!"

That fed Arlen the inspiration he required. The kid was ardent about rules, one of those who just shook and rattled at the idea of balking orders. He was arguing now because Arlen had been trying to convince him instead of giving him the boss voice and the boss attitude.

"Look here," he said, "ain't going to be a debate held. Fact is, we got off the train and changed the plan. Something about that you don't understand? You too dull-minded to realize that your pretty little schedule just got altered, boy? Not going to be a damn thing decided tonight, because there's no more trains passing through. So let's get on to this roadhouse and find a bed for the night."

Paul wanted to argue. He scowled again and then wet his lips and lifted his head as if a retort would be forthcoming. Arlen hit him with the stare then, a partner to the voice, perfected in places he'd rather not remember, and the kid couldn't hold his eyes.

"He said the boardinghouse was five miles away," Paul muttered.

"At what point between here and Alabama," Arlen said, "did you lose the use of your legs?"

4

It was a long, dark walk. The highway was bordered with scrub pines and tall grasses that rustled even when the wind was flat, and the summer night pressed down on them like a pair of strong hands, made each step feel like ten. They were both lugging bags, tossed to them by a sneering Wallace O'Connell as the train pulled away. They'd been at it for an hour, had probably gone four miles, when a car came up behind them and slowed. Cars had been passing occasionally, maybe five during the whole time they'd been walking, but this was the first that had slowed. Neither Arlen nor Paul had stuck out a thumb, and though the boy said, "Hey, they're stopping!" with delight in his voice, Arlen dropped his bags and put a hand in his pants pocket, near his knife. There were different reasons a car would stop for strangers on a lonely midnight highway, and some drifted far from acts of kindness.

The car was a newer-model sedan with gleaming chrome and whitewall tires. The window cranked down, and the driver called, "'Lo there." Cigarette smoke rolled out in a haze.

"Hello."

"I see two men with bags walking down this road at this hour, I figure they're either lost beyond hope or headed to Pearl's."

"Pearl's the name of a roadhouse farther up this highway?"

"Not but a mile ahead."

"That's good to hear," Arlen said. "Thanks. We'll carry on now."

"Why walk that last mile when you can ride?"

Arlen didn't much want that, but Paul stepped up close and said, "Yeah, why walk when we can ride? This is an Auburn."

"The kid knows sense when he hears it," the man with the shadowed face said, and then he slapped the side of the driver's door. "And he knows cars — this is indeed an Auburn, and it moves like you won't believe. Climb on in."

So they climbed in. The car was clean and new, and Paul was clearly impressed, running his palm over the seat and looking around with appreciation.

"Say, this is nice. The twelve cylinder, isn't it?"

"It is. Fastest damn car I've ever held the wheel of." To demonstrate, he accelerated — hard. The car's engine gave a throaty howl and they lunged forward. Paul gave a chuckle and the driver grinned. Tall guy, lean, with big knobby hands wrapped around the steering wheel.

"What's your name, friend?" Arlen said.

"Sorenson. Walt Sorenson." He tucked the cigarette back into his mouth and reached a hand out. Arlen clasped it, and then Paul, offering their own names.

"Wouldn't ordinarily so much as slow for any poor soul walking on this road at night," Sorenson said. "I'm in no hurry to have a knife stuck in my back."

Arlen released his hand from the knife in his pocket.

"Bad area?" he said.

"Isn't everyplace after the sun goes down? Can't trust the world anymore, you know? Was a time strangers helped strangers.

That time's gone. Too many people out to do harm, is my point. It's hard to pick good from bad, and takes too much energy trying. But then I see you two, with bags in your hands, and I say, *Walt, you'd be a bastard if you drove on by.* Where are you headed?"

Arlen kept quiet while Paul explained that they were CCC and had gotten off the train en route to a camp in the Keys.

"Why'd you leave the train?"

"Arlen wanted to get off," Paul said uncertainly. "He had a bad feeling."

"A bad feeling?"

"Let's not worry over it," Arlen said curtly. Lights glowed ahead of them then, a two-story building with a wide front porch coming into view. When Sorenson came thundering off the road and jerked the Auburn to a stop, Arlen could hear music from inside, somebody plucking at a guitar.

"Pearl's," Sorenson said, and then the conversation was done, and Arlen was grateful for that.

The only connection Arlen could see between Pearl and her name was that she was round. Plenty round. Looked to go every bit of three hundred pounds, in fact, and to call her an ugly woman would be an offense to the word — woman or ugly. She was in the midst of a profane shouting match. The argument sounded harsh but didn't seem to stir much true heat from anyone in the bar, including the participants. She cut it off fast when Walt Sorenson flagged her down and told her that the gentlemen with him would need a room for the night.

Arlen got some dollars out, and Paul started to reach in his own pocket but Arlen waved him off. He wasn't sure how much money Paul had on him, but it couldn't be much; the juniors in the CCC were required to send twenty-five of the thirty dollars they made each month directly home to help their parents. Pearl wouldn't even accept Arlen's money, though.

"Friend of Walt's," she said.

"Lady, we just met him ten minutes ago. Nobody owes us anything."

"Friend of Walt's," she repeated.

Paul was gawking around the bar. It was a rough-looking crowd. One man wore a long knife in a sheath at his belt, and another had a raw red gash down the length of one finger, the sort of thing that could be left behind by a tooth. It wasn't an old injury. At a table just inside the door, a man with a cigar pinched in the corner of his mouth was talking to a woman in a green dress that was cut so low the tops of her large white breasts were exposed completely. She had red hair and bored eyes.

Pearl led them up a set of stairs so narrow that she had to turn sideways to wedge her way along. She jerked open the first door they came to, then lit an oil lamp and waved her fat hand out over the two cots.

"Privy's outdoors," she said. "Wasn't the Astor family that built this, you might have noticed."

"It'll do fine," Arlen said.

She clomped back out the door and down the hall, and they could hear her let out a grunt as she started down the stairs. Paul caught Arlen's eye and grinned.

"Don't be getting any ideas," Arlen said. "She's too old for you."

"Oh, go on."

"I'm going downstairs to buy that fellow a drink. Thank him for the ride. You get some shut-eye."

Paul nodded at the wall and said, "Hear that? It's raining."

Yes, it was. Coming down soft but steady, would've soaked them to the bone if they'd still been out walking on the dark highway.

"Good thing we caught that ride," Paul said.

"Sure." Arlen pulled his bag up onto his bed and sorted through it until he found his canteen, unscrewed the cap, and shook the contents down, tugged a few bills out. He had $367 in it, savings accrued over the past twenty months. No fortune, but in this driven-to-its-knees economy, where men bartered heirlooms for bread, it felt close.

Outside, the rain gathered intensity.

Yes, Arlen thought, *it was a good thing we caught that ride.*

The bar was dim and dusty, with a crowd of men Arlen could smell easier than he could see bunched at one end, keeping conversation with Pearl. The guitar player had given up for the night, but the redheaded woman in the green dress was still at the table with her cigar-smoking companion, and Walt Sorenson sat alone at the far end of the bar, counting out small white balls with black numbers and placing them into a burlap bag. Arlen dropped onto a stool beside him and said, "Mind telling me what you're doing?"

Sorenson smiled. "You ever heard of bolita?"

"I have not," Arlen said. The woman in the green dress stood up and walked to the bar, her breasts wriggling like something come alive. Her hips matched the act, but the eyes stayed empty. She disappeared up the stairs, never casting a look back at the man with the cigar who followed her.

"Bolita," Sorenson said, "is a game of wagering. You should put in a dime, Mr.... what's your name? Wagner, was it?"

"Arlen Wagner, yes."

"Well, Arlen Wagner, I've developed what some might call an unusual ability — I can feel luck in the air. I mean, just taste it, like when you walk into a room where something good's been on the stove. And I'm telling you, sir, that luck rides with you tonight. There's no question about it. Luck rides with you."

Arlen thought of the station platform again, all those men with bone faces and bone hands climbing back onto the train. His mouth was dry.

"All right," he said. "Sure. I'll put in a dime."

"There you go. Now, pick yourself a number. One through one hundred."

He waited with a wolf's grin.

"One," Arlen said. "As in, how many times I'll try this game."

"Very nice, very nice." Sorenson chuckled and sorted through the balls until he found the number one. He held it up so Arlen could inspect it, then leaned it against his whiskey glass, which was now mostly ice. "I'll rest it right there so you can keep an eye on it."

"I'm going to expect such a game is illegal in this state," Arlen said.

"A good many of the best things are." Sorenson spent some time studying his betting sheet, cleared his throat, and called, "All right, boys, gather round, the losing is about to begin for most, and the winning for but a single soul."

He scooped the balls off the bar and into the bag. By now the crowd had gathered around Sorenson, and he wrapped the top of the bag until the balls were hidden from view, then gave it a ferocious shake.

"Here," he said. "Someone else take a try."

A man with skeptical eyes stepped forward and took the bag. He shook it for a long time. Sorenson took the bag back, opened the neck, and slid his right hand inside. He closed his eyes and let out a strange humming sound. This persisted for a moment as he felt around the inside, and then he snapped open one eye and told the crowd, "I've got to tune into the winner, you know. It's not so simple as just pulling one out. There's one man here who deserves to win tonight, one whose destiny is victory, and I must be sure that I hear his selection calling my name."

"You're so full of shit," one onlooker said, "I'm surprised it don't come out your ears."

Sorenson smiled, then snapped his hand out of the bag, his fist closed. "Gentlemen, I give you our winner."

He unfolded his hand and twisted the ball so the number was visible: *1*.

"And who had number one?"

Arlen lifted his hand, and a few of the men grumbled.

"He come in here with you," the one who'd shaken the bag said. "It's a damn swindle you're running."

"Ah, but you're wrong," Sorenson said, unbothered. "I've not met this man till this evening, and he'll tell you the same. But if that's how you feel, then I suggest another round, only this time our current winner must sit out."

There was no interest in further wagering.

"Hard to believe it here," Sorenson told Arlen, "but there are places where this little game is treated with respect. I've known men who became millionaires off this little game."

"Running it," Arlen said, "not playing it. And thanks for cheating me into the profit."

"Cheating?"

Arlen nodded at the glass of melting ice near Sorenson's hand. "You left the ball up there long enough to hold the cold. Then you could pick it out of the rest. It's a neat trick, but it may get your arm broken with the wrong crowd."

Sorenson gave a low chuckle. "You've got a sharp eye, Mr. Wagner."

Arlen lifted his hand and got Pearl's attention, asked for two whiskeys. When she'd shuffled off again, he said, "So is this your business, Sorenson? A traveling entertainment, that's what you are?"

"Oh, no. This little game is nothing more than a pastime."

"So what is it that you do?"

Sorenson smiled as Pearl set their drinks on the bar. "You're an inquisitive man. What I do has evolved a bit, but these days I'm an accounts manager."

"Accounts manager?"

"That's right, sir. I check in on clients all over the hellish back-woods of this forsaken Florida countryside. And once in a while, I get to the coast to do the same. I'll assure you, the ladies are of a finer breed on the coast." He nodded at Pearl's enormous rear end. "Ample evidence, you might say."

"Quick with a pun, Sorenson. Mighty quick."

"Quick with so many things."

He laughed at that, so Arlen laughed, too. Arlen's whiskey glass was empty, and Pearl had disappeared, so he slipped his flask out and poured his own. The flask was nearing empty now itself. Sorenson watched him and gave a soft sigh.

"It hasn't been so long since such an act was illegal."

"You don't appear to be a teetotaler, yet you say that with some sorrow."

"Sorrow for what's been lost, Mr. Wagner."

"And what was lost? Purity?" Arlen said with a snort.

"Purity, no. What was lost when Roosevelt kicked Prohibition in the ass was a business environment the sort of which we may never see again."

"Ah," Arlen said. "A bootlegger. That's what you are."

"Now? No, Mr. Wagner. You can't bootleg something that's openly bought and traded. So a new commodity must be found and..." He shrugged. "I just miss the simplicity of booze. But let's talk about you for a change. You and the young man departed a train in the middle of the night and lit out down an abandoned highway in an unfamiliar place. Due to a bad feel-ing, the boy said. It strikes me as a most exceptional decision."

"Paul said all that needed to be said. I had a bad feeling. End of story."

"I like it. Sounds ominous. A feeling of what? Impending doom?"

"I didn't see a black cat walking under a ladder or any such foolish shit," Arlen said, feeling anger rise, Sorenson watching him with calm interest. "If you had any idea..."

He let it die, and Sorenson said gently, "What *did* you see?"

Arlen shook his head. "Let's leave it at a bad feeling."

"And so we will. Make no mistake, Mr. Wagner, I'm a man who appreciates the art of the premonition."

"Mine are a little different than yours. Less manufactured."

"Than mine, sure. I've known others, though ... there's a village not far from here in which every resident claims to be a medium. The place is called Cassadaga. Anytime I pass close to the area, I pay a visit. A friend introduced me to a fortune-teller there. She's remarkable."

"What does she tell you? Winning numbers for your games?"

"Yesterday, she told me there was death in the rain."

"In the rain?"

"That's what she said. I asked her if it was my own death, and she said it was not. Then she told me, as she has before, that I worry too much about death. All that *dies,* she said, is the body. That's all. And she believes, quite firmly, that she can continue to communicate with those whose bodies are no more. Do you believe in such a thing?"

"Absolutely not," Arlen said, thinking, *I'd better not. Because if I do, then I've got something to answer for.*

"You say that with conviction," Sorenson said. "Yet you abandoned a train you needed to be on due to your own unusual perception."

"There's a world of difference there," Arlen said.

Sorenson had set his hat down on the bar and shed his jacket, revealing a sweat-stained white shirt and suspenders.

"The lad who travels with you was not in favor of the change of plans. He did not support the . . . bad feeling."

"He supported it enough," Arlen said. "He got off the train."

"Hell, man, you're *serious* about this, aren't you?"

Arlen turned to face him, the whiskey wrapping its arms around him now in such a way that he didn't fear the man's mocking.

"You think your fortune-teller can sense death coming?" he said. "Well, brother, I can *see* it. Tell you something else — I ain't ever wrong. *Ever.*"

Sorenson gazed at him without reaction. Arlen held the stare for a time and then turned away, at which point Sorenson finally spoke.

"I am most taken with games of chance and those who purport themselves as capable of beating them. And life, Mr. Wagner? That's the best game of chance in this world. You think you can beat it."

"No," Arlen said. "I do not think that."

"Sure you do. We'll see if you can. The fate of that train will tell the tale."

"It may not be the train," Arlen said, his voice starting to thicken with drink. "Could be something will happen that has nothing to do with the train. But the Keys aren't safe, damn it, and I want to keep that kid from going."

"You say that as if you suspect it will be difficult."

"He's determined. I'd like to get to Hillsborough County, to the CCC camp there. The boy doesn't belong down in the Keys."

"I see." Sorenson twirled his glass on the bar, watching the warm amber liquid devour his ice. Arlen had a passing notion that he was surprised such a bar even had ice; perhaps this was what Sorenson provided in these days of open liquor trade. "Well, Wagner, what I said during our game holds true — luck

33

rides with you tonight. Not only did you win the game, not only did you escape the train to the Keys, not only did you hitch with me just in time to avoid the rain, but you've found a ride to Hillsborough County. I'll make a few stops along the way, but by sundown I'll be within twenty miles. Can't pass on a free ride."

"Generous offer, but all the same, I think we'll stick to the trains."

"You wound me," Sorenson said. "Think logically—it's a five-mile hike back to the station and then you'll have to piece together a day of travel at considerable expense. You will also have to convince the lad to change his plans. He likes that car, Mr. Wagner. I imagine he'd like to drive it."

Arlen looked up at him and frowned. "Why so interested?" he said. "What's it to you, Sorenson?"

"There are plenty of reasons. For one, I find you a most fascinating man, you of the bad feelings, you, the seer of death. For another, I could use the company. These highways get lonesome, Mr. Wagner. And a third reason? My fortune-teller in Cassadaga, the one who warned me of death in the rain? Her guidance for me on this visit was quite limited—all she said was that I needed to be aware of travelers in need."

"You expect me to believe that, you're crazy."

"On the contrary," Sorenson said, "if you're anything close to the man I suspect you are, I know that you *will* believe it. Because it's the truth."

Arlen held his eyes for a time, then looked away without speaking.

"All right," he said. "We'll ride with you tomorrow."

5

H E DID NOT SLEEP WELL. In the room beside them, an ancient bed creaked a sad, hollow rhythm beneath first one man's grunting efforts and then another's. The redheaded woman who had once worn a green dress did not make a sound. Arlen lay in the dark and listened and wondered if Paul was awake. If he was, he didn't speak. By three Arlen's flask was empty and then so was the room beside them, the door swung shut one final time as the voices downstairs fell silent.

He dozed off sometime around four but slept in uneasy fits, jerking awake often to the sound of an unrelenting rain. It was sweltering in the constricted, windowless room, and Arlen's sweat soaked into the sheets as the night carried on and finally broke to dawn.

"Get on your feet," Arlen said, giving Paul a shake. "We've got a ride. Sorenson's going to take us south."

"To the Keys?"

"He isn't going that far. All I know is he's going south, and we can ride with him in that fancy car you liked so much. Beats waiting all day for a train."

Arlen felt a twinge at his own words. It wasn't a bald lie—Hillsborough County was indeed south, but it was also west, when the train lines that would carry them to the Keys were on the state's eastern shore.

They drove away in a gray, windy dawn, the Auburn gleaming as if freshly washed after the night of steady rain.

"Shouldn't take but five or six hours," Sorenson said. "I've a few stops to make along the way, but they'll be swift enough. I appreciate you joining me on this short sojourn."

Arlen winced, and Sorenson noted it. "What?" he said.

"Nothing," Arlen muttered. "You just…it reminded me of something my father used to say."

They're only dead to people like you, Arlen. Truth is they're carrying on, bound to a place where you can't yet follow. This life is but a sojourn.

"A story you'd like to share?" Sorenson said.

"No," Arlen said.

Their stops were roadhouses similar to Pearl's. At each of them, a large black case with two metal locks entered and exited the establishment with Sorenson. The stops were swift indeed, short disruptions as they drove through a green, saturated land. The ditches on either side of the road were swollen with muddy water. Arlen's father used to caution about dreams of muddy water, claiming they warned of impending trouble. Arlen wondered if his father had such a dream toward the end, or if dreams had failed him.

They pushed west as the heat continued to build and with it the thickness of the air. Sorenson had the windows cranked down on the Auburn, and out on the back roads he opened the engine up and let the big car run, Paul grinning as the speedometer hit seventy, eighty, ninety, one hundred. Sorenson let it fall off then but kept it closer to ninety than eighty for most of an hour. Their next stop was at a place called the Swamp. Unlike the previous roadhouses, this one seemed to be booming—the building was outfitted with electric lamps and glossy wood on the front patio, and cars filled the parking area already, new Plymouths and Chryslers and one Essex Terraplane that turned Paul's head.

"That one would blow your doors off, Mr. Sorenson," he said.

"You say."

"Oh, it's a fact."

"Busy place," Arlen said. "And one with some money."

"Casino inside," Sorenson said. "They do it right, too."

"Let's have a look," Paul said, but Arlen shook his head.

"We'll wait on him."

"Oh, it can't hurt to wander around in there a bit, Arlen."

"We'll wait."

They leaned against the Auburn and watched people come and go through the doors, women in dresses and heels, men in suits with drinks in their hands. *I guess we drove out of the Depression,* Arlen thought. *Be back in it another mile down the road, but somehow it doesn't exist right here. Must be nice.*

"This is what Key West is supposed to be like," Paul said. "Saloons all over the place, people having a good time just like here. That writer's down there, Hemingway, and I saw a picture of Dizzy Dean, taken on his vacation. All sorts of famous people pass through. Why, we could have a drink with them."

Arlen regarded him with surprise. He wouldn't have imagined a kid like Paul would give the first damn about saloons and Dizzy Dean. In his mind, the only thing the boy had been after in the Keys was work on the bridge. Well, that had no doubt been a naive, idealized notion. Paul was nineteen, probably wanted himself a taste of many things. All this time Arlen had seen the kid eyeing his flask, he'd assumed Paul was antiliquor. He was probably just curious.

When Sorenson returned, Arlen said, "Say, weren't you going to let the kid drive?"

"He probably won't want to if it isn't that Terraplane he's so sweet on."

"I'll drive," Paul said, and Sorenson grinned.

The funny thing was, once he got behind the wheel, he was scared to let the big motor run. Wouldn't take it beyond forty until Sorenson said, "Boy, if I'd wanted my mother to drive, I'd have brought her along." Then the kid finally laid into it, got them as high as sixty. Arlen wondered when Paul had last driven a car. Hell, if he'd *ever* driven a car. He handled it well, though, seemed comfortable behind the wheel even if hesitant of the engine's power.

"Mr. Sorenson?" Paul said after they'd gone about ten miles. "I thought we were going to head south today. We're driving due west."

Sorenson flicked his eyes over to Arlen, then looked back and said, "Didn't know I was required to stick to a specific compass point when I agreed to give y'all a ride."

"That's not what I'm saying, I was just wondering—"

"We'll be southbound shortly. Only one stop left. And it's on the beach."

"The beach? Now that's better. I've always wanted to see the ocean."

Arlen frowned. "Thought you grew up just south of New York."

"That's right."

"Hell, the ocean can't be but an hour from there at most."

"It's not," Paul said, and there was something different in his voice, an edge Arlen had never imagined him capable of. "I just never saw it, okay?"

"Okay," Arlen said. It struck him then how little he knew about the kid. His name, his age, his home. He knew those things and the undeniable fact that he was the closest thing to a mechanical genius Arlen had ever encountered.

Forty-five minutes later they caught a flash of blue, the expanse of the Gulf of Mexico ahead, and for the first time Paul seemed unsteady with the car, drifting across the center line for a blink before he brought it back. Sorenson told Paul that if he wanted to gawk at the water, he'd best give up the wheel.

It did look pretty. The sun had broken through — though there were dark clouds in the mirrors and more massing to the north — and the breakers glittered. There wasn't a boat in sight, the water an unbroken vastness of prehistoric power.

"Wow," Paul said. And then, softer, "That is something. It really is."

The road curled away from the coast again. There wasn't much development out here, wasn't much at all except for the road, in fact. Once, they crossed a set of train tracks — Paul going over the rails so gingerly Arlen thought he might get out and try to carry the Auburn across — but then those were gone and nothing showed ahead. Eventually they came to a four-way stop, pavement continuing south, dirt roads to the east and west, and Sorenson told Paul to turn right, west, back toward the Gulf.

They went maybe a mile down this mud track before the trees parted and the road went to something sandier, shells cracking beneath the tires. A moment later the water showed itself, and in front of the shore was a clapboard structure of white that had long since turned to gray. It was a rectangle with a smaller raised upper level, steep roofs all around. At the top of the second story was a small deck with fence rails surrounding it. A widow's walk. A porch ran the length of the house, and an old wooden sign swung in the wind above: *The Cypress House.*

"Tell you what," Sorenson said, "let's all go in here."

Paul passed him the keys and popped open the door, eager to step out and gawk at the sea. Arlen started out, too, but Sorenson put a hand on his arm.

"You might want to bring the bags in."

Arlen tilted his head. "Why?" They'd never been so much as invited in at any previous stop, and now Sorenson wanted the bags out of his car, too?

"This area," Sorenson said, and let the words hang.

Arlen looked around in every direction, saw nothing but the shore ahead and tangled trees and undergrowth behind.

"Looks peaceful to me," he said.

"Mr. Wagner," Sorenson said, and there was a bite in his words, "you ever been here before?"

"I've not."

Sorenson nodded. "Then perhaps you should reconsider my advice."

Arlen held his eyes for a moment and then turned without a word and grabbed the first bag and hauled it out with him. He tugged them all free from the Auburn and then hailed Paul to help carry them in, and while he worked he pretended not to notice that Sorenson had retrieved a small automatic from beneath the driver's seat and tucked it into his jacket pocket.

6

WHATEVER ILL FEELINGS Sorenson had about the Cypress House were not justified by their entrance into its humid, shadowed interior. They were standing in the middle of a long, narrow room without a soul inside. There was a fireplace on their left and a bar on their right. Behind the bar, liquor was displayed on thick wooden shelves, and atop the shelves was a massive brass-ringed and glass-faced mantelpiece clock that went about two feet in diameter and was clearly broken—according to the hands it was noon. Or midnight.

Between the bar and the fireplace were scattered a handful of tables, and the wall opposite them was composed of wide windows that looked out onto another porch and beyond that the ocean.

"Hello!" Sorenson bellowed once they'd stepped inside. Arlen set his bags down beside the door, and Paul followed suit. A minute after Sorenson's cry, they heard footsteps and then a figure rounded the corner from some unseen room Arlen took to be the kitchen and faced them across the bar.

It was a woman. Her silhouette stood out starkly against the light from the beach, but the front of her was lost to darkness.

"Walter," she said, in a voice that seemed to come from behind a gate with many locks.

"Becky, baby, how are ya?" Sorenson approached the bar with his big black case in his hand, and Arlen and Paul followed a few paces behind.

"Grand," the woman said in a tone that implied just the opposite. As they drew close enough to see her, Arlen felt the boy draw up taller at his side and understood the reason—she was a looker. She wore a simple white dress that had been washed many times, but beneath it the taut lines of her body curved clear and firm. Her face was sharp-featured and smooth, framed by honey-colored hair, and she regarded them with cool blue eyes.

"Who are your companions?" she said.

"Road-weary travelers, and parched," Sorenson said. His standard grandiose demeanor seemed to have risen a notch.

"I see."

"Might I have a pair of beers and one Coca-Cola?"

She didn't answer, just turned and slipped into the kitchen and then returned with two beers and a bottle of Coca-Cola.

"Thank you," Paul said, and even in the shadowed room Arlen could see red rise in the boy's cheeks. She was that kind of beautiful. The crippling kind. Arlen himself said not a word, just took a seat at the bar. She gave him no more than a flick of the eyes before returning her focus to Sorenson.

"You need to finish your beer, or can we handle our business?"

"No need to rush," he said, and was met with a frown that suggested she saw plenty of need.

"Well, when you're ready, I'll be in the back," she said. Arlen had the sense that she was unhappy Sorenson had brought strangers along.

"Aw, stay and talk a bit. I've neglected to make introductions. This here is Arlen Wagner, and his young companion is Paul Brickhill. They're CCC men."

"How lovely," she said in the same flat voice.

"And this," Sorenson said, "is beautiful Becky Cady, the pride of Corridor County."

"Rebecca," she said.

"Ah, you're Becky to me."

"But not to me," she said. "Walter, I'll be in the back."

She turned and went through a swinging door into the kitchen, and then it was just the three of them in the dim bar.

"Another dry county?" Arlen said.

Sorenson shook his head.

"Then what are you doing here?"

"I told you last night, Mr. Wagner, business isn't about booze these days."

Sorenson took a drink of his beer, and now Arlen could see that sweat was running down his face in thick rivulets, more sweat than the heat deserved. He looked over his shoulder at the door, had another drink, and then looked again.

"You expecting company?" Arlen said.

"Huh? Um, no."

Paul said, "Why's it called Corridor County?"

"The waterways," Sorenson answered. "There are inlets and estuaries all over the shore here, and they wind around and join the river about ten miles inland. It's a crazy tangled mess, though, and every storm that blows through shifts things around and puts up sandbars where there didn't used to be any. Nobody but a handful of locals can navigate the whole mess worth a shit."

He got to his feet. "If you'll excuse me, gentlemen."

He picked up the heavy black case and walked around the back of the bar and through the swinging door where Rebecca Cady had gone. Arlen looked at Paul, saw the question in the boy's eyes, and shrugged.

"Go look at your ocean," he said, hoping to distract the kid until Sorenson came back out and they could get on the road.

Paul got to his feet and walked over to the windows, gazed out at the sea, waves rolling in with their tops flattened by a freshening wind, and then went out on the porch. After a moment Arlen picked up his beer and followed. The smell of the sea rode toward them in warm, wet gusts, and seagulls screamed and circled the beach. South, there was nothing but sand and short dunes lined with clusters of grass, but to the north the shore seemed to curve inland and thickets of palms and strange green plants that looked like overgrown ferns traced what Arlen assumed was one of the inlets Sorenson had mentioned. He could see the roof of another structure through the trees. Some sort of boathouse, probably, sheltered from the pounding waves of the open water.

Paul stepped off the porch and walked down to the beach. He slid his shoes off and rolled his pants up to his knees. Arlen leaned on the weathered railing and felt a smile slide across his face as he watched the kid pick his way over the sand and down into the water, wade in until the waves broke over his knees and soaked his trousers. Paul seemed to have forgotten anyone else existed, just stood in the water, staring out at the line where sea met sky.

The wind was blowing steadily now, and that was probably why Arlen didn't hear the car. As it was, he caught a lucky angle. He'd turned back to glance in the bar, checking to see if Sorenson had reappeared, and saw a flash of movement through the windows at the opposite end of the building. It was gone then, and he took a few steps to the side and still couldn't see anything. After a glance back at Paul to make sure he was still standing in the surf, Arlen set his beer down on the rail and walked off the porch and around the side of the building. There, parked at the top of the sloping track that led down to the Cypress House, a black Plymouth sedan had pulled in beside the trees. The sun was shining off the glass and Arlen couldn't see anyone inside, but the car hadn't driven itself here.

He pulled back, leaning against the wall to get himself out of sight. Felt foolish doing it, but all the same he didn't want to be seen staring. Sorenson had been acting damn strange since the moment they'd arrived, and now someone had parked up at the top of that hill and stayed in the car as if waiting on something. It didn't feel right.

Paul was walking along the shore now, shin-deep in the water, his eyes still on the sea. Arlen went quietly back up the porch steps and then stepped inside the bar, taking care to move sideways, keeping out of view of the front windows.

"Hey, Sorenson," he called, voice soft.

Nobody answered. The place was empty.

"Damn it," he muttered, and then went around the bar and rapped his knuckles on the swinging door. "Sorenson!"

"Hang on, Wagner."

There was something in the man's voice Arlen hadn't heard before, and it gave him pause. For a few seconds he stood there on the other side of the swinging door, and then he said the hell with it and pushed through and stepped into the tiny kitchen. There was a grill and a stove on one side and a rack of shelves on the other and nobody in sight. Another door stood opposite, closed. He crossed to it and knocked again.

"Damn it, I said give us a min —"

"I think somebody's looking your car over," he said. "Or maybe Miss Cady's used to guests who park at the top of the hill and don't come inside."

There was a long silence, and then the door swung open and Sorenson stood before him with the black case wrapped under his arm. All the good humor and genteel demeanor had left his face.

"Where?" he said.

"Just where I said — top of the hill, above where you parked."

Sorenson shoved past him and walked through the swinging

45

door. He kept the case wrapped under his left arm, pressed against his side, but let his right hand drift under his jacket. Arlen paused just long enough to look back into the room, a cramped little office where Rebecca Cady stood with her hands folded in front of her and a blank look on her face, and then he followed. When he got out to the barroom, Sorenson was standing with the front door open, looking out.

"There's nobody there."

"Was a minute ago. Black Plymouth."

Sorenson reflected on that for a moment, then manufactured an uneasy grin and said, "Good thing I had you bring your bags in, see? This area is fraught with lazy crackers who'll steal anything they can lift."

Lazy crackers don't drive new Plymouths, Arlen thought.

"Where's the kid?" Sorenson asked.

"Down on the beach."

He nodded as if that pleased him, then said, "Why don't you bring him in? I'm going to drive the car down a little closer in case our visitor returns, and then we'll have another drink and head south."

"I don't need another drink. Let's just head."

"Not quite yet," Sorenson said, and then he stepped outside and let the thick wooden door bang shut behind him.

Arlen swore under his breath, wiped sweat off his forehead with the back of his hand, and then went onto the porch and hollered for Paul. The kid was nearly out of sight now, well down the beach, but he turned and lifted a hand and started back. Arlen picked his beer up off the rail and drank the rest of it while the boy returned and pulled on his socks and shoes. He jogged up to the porch.

"We leaving already?"

"Soon as we can," Arlen said. "Sorenson wants to linger, but I'm in favor of pushing on and—"

On the other side of the building, something exploded. A bang and a roar that came so fast they were just a heartbeat from simultaneous, and for a moment the beach disappeared in front of Arlen's eyes and he saw instead the dark forests of Belleau Wood, snarls of barbwire guarding the bases of the trees, corpses draped over them, grenades hurtling through the air. Then he blinked and found himself staring at Paul Brickhill, whose mouth hung agape.

"What was—"

Arlen ignored him, turned and ran back through the bar to the front door, opened it and then took a half step back and whispered, "Son of a bitch, Sorenson."

The Auburn was on fire. All of the glass had been blown out, and twisted, burning pieces of the seats lay on the hood. As Arlen watched, there was another explosion, flames shooting out of the engine compartment and filling the air with black smoke, and the thought of running back to the bar for a bucket of water died swiftly in his mind. He let the door swing shut and walked out onto the sandy soil and approached the Auburn with an arm held high to shield his face.

He was still fifteen feet from the car when he saw the body in the driver's seat. Black flesh peeling from white bone, hair curling with smoke above a suit jacket that lay across the body in smoldering strips. On the passenger seat beside the corpse, a black case with silver latches melted and dripped onto the floorboards.

Arlen turned and looked back at the bar and saw Rebecca Cady watching from the doorway.

"You got a phone?" he said.

"No."

"*No?*"

She shook her head. She was staring past him at the car, and her hand was tight on the door frame.

"Who does?"

She made a distracted gesture up the road and didn't answer.

"Well, let's go call the police," he said. His voice was so steady it seemed to come from another place, and he knew that it did. It came from over an ocean and within a field of wheat dotted with poppies red as roses, red as blood.

"Shouldn't we get some water or —"

"It's past the time for water."

She wet her lips and glanced backward, where Paul stood in the middle of the barroom, peering out, and said, "You two go on down the road and call for help, and I'll —"

"No," Arlen said. "We're all going together."

7

R EBECCA CADY HAD A TRUCK with a small cab and a bed surrounded by homemade fence rails. Arlen told Paul to climb
in the bed and then he got into the passenger seat as the woman
started up the truck without saying a word. She had her lips
pressed in a grim line and never glanced at the still-smoldering
Auburn as she drove past. At the top of the hill, Arlen saw a
place where the beach grass was matted down and tire tracks
showed in the sand.

"Who around here drives a black Plymouth?" he asked.

"I don't know." Rebecca Cady's tone was as flat now as it had
been during their introductions in the bar. If the idea of a man
being incinerated just outside her place of business was a concern, it was hard to tell.

"Well, you might want to be thinking on it," he said. "I suspect the sheriff is going to have plenty of questions, and that's
only going to be one of them. He'll also want to know what
Sorenson was doing at your place to begin with."

She was silent. The breeze blew in and fanned her hair back,
showing a slender, exquisite neck.

"You own the place?" Arlen asked.

"That's right."

"People die out there very often?"

"No."

"Well, you sure don't look rattled. And again, if I'm the sheriff, I'm going to be —"

"You're not the sheriff," she said, "and if I could offer any advice, it would be that you let me talk to him alone and you two go on your way."

"Go on our way? That man is dead and —"

"Dead he will stay," she said. "Whether you talk with the sheriff or not."

"Hell, no. There's not a chance, lady. I'll be talking to the law before I head out of this place."

He watched her for a long time, but she never looked over at him. They'd left the dirt road for the paved now, but there wasn't another vehicle in sight. It was isolated country, forested once you got away from the coast. They'd gone at least two miles down the paved stretch of road before a gap showed in the trees and a single gas pump appeared in a square of dusty earth. Rebecca Cady slowed the truck, and then they were past the trees and Arlen could see a service station set well back from the gas pump. There was a two-bay garage and a general store, with crates of oranges stacked beside the front door. Rebecca Cady pulled the truck in next to a delivery van and shut the engine off. Only then did she turn and look at Arlen.

"I'll go in now and call the sheriff, since that's what you want me to do."

"You're damned right it's what I *want* you to do. A man was killed!"

"Yes," she said. "Welcome to Corridor County, Mr. Wagner."

*   *   *

50

The sheriff told her to return to the Cypress House, and he was waiting on them when they arrived, standing beside the ruins of the Auburn while a young deputy with red hair poured pails of water onto the wreck. The flames were gone, but the metal steamed when the water touched it.

The sheriff had the look and charm of a cinder block — a shade over six feet but 250 at least, with gray hair and small, close-set brown eyes. His hands dangled at his sides beneath thick wrists and sunburned forearms. When they got out of the truck, he didn't say a word, just watched the three of them approach as the deputy emptied another pail of water onto the car in a hiss of steam. The sheriff didn't break the silence until they were standing at his side.

"Becky," he said then, "what in the world happened to your guest?"

"His car blew up," Rebecca Cady said. She was standing at Paul's side, facing the sheriff with her arms squeezed tightly across her chest, as if she'd found a cold breeze hiding in the ninety-degree day.

"So it did," the sheriff said. "So it did."

Arlen was struck by the man's voice. He'd expected the heavy southern drawl that seemed common in these parts, but the sheriff's accent had a touch of the Upper Midwest in it, Chicago or Minnesota or Wisconsin.

"Who are you boys?" the sheriff said, acknowledging their existence for the first time.

Arlen told it. Said they were CCC, had missed a train heading down to the Keys and caught a ride with the dead man.

"You'd never seen him before? Strangers, you say?"

"That's right. We'd just met him last evening, Mr....what was your name?"

"Tolliver," he said after a pause and a darkening of the eyes that suggested he didn't like Arlen treating the conversation as a two-way street, "but all you need to call me is Sheriff. Do you know Becky?"

"Just met her. Again, we'd come this way only because we hitched the ride. I've never set foot in this county before, and neither has Paul."

Tolliver pursed his lips and looked at his deputy, a freckle-faced kid with a sour scowl. He stared at him for a long time, like he was musing on something, and then he said, "Burt, put them in handcuffs and get them in the car."

Arlen said, "Whoa. Hold on, there. I just told you—"

Tolliver dipped one of his big hands to his belt and came out with a .45, held it loose, along his thigh.

"I know what you told me. I also know that Walt Sorenson, poor dead son of a bitch that he may be, was not the kind of man who took on riders he'd never met. So I'll give you two a chance to work on adjusting your story until you come out with the truth. Take another try right now if you'd like. Why were you riding with Sorenson?"

For a moment there was only silence, a light salty breeze blowing in, and then Arlen said, "A fortune-teller told him to be aware of travelers in need."

The sheriff nodded as if this were what he'd expected to hear. "It'll go that way, will it?" he said, and then snapped his chin at the deputy. "Burt."

The redheaded kid shook out a pair of handcuffs and advanced on Arlen. Paul Brickhill said, "Arlen, what...we didn't...Arlen," as the deputy grabbed on to Arlen's wrist and twisted it, and the big sheriff stood with the gun in his hand and a dare in his eyes. Rebecca Cady squeezed her arms tighter and stared past them all, over the top of the demolished car and off to the horizon, where clouds hung low over the water. She stood that way until both Arlen and Paul were in handcuffs and in the back of the sheriff's car.

8

PAUL TRIED TO TALK to Arlen when they were under way, but Tolliver said there'd be no conversation in the back unless someone wanted a skull-cracking. Arlen didn't say anything. It wasn't the first time he'd felt cuffs close around his wrists, and he knew the drill by now — you'd eat some shit, wait till they tired of feeding it to you, and then they'd kick you loose.

They drove past the service station where they'd called for Tolliver originally and on down the road. A few miles south they arrived in a small town laid out on a square, buildings lining a total of four roads and lasting for two blocks in each direction. A few of the signs indicated the place was called High Town, which was intriguing considering it was as flat a place as Arlen had seen. There were cars parked on the street but also two horse carts in view. The modern world had touched this place, yes, but it had made limited headway so far.

The deputy parked in front of a single-story building with clapboard added on to an older stone section in the rear. They went up the steps and into the station, and Tolliver said, "Keep the boy out here," and then led Arlen through a narrow hallway and out into a room where three small cells lined the back wall. He took a key from his belt and unfastened one of the doors and swung it open. Arlen went in without comment or objection.

"You walk around here like you been in a jail before," Tolliver said, facing him with his legs spread wide, a hint of a grin on his face.

"I've seen 'em."

"Prison, too?"

"Not a one. And I've never been charged with anything in my life except having a drink in my hand when it wasn't legal to do so."

"You say."

"It's the sort of thing can be checked on."

Tolliver cracked his knuckles, slowly and deliberately, and then said, "You call yourself Wagner."

"It's my name. Check on that, too."

"I believe it's pronounced Vagner," Tolliver said. "I believe I shot some men who may well have had the same name. I shot a lot of Germans in my day."

"So did I," Arlen said. "Probably more than you. And where I'm from, the name is Wagner."

Actually, it hadn't been. Arlen had pronounced it Vagner until his second day on the transport ship, when he determined it would be wise to alter that German sound, distancing him not only from the enemy but from his father. The latter felt like a more valuable gain than the former.

"Where might that be?" Tolliver said.

"All around," Arlen answered. "I've done some drifting."

Let the sheriff make his calls to Alabama, Georgia, Pennsylvania, Kentucky, or any of the other places Arlen had spent time over the years. Let him make calls to everywhere except Fayette County, West Virginia. The only secrets Arlen had worth hiding had been left there many years ago. The first blood on Arlen Wagner's hands hadn't come in the war.

"You want to keep drifting," Tolliver said, "you'll need to be on the other side of these bars. And for that to happen, I'm going to need to know the truth."

"Sheriff, you've already heard it."

Tolliver shook his head, the smile showing clearer now, as if this were what he'd expected, and it pleased him. He opened the door of the cell and stepped out, then swung it shut and locked it.

"I'll talk to the boy first. You think you're a hard case. He doesn't."

"He'll tell you what I will," Arlen said, "because it's all we can say. Let me tell you something else, Tolliver — you lay into the boy, I'll see it dealt with. You're the law here. You ain't the law all over."

"Nothing I enjoy more," Tolliver said, "then a handcuffed man who offers threats. I'll see you shortly."

Arlen leaned back on the cot until his head rested against the stone wall, wishing for his flask. This journey had been a mistake from the first. You didn't leave a good place to go to an unknown one. He'd let the kid talk him into it, and more than a year of comfort and steady work had lulled him, allowed him to think it was a fine time to move on, and the Keys a fine place to go. What he knew now was that from almost the moment they'd crossed the state line, trouble had swirled around them like an angry wind.

The sheriff wasn't with Paul Brickhill for long — twenty minutes, maybe — and when he came back he wasn't alone. There was a tall, broad-shouldered man in a suit and a white Panama hat at his side. He wore glasses that glittered under the overhead lights and turned his eyes into harsh white squares. Tolliver glanced at the man twice as they approached, and the look held a quality of deference. Tolliver was no longer in charge of the show.

The sheriff unlocked the cell and held the door so the new man could enter first. Then he stepped in behind him and banged the door shut.

"Arlen Wagner," the sheriff said, pronouncing it with the *V* again. "This here is Solomon Wade. He's the judge in Corridor County."

"You going to charge us?" Arlen said.

Solomon Wade blinked at Arlen from behind the glasses. They didn't seem to suit his face; he looked too harsh for them. He was young for a judge, but the youth didn't suggest a lack of assurance. Rather, every step and glance bespoke a man who was used to having command.

"What brings you to Florida?" he said as if Arlen hadn't spoken. His voice was thick with southern flavor, and soft, but still had a timbre that would hold men's attention, and hold it fast.

"I expect the sheriff has told you," Arlen said. "I came for work. We were bound for the Keys."

"This isn't the way to get there from Alabama."

"We had a detour."

"Bad time to head to the Keys," Wade said. "Bad time."

"Yeah?"

"Storm coming. It's all they're talking about on the radio. They're going to have a hurricane down south, down Miami way."

"A damned hurricane," Tolliver said under his breath, and a frown creased his broad face. He seemed genuinely distressed.

"All due respect," Arlen said, "but if we're going to talk about the weather, I'd like to be on the other side of these bars."

The sheriff looked at Solomon Wade and gave a rueful shake of his head, a *What did I tell you?* gesture.

"I'd likely imagine you would," Wade drawled. "But that's going to take some cooperation on your part."

"I've been cooperating."

"Al here disagrees," Wade said. "He suspects you of dishonesty."

"Al is wrong."

"Al is not often wrong. In my experience he's been a fine judge of character. And you, sir, will address him as Sheriff. I believe in a culture of respect in my jail. You don't show much of it."

"Everybody has an off day now and again," Arlen said.

Solomon Wade looked at Tolliver but didn't say anything. Tolliver ran a hand through his thinning gray hair. His shoulders were relaxed, his demeanor casual, as if they were all strangers on a train, pleasant but unfamiliar. He didn't appear to do so much as tense a muscle before he swung one of those meaty hands and caught Arlen flush on the side of the head. It was more slap than punch, but it rang Arlen's bell, knocked him sideways and put a flash of color in his eyes. He caught himself sliding off the cot, stood, and allowed a smile.

"Aw, hell," Tolliver said, "you're one of those kind. Enjoy being hit."

"No, Sheriff, I'm not."

"Just a cheerful son of a bitch, then?"

"Yes, sir."

He expected another blow, and Tolliver seemed prepared to administer one, but then Solomon Wade raised a hand.

"The boy sticks to his tale," he said. "And he's too damn green to be a good liar. I've got an expectation that the part about you all coming down from Alabama will check out well enough. What will not check out is the notion that Walt Sorenson drove you for a full day out of the goodness of his black heart. I'd be willing to believe, maybe, that he gave you a ride a mile up the highway. But the story the boy tells? Of you riding with him all day and making stops along the way at establishments that are well known to me? That don't carry water."

"It'll have to," Arlen said, wondering why in the hell the county judge seemed to be heading up the investigation.

Solomon Wade said, "Al," and at the one soft word, the sheriff put his right fist into Arlen's belly. A snake of cold-to-warm pain rippled through Arlen, and his knees tried to buckle, but Tolliver kept him upright and smiled in his face.

"So we begin," he said.

It went that way for an hour at least. Wade asked questions, and Arlen answered them, and when he couldn't, Tolliver swung. He was ox strong and knew all the soft spots, and it wasn't long before breathing was difficult and Arlen's kidneys were coiled flames.

Mostly Wade wanted to know where they'd gone and what had been said. He showed no interest at all in the explosion that had taken Sorenson's life. No mention was made of the Cypress House or of Rebecca Cady. No, just questions of what Sorenson had said and where he'd stopped and whether he'd had any money on his person. Arlen answered what he could, and he didn't resist the blows. Tolliver had a gun on one side of his belt and a hickory billy club on the other and a deputy waiting outside. Giving him even a taste of the fight he wanted was going to work out poorly in the end, and so even as Arlen marked the weaknesses in the larger man's approach, saw the openings and envisioned the bloody shattering of that broad nose, he kept his hands down and took what was offered.

Tolliver was a strong man but not a fit one. Before long the exertion of knocking Arlen's ass around the hot, clammy room had taken its toll, and he was breathing damn near as hard as Arlen and mopping sweat from his face and neck.

Wade reached up and adjusted his glasses. "Doesn't seem to have been very productive."

"He's a stubborn son of a bitch, I'll give you that," Tolliver said.

"Could be he's telling the truth."

"You think?"

Wade shook his head.

"That's where I landed, too," Tolliver said. "Shall I keep at it?"

"No." Wade came off the bars and looked down at Arlen as if he were studying a carcass. "We'll let him sleep, let him get used to the way that cot feels and stare at those bars and begin asking himself if it's worth it. We'll let him remember that if we're so inclined, it can be arranged for him to stay here a powerful long time."

He tilted his head at the cell door, and Tolliver opened it and Wade stepped out, then turned and looked back at Arlen with cold eyes.

"On behalf of the good people of Corridor County, we'd like to thank you for being such a helpful witness, Mr. Wagner."

Arlen dragged in some of the dusty air and didn't answer. Tolliver locked the cell and followed Wade out the door. For a long time after they were gone, Arlen stayed down on the floor, sweat dripping into his eyes and salting the corners of his mouth. Outside, the wind gusted hard against the stone wall and found it solid. Still it pushed, though, undeterred, driving on as night settled and the slanted light in the empty jail edged toward gray dusk.

9

THEY BROUGHT PAUL BRICKHILL in before it was full night. By then Arlen was back on the cot and breathing normally, and the deputy locked Paul in the cell next to him and brought them each a plate of buttered bread and a mug of water. When he was gone, Arlen said, "How rough did they go on you?"

"He did some shouting."

"That's all?"

"Yes. Why? They didn't try anything more than that on you, did they?"

"No," Arlen said. "No. Was the judge there?"

"Yeah. He didn't say much. He just listened. But I don't know why he was even there. I mean, you don't think... Arlen, there's no way they'll keep us here, is there? We weren't anything but bystanders, we'd—"

"Settle down," Arlen said. "They'll kick us loose soon enough."

Paul said, "We should've taken our chances on that train."

Neither of them spoke much after that.

*   *   *

Night passed and dawn rose and with it the heat, and no one set foot in the jail. Paul couldn't sit still — he paced the narrow cell most of the night and then in the morning began to do push-ups on the floor, grunting out the count as he went. Poor as this predicament was, Arlen still couldn't help grinning. The kid was acting like a con from some prison flicker. Before long he'd probably start laying escape plans, set to work sawing on his cell bars with his fingernails.

"Aren't they going to feed us any breakfast?" Paul said when he tired of exercising. "That's a legal requirement, Arlen! They can't deny a man food."

"They'll feed us."

"We should have a lawyer. Not one we have to pay for either, but one they provide. You know, to protect our rights."

"Uh-huh."

At noon the sheriff and deputy brought them their meals: buttered bread and a strip of beef so tough it ate like jerky and tasted like boot leather. They remained in the room while the inmates ate. The redheaded deputy stood with his arms folded and glared into the cells, and Tolliver sat on a stool in the corner of the room and read a newspaper. At one point he gave a grunt of disgust and shook his head.

"If they had two boys who threw like Mel Harder, my Indians would win the pennant going away, Burt," he told the deputy. "Win it by ten games."

Arlen, chewing his stale bread, heard that and thought, *Cleveland*. That's where Tolliver was from. He surely wasn't local — both his voice and his sunburned skin spoke of a life spent far north of this place. How did a man from Cleveland find himself as sheriff of a backwater Florida county, though?

When they were finished eating, the deputy gathered their

plates and Tolliver crumpled the newspaper and asked without interest whether they'd like to offer any changes to their stories. They did not. Paul inquired — a great deal more tentatively than he had with Arlen — why they were still in the jail if they hadn't been charged with anything.

"Have to ask the judge about that."

"When will he be back? I don't believe it's legal to keep us —"

"You know who decides what's legal?" Tolliver said. "Solomon Wade."

That was the end of it. Arlen never said a word. When the sheriff was gone, Paul said, "Arlen, this isn't right."

Arlen said, "Kid, you been around long enough to know ain't much about this world that's right. Leastwise not lately."

"They could keep us locked up in here for weeks. Shoot, for months."

"It won't be months," Arlen said, "and it won't be weeks."

"How in the hell are you so sure?" the kid snapped with an unnatural harshness. "You see that in your head, too, like the dead men on that train?"

"No," Arlen said. "This one's more of a guess."

It was quiet, and then Paul said, "Arlen, I'm sorry. It's just that —"

"I know," Arlen said. "For what it's worth, kid, I'm sorry, too. But you'll see a lot more of this in your time. Foul deeds done by men who have themselves some power. They'll beat on you in some way or another just 'cause they can, and most times they won't answer for it."

"When we get out of here," Paul said, "I just want to get back to one of the camps. Doesn't even have to be the Keys. I just want to get back to a CCC camp."

That brought some comfort to Arlen. He said, "We're going back to Flagg Mountain. It isn't wise to stay in Florida after this.

We'll have trouble even if we don't deserve it. Word gets around."

"When do you think we'll be back?"

"End of the week at the latest."

"That sounds good," Paul said. "Be nice to be back by Friday. Today's Monday, right? Today's Labor Day. Some holiday we had."

He was right, Arlen realized. It was the end of the holiday now, the end of Labor Day, 1935.

Arlen had felt some swelter in his time, but not much that rivaled the way that jail got by midafternoon. The back wall faced west, and the sun came on and baked into the stone and there wasn't so much as an open window to let the heat breathe. Paul Brickhill shifted and muttered and paced, and Arlen lay on the cot and felt the sweat bead on his flesh and waited for Tolliver's return.

It never came. That evening a new deputy brought them food, and then it was night and they were still in their cells. The next morning Arlen woke to the sound of rain, stretched, and ran a hand over his face. When he did it, he winced. The stubble was thickening up. Arlen shaved every morning, no matter what, refused to miss it. He hated to see the hint of a beard when he looked in the mirror. Even a touch of dark shadow on his broad jaw changed his face, made him look so much like his father it was frightening. Isaac Wagner had always worn a beard, and because of it, Arlen stayed clean-shaven. Less he resembled that man, the better.

He was still on his back, studying moisture marks that seemed to be darkening in the old ceiling, when there came the sound of a key in the door and he sat up to see Solomon Wade stepping through.

"Paul," Arlen said in a low voice.

"Yeah."

He'd just wanted to make sure the kid was awake. The judge walked over to Arlen's cell and stood leaning forward with his hands wrapped around the bars. At the sight of him, Paul and his worries about prisoners' rights had fallen silent; he offered nary a question.

"Those beds aren't too bad, are they?" Wade said.

"I've had better," Arlen said, "and I've had worse."

"Ain't that the truth." Wade twisted his head to study Paul. "You know there's men all over this country don't have a bed for the night. Women and children, too."

Paul said, "Yes, sir. I know."

Wade nodded. "Just so we're clear on that. Wanted to be sure y'all had a sense of appreciation."

"Yes, sir."

"You have a sense of appreciation?"

"Yes, sir."

"Well, I'm glad to hear it. Because I was worried you were lacking in appreciation after I heard from the sheriff. Said there'd been talk of lawyers and lawfulness and a general quality of bitching, not a hint of gratitude in the air."

"He was mistaken," Arlen said.

"You calling the sheriff a liar?" Wade said, swiveling to look at Arlen.

"I'm not."

"A fool, then?"

"No, sir. Just mistaken."

Wade nodded sagely, as if this were a philosophers' debate of intense interest.

"I've made some calls," he said. "Seems the CCC actually recollects the two of you. So does a train station attendant out in Bradford County."

"Good to hear," Arlen said, still wondering why in the hell a judge would be making calls in an investigation. Seemed like Tolliver's job.

"Not a one of them answered the question I needed answered," Wade said, "which is what you did to find yourself inside Walt Sorenson's Auburn on the day of his demise. I'll tell you something — it's a question that vexes me."

"If we could ease your suffering," Arlen said, "we surely would."

Wade cocked his head sideways and gazed in at Arlen. "Why'd you get off that train? Station attendant told me you didn't miss the train, you just got off and didn't get back on."

"I didn't like the look of the crowd we were traveling with," Arlen said. That was true enough.

"Well, I'll tell you something: you have fool's luck watching over you."

The words gave Arlen a tingle, one that started low in his back and shivered all the way up his spine and tightened the muscles in his neck.

"Train you were on was bound for the Keys," Wade said. "Would've put you off down there, what, late afternoon day before yesterday."

He dropped his hands from the bars. "You know what happened to the Keys last night?"

He waited, so Arlen said, "No. We've been in here. Nobody kept us posted on the news."

"Well, let me get you posted, then — the Keys are *gone.*"

Paul said, "What do you mean, gone?"

"I mean obliterated. Nothing left but sand and shells. And blood."

"The hurricane?" Paul said, voice soft.

"'Hurricane' isn't even the right word," Wade said. "That's what they'll call it, yes, but sounds like this was more devil than storm. I've been listening to the radio reports; they say they've got bodies in the trees down there. Whole towns blown to the ground, men and women and children swept out to sea. They sent a rescue train, and it was torn right off the tracks."

Arlen couldn't find his voice. Solomon Wade was staring in at him like he wanted to hear a response, but Arlen simply couldn't muster one.

"They say it's coming here now," Wade said. "This rain's the first of it. Wind'll come next, and with it? We'll have to wait and see. Could be as bad as what the Keys got, could be that it's tasted enough blood by now. Either way, I ain't got time to deal with you sorry bastards. But if a complaint rises to your lips about your stay here in Corridor County, you remember where you'd be if we *hadn't* locked your asses up. You remember that."

10

T HE SHERIFF WAS WAITING in the car, parked just in front of the station, no more than fifteen steps from the door. Even so, they were soaked by the time they fell into the backseat. The rain was coming down in a way that made Arlen wonder if the power of gravity had been increased while they'd waited in the jail; things didn't fall from the sky now, they plummeted.

Tolliver didn't say a word to them as they sat dripping in the back of the car, just put it in gear and drove slowly away from the center of High Town, back into the shrouded woods that today looked more black than green. Arlen watched the rain come down, pouring so furiously the sheriff had to keep the car at a crawl because he couldn't see out of the windshield, and wondered how in the hell they were going to get to a train station today. Be a mighty wet walk. And if there was a hurricane on the way . . .

Shit, hurricane or not, he wanted out, and he wanted out *now*. Regardless of the rain, the wind didn't seem all that powerful yet, had the trees swaying and shaking but not stretching out sideways the way they would when it really began to blow, like they were roaring mad at the roots that bound them to the earth, determined to get free. He'd never seen a true coastal hurricane, but he'd been in Alabama in '28 when the remnants of a bad one blew out in the wooded country where he'd been staying. The sheer power of that storm, the ferocity of the wind, had lingered in his mind. It wasn't the sort of thing you wanted to experience hiking down the highway. No, they'd best grab their bags and hitch whatever ride they could, get inland and find housing for the night.

"I've never seen rain like this," Paul said. He had one hand on the seat in front of him, squeezing it as he stared out the window and into the downpour.

"It's heavy," Arlen agreed.

They limped along a ribbon of gray that looked more like a creek bed than a road. Here and there the sheriff slowed and eased them one way or the other to avoid washouts of mud and gravel. He moved his hands on the wheel constantly, shifting their positions as if he weren't sure which one worked best, and Arlen realized he didn't like the rain any more than Paul did. He was breathing shallowly and there was sweat on his face. Twice he swore at the storm, and his voice was uneasy. This was the first hurricane he'd seen. Arlen was sure of it, and with that recognition the old questions returned: How had he found his way down here, and how had he gotten elected sheriff in a place where strangers had to be scarce?

"Hey, Arlen," Paul said.

"Yeah?"

"What the judge said about the hurricane . . . you think the men we were with on the train . . . you think they died?"

Arlen turned his head from the kid, looked back out the window, and said, "No. I don't."

"That's a lie," Paul said softly. "You *know* they did. You always knew it."

68

There were answers for that, but Arlen didn't offer any of them.

Down near the Gulf, without the woods as a screen, the rain actually seemed less imposing. The sheer expanse of gray sky lightened things up, and the ocean winds pushed the rain sideways and sprayed it around. There were no cars parked in front of the inn, but lights showed inside. The sheriff drove them to the top of the hill, just where the Plymouth had parked, and then said, "Get out. I'm not trying the hill in this mud."

"It's been a real pleasure," Arlen said. He pushed open his door and felt a spray of rain drill into his face, stepped out and let the wind swing the door shut as he walked for the inn. He intended to go all the way down there at a stroll — couldn't get much wetter — but then Paul passed him at a run and Arlen thought, *What the hell,* and followed suit.

Paul beat him to the door and jerked it open, but Arlen slid on the wet boards of the front porch and knocked right into the kid. They fell through the door together, stumbling, and by the time they had it shut they were both laughing, acting like a couple of schoolboys instead of two men who'd just been released from the county jail.

"Well, we're out," Paul said. "I didn't think I'd ever be so happy to stand outside and get rained on!"

"You'd have thought we were in there for ten years, way you talk."

The kid grinned and wiped rain from his face. "Felt close enough to me."

Arlen was sweeping his palms over his clothes, trying to shed the water, when he looked over Paul's shoulder and finally saw the woman. He'd thought the room was empty when they entered, but Rebecca Cady stood in the corner nearest them, a hammer in her right hand. When he saw her, neither of them spoke. Then Paul followed his eyes and spotted her and blurted out, "Hey."

"Hey," she said.

"The sheriff just dropped us off," Arlen said. "We had a nice couple nights in jail. Evidently it didn't matter to them that we were in here with you when Sorenson's car blew up."

"I didn't expect it would," she said, stepping forward and dropping a handful of nails onto the bar, then setting the hammer down.

"Don't seem awful concerned," Arlen said.

"Would my concern mean much? You seem to hold me responsible."

"I'm just wanting to let you know that we're damn lucky the judge didn't decide to keep us in those cells until the end of the year."

Something changed in her face. "You met the judge? Solomon Wade?"

Arlen nodded. "That's right. You a friend of his?"

That put fury in her eyes. "No."

There was something odd here, but Arlen had no wish to pursue it.

"We'll take our bags," he said shortly, "and be on our way. I'd appreciate it if you'd give us a ride to a train station."

"I'm not driving you anywhere in this weather."

"Seems the right thing to do. We were visiting on your property when our last ride was killed and we ended up in jail."

"That may be," she said, "but it was not my fault and is not my responsibility. You were Walter's guests, not mine. I didn't invite you here."

"Hell of a way to run a tavern," Arlen said. "Real sense of hospitality."

Paul shifted uneasily, touched Arlen's arm, and said, "It isn't any of her doing. Let's just find our own way."

Arlen turned and waved his arm at the wide window facing the beach, where rain drummed off the sea and wisps of pale fog hung over the water.

"Find our own way through that? It's many miles of walking, Paul. She's got a truck. She could—"

"She *could* do a lot of things," Rebecca Cady said, pulling her shoulders back and tightening one slender hand back around the hammer, "but she won't. Your bags are behind the bar. Take them and go."

She and Arlen stood and stared at each other with naked dislike, but she kept her head high and those blue eyes firm on his. *Hell with it,* he thought, *no use arguing with the likes of her. We'll have ourselves a wet walk, but it'll take us away from here, and that's the only thing I want right now. That, and a drink.*

"Fine," he said. "Let it never be said that you're lacking in generosity, Miss Cady."

She didn't answer, and he walked around the bar to find their bags. They were stacked back by the swinging door that led into the tiny kitchen. Arlen sorted out his and saw immediately that the contents had been disrupted.

"Sheriff and his deputy did that," she said.

"They never touched our belongings. Didn't set a foot inside the door."

"They came back. After you were in the jail, they came back. To talk to me." She gave him a long look, enough pause to let him imagine what Tolliver might have been like with her, and then said, "They tore through all your things and left them on my floor. I put them back as well as I could."

"Thank you," Paul said, joining Arlen behind the bar. Arlen just grunted, fingers searching through his shirts and under his jacket for the canteen. It was there. He withdrew it, unscrewed the cap, and tilted it.

There was no familiar rustle of paper. He shook it, feeling a cold rope tighten around his throat, and then turned it all the way upside down and reached inside with his index finger, slid it in all directions.

Nothing.

He stood there with the canteen in his hand as Paul shuffled around beside him. At length the boy went still, too, and then spoke in a soft voice.

"Arlen...my money's gone. All I had."

"Yes."

Paul looked up. "You, too? They took —"

"Yes," he said, and turned to look back at Rebecca Cady. "Someone did. Someone stole every dime we had."

She held her palms up. "I didn't *touch* your money."

"Did you see them steal it?"

"No."

"I find that hard to believe."

"The sheriff talked to me while the deputy went through your things."

"Easy story for you to tell," Arlen said.

She smiled. It was the first time he'd ever seen her smile, and even though this one was anything but an expression of pleasure, it stung him. She was something beyond beautiful.

"You want to see how much money I have," she said, "you're more than welcome to search the place."

Arlen didn't answer. He dropped the canteen down on top of his bag and leaned on the bar and stared out the windows into the building storm. He'd been worried enough about getting to a train station. Now they had no means of obtaining tickets once they got there. Outside the rain fell relentlessly and the wind had already begun to rise. It was miles just to get back to High Town, and what waited there for them? A sheriff who'd shown little interest in legality the first time he'd locked them up.

Almost four hundred dollars, he thought. *Nearly two years of saving, with no goal in mind but to keep this dark damned world at bay. Gone, gone, gone.*

"Arlen," Paul said. "What are we going to do?"

The row of liquor bottles stood before him, glittering. He found a bottle of whiskey and took it off the shelf and located a glass and poured.

Paul said, "Arlen?"

He took a long drink, closing his eyes when he felt the wet heat spread through his chest.

"We'll take advantage of Miss Cady's hospitality."

Rebecca Cady didn't say a word.

"What do you mean?" Paul said.

"We'll wait here for the rain to break. Then we'll start walking."

"Could be a long wait."

"Yes," Arlen said, topping the glass off. "It could."

II

IT WAS AN AFTERNOON of pouring—for the rain, and Arlen. He sat at a table beside the cold, empty fireplace and drank whiskey and didn't speak. After a few glasses the gentle burn turned to a pleasant, protective fog, and he put his feet up on the table and lifted his glass to the storm in a toast. *Come on in, you big bitch. Let's see what you can do. No worse than what's already been done to me. Think I'm scared of some wind and rain? Then you weren't in the Wood, friend. You weren't there when the gas went off and the men too slow with their masks ended up choking on their own insides, spitting and sneezing out pieces of pink and gray while I watched it all with a gun in my hands. No, I'm not scared of some wind and rain.*

Paul had wandered off somewhere. He and Rebecca Cady both. Hell with her. Arlen still wasn't certain she hadn't stolen the money herself, but she damn sure wouldn't be telling him to leave until this storm was past. He wasn't about to go walking down that dirt road in the rain without so much as a nickel in his pocket, turned into just another beggar in a country full of them, no better off than the migrant pickers or hoboes in search of a breadline.

Three hundred sixty-seven dollars. Three hundred sixty-seven...

It was his own fault. Hid his money in a canteen, like a child saving coins for the candy store. Back at Flagg Mountain, though, it had been safe enough. Safer than the banks, where your only question was what would happen first: Would the bank fail or get robbed? Either way, you lost. His canteen had looked more secure.

In a small room on the other side of the bar, something shook and rattled. The generator, probably. He'd not paused to think about it until now, but the place was lit with electric lights, there'd been an icebox in the kitchen behind the bar, and a fan hummed and pushed warm air around the room. There were no electric lines out here, so the Cypress House had to have one of those kerosene generators. They cost some dollars, though, and this place didn't seem to be thriving. So where'd the cash come from?

He sat with his head against the stone that surrounded the fireplace and closed his eyes, trying to focus on the feeling of the liquor in his belly. Outside, the wind had pulled something loose and was banging it against the house. An incessant hammering. He scowled and snapped his eyes open, wishing Paul were here so he could tell him to find the source of that damn noise and make it stop. That was when he saw that his view of the ocean had been cut in half and understood the hammering sound was truly hammering. Paul was out there with Rebecca Cady, out in the rain, nailing sheets of plywood over the windows. She was holding the boards in place while he drove the nails, and even under the overhang of the porch the rain had found her and drenched her. That dark blond hair hung in wet tangles along her neck and shoulders, and the pale blue dress she wore was pressed tight to her body, her breasts pushing back against the wet fabric. Arlen stared at her for a moment and felt a stirring, then frowned and looked away and took another sip of the whiskey.

Beautiful, yes. The sort of gorgeous that haunted men, chased them over oceans and never left their minds, not even when they wanted a respite. But was she trustworthy? No. Arlen was sure of that. Whatever had led her out here was nothing honest. Whatever paid for the electric generator and the icebox and the liquor behind the bar, whatever brought someone like Walt Sorenson on a long drive to see her, it wasn't on the level.

Shadows deepened around the room, all but the last window on the ocean side boarded up now. Arlen cast one more glance that way, and when he did he saw Rebecca Cady staring in at him as water dripped out of her hair and ran along her cheekbones, tracing her jaw. She looked him full in the eyes.

Go out there and help.

The thought flicked through his mind, and he shook it off. Be damned if he'd help this woman who'd shown no inclination to help them, who may well have stolen from them, who'd stood in silence as the sheriff put them in handcuffs. Let her work in the rain. He'd stay inside with the whiskey.

By late afternoon Arlen's head was beginning to pound, that pleasant fog turning into something with teeth, and he went in search of a privy. He'd seen no outhouse; seemed this place had indoor plumbing to complement its lights.

He found the bathroom upstairs, full of white tile and a ceramic toilet and a large claw-foot tub. He'd relieved himself and turned to the sink before he caught a glimpse in the mirror and stopped short.

His beard, always swift-growing, had filled in his face with nearly three days of shadow, the same dark brown shade of his hair and eyes, covering weathered skin turned brown by the sun and wind.

You look just like him. Look just like the crazy old bastard.

He braced his hands on the sink and leaned close to the mirror, fascinated by the way a living man's face could so resemble a dead man's. He hardly trusted his own eyes in the mirror; were they Arlen Wagner's or Isaac Wagner's?

The sight of the undertaker's shop came back to him then, the coffins lining the wall, the sound of his father's chisel working the wood, shaping final homes. And his voice...his conversations. With them. With the dead.

Arlen shook his head, ran water over his hands and splashed it onto his face, blinking it out of his eyes. He kept his head turned away from the mirror and went downstairs in search of his razor.

Yes, it was time to shave.

He was drunk by the time they finished working. Sitting back by the fireplace, talking to himself with his head down on the table. Eventually Paul came over and told Arlen he needed to lie down.

"Go on, then," Arlen said, that or something close to it, but evidently the boy had been referring to him, because he got his hands under Arlen's arms and heaved him to his feet. Arlen didn't like that, and he tried to shove him away and prove that he could stand on his own two, thank you very much. When he did it, though, he knocked the ladder-back chair over and tripped on its legs, would've sprawled right into the fireplace if Paul hadn't caught him. He stopped struggling then, let the boy wrestle him upright and leaned his weight onto the kid's side as they moved across the room. Rebecca Cady stood behind the bar in front of the electric fan, drying her hair and dress, and she watched Arlen with knowing eyes. He grinned at her, a wide, mocking smile. It earned no response.

The stairs were difficult, but Arlen had traversed stairs on unsteady legs before, and this time he had Paul to help. At the top, he stopped and gripped the railing because the building had taken to tilting and swirling around him, and he thought it prudent to hold off on any further steps. Paul kept pushing him ahead, though, down the hallway and past the bathroom, and then he opened one of the closed doors and guided Arlen into a hot, dusty room with a bed. It was stifling, and Arlen growled at the boy to open the window, let some air in.

"It's boarded up. They're all boarded up."

That was foolishness; why in the hell would anybody put boards over a window in a place so hellish hot as this? Arlen was ready to raise the question when the boy stepped out from under him and let him tumble down onto the bed, and it was soft, so soft. He forgot his planned remark and pulled himself higher on the bed, using his elbows to move, got his boots kicked off.

"We're leaving," he said.

"Not yet," Paul said.

"No, I'll rest, but then…we're leaving, Paul. Got to leave. Got to."

Paul was standing in the doorway, staring at him with a frown. "Those men from the train…they died in the storm, didn't they, Arlen?"

Arlen looked into the kid's eyes and for a moment felt as if he'd stared his way into some small circle of sobriety. The men from the train. Wallace O'Connell and the rest who'd climbed back on board with laughter on their lips…yes, they were dead.

"You already asked me that," Arlen mumbled.

"I know it. And you said you didn't think they were dead, but honestly you're sure of it. That night at the station, you were right."

The kid had begun to shift in front of Arlen's eyes, tilting first one way and then the other, and there were three or four versions of him now, each one staring with intense eyes.

78

"How did you?" Paul said. "How in the hell did you know?"

Arlen flopped his head back down on the bed and squeezed his eyes shut. "Go away. Lemme sleep."

Paul didn't say anything. There was no sound from the doorway, and after enough time had passed Arlen was sure he'd left, but then he heard a footstep followed by the thud of the door swinging shut and knew the kid had been standing there the whole time, staring at him.

How in the hell did you know?

He just knew, damn it. Wasn't a thing could be said to explain it; Arlen Wagner saw the dead, knew when the hour tolled and the lives of men both friend and stranger would come to a close.

They didn't have to die, he thought. *The selfish bastards. All I can do is give a word of warning. The boy believed me simply because he is a boy. Grown men aren't allowed to believe such tales, even when they must. Even when it's all that can save them, they won't allow themselves to believe.*

He thought of Walt Sorenson leaning close to him at the roadhouse the night they'd met, that story of the fortune-teller who'd seen death in the rain and told him to be aware of travelers in need.

He might have believed, Arlen thought. *He was one of the few who might have believed, and I didn't see a damn thing before he died. Couldn't warn him.*

Why couldn't he? The man had died; Arlen had watched his body burn, had seen his flesh melt from his bones. Why hadn't Arlen been offered any warning? Why hadn't he looked into Sorenson's eyes and seen smoke?

It's this place, he thought. *There's something wrong with this place. Death hides here, even from me.*

The Cypress House, it was called. The Cypress House. That brought back memories, too. Not of a highway tavern, though. No, no. The cypress houses of Arlen's youth had been quite different than that. They'd been houses of

death

another sort entirely. The last Pope was in one now. Every Pope who'd passed on was, as far as Arlen knew. Always would be. Cypress wood was required in the sacred burial rites of many faiths in many lands. The branches of the trees themselves were symbols of

death

mourning. Arlen's father had carved them many times. The trees were not an uncommon symbol among German grave-stones. The leaves stayed evergreen even after the tree had been felled, and this was believed to be a sign of spiritual immortality, a representation of the insignificance of the body's passing. It went back to the Romans or the Greeks or some such, went back countless years, this idea of the cypress as an emblem of

death

morbid significance. What a terrible name for an inn. The Cypress House. He was edging toward sleep in a cypress house. He was edging toward —

death a coffin sleep in a cypress house death you are edging toward death

"We're leaving soon as we can," Arlen said, speaking to no one. "Soon as we can, we're going home." Then he brought his hands up and dropped them over his face, because keeping his eyes shut in this room with the boarded-up windows still didn't offer enough darkness.

12

H IS SLEEP WAS RESTLESS and oppressive, the tossing-and-turning, half-conscious slumber of a drunk. Dreams blurred with reality, and coherent thoughts spun a tangled dance with dark visions and memories. Men with skeletal faces leered at him, then vanished and turned back into the dark walls of the room before another blink conjured up a rattlesnake coiled on a slab of West Virginia stone and another brought forth a slick of burgundy liquid on soil in France, mustard gas after it had settled to earth.

He heard Paul's voice and Rebecca Cady's and tried to listen to them, but they became his father's voice and then Edwin Main's, the man who'd come to kill his father many years ago. Life was rushing past, stacking days upon days, but still some things wouldn't stay buried. Not Isaac's face, not his voice.

You're all I have in this *world, son, that death can't take. This world isn't anything but a sojourn, to be sure, but death removes every trace unless you've taken pains to leave one behind. You're my trace, Arlen.*

Isaac Wagner's bearded face split into a smile of crooked teeth, and he started a laugh that ended in a howl. The howl went on and on, a howl of madness, a howl of... wind.

The wind was roaring now, pushing at the walls of the Cypress House, the building shuddering in its grasp. Arlen tried to open his eyes, but the lids slid down again. He had to get on his feet, had to get out of here. There was something wrong in this place, terribly wrong, and he'd brought Paul Brickhill here and now was responsible for getting him out. They had to get out. It was time to get on his feet, and then they could hike to a train station... but he had no money. Someone had taken his money. His protection from hard times was gone, taken from him so easily when it had been so hard to build.

A voice whispered again, and he expected Isaac's and cried out against it, but this voice was disembodied, distant.

The seawall may not hold... most of the water has been drawn out of Tampa Bay... the storm will be weaker than when it passed through the Keys, but if the seawall fails...

A radio. They were listening to a radio. Let them listen; listening wouldn't change a thing. The storm would do what it would do, and they would be here for it. He had nowhere else to go. He was but another soldier in the trenches again, in a place where the trenches were filled with desperate, lost men.

He woke when the wind reached a scream. The door swung open, and he spun with a grunt and found himself facing Paul Brickhill.

"Arlen? Rebecca says you'd best come downstairs. It's getting close."

Arlen just stared at the kid for a moment, too disoriented to speak or move. Then he managed a nod and struggled out of bed. A blanket was snarled around his foot and he almost fell, but caught himself and tore free. The motion set off a bolt of pain that began in his head and ended in his gut, nausea sliding in behind it. He bent over, bracing his forearms on his knees, and sucked in a few breaths until it passed. Paul moved from the door as if to help, but Arlen held a hand up, breathed a few more times, and then straightened. His eyelids scraped like sandpaper with each blink, and his throat was dry and scorched.

"Sorry," he said, his voice harsh as a rasp on a cedar plank. "I shouldn't have...I didn't mean to drink like that. It's just the money was gone and I—"

Something tore on the side of the house, and Paul looked at the window as if he might be able to see through the boards to the other side.

"Let's get on downstairs, Arlen."

"Time is it?"

"Noon."

Noon. He'd been up here for an entire night and morning.

They went down the steps and out into the barroom. The electric lights were still on and the fan still blowing, but even so the room was dark and hot with all the windows and doors sealed. Rebecca Cady was sitting with a radio at a table in front of the bar. The radio was off. She looked up as they entered, let her eyes hang on Arlen's for a moment, and then said, "The water's coming up."

"Out of the ocean?" Paul said it like he didn't believe it.

She nodded.

Paul crossed the room and went to one of the windows. Arlen noticed now that there was a jagged shaft of gray light where a piece of the board had been torn away. Paul put his face to the glass and stared at the beach.

"How high will it get?" he said. "It's getting close to the porch."

He was trying to say it calmly enough, but there was a tremor in his voice.

"I'm not sure how high it will go," Rebecca Cady said. There was no tremor in hers.

Arlen crossed the room and joined Paul at the window, nudged him aside and looked out at the shore. The palm trees to the side of the back porch were bent at an incomprehensible angle — how the trunks didn't split, he couldn't imagine — and the Gulf of Mexico had turned into a wild, thrashing expanse of gray water speckled with white froth. Where the beach had once ended, now there was only water, furious water, pushed ahead by the wind and climbing with ease. The waves splashed no more than twenty feet from the base of the porch now, and even as Arlen watched, they seemed to grow closer.

"House is raised?" he said.

"Yes," Rebecca Cady said.

"By how much?"

"Three feet," Paul said quietly. "Block pylons. It'll move through them instead of around the sides of the house. Higher than that, it'll be on the porch."

Arlen didn't answer, still looking out at the water. A frond tore loose from one of the palms and snapped through the air, plastered onto the window just below Arlen's eye with such force that he gave an involuntary jerk. The wind's scream rose, as if it were laughing at him as it flattened the tops on the waves in the tossing sea. He stepped back from the window and shook his head. How could anything unseen have such savage strength? You could only watch its effects; the beast itself was invisible.

He followed Paul to the table and sat with Rebecca Cady, each of them listening to the sounds of the storm. He nodded at the radio.

"What do they say?"

"That it's here."

"That's all they say?"

"The seawall failed in Tampa. There's flooding."

"How far away is that?"

"Fifty miles south. That's nothing like what happened in the Keys. They still don't have a death toll settled on."

Arlen and Paul looked at each other until something crashed against the back of the house and gave them an excuse to turn away.

"Why don't you turn it back on?" Arlen said, pointing at the radio.

"Saving the batteries."

"I can't believe your lights are still on."

"It's a good generator."

"Sure is," Arlen agreed. "How'd you pay for it, with no business?"

This time her silence lingered. He'd just about given up on a response when she said, "My father put that in. Things were different then."

"Where is he now?"

"In a coffin."

"A lot of good men are," Arlen said.

She scowled and turned away. Arlen said, "Is there beer in that icebox?"

"I should think the last thing you'd need right now is another drink."

"Actually, the *one* thing I need right now is another drink."

He stood up and walked around the bar and into the kitchen, found the icebox. He took a bottle of beer out, then hesitated and withdrew two more.

When he came back, he set a bottle down in front of Paul, then in front of Rebecca Cady. Both of them looked at him like he was crazy, and he shrugged. The wind shrieked around the house, and Paul reached out tentatively and touched his beer, then moved his hand away when Rebecca Cady shifted her eyes to him.

"Go on," Arlen said, "just one ain't going to bite you. It's a hurricane, son. If that isn't a special occasion, what is?"

It wasn't strong stuff, but it was enough to settle Arlen's stomach and ease his headache. Paul let the bottle sit untouched in front of him for a few minutes and then lifted it and took a small swallow.

About ten minutes went by, and then there came a crash and a tearing from the back porch. Arlen and Paul got to their feet and went to the small exposed portion of glass to look out. One of the porch railings had ripped free and blown into the back wall, and the corresponding roof support had buckled. The porch roof was still standing, but on just three legs now.

"That porch is almost finished," Paul whispered. "I wonder what's happening to that dock and the boathouse up in the inlet."

Before Arlen could answer, there was another crash, this one far louder and on the southern side of the house, out of sight at their angle. The entire building trembled with impact, and then the lights went out. There wasn't so much as a flicker; they simply snapped off. The electric fan whirled down to a crawl and then a stop, and now there were no sounds but the storm.

Arlen led the way back, picking past chairs and tables that existed as shadows. Rebecca Cady was where they'd left her, and though she hadn't said a word, she was moving in the darkness. It took Arlen a minute to realize that she'd begun to drink the beer.

13

IT WENT ON THROUGH the afternoon and into the evening—wind and rain and the sounds of the house threatening to break up around them. One of the back windows splintered from the squeezing and shifting of the frame, then fell to the floor in shards when another gust shook the house. Paul and Arlen set to work cleaning up the glass and waiting on the rest of the windows to go, but they never did. The storm surge covered the beach and reached the porch and sloshed under the house. They could hear it moving beneath the floor, and Rebecca Cady kept her eyes downcast for at least an hour, looking for signs of it, expecting the water to begin seeping through. It didn't rise high enough, though. Now and then a particularly inspired wave would splash up onto the edge of the porch, but it never made the door.

The three of them went out onto the front porch once, with the building offering shelter between them and the wind, and took in the yard. Everything was awash with water, the sea moving all around them, as if they stood aboard a ship rather than a porch. The heavy Cypress House sign banged on its iron chains.

Up the hill, the trees bent almost to the earth and the under-growth had been picked clean by the wind. The air was thick with spray and sand, peppering the trees.

"You ever seen one like this before?" Paul shouted in Rebecca Cady's ear, his hand cupped to the side of her face. She shook her head.

It didn't begin to lessen until evening, and then it was subtle — the wind shriek losing its voice just a bit, as if its lungs were worn from the day's ravings. An hour later it was noticeably calmer, and the rain had faded to an ordinary, steady summer shower as the ocean mustered a slow retreat, as if displeased with the results of its reconnaissance mission on land. Maybe it would invade sometime, but it wouldn't be now and wouldn't be here.

As the storm eased away, real darkness settled in, and Rebecca lit more oil lamps. She had two lanterns, and around nine that evening, when the wind dangers seemed past, she lit them both and handed one to Paul and kept the other herself, and they all went outside.

The yard was littered with pieces of siding and porch rails and shingles. The back porch was in shambles, but the roof had held; the widow's walk deck hadn't fared so well.

Rebecca Cady looked everything over without comment and then said she wanted to go to the boathouse. She led the way, holding the lantern out in front of her body, picking over branches and planks and other debris. There was a narrow path that led north from the house and into the palms. It curved away from the Gulf, then opened up on an inlet that appeared to wind back into ever deeper undergrowth. The boathouse stood before them, little more than a tall shed built out onto the dock. Most of its roof was gone. Rebecca walked to the edge of the dock and lifted the lantern high. A third of the floor planks were missing, but the pilings that supported them were intact.

"You have anything in that boathouse?" Arlen asked.

"It was moved," she said shortly, and then turned and started back to the house. "Let's look at the generator."

"We might be able to get it running again tonight," Paul said, full of forced optimism.

That idea lasted for the amount of time it took them to get back to the house. The generator was in an enclosure that had been constructed on the north side of the building. Where it had once stood, nothing was visible but tangled branches. A tree of at least forty feet in length—it was some sort of coastal pine whose branches and needles had been pruned away by the storm—had blown directly into the side of the building, crushing the shed. The smell of fuel hung in the air, and when Paul leaned over the tree and lifted his lantern, a piece of an engine became visible.

"It's ruined," Rebecca Cady said. "Destroyed."

Paul set his lantern on the ground and tried to heave the tree off the generator. After watching him struggle for a few seconds, Arlen fell in to help, and they rolled the tree back enough to see the damage more clearly. It looked to Arlen to be catastrophic—the generator had been broken into pieces and was now covered with wet sand. He could see a metal plate with the words "Delco-Light" stamped onto the side. Arlen was a damn fine carpenter, but he was no mechanic, and even a great one wouldn't be able to put this wreck back together.

"Going to need a new one," he said.

"I can't afford one." She looked up from the ruined generator and out at the rest of her property—shanks of damaged siding littered the yard, pieces of the back porch lay half buried in the sandy hill above the inn, the bed rails from her truck had been ripped off and deposited somewhere in the darkness.

"We'll get it cleaned up," Paul said, and Arlen looked at him with wide eyes. The hell they would. They were leaving.

"I can take care of it," she said.

"No, you can't. You going to rebuild that porch?" He shook his head. "We won't leave until it's cleaned up."

Arlen said, "Have you lost your senses?"

"We have to stay long enough to help—"

"We don't have to stay long enough for anything! I don't recall that we invited the hurricane here, and I'll be damned if I take any sense of neighborly kindness at a place where I was jailed and robbed. We're leaving in the morning."

Paul shook his head, and Arlen wanted to knock it right off his shoulders.

"We came in together," Paul said. "That doesn't mean we have to leave together. I'm staying at least long enough to help her get this place cleaned up."

They stood there for a while in the lantern light and the soft rain, looking out at the inn that was now bound by darkness.

"Come on," Arlen said at last. "Won't be able to do anything out here till daylight, and there's no use burning the lantern fuel. Way that generator looks, you're going to need it."

Nobody came by to check on the Cypress House until the next morning, and then it was a man in a white panel van. Arlen was in the bathroom and Paul and Rebecca Cady were already outside, pulling the boards off the windows. They hadn't reached the second floor yet, so when Arlen heard the sound of the approaching engine, he had to go downstairs to see the source. The van had parked and the driver got out, a short, squat man in a watch cap. He stood with his hands on his hips, looked around the tavern, and shook his head.

Arlen opened the door and stepped out onto the porch, lifting a hand. The man lifted one in response and walked up to join him. "How'd you folks fare?"

"Well enough," Arlen answered, "but it's not my place."

"Oh, I know that," the visitor said. He had a heavy drawl, a spray of freckles across his face, blue eyes that held good humor. "Y'all are the criminals."

Arlen raised his eyebrows, and the man laughed.

"You best expect that to be known by now. Think a pesky thing like a hurricane will keep folks from talking?" He put out a hand. "Thomas Barrett. I reckon you're Wagner, not Brickhill."

Arlen didn't take his hand, and Barrett laughed again. "Relax. I'm nothing but a delivery driver. You can put away your guns."

"Sorry," Arlen said, finally reaching out to accept the handshake, "but I'm a bit leery of folks out here. They kill some men, lock others up, and probably steal from everyone."

Barrett's smile went sour as he pulled his hand back. "Ain't everybody around here that'll do you that way."

"I'd hope not. But it's who I've met so far."

Barrett nodded. "You met the sheriff, and maybe you met the judge?"

"That's right. What do you know about them?"

"Enough to stay out of their way. Enough to know that most folks with half a mind are scared witless of them."

"They're elected positions, aren't they?"

Barrett threw his head back and gave a bull snort. "Elected, sure. And I ran against Tolliver for sheriff, so you ever want to hear about Corridor County politics, I can talk on it. But you probably don't, and I probably shouldn't."

"I got the impression he was from Cleveland."

Barrett gave him a surprised glance and a nod. "You had the right impression."

"How in the hell did he become sheriff down here, then?"

Barrett's smile was forced this time. "I wouldn't waste your thoughts worrying on a thing like that. It's Corridor County's problem, not yours."

"Is High Town really all there is to the county?"

"Most people are scattered. You know, live in the woods or out at places like this. Was a lumber mill outside of High Town that kept the place alive, but it went under five years ago, and, all told, a few thousand people probably went with it. Workers and their families and such. Take away the only real industry in a place like this, and it empties out powerful fast."

"So what do people out here do now?"

"They try to get by," Barrett said. "Just like Becky."

"How'd she end up alone in this place?"

"Was owned by her parents. They came down from Georgia years back to try and build a sport fishing business. It didn't take. Her mother drowned right out from the house. Some said it was tides that caught her, others believed she went willingly enough. Tired of her husband's methods of getting ahead."

"What methods were those?"

Barrett gave him a long look, then turned away and said, "A few years later, Rebecca's daddy took his boat out, lost the engines, and then lost himself. They found the boat but not him. All that was left of her family by then was her brother, and he's in prison."

At that moment Rebecca Cady appeared around the side of the house, wiping her hands on a towel.

"Hello, Tom."

"Becky, you survive all right?"

"Better than the inn," she said, and then added, "Stop calling me Becky."

"I know, I know. Is there anything left of the back porch?"

"Not much. I lost the generator, too. No icebox."

Barrett groaned. "Can it be fixed?"

"Probably not. You can have a look if you'd like."

"I'll do that." He turned to Arlen and winked. "We'll talk in a minute, gunslinger. Don't shoot me in the back now, hear?"

"Awful witty boy, aren't you?" Arlen said, and Barrett gave another of his loud laughs and walked away. Arlen went in search of Paul.

He found him up on the ladder on the side of the house. He'd gotten the boards off the windows and was now nailing a torn piece of the wooden siding back into place. Arlen called for him to come down.

"We've got a job," Paul said before his feet had even touched ground.

"I'm sorry?"

"Here," Paul said triumphantly. "I talked her into it this morning. She sure needs the help, and we sure need the money. I know you don't want to stay, but it's a different tune if we're getting paid, right?"

"What we need is a *ride,* boy, and there's one out front."

Paul frowned. "A ride where, Arlen? We don't have enough money for a meal, much less a train ticket. You want to walk all the way back to Alabama? Rebecca said she could pay us ten dollars each if we get this place cleaned up and the porch put back together. Shouldn't take more than a few days. That's enough for train tickets at least."

Arlen stared at him. "Paul...you remember where you are? You remember what happened to the man who drove us down here?"

"Arlen, it's not like *she* blew his car up!"

"I don't care if she did or not, he ended up dead and we ended up in jail and this ain't a place I intend to stay around."

"So where are you going to go?"

"Away," Arlen said. "Hitch a ride into a town and figure it out."

"Wouldn't you rather do that with a few dollars in your pocket?"

"They're probably my own dollars," Arlen snapped. "I'm still not sure she didn't steal it herself."

Paul sighed and shook his head again. "You know that's not the case."

"I don't *know* a damn thing, son! Neither do you."

"Arlen, she's here by herself. We can't just leave. It isn't right. I mean, if she were my mother and somebody walked off and left—"

"You aren't confusing her for your mother," Arlen said. "I've seen the way you look at her."

Paul flushed and looked down, twirled the hammer in his hands. "I got off that train when you asked me to."

"Aren't you glad you did?"

"*Yes*. But now I'm asking you: stick for a few days. Just long enough to help her get this place put together."

Arlen stepped back and ran a hand over his face. He didn't want to leave the kid here on his own. Not in this place.

"Listen," he said, his voice sharpening in a way that brought Paul's eyes up. "You wouldn't lie to me, would you, son? Look me in the face and lie?"

"No. Of course not."

"All right. So when you tell me we'll stay just long enough to get the tavern cleaned up, and then we'll go back to Alabama... that's the truth?"

"Yes."

Arlen said, "Shit," and sighed.

"Won't be so bad," Paul said. "Working right on the ocean like this? It'll almost be a vacation."

"Just find me another hammer," Arlen said. "Faster we work, faster we can leave."

They walked back to the front of the house together in search of the second hammer. Barrett was leaving, pulling away in his van with a honk and a wave, and Rebecca stood on the front porch with a newspaper in her hands and a grim look on her face. She glanced up at them, said nothing, and passed the paper to Arlen. The front page was half covered by an enormous head-line that shrieked: 1,000 PREDICTED DEATH TOLL IN KEYS.

Below that, a promise of the "complete hurricane carnage in pictures" stood above a photograph of corpses stacked on the front of a ship.

Arlen didn't want to see the complete hurricane carnage in pictures. Nor did he want to read about the dead. Paul had seen the look on his face, though, and he said, "What's wrong?"

"Nothing."

Paul came up and looked over Arlen's shoulder at the photograph of the dead men and that headline. One thousand predicted dead. One thousand.

"Let me see," Paul said, his voice hushed. Arlen passed it over, fished a cigarette out and lit it and smoked with his back to the boy and the newspaper. Every now and then Paul would let out a murmur of horror or pain. Rebecca had joined him and was reading at his side.

"Arlen," Paul said, "most of these pictures are of the veterans' camps. They were just waiting there for it. Waiting in tents and shacks."

"Yeah."

"It's got an editorial in here someone wrote for the *Washington Post*. Says it was a tragedy, but then says that the men in those camps were 'drifters, psychopathic cases, or habitual trouble-makers.'"

Arlen lowered his cigarette and smashed it out on the deck rail. He'd heard the camps were rough. It's why the CCC hadn't wanted to send juniors. But something else those men were, every last one of them? Veterans. Soldiers. Men who'd listened to Washington when Washington told them to go across an ocean and pour their blood into the soil of a place they knew nothing about, men who'd taken bullets and bayonets and breathed in mustard gas. Heroes, Washington had called them back in '18 and '19, the war won and the economy strong. Now they were "drifters, psychopathic cases, or habitual trouble-makers."

"You think those men on our train died?" Paul said.

"Yes," Arlen said. It was the first time he'd given the boy a flat, honest answer on that question. The dead deserved that much right now. They deserved a little honesty.

Rebecca had been staring at Arlen, but when he looked over she turned away. Paul folded the paper, but Arlen shook his head, took it from the boy, and lit a match and held it to the edge, watched as the flame caught and licked along until the rolled paper was a torch in his hand. Then he dropped it out into the sand, and they watched it burn down to embers.

Part Two

CORRIDOR COUNTY

14

SOLOMON WADE MADE HIS first appearance the next day. By then they'd gotten the yard cleared and all the damaged siding repaired and had turned to the back porch. The railing could be salvaged, but many of the spindles were lost and the pillar that supported the roof had been smashed and sheared in half. They got the railings in place easily enough and then Arlen went to the roof pillar, turned the pieces over in his hands and studied them, looking at the jagged ends.

"Won't fit together anymore," Paul said. "There's some scrap wood around but nothing like that."

"Got to make it work, then," Arlen said, eyeing the uneven fit of the broken wood. "If we shave it down and smooth it, we can drive nails in like this" — he indicated the angle with his index finger — "and make it solid. Will it look perfect? Nah. But it'll hold. Problem is, we'll lose some length, so we'll have to cut a block to put between this piece and the rail. Maybe put it between this piece and the roof, actually. That'll hide it better."

It was nearing noon and had been, much as Arlen was loath to admit it, not an altogether bad day. He enjoyed working with the boy, and they'd made swift progress. All things considered, he was in fairly good spirits when he went around the side of the house in search of a drill and heard the clatter of an engine and saw the visitor approaching.

Rebecca Cady was also on the south side of the house, using a shovel to move sand out from under the foundation, where it had been heaped by the wind. Give her this much: she'd worked hard and without complaint alongside them. At the sound of the car, she straightened without much interest, but when she got a glimpse of it, her body went tight.

It was a steel-gray Ford coupe, and it rumbled right down the hill and into the yard, parked beside the truck. The engine shut off and the driver stepped out, and when Arlen saw who it was, he cursed himself instantly. They shouldn't have lingered to give Solomon Wade another crack at them. It was begging for trouble.

The only thing that reassured him was that Wade appeared to be alone, not accompanied by Sheriff Tolliver.

Wade had a cigarette in his mouth, and now he removed it and blew smoke and studied the house with a quality of ownership. He removed his white Panama hat and fanned himself and shifted his gaze their way. He took his time walking down to them, looking around the property and smoking his cigarette and not saying a word. When he was close enough, he came to a stop and stared at Arlen. Behind his glasses his eyes were gray, reminded Arlen of the color of the sea as it had crawled up the beach in the storm.

"I expected you would have left my county by now."

"Hurricane slowed us down a touch," Arlen said.

Wade showed no reaction. At that moment Paul rounded the corner, half of the broken porch support in his hand, and everyone turned to face him. He pulled back and swung the piece of wood around in front of him, as if to ward off their stares. He looked as thrilled at the sight of Wade as Arlen had been.

"They're helping me with repairs," Rebecca said.

"I gathered that."

"And their money was stolen. Sometime after Tolliver arrested them, all of their money was stolen."

"Is that so?" he said without apparent interest. "How's the dock?"

"Nearly ruined. Same with the boathouse."

His scowl said that was of personal annoyance.

"There's a lot to be done," she said.

"Well, get the tavern cleaned up first, and get it done fast. You'll be having visitors soon. Friends of mine."

"Solomon"—she waved her hand at the building behind them—"you see what this place looks like? I can't be ready for anyone."

"They won't mind the condition."

"There was a *hurricane*—"

"I am aware. But it's gone now."

Paul Brickhill shifted the piece of wood in his hands and frowned at Wade, disliking the judge's tone. Arlen watched it and saw what he'd already suspected—the boy was beyond smitten with Rebecca Cady.

"I don't have electricity," she said. "No lights, no icebox, no—"

"Then put out some oil lamps," Wade said. "They'll be down Monday evening, and you need to be ready to receive them."

"Hey," Paul said, "she just told you..."

He didn't finish the sentence. Both Arlen and Solomon Wade turned to him with daggers in their eyes, daggers carried for different purposes, and Rebecca Cady laid her hand on his arm, the word "stop" clear in the touch.

"Son," Wade said, "do you remember that cell?"

It seemed a rhetorical question, but Wade held the boy's eyes until it became clear he wanted an answer. Paul managed a nod.

"I hope that you do," Wade said. "It would serve you well to remember."

They all regarded one another in silence, and then the judge dropped his cigarette into the sand and ground it out with his shoe.

"Becky? Be ready for my guests." He turned to Arlen then and said, "Mr. Wagner, walk on up to the car with me."

Arlen did as he said. They left Paul and Rebecca behind and walked in silence until they reached the Ford. When they got there, Wade pulled open the driver's door and stood with one foot resting in the car and one on the ground, his arm leaning against the roof. He put the Panama back on his head.

"Shame to hear about the loss of your savings," he said. "Tough country right now for a man with no dollars."

He was staring back up at the inn, where Paul was watching them and Rebecca was pretending not to.

"I'd expect," Wade continued, "that you'd like to have that cash back."

He was waiting for an answer again, just as he had with Paul. Arlen said, "I expect you're right."

Wade nodded. "Now of course I know nothing of the circumstance of your loss. I don't know how much money you carried, if there even was any money."

"Of course not," Arlen said, wanting to smash those glasses back into Wade's face.

"But I do know of a way that your loss could be made up. I have some sway in this county, and I believe I could see that you're reimbursed."

"On what condition?" Arlen said. "Because you're damn sure not making that offer without a string on it."

"On the condition that you do what you should have done all along, and tell me the truth about Walter Sorenson."

"Judge," Arlen said, "you've heard the truth. Heard it over and over. I can't make you believe it."

Wade gave a little sigh, as if this were expected but still disappointing.

"You believe you're making a stand, Mr. Wagner, and, like so many foolish men, you believe that making a stand, even at the loss of a few dollars, is worth something. It's a sad, silly notion. You couldn't fathom the amount of money that passes through this place. Tell me, where do you think it goes?"

"Right into your pockets," Arlen said, and Wade smiled and shook his head.

"You make my point for me. You possess a staggering lack of understanding of the world. The dollars that pass through my hands, Wagner, they rise and disappear like smoke. Then men you'd never imagine are connected to a place like Corridor County fill their lungs deep with it. You know my role in all that?"

Arlen didn't say anything.

"I am," Solomon Wade said, "the match."

He shook out a cigarette, put it between his lips, then struck a match theatrically and lit the cigarette. When the tip glowed red, he inhaled and then blew smoke into Arlen's eyes.

"Those men I speak of," he said, "they need their smoke. I provide it. Someday, a day not far off, I will breathe of it myself."

He leveled his gaze at Arlen. "I suspect you believe that you can carry on out of this place and out of my reach, Mr. Wagner. Believe that once you've made a few dollars from Miss Cady here, you can just go back to Alabama or West Virginia."

Arlen bristled. He had never spoken of his home state. Not to the judge or the sheriff. In fact, he rarely spoke of Fayette County to anyone.

Wade looked at him and nodded. "Yes, I know where you're from. The boy, too. And if I desire, I can tamper with his life same as yours. Hell, I'm one phone call away from bringing shame down on his family."

"What do you know about his family?"

"More than you, probably. His old man used to work in a silk factory in Paterson. Got into an accident, lost the use of his legs. Was in a wheelchair until he killed himself on some bad hooch."

"I don't see any shame in that," Arlen said. "I just see some sorrow."

"Sure. Thing is, with no father around to work, his mother had to. Pretty woman, his mother, or so I've been told. She took to waitressing at a few supper clubs. They aren't the sort of clubs where you want your mother waitressing, you know? She's not getting paid for delivering steak and potatoes. Be easy enough to send some local police down to make life hard on her."

Arlen felt a slow, liquid heat spreading through his body. "Listen," he said, "you want to stick your short, sorry pecker into my life, have at it, Judge. But you tamper with that boy's mother? With that boy, period? Wade, I'll cut your damn throat. Think that's a lie? I will cut your throat, you son of a bitch."

Wade's voice was cool. "You're an ignorant man, Mr. Wagner. Not a brave one—just stupid. We can stand here and trade threats, but when the time comes to deliver on them? That won't be a pleasant day for you." He nodded at the inn. "Go on back to work. Go on back and hope I don't have cause to venture your way again. Pray for it."

15

IT WAS MIDAFTERNOON BEFORE Arlen had the opportunity to
get Rebecca Cady alone for a few minutes. Paul was immersed
in work on the porch, the rest of the world vanishing from his
mind the way it always seemed to when he was on a job, and
when Arlen heard Rebecca moving around inside the barroom,
he told Paul he needed a drink of water and then went inside.

She was cleaning the bar with a wet rag and merely glanced at
him. Only after he'd stood and watched her for a few minutes
did she look back up.

"Can I help you?"

"I hope so. We've been helping you, so I figured you might do
the same."

"Well, what is it?"

"Why did the judge come out here?" Arlen asked.

Her face darkened, and she looked back down at the glossy
bar top.

"You heard him. He's going to rent the place on Monday
night."

"I heard that he was sending people down here Monday

night," Arlen said. "I didn't hear a word about *renting,* though. Which brings to mind another question: where in the hell is your business? You know, customers?"

"There was a hurricane."

"So you're telling me that a few days from now, when people have settled from the storm, this place will be busy?"

She didn't answer.

"That's what I figured," he said. "Now tell me about Solomon Wade."

"I've got nothing to tell. You've met him and you've met the sheriff. You should be able to gather plenty from that."

"I've gathered that they're crooked as snake tracks, sure. I'd like to know what in the hell it is they're up to, though, and where Sorenson figured in."

"I'd have no way of knowing."

"I don't believe that. As soon as the poor bastard blew up, you suggested we leave and let you handle the sheriff. Just as if you knew what might happen."

"I knew there was a chance you'd be treated unfairly."

"Treated unfairly," Arlen echoed, nodding. "You mean locked up, beaten, robbed? That's what you knew there was a chance of?"

She held his eyes.

"Sorenson was a bootlegger," he said. "But this isn't a dry county. What was his business here?"

"I couldn't say."

"That's a damned lie and you know it."

She looked away, then back to him, and said, "What did Wade tell you when you were talking at his car?"

"That he might have a way of finding our money if we told him what he wants to know about Sorenson. Trouble is, we don't know anything."

"Really?"

"Really. You do, though. You probably know a hell of a lot. Care to tell me what a man from Cleveland's doing as sheriff of a place where visitors from the north are about as common as penguins? Care to tell me what it is brings men like those two to a backwater like this, what brought your father to it, what put your brother in—"

"Don't you speak of my family," she said, and her voice was so low and cold that she seemed truly dangerous.

He studied her, then nodded and said, "I'll keep such questions to myself. They're of no concern to me. Solomon Wade and his thug sheriff are."

She dropped her gaze, and when she spoke again her voice was soft and measured. "You should be careful with Solomon Wade. Whether you're here or somewhere else, you should be careful with Solomon Wade."

It was a different version of the same speech Wade himself had given.

"I'm wondering," Arlen said, "why all of these boys seem to spend so much time at your place? What are *you* doing here?"

She picked up the rag and began to scrub again, rubbing so hard that the muscles in her arm stood out.

"As you already said, my private affairs are of no concern to you."

He watched her for a long time, waiting for more, but she didn't look up again. At length he turned and went back outside.

They finished the porch roof by noon on Sunday, and as they stood in the sand surveying their work, Arlen was unable to avoid feeling a small tug of satisfaction at the way the job looked. For what they'd had to work with, it was damn fine construction.

"Could leave," he suggested. "Most everything's done now."

"We're not even close to done," Paul said, smearing sweat around his face with a rag. He looked older, with his skin burned dark brown and his hair a few weeks past cutting. "Haven't even started on the widow's walk or the generator."

Arlen stopped with a cigarette halfway to his mouth. "The *generator?* Have you lost your senses?"

"She can't buy a new one," Paul said calmly. "So I'd say that one will need fixing."

"Son, ain't a mechanic alive can put that thing back together now, and neither of us is a mechanic. You've got to know what you're doing to work on one that's solid, let alone one that's been busted up into a hundred pieces. That thing's covered in sand and grit and—"

"I've got it cleaned up. Come have a look."

So they went around to the front porch, and Paul pulled free a tarpaulin and there were the pieces of the generator, all neat and tidy.

"When'd you do that?"

"Been getting up early," Paul said, dropping to one knee and running a fingertip over one of the flywheels. "Brushed all the sand off and then wiped it down with a rag and oil, because that salt water would rust it awfully fast, I think."

"Any chance the thing came with some sort of a book? A manual?"

"She said she never saw one. But she has all the tools for it."

Arlen stared down at the mess and shook his head. "You ever worked on an engine before in your life?"

"No. But the way it works is, it charges that bank of batteries," Paul said, pointing at a row of batteries stacked against the back wall. "All of them seem fine. The exhaust pipe is still solid, too."

"Great. But the *engine* is not. Not to mention that however it was connected to the house is no more than a memory."

"Well, let me show you what I've done. There were two plugs

on the frame, and I got those out and then the frame came off and I could get at the flywheel and the camshaft and the main bearing. All of those are intact."

"How in the hell do you even know what they are?"

Paul shrugged. "I've read a lot about engines. My point is, the main assembly of this thing is fine. So now that I've got it cleaned up, it's just a matter of figuring out how it went together in the first place. That'll be common sense."

"Sure," Arlen said, looking down at the gears and wrenches and belts scattered on the porch floor. "Common sense."

"I got the inspection plate off," Paul said, oblivious to Arlen now, focused on the machine, "and you can see the connecting rods in here. Looks like they got loosened up when it was knocked around. See here, when I move the crankshaft? It's wiggling down at the bearing. That shouldn't happen. It needs to be tight. So I've got to get those tightened up before we try and run it again."

"Even supposing you get the thing in a condition that it *could* run again," Arlen said, "you've got to get it set up so it actually feeds power the way it used to. Those wires were all torn apart."

"Oh, that'll be easy. Just a matter of looking, seeing how it makes sense."

"I suppose that leaves me to that damn widow's walk myself?"

Paul's lack of response allowed that it did, and Arlen walked out into the yard, grumbling and swearing, and stared up at the peak of the roof. The widow's walk was perched onto the back, affording an expansive view of the Gulf, and all except for one corner piling had been torn off. They'd gathered the pieces from out in the yard and stacked them up alongside the house. Even from down here, Arlen could tell that it was going to be awkward and dangerous work.

He found the stairs to the attic, sweat springing out of his pores as he climbed into the dank, closed space. It was so dark he had to feel around with his hands to locate the trapdoor, but it opened easily enough and he poked his head up through the roof and into fresh air. He'd never been unsettled by heights, but this roof was pitched steeply, and he felt a swirl of doubt as he climbed out onto it, keeping a tight hand on the braces of the door frame. Ordinarily the railings would keep you from tumbling off, but they were stacked on the ground now, nothing between him and a broken spine but a few bounces off the shingles.

Had to admit, though — once he was up here, the view was stunning, like being in a lighthouse. He could see out into the sea and along the shore. This was his first realization of just how damn isolated the inn was. To the south the beach ran on unbroken, and to the north the trees grew thick along the winding inlet. No such thing as a neighbor. He turned to look east, inland, and saw the boat in the inlet.

It was positioned around a bend, where there was a slot in the trees that afforded a view of the house. The boat was flat-bottomed, outfitted only with oars — a craft you could move damn near silently if you knew how to use it. There was only one man inside. From here, all Arlen could tell was that he was an older man: stringy gray hair showed along his neck down to his shoulders.

Don't stare, he thought. *He'll know that you've seen him.*

He turned away and got busy taking measurements for the roof deck, working with his back to the inlet for a while. When he finally turned around and risked a glance, the boat was gone.

That night they all sat together on the porch, as had become their custom, and ate dinner as the sun went fat and red in the west and slipped down toward the horizon line. It moved at a crawl right until the bottom edge touched the water, and then it was as if something greedy were waiting for it on the other side, snatched it away quick, leaving only a crimson smear on the horizon.

"This place sure is something," Paul said, stretched out on the porch floor with the already empty plate on his lap. "It's beautiful."

Rebecca nodded but didn't speak, and he turned to her.

"Why doesn't anyone ever come out here?"

"Excuse me?"

"Well ... why don't you have any customers?"

She looked away from him. "Corridor County is a very rural place. There aren't a lot of people. Less now that the lumber mill closed."

"Well, still, *somebody* has to live around here."

"I don't have much business from locals. Mostly people who rent it out for a few days at a time. There's less of that now. Hard times."

"Have you always been out here alone?"

"Not always." Her voice was tight. "Tell me, where are you from?"

If Paul sensed that the redirecting of the conversation was intentional, he didn't show it.

"New Jersey. Town called Paterson. Back there, we'd be sitting in an alley and looking at trash cans if we wanted to eat outside."

"You don't care for it?"

He looked uncomfortable. "I don't know. It's just a place ... doesn't look anything like this, though." Then, after a pause, "But there's a bridge you ought to see. Just up from the waterfalls."

Rebecca Cady laughed, and Paul looked perplexed.

"I'm sorry," she said. "I just thought it was amusing that you'd mention a bridge before you would a waterfall."

He shrugged. "I just like it, that's all."

Arlen smiled and sipped his beer. She didn't know him yet. With the exception of the ocean in front of them, Arlen had never known the boy to show the slightest interest in the natural world, only in man-made structures. He was mighty American in that way: show him a river, he'd want to see a bridge; show him a mountain, he'd wonder how you could get a tunnel through it. For all his carpentry experience, Arlen didn't have the same mind-set. The older he got, the more he wished people would leave things alone. As a boy he'd watched the hills around his hometown blasted open with dynamite, laced with gouges that looked like wounds of the flesh, and in their own way they were exactly that. Had watched the skies above them turn black with soot and coal smoke, the stretches of ancient forests replaced by stump fields. No, he wasn't the conquering sort. That was one of the things he'd liked so much about the CCC. Back at Flagg Mountain, they'd spent weeks at hard labor to build a tower. Its purpose? To afford a view of the beauty around it. That was all. Arlen loved that damn tower.

He didn't know for certain what he'd even have thought of the bridge in the Keys, that attempt for road to conquer water. Maybe it would've been impressive. Maybe it would've been heartbreaking.

"Did you always live in Paterson?" Rebecca was asking Paul, and Arlen looked back at the boy, realizing Arlen himself didn't know the answer to this one.

"Yes." Paul got to his feet and set the plate aside. "I'm going to go for a walk before it gets too dark."

He left without another word, headed south with his hands in his pockets and his shoulders hunched. Rebecca Cady said, "Did I say something wrong?"

"I think you both did."

"Pardon?"

"You didn't want to answer questions about yourself," he said, "and neither did Paul. Everybody's got a few things they'd like to keep quiet on."

He finished the warm beer and tilted his head and studied her. Her face was lit with fading sunset glow, and it made her blond hair look red.

"Can you really see the dead?" she asked. The question hit him like a punch.

"Paul told me about the train," she said when he didn't answer. "Why you two got off."

"Wasn't his place to tell you that."

"Don't be angry with him. He was just fascinated by it. Maybe a little frightened, especially after reading that newspaper article and learning what happened to the men who stayed on the train. He told me you see smoke or —"

"I don't know why we're talking about this."

"I just wanted to hear what it's like," she said.

"I can't tell you what it's like. You won't believe it if I try, and I don't give a damn what you think. It's a waste of everybody's time."

"I might believe it."

"You wouldn't."

"You can see death before it happens," she said. "That's what Paul said."

He didn't answer.

"Did you see anything with Walter Sorenson?" she asked.

He studied her for a long time before saying, "No, I didn't."

"Why do you think that was?"

"I'm not sure. But I suspect it's got something to do with this place."

"This place?"

"That's right. There's something wrong here."

He could see her throat move when she swallowed. She said, "You can feel that?"

"Sure," he said. "Can't you?"

She said, "I'm not part of it. You think that I am, but I'm not. When I arrived, it was with the expectation that I'd be leaving soon, just like you."

"That some kind of warning?"

She didn't reply.

"Answer the question I asked," he said. "Do you feel like there's something wrong with this place?"

"Of course. It hangs in the air like the salt smell from the water. But I don't need to have *feelings* about it. I've been here far too long for that. You have bad feelings; I have bad memories."

They fell silent after that. Eventually he said, "As long as everybody's trading questions, I have one for you. Why don't you like to be called Becky?"

She'd bristled every time someone said it, from Sorenson to Barrett, the delivery driver. It seemed to Arlen to go well beyond a dislike of the nickname.

She looked at him with a steady gaze, but something in her face faltered. He felt, for just a moment, as if she were about to tell him things that had gone unsaid for too long. As if she kept a silence that pained her. He knew about that. He had his own untold tale, guarded for years, but somehow, on this porch, lit by the fading sun and warmed by the Gulf breeze, he wanted to tell it to her. That last part was key. To *her*.

She turned from him, though, and when she spoke her voice was distant and her eyes were on the sea.

"People used to call me that," she said. "Different people in a different place. I'm not that person anymore, so that name...it doesn't suit me these days. It's not mine, not anymore."

She rose then and walked to the end of the porch and stood with her back to him as the last smears of red light faded, and though they shared the shadowed space, they were each alone with their silent sorrows.

16

REBECCA WAITED UNTIL THE next morning to try to get rid of them. She came out onto the porch, where Paul was working on the generator and Arlen was sanding down pieces of the broken railing from the roof deck, and held out a slim stack of worn dollar bills.

"Here," she said. "You've earned it, and I don't want to make you stay any longer. I can drive you into High Town, let you find a ride from there."

Arlen just sat back on his heels and didn't speak. Paul looked from the money in her hand to her face and frowned.

"We're not finished," he said.

"You've done enough. You've done more than enough."

He shook his head. "No. I'm going to get this generator running again."

"There's no need to—"

"You trying to run us off because the judge's friends are coming?"

That stopped her.

"No, it's just...you've both already done enough," she fumbled. "You were a big help, but you've done enough, and I can't afford to keep you on anymore. So please take the money and I'll drive you—"

"I'm going to finish this job."

She stared at him, then slowly folded her hand over the bills. Her eyes were still on Paul, but they'd gone distant.

"Listen to me," she said. "It might be best if you weren't around tonight."

"Why? Who are these guys? Are you in some kind of trouble?"

Arlen said, "Paul, it ain't your concern," but the boy never looked at him.

"Are you in some kind of trouble?" he repeated.

"No, I'm not. But when Solomon Wade rents this place out, he wants it empty. It's supposed to be for his friends; no one else is allowed."

"Well," Paul said, "we're here."

"All right," she said, "then you stay in the boathouse tonight."

"The boathouse?" Paul said. "It doesn't even have a roof."

"You're the one who won't leave; you can deal without a roof for one night." She snapped it at him, and Paul's jaw tightened and he looked away.

That'll do it, Arlen thought. *He's going to say enough is enough, finally, and take that money from her hand and we'll be on our way...*

But Paul said, "Fine. We'll stay in the boathouse."

Rebecca lifted a hand to the side of her face, and for a moment, just a blink, it was the gesture of some other woman, a gesture of someone vulnerable. Then she seemed to catch herself and pushed her hair back over her ear as if that's what she'd been planning to do all the time.

* * *

That was the last that was said about it. Paul continued to battle with the generator. By midafternoon he was satisfied that the mechanical workings were solid again and began to put the pieces back together. Arlen watched him do it, rebuilding something he'd never built in the first place, working without benefit of a manual or diagram, and shook his head. The kid was a natural, no question. He still didn't think the thing would ever work again, though.

By five he had the generator together and hollered at Arlen to come down so they could test it. He came over and watched as Paul filled the tank with gasoline and explained that he had it connected to the battery bank, and once he was sure it would work all they'd have to do is wire it back into the house and build a new enclosure for it. Rebecca came out while he was talking, and as soon as she arrived Paul's voice deepened and his speaking became more authoritative, as if he'd been repairing generators all his life. Arlen lit a cigarette to hide a grin.

"Here we go," Paul said, and then he made some adjustment, which Arlen figured was to the throttle, with his left hand while turning the crank with his right.

Nothing happened. There wasn't a sound but the turning of the hand crank, not so much as a gurgle or cough of gasoline power. Paul frowned and jiggled the throttle and spun the crank faster, sweat beading on his forehead. Still nothing. He dropped his hand from the crank and stepped back.

"Give it a minute," Rebecca said. "Maybe you just need to crank longer."

He shook his head. "It's not even trying. Something's still wrong. It wouldn't even try to start."

His voice was his own again, softer and younger. Arlen blew

out some smoke and said, "You did more than I thought you could just getting it put back into one piece. Getting it to run is a mighty tall order."

Paul didn't answer, dropped to his knees and picked up a screwdriver and set to work removing the inspection plate again.

Rebecca said, "You may not be able to get it, Paul. It may just be ruined."

"It's not ruined," he said, but she'd stopped looking at him and the generator, was instead staring up the road and into the dark trees. She wet her lips.

"You'll have to stop soon," she said. "I need you to be gone by the time the...guests arrive."

"Right," Paul said. "The guests."

Her "guests" had arrived in three vehicles that came in succession, like the funeral procession of an unpopular man. The cars pulled in and parked, and their occupants began to pile out. The first was a battered truck, with dents all over the door panels, and the last was the sheriff's car. Between them was a shining black Plymouth.

Arlen and Paul watched from the trees, silent. It felt like the war again to Arlen, crouched in the brush with a comrade, treachery nearby. When he saw the Plymouth, his throat tightened, and he thought for a moment that he ought to get the license number. Who would he give it to, though? Sheriff Tolliver? Judge Solomon Wade? No, he didn't need to have any more knowledge of that car.

A man and three boys who couldn't be out of their teens filled the lead vehicle. Country folk. Wore clothes you wouldn't see in a department store, the sort that you ordered from a farm-supply catalog, with tattered hats that had been kicked around in the dust a time or two. The man had a thin string of gray hair that hung down past his neck. The watcher from the boat in the inlet. The three boys followed at his heels like obedient but wary dogs.

There was only one man in the Plymouth, a sharp-looking, tidy boy in a suit. Tolliver had also traveled alone, no deputy along for this ride. He stood in the yard and looked around with a suspicious stare while the rest of the group went inside. His gaze floated over the trees where Arlen and Paul hid, but he did not see them. At length he followed the others into the Cypress House, and then they were gone from view, hidden behind the closed door.

"I don't like this," Paul whispered. "We ought not leave her—"

"Shut up," Arlen said, his own nerves making his voice harsh. "We'll do as she asked. She knows what to expect; we don't. You in a hurry to chat with the sheriff again?"

That quieted him, and they slipped out of the trees and back down to the dock. Paul settled on one of the floor planks, with his feet dangling in the gap where others were missing.

"We could fix this dock easy enough, if she had the lumber," he said.

"I expect we could."

"And isn't anything to that boathouse but basic carpentry— roof repairs, wall reinforcements, that sort of thing."

"Sure isn't."

"So we could do it."

"Sure could." Arlen was distracted, thinking of that group up at the inn.

He lit a cigarette and looked at the boy's slumped shoulders and then out at the wooded inlet. The sun had disappeared, vanished beneath the waves of the Gulf, but a faint pink smudge along the horizon remained, fading fast to shadow. The air was the sort of warm that made you comfortable, ready to stretch out and watch the stars rise as your eyelids became heavy.

A heron slid in, sleek and swift as a bullet, then hit the shore across from them and stood on spindly legs, studying the water. If you looked away from it and then back, the bird was tough to find, a pencil-thin shadow amid the backdrop of plants. Deeper in the woods, insects trilled and creatures rustled.

"She's ready to pay us," Arlen said. "And it won't be much, but it'll put us on a train and send us back to Flagg Mountain."

"Arlen," Paul said as the last glowing remnants of the sun slid beneath black water, "I can't leave her."

"Can't leave her?"

Paul nodded, still with his back to Arlen. "Rebecca. I can't leave her."

Arlen closed his eyes and sucked deep at the cigarette, too deep, enough so the smoke that touched his throat was hot and harsh. He swallowed down the cough that wanted to rise, kept his eyes squeezed shut.

"Tell me why."

"You know why."

"Paul...that's a mighty beautiful woman. One could have a son near as old as you. And I understand what you see in her. She's the kind that would weaken the knees of most men. But she's also in a situation that you can't be a part of."

"What do you mean? What do you know about it?"

"Those men up there, son, they aren't good men. And Wade? You think he's running a legitimate business through here? Hell, the man we rode in with was a damned bootlegger. What do I know about the details of her situation? Nary a thing. But I know the gist, and that's enough."

"Even so, I'm not leaving her. I feel like I've been traveling through time to get here, Arlen, just to find her. And now that I have...I can't leave."

Paul's voice was thick, and the sound of it made Arlen open his eyes and look at the boy and then away, out across the dark waters and into the breeze that fanned toward them from the west.

"Son, she's more than ten years older than you. Fifteen, maybe. She's a grown woman."

"That doesn't mean a thing. She's alone out here, Arlen, and I can tell she's awful tired of being alone. I can see that clear as anything."

"She made the choice to stay out here."

"I don't know that she did. Lots of people in this country are doing things they didn't *choose* to do, things they have to do. And I'll tell you something else: she doesn't show it, but she's scared. I saw that the day before the hurricane came in, when I helped her board up the windows."

"Lots of people are scared of hurricanes."

"She's scared," Paul repeated, "but it's not of a hurricane."

Arlen didn't say anything. Paul turned and faced him, his jaw set.

"She's lonely, and she likes me." As if that ended the discussion.

"She does like you. I can see that. But it's in a different way than—"

"How do *you* know?" Paul snapped. "How do you know what she feels? You married? You ever been married?"

There was a long silence, and then Arlen said gently, "You're fixing to marry her?"

"Oh, I don't know. Don't twist my words on me like that. I'll make that easy on you, and we both know it. What I'm saying is that I like her. I like her in a way... Arlen, I can't even tell you the way."

Arlen understood, though. Had seen it rising since they'd landed at the Cypress House, but now that Paul was trying to put it into words it set off a warning in his head, a sense of a new trouble joining those he already had.

"I get it," he said. "But you're asking for trouble. You won't take anything from this but—"

"I can't leave her, Arlen."

The thick, choked sound was gone from his voice now, and there was the ring of finality to the words. He looked Arlen in the eye when he said them, held the look, and then turned and stared back across the inlet. The heron had moved on a fish in the shallows, moved with a splash and flourish, then stepped back. Its beak was empty. Swing and a miss.

"I thought we'd agreed on returning to Flagg," Arlen said.

"I know it, and there isn't anything makes me feel worse than arguing with you. But, Arlen?" He turned and looked at him again, and in the shadows he seemed more man than boy, had the weariness of an adult in his countenance. "I cannot leave her. Okay? I'm going to stay."

"What if she won't have you?"

"She'll have me. She needs this dock fixed, and then the boat-house, and I'll be damned what anybody says, I can make that generator run. I can do it. There are things for me to do, and they'll let me show her...show her..."

"That she needs you," Arlen said softly.

"Yeah."

Arlen's chest filled and he blew out air, but this time the ciga-rette was still held down against his side. Darkness had shrouded them, and the cacophony of buzzing insects from the woods had increased as the daylight faded. Out in the inlet, the heron was marking new territory, ready for another strike.

"I brought you down here," Arlen said. "It was me who brought you south, and it was me who took you off the train. Was also me who put you in Sorenson's fancy car and dragged you this way, and I'm not going to leave you here now."

He felt, as he often had since the start of this journey, like a man pushed by unseen but powerful currents.

"You don't need to stay," Paul said.

"I'm not leaving you here alone. You're no fool, boy; there's trouble up there and you know it. I won't leave you alone in such a place."

Paul said, "Thank you."

"Shit," Arlen said, and fumbled in the dark for another cigarette.

It was quiet for a moment, nothing but the night sounds around them, and then Paul said, "You don't think she can ever love me."

Arlen said nothing.

"I think she can," Paul said. "But it'll take some time. It'll take a chance for me to show her who I really am. Who I can be. But I think..."

His words trailed off, and Arlen didn't spur them back into life or add to them. He just leaned against the mangled side of the boathouse and smoked his cigarette, and the boy looked out across the inlet as the heron struck and missed once, and then again, and then it was too dark to see all the way over to him.

17

THEY SPENT AN HOUR OR TWO sitting and talking about insignificant things but both of them jerking at every sound, their minds back at the Cypress House. Once, Paul started to mosey that way, said he had to relieve himself. Arlen pointed into the trees.

"All the privacy you need right there. Don't you even think about going back up into the view of that tavern unless you want to cause trouble for her."

That seemed to convince him. He went off into the bushes and pissed.

"Think she's okay?" he said when he returned.

"I know she is," Arlen said. "She's run this place on her own for a time, Paul. She's had men like that visit more than once, and she's handled herself fine. Don't trouble yourself over it. It's a normal night for her."

He wasn't sure of that, but he needed the boy to be. He took his flask from his pocket and uncapped it and offered it to Paul.

"Sip a little."

"No, I'm fine."

"Go on," he said. "You've earned it tonight, Paul. It'll ease your worry."

After a hesitation, Paul accepted the flask and drank. They passed it back and forth as they sat on the floor of the boathouse, which was now like a lean-to shelter, open to the night sky on one side. Just to Paul's left, the water from the inlet lapped gently inside the boathouse.

"This isn't such a bad spot to spend a night," he said at length, his voice beginning to show the booze. "Hear that ocean, see those stars?"

Arlen didn't say anything. After a while the boy slumped down against the pile of blankets. Arlen lit a cigarette and let the sound of wind and water fill the silence. By the time the cigarette had burned down to his fingertips, he could tell the kid was already asleep. He always went down hard and fast, the way the boys in the CCC had—you worked them enough during the day, and they forgot their homesickness and orneriness as soon as their heads touched the pillows—but he was also unfamiliar with drink, and it would help to keep him down. Arlen had been counting on this.

He got quietly to his feet and left the dock and started up the sandy path to the tavern. By the time he reached the end of the trail, he could see the flickering light of oil lamps from the main barroom. All of the cars were still parked out in the yard.

He hesitated and looked up at the cars and wondered what the best approach was. If he really worked at being unseen, crept around staying low and in the shadows, he suspected he could do it. The problem then was with the off chance that they came bumbling out of the bar at just the wrong time and caught him. No, better to just walk up to the cars as casually as he could, and if someone came out and saw him, he'd feign ignorance, explain that they were staying at the boathouse and that he couldn't sleep. Be easy to present as the truth, because mostly it was.

He circled around to the Plymouth and had just removed a matchbook so he could put some light on the license plate when something moved in the corner of his eye. He spun back with his fists raised and heart thundering.

There was a woman inside the sheriff's car. Sitting in the passenger seat, staring through the shadowed glass at Arlen without expression.

For a moment he stayed there with his hands clenched into fists, and then he dropped them, looked once at the tavern, and approached the car, making a rolling gesture with his hand, indicating that she should lower the window. She did so, and he could hear a strange tinkling noise. It wasn't until he stepped closer and knelt beside the door that he understood—she was wearing handcuffs.

"What are you doing out here?" he whispered.

"I'm waiting," she said, "for them to finish bargaining."

"Over what?"

"My life."

He ran a hand over his jaw and stared at her, looking from the handcuffs back to her face. She was a beautiful woman, with full lips and hair so dark it looked like oil spilled across the front of her dress, which was a pale yellow. Beneath the clasps of steel, her arms were slender and elegant.

"What are you talking about?" Arlen said. "Who are you?"

"My name is Gwen."

"I don't mean your name, I mean what in the hell you're doing here, with men like that. Why does that son of a bitch have you in chains?"

"I'm leverage," she said, and for the first time he heard clear emotion in her words. Not fear but sorrow. The sort that rose up from the core.

"How?"

"There's a man inside who loves me," she said. "And they

know that. They intend…I believe they intend to test the strength of his love."

"The fellow who drove the Plymouth?"

"Yes. David."

"Why do they have you out here, instead of in with them?"

"I was inside, once. So he could see me. Then Tate asked the sheriff to take me back out. I believe I unsettle him."

Her voice was eerie, faint but firm and entirely matter-of-fact.

"Who is Tate? He the older guy? Long gray hair?"

"Yes. The three with him are his sons. A family of vipers. You and the boy will need to be careful with them, Mr. Wagner."

When she said his name he tightened his hand around the door frame.

"You know me, eh? Tolliver's been telling his tales."

"These men aren't concerned with you," she said as if he hadn't spoken, "yet. But they will be the longer you linger."

"I don't intend to linger. I've been trying to get—"

"Give me your hand," she said.

"What?"

"You heard me." Her whisper now held urgency.

The wind picked up, blowing cool off the water, and Arlen's flesh prickled. He was looking into her eyes, and while he meant to object he could not. He released the door frame and extended his right hand, and she lifted both of hers, the cuffs rattling, and grasped it. His breath caught at the touch, her slim hands cool against his, her fingers gliding over his palm.

"You're the girl from Cassadaga," he said. "Sorenson's girl."

The fortune-teller, the palm reader. The one who'd told Sorenson to watch for travelers in need.

"I'm a girl from Cassadaga," she said. "But not Sorenson's. I already told you—I love the man in that house. David. And he loves me, and that will be our downfall, Mr. Wagner. Love is a powerful thing, and like all powerful things, it can be used to harm."

She was rubbing his palm lightly with her fingertips.

"You fell in love with the wrong sort of boy," Arlen said.

"Shh. I'm trying to see whether you're—"

"Stop it," he said suddenly, his voice rough, and he jerked his hand free. "I won't have that bullshit. You can't tell a damn thing from that."

She frowned but didn't respond to his harshness.

"You're the boy's guardian," she said. "And you know that he won't fare well in this place. I can tell that. You understand the danger and—"

"I told you to stop it," he said. "You want to talk truth, lady, I'll talk it with you, but I'm not inclined to sit here and listen to foolishness."

"Of course not. You've tried long and hard to block the things you need to hear. At some point you're going to have to listen."

"What I will *listen* to is you explaining what happened to Walter Sorenson and what's going on inside that..." His voice trailed off. He didn't even get his mouth closed, just knelt there slack-jawed, staring into the dark of the sheriff's car.

The glittering silver handcuffs were now resting on thin shafts of bone.

"What?" she said, and he raised his eyes, hoping to see those sculpted, full lips. A skull stared back at him.

No words came. The skull tilted and studied him, then said, in a soft and sad voice, "It's happened now, hasn't it? He's told them. It's done."

Arlen couldn't answer.

She said, "You can see it in me. You truly have gifts beyond measure."

Finally, he spoke. Said, "Lady, you've got to get out of that car."

The skull shook slowly back and forth. "No."

"*Yes.* You have got to get out of that car and—"

"They'll find me," she said. "And it will end the same for me, only it will also be bad for you and the boy. And for Rebecca. I won't initiate such things."

"Lady," he said, "Gwen, you've got to understand something. They're going to kill you."

"They always were," she said. "It just took some time to confirm it."

He couldn't bear to look at the skull anymore. He pulled out his matchbook and struck a match and leaned into the car, held it close to her. In the flickering light, flesh spread like butter over the bones and she was whole again. Whole except for the whirling pools of gray smoke where her eyes belonged.

"Come on," he said. "We're leaving. We're going to run. All three of us. I'll get the boy up here and we'll run."

"You can't run from them," she said. "I hope you understand that. You're going to need to. There will be no running from what lies ahead."

"Quiet," he said. "We're going now." The match had burned down to his fingers, and he shook it out and reached for the door handle.

"No!" she said, and she took the handle in her bone fingers and pulled back against his efforts.

"Get out of the car!"

"Leave me," she hissed.

"I won't. Get out of the damn car."

He got the door partially opened, but then, with surprising strength, she slammed it back. The sound of metal on metal rang out loud in the still night. She said, "Hide. *Now*."

He did not argue this time. He knew that he could not. He dropped to the grass and rolled forward, toward the Plymouth, as the front door of the Cypress House banged open and footsteps slapped onto the porch and someone called for a lantern. It was still dark back by the cars, and Arlen wriggled forward until he was entirely beneath the Plymouth. He was there when Tolliver tramped past him, nothing showing but a pair of boots and the angled glow of a lantern.

"You were told not to move," the sheriff was saying. "Not to make a sound. Think you'll be able to take so much as a step, chained like that?"

She was chained to the car, Arlen realized. Maybe at the feet. She couldn't have run if she wanted to.

"We're about done, darling," Tolliver said, his voice so rich with mocking menace that Arlen clenched his teeth together, willing down the urge to roll out from under the Plymouth and start swinging. There were more men inside. All of them probably armed.

"We'll be on our way soon. We'll be taking you home. But if you move again, make a sound again, I'll put a bullet in your beautiful face. Understand?"

There was a long pause, and then Tolliver passed the Plymouth a second time. Arlen waited until he'd heard his boots on the porch and the sound of the door closing, and then he slid back out from under the car. He crept around to the sheriff's car and stared in at her. The skull face regarded him.

"They're going to need you," the woman named Gwen said. "Paul and Rebecca. You can't leave them here. They need you."

There were loud voices inside again. She looked in that direction, then back to him, and said, "Go. You can't be caught here. Go now."

He backed into the trees without answering, unsure of himself. He was there, among the storm-torn mangroves, when they all came out of the tavern. Sheriff Tolliver and the gray-haired man she had called Tate led the way. The three boys followed — dragging the man from the Plymouth between them. He could not hold his own footing, and though he mumbled constantly he could not make intelligible words. It sounded as if he were trying to speak without lips or teeth.

They loaded him back into the Plymouth, but this time he was in the backseat, and this time all three of Tate's boys rode with him. Tate fired up the truck as Tolliver leaned in the Plymouth window with an inspector's stare, spoke to the boy at the wheel, and then moved back to his own car. He climbed in and started the engine and led the procession out of the yard and up the road.

Arlen searched for the girl in the darkness, hoping that her appearance would change as they left this place. It was too dark, though. He couldn't see a thing.

18

HE WENT TO THE BOATHOUSE to check on Paul first. The boy slept soundly, curled up against the stack of old blankets, water lapping at the dock pylons beneath him. It was pitch-black, but the later it got the louder the night seemed — insects and nocturnal animals and wind sounds filling the trees all around the inlet. To the east, farther inland, the woods thickened, a mass of weaving silhouettes against the night sky. Arlen thought that if he lived in this part of the country, he'd want to hug the coast as much as possible, where things were open and bright and you could see what was coming.

He picked the flask up from where it lay on the dock and had a long drink. Then he capped it and walked back to the inn. The lights were still glowing, and he could hear a scraping sound. He swung open the door and stepped inside, and Rebecca Cady gave a shout of fear.

She was standing in the center of the barroom with a mop in her hands, and when he opened the door she pulled the mop back and brandished it like a weapon. Then her shoulders sagged and she dropped it back to the floor.

"What are you doing? I told you to stay out!"

He stood in the doorway and looked around the room. Everything was as it had been, except that the floor around the fireplace was shining with soapy water.

"Late for washing the floors, isn't it?"

"Get out."

He let the door swing shut behind him. There was a strange smell in the air. Kerosene and cleansers, yes, but there was something else to it. A faint copper tinge. He felt his stomach stir and the muscles in his neck go tight.

"How was the party?"

"It wasn't a party." The mop was shaking in her hands. She tightened her grip, trying to still it, but that only seemed to intensify the rattling. As she stood there and stared at him, a tear leaked out of her right eye and glided down her cheek, dripped off her jaw, and fell to the wet floor.

"What in the hell happened?" Arlen said, walking toward her.

"Get out!"

He stopped halfway across the room. She pulled her shoulders back and gave him a look that would have been cold and strong if not for the tears.

"Maybe if you want me out of here so bad, you should go call the sheriff," he said. "My guess is he'll see that I'm gone fast enough. Me and the boy both. And he'll probably help you clean the floor."

He had edged closer to her, was only a few feet away now. He looked from her face down into the pail at her feet. Even in the dim glow of the oil lamps, the crimson tint was clear. There was a lot of blood in that water.

"I'd like you to leave." Her voice was shaking, and Arlen had the sense that if he reached out and laid one fingertip against her skin, she'd collapse.

"Did you see her?" he asked.

"What?"

"The woman they brought in. Her name was Gwen. Did you see her?"

She shook her head, and another tear fell free.

"They had her in handcuffs," he said. "Chained up in the sheriff's car. They went all the way to Cassadaga to find her."

"I was upstairs," she said in a whisper so faint he could scarcely hear it. "I always stay upstairs. I don't want to see any of them. I don't want to hear…anything."

"Like the sounds of that man getting beaten within an inch of his life?" Arlen asked. "You didn't hear that upstairs?"

Her face was wet with tears now.

"I can't speak to you about this," she said. "I *can't*. Just promise me that you'll leave. That you'll take Paul and go. You don't belong here. You shouldn't be here. Leave."

"All right," he said. "You want us gone, I'll see that it happens. But something to remember? If we're not around, it means you're here alone."

He watched her eyes break from his and go to the pail of bloody water.

"The mess you've got on your hands," he said, "isn't the sort you clean up with a mop."

19

H E WOKE TO THE sound of the generator.
It was well into the morning, and he lay on his stomach on the boathouse floor. Somehow he'd thrashed his way off the blanket in his sleep, and his cheek was pressed to the bare boards. He was lucky he hadn't pitched himself into the water. Dreams of a woman in a yellow dress had stalked him.

He pushed himself upright now and blinked and cocked his head, listening. Yes, it was definitely the generator; he could hear the distinctive hammering of the cylinders. The timing was off, making it sound like the motor had a limp, but it was running. The damn thing was running.

He got up slowly, feeling stiffness in every joint, then leaned off the edge of the dock and splashed briny water into his face, licking the salt off his lips. He groaned and rolled his head around on his neck and then started up the path. In the yard, he could see the indentations the cars had left the night before. He thought of the sheriff's car and the woman in handcuffs and the way he'd let them drive off into the darkness, and he felt his chest tighten.

In front of the porch, Paul stood beside the generator with a wide grin on his face. Rebecca Cady had her hands at her temples as if she couldn't believe it. When Arlen joined them, Paul kept smiling but didn't say a word.

"I figured it out last night," he said finally. "Woke up at dawn, thinking that everything was ready to move the way it should mechanically. I had all that done right. But it wasn't even catching, and so I thought the problem had to be in the electrical. It's an electrical ignition, you know. You turn that crank to make the current that fires the ignition, and then the batteries take over. The engine charges the batteries."

"I get it," Arlen said. "But what did you *do?*"

"Checked the cutouts to see if the circuit was alive or if one of them was open. Turned out two of them were. I closed them, and it started on the first try."

"Hell of a job," Arlen said, but he was looking at Rebecca Cady instead of the generator. The gaze she returned was as cool as winter wind. No trace of the nearly broken woman that had showed last night in the trembling hands that held the mop, in the tears that slid down her face.

"I've got to adjust the timing," Paul said, shutting the generator off, the bangs slowing and then silencing altogether. "But I'll wait until we have it back in place to do that. Then we'll need to get that little shed put back together."

"I guess we have a full day ahead of us," Arlen said.

Rebecca didn't offer a word of objection. *I'd like you to leave,* she'd screamed at him last night, but now she stood by silently.

Paul was right, Arlen thought. *She's scared, and she doesn't want to be alone anymore. Won't tell anybody a damn thing, though, so she's nearly as alone now as she would be if we were gone. You can't find much company from inside a padlocked, stone-walled fortress.*

He had to get her to talk. If they were spending so much as another night in this place, he had to understand what in the hell was going on. And they'd be spending another night, because what he'd told her before was bullshit—he couldn't convince the boy to leave. Not anymore. Paul was anchored here by a love that Rebecca didn't even see.

Love is a powerful thing, and like all powerful things, it can be used to harm, the woman named Gwen had said the previous night, just before her face became a skull. The memory left Arlen wishing for his flask, even though he hadn't yet tasted coffee.

"Going to need lumber," he said, just to fill the air with talk. "Not much left of that generator shed that'll be usable."

"Going to need some for the dock and boathouse, too," Paul said.

If she wanted them gone, now was the time to say so.

"I've got enough money to get it started at least," she said. "If you know what you'll need, I can give you enough to get it started."

So there it was. They were staying. The proclamation had been issued quietly, but it rang loud and clear to Arlen, and from the satisfied smile he saw on Paul's face, he knew the boy had registered the implication, too.

"We'll take some measurements," Paul said, "and figure out what we need. It shouldn't be too expensive to get started. We'll build that generator shed first and then work on the dock. I think that would make the most sense."

Off he went, talking a mile a minute. Rebecca Cady was responding, but Arlen was no longer listening to either of them, was instead gazing up at the house and the empty expanse of sand and sea behind it.

It was supposed to be an hour, he thought. *Maybe less. Time enough for a beer and whatever business Walt Sorenson had to conduct, and then we were moving on down the road.*

This wasn't a world you planned your way through, though. He'd known that much for many a year.

*   *   *

It was nearing noon when Thomas Barrett's panel van pulled into the yard. Rebecca talked to him briefly and then waved a hand, calling for them.

"So you boys going to be visiting a little longer, huh?" Barrett said when they walked over, the mellow grin on his face the same as always.

"We got no money," Arlen said. "Might as well make some."

"Good sense. Becky here tells me y'all'll be needing some lumber."

"That's right," Paul said. "We've got it all written down."

"Well, I told her I'd be happy to pick it up for a small charge, but I'll need a hand loading."

"Paul can go along," Arlen said.

Paul frowned. "I was going to wire that generator back in."

"It'll hold," Arlen said. "My back ain't up to heavy lifting today, not after sleeping down in the boathouse. Go on and show off your muscles."

Rebecca passed Barrett a tightly folded roll of bills, all of which looked to be singles, and he slipped them into his pocket and winked at Paul.

"Ready to go blow this on booze and loose women?"

The two of them were off. Arlen watched the van pull away, and by the time he turned back to Rebecca, she was already gone. He gave a grim smile, thinking, *Not going to be that easy, gorgeous. You and I are going to talk.*

She was back in the barroom, cleaning the stools with a rag that reeked of some powerful disinfectant. She didn't hear him enter, and Arlen watched her work, scrubbing furiously at the nicked legs of the old bar stools.

"Blood get on those, too?" he said.

She gave a start, then saw who it was, and her eyes hardened and her hand tightened around the rag. A drop of the cleaning fluid dripped onto the floor.

"I thought I was paying you to fix things," she said. "Not stand around in the dark watching me."

"There are lots of things around here need fixing," he said with a nod, stepping closer. "I'm just trying to get a sense of all of them."

She hesitated a moment, down on her hands and knees, and then got to her feet with a small sigh and stood with her back against the bar.

"There was a fight. It's not uncommon when those men get together. People get hurt."

"People got hurt," Arlen said, "but that was no fight."

"I have no idea what happened," she said. "I was upstairs, trying not to hear it. That's what I always do."

"I believe that, but you know damn well that whatever happened in here last night wasn't a fight."

"You think I should call the sheriff?" she said, scorn clear in her voice. "Or maybe call Judge Solomon Wade himself?"

"There are other people to call."

She didn't answer.

"If we're staying here," he said, "I'm going to need to be told the truth about some things."

"Why?"

The abruptness of the question startled him. He leaned his head back, staring at her, and said, "Because I don't want you to be mopping up me or Paul Brickhill next time around."

"I don't know why you're staying," she said. "You should go. Don't you understand that? Even *I* understand it."

"You want us gone?"

Her jaw trembled for an instant before she said, "You know that I don't, you said it last night. If you're gone, I'm alone again. With them."

"If you don't talk to me, you're damn near that alone anyhow."

"No," she said. "I'm nowhere near as alone as that."

You can't leave them here, the woman from Cassadaga had told him. *They need you.*

"I can't help you," he said, "if you won't speak the truth."

"I've told no lies."

"You've told *nothing,* period."

"My problems are my own. I don't need to share them."

Her face floated there just before his, those smooth lines and endless eyes.

"But you're right about this place," she said. "It's filled with trouble. I'm filled with trouble. You don't need any of it, and Paul certainly doesn't. The best thing for both of you would be to—"

He leaned down and kissed her. Lifted his hand to the back of her neck and kissed her on the lips just as smoothly and sweetly as he could.

She stepped back and struck him.

Her slap caught him high on the left side of his face. He stood where he was and stared as she hissed, "That's what you want? Is that all you want?"

She moved away from him in a rush, went around the bar and through the swinging door into the kitchen, and then he was alone with the imprint of her slap stinging on his cheek.

20

He couldn't say why he'd done it. Hadn't been thought-out, planned. No, he'd just been looking at her face and seeing those lips and…hell, what a mistake.

He went outside and stared at the wires coming out of the generator and knew damn well that he wouldn't make any progress without Paul there. He walked down to the dock and set to work tearing some of the damaged planking free and stacking it on the shore. He worked hard and angry, frustrated and embarrassed with himself for what had happened. What would the boy have thought if he'd seen it?

While he was working, he thought he heard a boat. A faint sound, but he'd have bet money it was the creaking of a set of oars working in their oarlocks. He straightened and stared up the inlet, but it curled away from him, and the trees with their draperies of Spanish moss screened what lay beyond. He waited for a time and didn't see anything, and then he returned to work.

It was more than an hour before Paul and Thomas Barrett made it back. The panel van had been replaced by an old pickup that was so loaded with lumber, it flattened the tires.

"Enough for the dock and the generator shed," Barrett told Arlen when he walked up to join them. "Won't be enough for the boathouse, but it'll do the rest."

"That's a start. Hey, Paul? Why don't you look at that generator while I get this unloaded. I couldn't make heads or tails out of that."

"Your back's feeling better?"

"Yeah," Arlen said. Rebecca had come out on the porch to watch them, and he didn't look her way.

Paul went off to the generator, and Barrett hung around to help Arlen with the boards. They unloaded the lumber and carried it down to the boathouse. By the time they got back from the last load, the generator was running again, and Rebecca Cady stood on the porch with a rare smile on her face.

"I'll be able to use some eggs and milk tomorrow," she told Barrett. "I can finally keep them cool again. He actually got it to work."

Barrett left then, promising to return with the perishables the next day, and Arlen and Paul got to work rebuilding the enclosure for the generator. Paul insisted on making it wider than the original, which made sense because it allowed you to move around and access the thing if there were problems. He'd gotten the timing adjusted, and the cylinders were firing smoothly and accurately. Arlen watched it hammer away and thought there weren't many men in the world who could put a thing like that back together without any training or experience with engines — hell, without so much as an instruction or a diagram. Looking at the generator, Arlen realized he was feeling a small surge of pride. That was undeserved — he couldn't take any credit for the kid's success. It was there all the same, though. He was proud of him.

At sunset they joined Rebecca on the back porch and ate dinner, Arlen sipping a cold beer.

"First I can really appreciate of the boy's contributions," he said to Rebecca. "Beer sure does taste better once it's been chilled."

Paul frowned when he said that, and Arlen assumed it was related in some way to drinking, but a few minutes later when Rebecca had gone inside in search of salt, Paul said, "I'd appreciate it if you wouldn't call me that in front of her."

Arlen stared at him. "Call you what?"

"The boy."

Arlen raised his eyebrows and gave a little nod.

"That's not how I want her to think of me," Paul said. "Understand?"

"Sure," Arlen said. "Won't happen again."

He was starting to worry about Paul's infatuation, though. It was none of his business, but he didn't for a minute believe Rebecca Cady did—or would—think of him as a man, let alone as a romantic interest. She treated him with affection, yes, but it wasn't in the way the kid was hoping.

Rebecca had just stepped back out with saltshaker in hand when they heard a car pulling in. Arlen looked up at her and saw a shadow pass across her face. She set the salt down and went back inside but hadn't even made it across the barroom when the front door opened and two men stepped through. What was left of the sun was shining off the windows and it was impossible to look through and see them clearly, but Arlen was certain the one who'd entered first was Solomon Wade, because he could see the outline of the white Panama hat. Wade said something to Rebecca, and then they came back out onto the porch.

The judge's companion tonight was the man called Tate. He had a wide leather belt like the kind issued to police, with a holstered pistol hanging off one side and a sheathed knife on the other. Wade appeared to be unarmed, wearing dark pants and a shirt with suspenders, no jacket, wire-rimmed glasses over his eyes. He looked like a small-town banker.

"You two haven't found your way up the road yet?" Wade said. He'd taken Rebecca's chair, sat facing Arlen. Rebecca was standing back by the door, and Tate had circled around behind Paul and was leaning on the railing, the one they'd just repaired. Paul shifted uneasily, as if he didn't like having Tate behind him. Arlen didn't like it either.

"What's keeping y'all in Corridor County?" Wade asked when no one responded to him.

"They're helping me," Rebecca said from the doorway. "I told you that, Solomon. I needed help and—"

"I was asking them," Wade said.

Arlen took a long drink of his beer. "Maybe you didn't catch it the last time you were out here and spoke to us, but we were robbed. Tough to move on down the road without a single dollar."

Wade gave him a long, cold stare. Arlen wanted to meet his gaze, but he also couldn't help glancing at Tate every few seconds. There was something damned unsettling about the old bastard. He had a face like untreated saddle leather, dark eyes, strings of unkempt gray hair trailing along his neck and down to his shoulders. There were scars over almost every inch of the backs of his hands, a variety of colors and textures to them, souvenirs of different incidents. When the breeze pushed in off the Gulf, Arlen could smell the odor of stale sweat coming from him.

"So you want to make some money before you move on," Wade said. He had a distant way of speaking, as if he always had minimal interest in the conversation.

"Want to," Arlen said, "and need to."

Wade blinked and looked out at the sea, purple and black filling in around the edges now, a shrinking pool of orange in the center.

"I believe you were offered a chance to make your money back overnight. I believe you passed on the opportunity."

Paul turned his head and looked at Arlen, a frown on his face.

"There was no opportunity," Arlen said. "You tried to bribe me with my own dollars, and what you wanted, I didn't have. I still don't."

"Supposing you made back your losses as well as an additional profit, might you be inclined to reconsider?"

Arlen looked at him for a long time. Then he said, "No."

"What do you mean, no?"

It was the first time Wade had shown any spark of emotion. His eyes had narrowed behind the glasses.

"Even if I'd been holding out on you," Arlen said, "I wouldn't tell you a damn thing now. I don't like being pushed around, by money or muscle."

He'd spent most of his life without money in his wallet; he had not and would not spend any of it being run around by men like Solomon Wade. The man wanted him to cower like a whipped dog, expected him to. After all the things Arlen had seen in this life, he'd be damned if he'd cower for this son of a bitch.

"You know who you are?" he said. "You're Edwin Main."

Wade tilted his head and stared. "What?"

"A man I used to know back home. You remind me of him."

Arlen could remember going to get the sheriff, walking down the street with his legs trembling and two faces trapped in his mind: his father's bearded one and a dead woman's pale-lipped one. When the law came back, it came with Edwin Main, who wasn't a member of it but thought he was and had the rest of the town convinced of the same.

When Arlen spoke again, his voice was harder than he'd heard it in years.

"We've told you again and again all that we can tell you about Sorenson — nothing. You tried to beat it out, threaten it out, and buy it out. How you can be so damned stupid not to realize that we've been telling the truth the whole time, I don't know. But I'm done with it. And something you need to understand, Wade? I've been around for a while, done a lot of hard living, seen a lot of tough boys. You ain't the first."

Wade didn't answer. Arlen hadn't seen Tate move, but the older man's hand was resting high on his thigh now, near the pistol.

"Your business is of no interest to me," Arlen said. "None. Nor to the...nor to Paul. But I'll tell you something else: ours ought not to be of any interest to you. It better not be."

It was quiet for a long time. The sun was all the way gone now, the porch covered in darkness. Wade finally spoke.

"Fourteen days left," he said. "You be ready for him?"

Arlen didn't understand what in the hell he was talking about. Then Rebecca Cady spoke, and it became clear the comment had been intended for her.

"You know the answer," she said. Her voice was strained.

Wade nodded congenially. "Yes, I do. I just wanted you to know I can keep track of the days, too."

He stood up, scraping his chair back across the porch floor. "Becky, let's take a moment inside. In private. Just you, me, and Mr. McGrath."

McGrath was apparently Tate's last name. The three of them started for the door, but Arlen interrupted.

"Hold on. You can stay right out here and have your talk."

Wade spun back to him. "You were just telling me the virtues of minding your life while I mind my own. Weren't you?"

Arlen ran his tongue along the inside of his lip and stared at him but didn't say anything. Wade gave a short nod and pulled the door open and went inside.

"Who do you think he really is?" Paul said in a whisper when they were alone. "Doesn't behave like a judge."

I am the match, Wade had said.

"He's a big fish," Arlen said, "in a small pond. Sharp teeth, though. Even the ones in the small ponds got their teeth."

He was watching them through the shadowed glass. Wade was standing close to Rebecca, talking to her, while Tate McGrath floated around in silence. Arlen thought of McGrath's three sons and the man they'd loaded into the black Plymouth the previous night, of the way his legs wouldn't support his weight and his mouth couldn't form words. He thought of the woman in the yellow dress.

Rebecca's face was flat, betraying no emotion. She turned away from Wade and lit an oil lamp while he talked, the light throwing a pale glow across his face, making his glasses shine again. At length he turned to Tate and snapped a few words, and the older man went out through the front door. He was gone for only a minute, and when he came back he had a box in his hands, what looked like a large wooden cigar box wrapped with twine. He set it on the bar in front of Rebecca, who kept her eyes down and didn't look at it.

Wade leaned close, his face within inches of hers, and he spoke softly into her ear, tapping the box with his index finger as he talked. Still she didn't look up. Wade wrapped his fingers in her hair and pulled slowly, until her chin lifted.

"Hey," Paul said, "what's he doing? That son of a bitch."

Arlen said, *"Paul,"* but it was too late: the kid was out of his chair and through the door. Arlen swore and went after him.

Solomon Wade still had a fistful of Rebecca's hair, and he turned to them and a small smile showed on his face as Paul rushed forward.

"Get your hands off her," Paul was saying. "Damn you, take your hands off—"

Tate McGrath stepped in front of Wade and swung. He hit Paul square in the forehead with the punch, stepping into it, a good solid crack that sounded as if someone had dropped a clay pot. Paul's feet went out from beneath him, and he fell straight backward. He got his hands out, kept his head from drilling into the floorboards. Rebecca Cady gave a little cry when he went down.

Paul struggled to his feet, unsteady, and charged back at McGrath, who sidestepped the rush, hooked his right hand around Paul's arm, and sent him spinning into one of the tables. He went down again, this time in a clattering mess, taking three chairs and the table with him.

McGrath walked to one of the chairs and lifted his foot and brought it down hard, shearing the leg right off the chair. He reached down and picked it up, a heavy chunk of wood, and then he advanced on Paul, bouncing the wood in his hand, as Arlen finally caught up to them.

McGrath heard him coming and whirled to strike, but Arlen had just bent to pick up what was left of the chair and he used it to block the blow. He shoved ahead, holding the chair, and McGrath twisted, trying to clear away from it. Arlen leaned his weight forward, bracing the chair with his left arm, and then reached down for McGrath's waist with his right, made one quick clean grab and came up with McGrath's own knife.

McGrath gave a grunt and tried to go for his pistol, but Arlen shoved the chair into his face and then dropped it entirely as the older man stumbled back. By the time McGrath had regained his balance, Arlen had his greasy hair in one hand and the knife at his throat with the other.

He jerked on the hair and maneuvered McGrath sideways so that the whole room was visible. Paul had gotten to his feet, breathing hard, but Wade hadn't so much as moved. He still had hold of Rebecca's hair, but he hadn't stepped toward the brawl.

"Seems like the way schoolgirls would fight," Arlen said. "Here we are, both hanging on to somebody's pretty locks."

McGrath was breathing hard through his nose. The blade of

the knife was firm against the worn, sunburned skin of his throat.

"What do you say, Wade?" Arlen said. "You let go of your lady, I'll let go of mine."

Wade's face showed no change in expression, but he released Rebecca's hair. She stepped back quickly, went around the side of the bar.

"Let him go, Arlen," she said.

"I guess I will," Arlen said. "I was thinking I might dance with him a little longer, but maybe not."

He gave another twist of McGrath's hair and leaned his face down.

"I let you go, you can reach for that pistol," he said. "I don't want that to happen. So you're going to stand where you are and let the kid take the gun off your belt. You're not going to move an inch while it happens."

McGrath made no response. Arlen said, "Paul."

Paul came forward, moving as reluctantly as if he'd been asked to handle a snake, and reached down and got the gun out of the holster.

"Hang on to it and go stand by the door," Arlen said. "We'll give Mr. McGrath his toys in just a minute."

He waited until Paul was at the door and then he dropped the knife from Tate McGrath's throat and shoved him away, taking a step back as he did. McGrath straightened and looked at him, and for a moment Arlen was sure he was going to try, even with Arlen holding the knife and Paul holding the gun. Tate McGrath was the sort of alley cat who fought dogs of his own volition. By holding his own knife to his throat, Arlen had just bought a lifetime of hatred.

"Wouldn't be wise," he said as McGrath took a circling step toward him.

"Tate," Wade snapped, and McGrath came to a stop. "I've seen more than enough wrestling for one night. Mr. Wagner seems to have a mighty confused idea of what it means to mind his own business, but that's all right. We'll give him a chance to figure it out. I'm pretty sure he'll take to it quickly."

Wade was looking at Arlen, but Arlen wouldn't take his eyes off McGrath.

"I'm a mighty fast learner," he said. "Now are you boys ready to head out for the night, or do I need to hang on to this knife much longer?"

"We're on our way," Wade said. "You can give him his knife."

Arlen shook his head. "Not until you're in the car."

Wade shrugged. He turned to Rebecca and extended his hand, touched her cheek gently. She grimaced.

"You remember our chat," he said, and then he turned and walked toward the door. When he reached Paul he slowed and stared down into the boy's face, then laid a hand on his shoulder. "Watch who you travel with, son," he said. "Bad company can be disastrous."

Arlen had been keeping his attention on Tate McGrath, but now, as Arlen watched Wade talk to Paul, the backwoodsman fell from his mind entirely.

Paul's eyes had just filled with smoke.

It twisted in the sockets, two gray whirlpools set high on his face. Arlen felt something clench in his throat and he took a step forward and raised the knife.

Paul turned the smoke-eyes to face him, and Wade gave the boy a pat on the shoulder and then released his grip and looked back at Arlen. The instant his hand left Paul's shoulder, the smoke vanished.

Arlen stopped where he was, halfway across the room, knife in hand.

Wade said, "What are you doing?"

"Step back from him," Arlen said. His voice was unsteady.

Wade gave him an unpleasant look but stepped away. Paul's brown eyes regarded Arlen with curiosity.

"Let's go, Tate," Wade said, and then he stepped through the door. McGrath followed, and Arlen kept staring at Paul. There was no smoke now, but there had been. He was certain that there had been. Why had it disappeared so quickly?

"Give me the gun," Arlen said. Both Paul and Rebecca were watching him with a measure of confusion. Paul passed the gun over, and then Arlen went out to Tate McGrath's truck. Tate was behind the wheel, Wade in the passenger seat. Arlen tossed the knife and the gun down in the bed, and then he banged his hand off the side of the truck and stepped back.

"Y'all have a nice evening now," he called.

"You'll see us again," Solomon Wade said. "And there will come a time when you will regret tonight's decision."

"I've never been one for regrets," Arlen said, and then he turned and walked back to the Cypress House. The whole way, there was a tightness through his back and he was ready for the sound of the truck door opening, Tate McGrath stepping back out and going for the gun. The only sound that came, though, was the truck rattling off down the road.

It had been Wade's touch, Arlen realized as he stepped onto the porch. Smoke had filled Paul's eyes when Wade laid a hand on his shoulder; it had vanished as soon as the hand was removed.

But the smoke had been there. He was certain of that, and of what it meant.

21

P AUL HAD A THICK red lump swelling on his forehead, just above his eye. He sat on a bar stool while Rebecca ran a cool rag over his face and inspected the wound. Arlen could see the boy's breathing stagger when her fingertips slid over his skin. It wasn't from pain.

"You okay?" he said.

"Yeah," Paul mumbled. "I wasn't expecting him to come on that fast. Once I got my bearings, I'd have been all right."

"Sure," Arlen said, knowing that Tate probably would have beaten the boy within an inch of his life if he'd been allowed to start swinging that chair leg.

"Thank you for stepping in," Paul said. "I shouldn't have needed your help, but—"

"You were going to need somebody's help. I would have, too, with that old bastard. Only reason I was able to get away with what I did was that he was paying attention to you. That's a mean son of a bitch, Paul, and a dangerous one. You see him again, you stay the hell away from him."

A family of vipers, the woman named Gwen had said. Tate

surely seemed to be, and tonight he'd traveled alone. If he'd brought those boys of his along, it might have been a very bloody evening.

"Tate's awful," Rebecca said. It was the first time she'd spoken. "He's a terrible human being. Just like Solomon."

"Why do you let them come around here?" Paul said.

She didn't answer. Arlen went behind the bar to pour a glass of whiskey. His hands were trembling and he shifted so they wouldn't see. When he turned back, he noticed that the cigar box was missing from the top of the bar. She'd already moved it.

"Hey, Arlen," Paul said.

"Yeah?"

"Who was Edwin Main?"

Rebecca looked up at that, too, looked Arlen in the eyes for the first time since that afternoon.

"Nobody, Paul. He was nobody."

Silence overcame them quickly. Arlen's mind was lost to the sudden appearance of smoke in Paul's eyes, and Rebecca was quiet, with Paul trying too hard to lure her back into conversation. She went upstairs early, but not without first giving his arm a squeeze and telling him to take care of his forehead. He stuttered out something about not being able to feel a thing, giving her the tough-guy routine, but she was already moving up the stairs.

The two of them sat there in silence for a while, and then Paul went out to the porch. Arlen could see him through the windows, leaning on the rail and staring out at the dark water. He went to the bar and poured two glasses of whiskey, one tall and one quite short, mixing a touch of water in the short glass to level them out. Then he took the two glasses and went out on the porch.

"Here," he said, handing the watered-down whiskey to Paul. "After a man gets in a fight, a man deserves a drink."

Paul stared at the glass for a moment and then a smile slid over his face and he nodded and took it from Arlen's hand.

"Thanks."

Arlen drank his whiskey and pretended not to notice when the boy's eyes began to water after his first sip. They stood there together and listened to the waves breaking.

"What do you think those guys are doing out here?" Paul said eventually.

"I don't know, and like I told 'em tonight—I don't care. It's got nothing to do with us."

"Well, I do care. Because they're—"

"Yeah," Arlen said. "Because they're bothering her. I get it."

Paul frowned and fell silent.

"You been gone from Flagg for a while," Arlen said. "Your mother know where you are? You written her?"

Paul blinked at him. "What?"

"Does she think you're still in Alabama, son?"

"I, uh, I don't know. I told her I was going to try to get down to the Keys."

"Well, shit, if she's been reading about that hurricane, she's probably worried. Show some respect; sit down and write a letter."

"She doesn't do much writing herself," Paul said, "and I doubt she's real concerned about me."

There was bridling resentment in his voice.

"But is she counting on your CCC checks?" Arlen said. "I bet she is."

"Sure she is. And the first time I'll hear from her is when she notices the money's stopped coming in."

Arlen took a sip of the whiskey and said, "You're not making money here, son. You need to find your way back to a camp and do another CCC hitch."

"No." Paul shook his head. "I'm staying."

"It's time we leave."

"You know I'm not going to do that."

"Paul," Arlen said, "I don't think you understand. . . . You need to leave this place. It's just like the train, son. I can feel it."

Paul lifted his head and stared at him. "What?"

Arlen nodded.

"You mean right now? You can see it in me right now?"

"Not now. Before. When they were here."

Paul was quiet for a moment before saying, "Well, it was probably that fight. Maybe he would have cut me or shot me or something."

"It was after the fight. When Wade touched your shoulder."

Paul frowned.

"You know I'm not lying," Arlen said. "You know it's the truth, Paul. You saw what happened to those men from the train."

"When he touched my shoulder?"

Arlen nodded.

"Well," Paul said after a lengthy pause, "it's gone now, right?"

"Yes, but that's not the point."

"Sure it is. Whatever was there, it passed. It's gone now."

"Paul, that's not how it—"

"Stop it," Paul said. "I don't want to hear it. It's gone, okay? It's gone!"

He turned and stomped back inside the Cypress House.

That night Arlen spent some time lying in the dark, watching the patterns of shadow shift as the moon rose, sipping from the flask and adjusting his position constantly on the bed, as if sleep were just one angle-change away. By now he knew the routine too well, though, and gave up earlier than usual, got to his feet and dressed again, walked downstairs and topped the flask off before going outside.

For a time he stood just below the porch and smoked a cigarette and watched the waves. Their tops sparkled as they broke.
When the cigarette was gone he began to walk, heading south.
He walked for a long time, sticking close to the waterline, his
hands in his pockets and his mind dancing among Solomon
Wade and Edwin Main and his father. Paul was in there, too,
and Rebecca Cady, and every now and then someone else would
slip through those chinks that even the whiskey was unable to
caulk. When an unusually strong wave drove far enough up the
shore to catch his feet, he finally came to a stop, looked around to
see that the moon was much higher and the Cypress House was
nowhere in sight. The coastal forest had encroached quietly
around him, the stretch of beach much narrower here, the trees
leaning close to the sea. He turned and started back.

Eventually the silhouette of the Cypress House showed. He
had the passing thought that he needed to finish the widow's
walk, and then he saw something moving along the beach and
everything else faded from his mind.

It was a shimmering white shape that seemed to emerge from
the waterline, and for one short, frozen-heart moment he had
visions of all the stories of ghosts and haints that he'd heard in
his boyhood. Then the figure turned, and he saw that it was
Rebecca Cady. She was wearing a white gown, and she'd walked
all the way down to the water's edge and was now wading into
the surf.

He advanced slowly, grateful for the sand that allowed silent
steps. He could see that she was holding something in her hands
but couldn't make out what. She stood for a moment as if in hesitation, then backed out of the water and set the object down in
the sand. It looked like the cigar box Wade had given her.

She dipped her hands and grasped the hem of her gown and
lifted it up her body and over her head and then it was off and
she was standing naked on the sand. Arlen felt his breath catch,

a flush rising through him. She was a tall woman, and somehow both soft and absent of fat, each curve sublime and sculpted. Even in the moonlight, her body was enough to numb his brain. He stood dumbly and stared as she picked the box up and went back into the sea.

She paused when the water reached her knees, as if adjusting to the temperature, and then stepped out deeper, lifting the box as she went. When the water reached her breasts, she stopped and, for just a moment, stood with the box over her head and the waves breaking high enough to drench the ends of her hair. Then she pivoted back toward the shore and whirled out to sea again, flinging the box away from her.

She didn't get it far. The wind was working against her, and her motion was awkward. The box tumbled maybe fifteen feet out into the sea and landed flat, barely making a splash. For a few seconds it floated, riding back toward shore with the swells, almost all the way to where she stood, and then it began to sink and disappeared from sight.

Rebecca Cady stayed in the water and watched it. She looked for a long time at the place where it had vanished, and then she turned and waded back out of the sea and onto the beach.

For a while she stood on the sand, her head bowed, letting the wind fan over her body and dry her skin. Arlen's throat felt thick, watching her. He didn't move, just stood where he was until she'd picked up the gown and pulled it over her head and walked up to the house.

Only when he was sure she would be back in her room did he slip off his shoes and remove his shirt and trousers and venture into the water in search of the box.

22

IT WAS PAST MIDNIGHT when he found it. He'd seen the spot clearly enough where it entered the water, marked it the best that he could, but it was a big ocean and things shifted as they sank. He went up and down the short stretch of shore where it had to have ended up, walking carefully, dragging his feet through the rough sand, waiting for the telltale feel of the wooden box. He didn't like being out in the dark, with so many unseen creatures circling the waters around him. Sharks were like alligators, prehistoric beasts that had somehow managed to last through one world and into the next. At least you could see their fins in daylight. Out here in the dark, one of them could be at his side and he wouldn't know.

He looked for more than an hour and didn't find anything. Tired, he went back to the beach and sat in the sand. The air was warm, but the breeze chilled the moisture on his skin and soon had him ready to return to the water.

He was still searching but the expectation of success was dimming in his mind when the side of his right foot thumped against something solid. He paused and dragged his foot back and felt the impact again, dipped and let a wave slap over his head, drenching him, as he felt with his hands. As soon as his fingers made contact, he knew this had to be it. He pulled it from the sand and broke the surface again, then waded out of the surf.

There was a book of matches in his pants pocket, and he went back up and sat in the sand again and took them out. The twine was still there, and Rebecca had used it to secure a flat stone to the box, ensuring that it would sink. He untied it, lit a match, and opened the lid. He was kneeling in the sand now, and when the match light caught the inside of the box and revealed its contents, he stumbled upright and backward. The match dropped into the sand and snuffed out. He stood where he was for a moment, then took a deep breath, lit another match, and bent for a second look.

Inside the box was a pair of hands.

They'd been severed just above the wrists, cut with a clean chop from a cleaver or an ax, not sawed away. What blood had been in the hands had long since drained, maybe before they were put into the box, maybe once the seawater found its way inside; what was left was swollen gray flesh with strings of muscle and shards of bone exposed at the bottoms. They were a man's hands, but the decomposing flesh hid any clue as to what kind of man; details like calluses or scars or carefully tended fingernails were now impossible to detect.

The match burned down and scorched his fingers, and then he dropped that one, too, closed the lid of the box, and sat down heavily in the sand. He found his flask and took a long drink and then fastened the cap and sat staring at the box as the wind drove hard across the water. He stared for a long time and then got to his feet and walked to the house and found the shovel.

Back at the beach, he gathered the box, feeling a prickle of horror as he heard the contents slide around inside, and then walked down the shore with the box in one hand and the shovel in the other. He walked until he found a tree that had been broken in half by the hurricane, and then he carefully marked five paces out from it and began to dig. When the hole was about three feet deep, he dropped the box into the center and filled it back in with sand. He smoothed the surface with the underside of the shovel's blade, then spent some time walking back and forth over the top, until he was satisfied that the disturbed ground would be nearly impossible to spot.

When he was done, he walked back to the house and replaced the shovel. He paused on the porch and smoked a cigarette in the dark, and then he opened the door and went inside to find Rebecca Cady.

Her room was dark and the door was closed. There was no sound inside but the occasional creaking of the house in the wind. Paul's room was directly next to hers, but it was silent as well. Arlen opened the door as softly as he could, looked inside and saw the outline of her body on the bed. Her chest rose and fell slowly. She was asleep.

He crossed the room until he was standing at the side of her bed. There was a chair next to the bed, and a pair of pistols rested on it. He stared at them for a few seconds, and then he reached out and laid his hand on her shoulder.

She came awake with a start, was about to let out a cry, but he moved his hand to her mouth in time to muffle it. She twisted to the side and reached for the chair where the pistols lay, but he blocked that with his hip and said, "Easy."

She bit his hand.

It was a damn good bite, one that broke the flesh and made him grunt with pain. He jerked away and stepped back and she went for the guns again, but he kept in front of the chair.

"*Get out*. What are you—"

"You lost your box in the ocean," he said in a low voice, conscious of Paul in the room next to them, wanting very much for the boy to sleep through this. "I went in and found it for you."

She went still and silent. She was propped up on the heels of her hands now, pushed back against the headboard, lit by the moon glow.

"I think it's time we talk," Arlen said. "At least it's time I talk to somebody. You got a chance for it to be you. Pass, and I'll find someone else."

She said, "All right. We'll talk."

"Downstairs," he said. "We don't need Paul waking up for this."

"I'll be down in a minute."

Arlen smiled in the dark and shook his head.

"We'll go on down together," he said. "I'd like to make sure those pistols don't make the trip with you."

23

THEY WENT DOWNSTAIRS and she motioned at one of the tables in the barroom, but he shook his head.

"Outside. Like I said, I don't want to wake the boy."

So they went out on the porch, and Arlen leaned against the railing and faced her, his hand oozing blood from the bite. She didn't sit but stood with her arms folded under her breasts. The breeze had cooled, and her nipples budded against the thin fabric of the gown.

She cleaned a pool of blood off the floor and didn't call anyone to report the crime, Arlen thought. *She threw a pair of severed hands into the ocean and wouldn't have said a word about that either. Don't you look at her, Wagner. Don't you dare let yourself keep looking at her like that. It's only trouble.*

"I was out on the beach," he said. "I saw you go in the water and throw Wade's box out there, and I figured I ought to see what was in it. Took a damn long time to find the thing, but I did."

"You were watching me?" she said, squeezing herself tighter.

"That's right," he said. "But I'm a lot more interested in that box than I am in your body. It's a fine-looking body, even in the dark, but I don't give a damn. I want to hear what in the hell it is that Solomon Wade is doing out here, and why you're letting it happen. And I want to hear the truth."

She was quiet, looking past him at the moonlit sea.

"You got one chance to tell it," he said. "Otherwise, I'll be back with the law. It won't be Tolliver either. There's real law in places not far off."

She dropped into a chair as if the strength had left her legs, leaned forward and clasped her hands together, like a woman in prayer.

"It's my brother."

"Your brother?"

"He's in prison," she said. "Raiford. He's only twenty years old. It was working with Solomon Wade that got him into trouble."

"That experience made you eager to work with him yourself?"

She looked up at him. "If I don't, Solomon will have Owen killed. He's done it before. I can show you newspaper articles if you'd like. There are at least three men who have been killed in prisons or work camps in this state because Solomon Wade ordered it to happen."

"That shows up in the papers?"

"Of course not. But I can show you articles about the men who died, and then I can tell you the truth about why they died, and how."

"He's a judge," Arlen said. "A crooked one, sure, but still a judge. He's not some sort of Al Capone or —"

But she was shaking her head.

"He's as dangerous as anyone in the state."

"Who in the hell is he?" Arlen said. "How does a backwoods county judge like that get so much power?"

"He's not a backwoods county judge," she said. "He's a hand-picked choice of evil men, sent here from New Orleans."

"Why? What was here for him?"

"Smuggling."

"What's he into now? It isn't rum-running these days."

"Morphine. Or that's what he calls it. Heroin."

"What's the difference?"

"Strength. One grain of heroin is the same as three grains of morphine."

"You seem to know a lot about it."

"Yes," she said simply.

"He brings this in from Cuba?"

"That's right. Hidden in orange crates. The crates are dropped off in my inlet, loaded up in trucks, and taken to New Orleans, Memphis, and Kansas City. My brother was driving one of them when he was arrested. He refused to talk to the police, because to do so would implicate my father and Wade. So he told a pretty lie and now he sits in Raiford with no idea that Solomon Wade, his trusted boss, is using his life as blackmail."

"This is still happening?" Arlen said. "The smuggling, here?"

"Yes. Every six weeks or so. A lot of drugs come through this inlet. And a lot of money."

"Solomon suggested as much to me," Arlen said. "You said he was handpicked by people in New Orleans, but judge is an elected position. As is sheriff. How did those two come from other places and get themselves elected?"

"Bribes, swindling, and intimidation," she said. "Solomon was the first. Then he brought Tolliver down from Cleveland and got him elected the same way. They don't answer to the people of this county or anyone in the entire state; they answer to New Orleans, New York, and Chicago. I don't think smuggling has anything to do with Solomon wanting to be a judge, though. It has to do with power, and background. He's building both. What he wants won't be found in Corridor County. He intends to go far beyond that."

"And you're helping him lay the foundation."

"I just told you why! It's not as if I made some decision to—"

"Whose hands were they?" he said.

"What?"

"The hands in the box. Who do they belong to? That man in the Plymouth who came by last night?"

"Yes. Tate McGrath killed him, I'm sure. Tate and his sons. His name was David Franklin. From Tampa. He worked with Walter Sorenson."

"Doing what?"

"Collections. Bookkeeping. They were the money men."

"I get the feeling," Arlen said, "that Mr. Franklin tried to get more than his share. Apparently Wade and his boys didn't appreciate that he melted Walt Sorenson in his attempt."

She turned away as if feeling ill.

"Why would they bring the hands to you tonight?" he asked.

"That's Solomon's idea of a message. He's reminding me of his power."

"But why would you care about this David Franklin?"

"Because," she said, her voice dipping to a near whisper, "we do the same sort of work for Solomon. He's reminding me to do it right."

Neither of them spoke for a while then. The wind blew and the waves broke and they sat in silence.

"There was a woman with Franklin last night. Do you know—"

"I have no idea what happened to her," she said.

But they both knew.

Arlen took out a cigarette and lit it and smoked. "This is why you stayed," he said. "Because you believe that if you leave, he'll have your brother killed."

"I don't believe it. I *know* it."

"So this place has value to Solomon," he said, "because he can let his boys meet out here, bring in visitors to talk about things that can't be overheard, maybe kill a man or two. You'll keep silent because you're worried for your brother."

"That's right."

He smiled in the darkness and tapped ash from the cigarette. "Do you truly take me for a fool?"

She pulled her head back. "What?"

"I'm supposed to believe that's all there is?" he said. "That's the most ignorant thing I've ever heard in my life. It's not worth the risk to him. There are a thousand places you could land a boat offshore here and smuggle into these creeks. There are a thousand places you could hold meetings. Hell, if he's so damned determined that *this* be the spot, he'd run you off from it and take over."

She ran her fingertips across her cheekbone and said, "Long enough ago, he might have done that. He didn't have to, though. He had my father working for him willingly. My father and my brother. And there aren't a thousand places like this, not with a deep-water inlet. You can bring a large boat in here and get trucks right down to it, unload quick, and the whole place is such a jungle that it would be almost impossible for anyone to watch you do it, for anyone to surprise you. No, this is actually the *perfect* place for Solomon Wade."

"Your father was partners with him."

She nodded. "For a time. Back when it was only liquor and people weren't being killed and he thought Wade was someone he could trust."

"So your father, he just allowed the smuggling to go on, is that it? Pretended not to know what they were doing, took a cut to keep his mouth shut?"

"He did a little more than that. Tate McGrath's no mathematician. Solomon needed somebody who could think, somebody who could handle the dollars, the *real* dollars."

"Your father did those things."

"He did," she said, "and now I do."

He looked at her for a time and then stretched his neck first one way and then the other, felt the stiff joints pop.

"I don't believe that," he said. "I don't believe a woman like you could be forced into doing so much for a man like that based on nothing more than intimidation. Someone like you? Shit, you'd have called the governor by now. Called old J. Edgar Hoover himself, had all of them down at Raiford, hauling your baby brother out while they fastened shackles around Wade."

"Nothing more than intimidation," she echoed. "Nothing more."

"That's all it sounds like to me, and you don't seem the type to crumble under it as completely as you're wanting me to believe."

She lifted her chin and gave him that challenging stare she had. Her shoulders were pulled back and he could see her breasts pushing at the gown and the smooth lines of her sides swerving out into her hips, could see her hair tracing her neck. When he took another drag off his cigarette, he held the smoke longer than he intended. Almost like he'd forgotten it was there.

"Okay," he said. "You've made your decisions. Something you need to understand? I'm about to make mine."

She was silent.

"There any reason I shouldn't walk up the road with that cute little box, show it to the law, and tell them what I've seen?"

"Where is the box?"

"That ain't the question, honey."

"It's *my* question. Where is the box?"

He grinned at her and shook his head.

It went quiet again. They listened to the water break on the beach, and Arlen finished his cigarette and put it out under his toe.

"I've told you all I care to tell you," she said. "This isn't a game. My brother will die. He's the same age as Paul, almost. Ten months older."

"And he's almost out," Arlen said.

"How do you know that?"

"I only look ignorant, Miss Cady. Solomon told you fourteen days left. I suspect he meant until your brother gets out. Am I right?"

Her silence told him that he was.

"So he'll come back," Arlen said. "That's your idea at least. Then what?"

"I've got a plan."

"Many of the dead people I've known did."

"You've such an encouraging touch."

"Is that what you need? Encouragement?"

"What I need," she said, "is to be left alone again."

"Bullshit. Last thing in the world you want is to be left alone. You could've sent us off days ago, but you didn't. You let us linger."

She was quiet.

"Well," he said, "I suppose I'll have to do some thinking."

"What have you done with that box?" she said.

"It's in a place of my control. Don't get any bright ideas about having Wade hang me up by my toenails to find out where."

"I wouldn't do that."

"You'd do damn near anything you *decide* to do," he said. "That much has been made clear."

She went quiet again, and he realized that she was crying. Hardly making a sound, but her cheeks were damp and her breathing unsteady.

"Like I said," he told her, the edge dulling from his voice, "I've got my own decisions to make."

They sat there for a long time in the silent dark, and eventually he stepped away from the railing and went to the door and held it open. She hesitated but then rose and walked inside. Her body passed close to him, almost brushing him, and he could smell her hair, clean and with some hint of flowers.

She turned to him, still standing very close, her chest inches from his, and said, "So what do you expect me to do? Go upstairs and wait for you to think?"

"You can do that," he said, "or you can kill me while I sleep. Let me know what you decide."

24

She came into his room just before dawn. He'd finally found sleep; the flask still lay in his hand, held against his side the way a child holds a dear toy. He wasn't sure what sound stirred him or even if one had. He just opened his eyes and she was there, the white gown almost all that showed of her in the dark. The sky hadn't begun to lighten yet, but he knew it must be close to morning. For a moment he didn't speak, just looked at her and then dropped his eyes to her hands, thinking of the pistols. Her hands were empty.

"You don't believe that Wade's intimidation is enough to keep me here," she said. "Enough to keep me working for him. That's what you said."

He didn't answer, just pushed up in bed. He was bare-chested, and the room that always felt too warm now seemed cool.

"You asked why he didn't just run us off and take the place over for himself," she said. "Do you know how much I would love to have him do that? I'd *give* him the property, sign it over to him without a dime in return. That's not enough for him, though. Not at this point. This family has been connected to him for too long. We're either working for him or we're working against him. That's how he sees it at least. The minute I try to leave this place, even if I want nothing more than peace, he will view it as a threat. And I can tell you something about how he handles threats."

She went quiet for a moment, and when she continued her voice was lower, more controlled.

"Solomon's had help at the Cypress House for years. Since not long after my father built it. My father thought he was financially secure and found out he wasn't. He lost his savings, and he couldn't make any money here. It was a foolish idea from the start. This place is too far from anywhere to make a success. So what if you can catch fish? You can catch fish anywhere."

Her face was beginning to take shape in the gloom.

"I stayed in Savannah when they moved here. My brother was just a boy, so he went along, but I was grown and I stayed there. They'd been down for only a few years before my mother died. Drowned just out from the beach."

Arlen remembered the way his mother had looked at the end, body and mind ravaged by fever, her eyes so far from the woman he'd known that he couldn't look into them.

"My father was devastated, and he needed help with my brother. I came down for a time, stayed for just over a year. When the lumber company in High Town went under, they killed off the railroad spur and this place was truly isolated. I couldn't stand it anymore, and I left. I hated it here. *Hated* it. I moved back to Savannah. I was there for five years."

She paused, and he was about to ask why she'd returned, but something told him not to speak. Just let her talk.

"During that time my father worked with Wade. After Prohibition ended, things got worse. The people involved were more ruthless, my father's role more important. He was scared of it, then. After getting in so deeply, he decided he was scared. He began writing me letters, telling me that I needed to help him convince Owen to come and live with me in Georgia, that Owen couldn't stay in this place anymore. I tried to talk to my brother, and I was ignored. Then he was arrested."

A soft breeze slid in through the open window and flattened the sheet against Arlen's thigh.

"I left Savannah and came back. Thinking"—her voice hitched slightly—"that I would save them."

In his room at the far end of the hall, Paul coughed and muttered. It brought Rebecca up, held her silent. The moon painted her shadow on the wall.

"My father was terribly depressed. Near suicidal. He blamed himself for Owen's situation, and he felt trapped here. He said anyone who betrayed Solomon Wade paid for it. That he'd follow you, find you no matter how long it took, and kill you. I didn't believe that."

This time she was quiet much longer.

Arlen said, "Tell me the rest. I don't care how hard it is. You've got to tell me the rest."

"It was my idea," she said finally, her voice unsteady now. "My father was willing to try, but it was my idea. He kept talking about how the only way you escaped Solomon was through death. I told him we'd use that. He was going to take the boat out and sink it. Fake his death. He would leave, go to a place we'd agreed upon, but I'd have to stay for a while. For it to fool Wade, I would have to stay here at least long enough to make it look like we hadn't run. I'd sell the inn, and when my brother was released, there'd be no reason for him to return here. It wouldn't concern anyone when we decided to leave Corridor County once my father was dead. It would seem logical."

"Your father actually did drown, though," he said. "That's what Thomas Barrett told me. So did he drown trying to scuttle the boat?"

"You don't drown with your throat cut."

He was silent for a time, and then he said, "No, you don't. How can you be sure that's what happened, though?"

"I saw the body. Who do you think was supposed to get him off the boat before he sank it?"

"You didn't tell anyone."

"You have trouble believing that," she said. "I'm sure you've never seen your own father with his throat cut because of the way you handled a situation."

No, not with his throat cut, Arlen thought. *I saw my father spilling blood into the dust from a bullet, though, and you better believe it was because of the way I handled the situation. Difference was, I was right. Edwin Main might have been corrupt, but I did what was right. My father was dangerous. Insane.*

"By the time I got back here," she said when he didn't respond, "Solomon Wade was waiting. His message was simple: either I did what was asked, or my brother would end up like my father."

Another sound from Paul's room, this time a garbled sort of cry. Talking in his sleep. Trapped in a nightmare.

"Is your brother aware of any of this?"

"No. How could I tell him while he was in prison?"

"He knows your father is dead, though."

"Yes. But he believes that he drowned."

"And you believe he'll be killed if you leave or seek help."

"I think that's obvious." She shifted her weight, the floor creaking beneath her, and said, "You want to know why Solomon Wade killed my father? It's not just because what he knew made him a threat. I don't think it had anything to do with that, really. It was the idea that he thought he could slip out of Wade's control. The idea that he thought Wade had anything but total power over him."

It went quiet again, and the morning wind worked through the window and swirled her gown around her feet.

"You wanted to know my reasons," she said. "You wanted to know why I haven't gone to someone for help. Said you couldn't believe a woman like me would be intimidated into such an agreement with Solomon Wade."

She took a step closer to him, so he could see her face clearly, and said, "Do you believe it now?"

He nodded. "You've been waiting for him to get out. Waiting for Owen."

"Yes."

"He's almost out. He'll be coming back."

"Yes."

"And then?"

She wet her lips and broke eye contact.

"It would seem to me," he said, "whatever plan you've got, it's going to need to be a damn good one."

"We'll be leaving," she said.

"You don't think Wade's expecting that?"

"I know that he is."

Arlen let his silence speak for him.

"Well, what do you propose?" she said. "Stay? Live the rest of our lives with a gun to our heads?"

"No, I wouldn't propose that. But you'd better not make a mistake."

"After the last six months of my life," she said, "surely you don't really believe you need to explain that to me."

He gave that a nod.

"Well, there you are," she said. "My reasons. You said you had your own decision to make. You can make it with those in your mind."

He was waiting for more, expecting her to say something else, to implore him toward silence or trust, but instead she turned and walked almost soundlessly across the floor, opened the door, and slipped back out of the room.

25

THE NEXT MORNING they finished the generator shed and began work on the dock, and Arlen's eyes wandered constantly, looking for Solomon Wade or Sheriff Tolliver or Tate McGrath and his sons. No one came. Paul sensed his distraction and asked after it, and Arlen dismissed it as a headache. He had a bandage on his hand from Rebecca's bite, but Paul didn't inquire about that.

She'd asked nothing of him. Told him her story and slipped back out of the room. What she wanted, evidently, was only his silence. She wanted her fourteen — now thirteen — days to wait until her brother's release. No other help had been requested, no other plan shared.

It was at lunch that Paul asked about the clock.

The thing was massive, with a brass frame set in a beautiful piece of walnut that sloped away on both sides, its hands stopped dead on midnight. Arlen had seen it the day they'd entered with Sorenson but paid little attention to it then or anytime else.

"My mother ordered that clock," Rebecca said, and though

her eyes were empty her voice seemed to be coming from some-where out at sea. "She loved it. It's been broken for years now."

"Maybe I'll have a look," Paul said.

"I think you'd have to know about clocks."

"That's what we all said about the generator, too," Arlen pointed out.

"Exactly," Paul said. "Arlen, help me get that down?"

The kid wanted so badly to have something to do for her. *Let me help you* seemed to issue forth from him like a constant shout, as if by helping her enough he'd convince her of something. *I'll show her that she needs me,* he'd said. Now Arlen wanted to grab him and shake him and shout that he had no damn idea what she needed and what it could cost him. Her needs went beyond any that Paul could imagine. Her needs involved people who cut off a man's hands and presented them to her in a box wrapped with twine, like a gift.

"Arlen?"

"Yeah," Arlen said, blinking back into the moment. "Sure."

They brought a ladder in and, with Paul on the ladder and Arlen standing on the bar, got the whole piece down. It weighed less than the generator but not by much. Paul studied the casing and then went in search of a screwdriver. When he was gone, it was just Rebecca and Arlen in the barroom. She looked at him in silence for a few seconds and then said, "You're still here."

"Wondering about my decision," he said. "That it?"

"Yes."

"Here's a start on it," he said. "There are two pistols on the chair beside your bed. I'd like one of them."

"What?"

"Seems like a fair gesture of trust to me," he said.

Paul's footsteps slapped off the floor, and then the door to the kitchen banged open and he was back with them, in mid-sentence and midstride, discussing his theories on the clock's malfunction before he'd even gotten the case off. When he'd knelt on the floor above it and ducked his head, Arlen stared back at Rebecca Cady, a look in his eyes that said, *The rest is up to you.*

She turned away.

All day long they worked, speaking to each other as if nothing lay between them. All day long Arlen watched the road for Wade and McGrath, and all day long he considered the countless reasons for gathering his bags and walking away from this place.

When darkness fell, his bags were where they'd been for days.

She came for him in the night.

He was in the chair at the window, had dozed off, and the sound of the door opening woke him. He could see her reflection in the glass as she entered. The pistol was in her left hand, looking big and ugly.

"Do you ever sleep?" she said, apparently thinking that because he was in the chair he'd been awake.

"I used to."

He still hadn't turned, and after a short hesitation she crossed the room to him. When she reached the chair, she didn't say anything at first, just joined him in staring out at the sea. Then, still silent, she switched the gun from her left hand to her right and extended it to him.

He didn't move to take it.

"There are bullets inside, if they make you feel better. I can give you more if you want them."

He stared at the horizon line. Even in the dark of full night, you could make out the distinction once your eyes had adjusted. Shades of gray.

"Well?" she said, and gave the gun a little shake.

"You intend to leave," Arlen said, not moving his hands from his lap, letting the big Smith & Wesson float in the air in front of his chest.

"What?"

"When your brother is released, you intend to leave."

"That's right."

"He'll look for you," Arlen said. "And you want to know something else? He'll look for me and Paul."

"It has nothing to do with you."

"It didn't."

"It doesn't now."

"Like hell. It does now, and it will then."

She moved the gun away, dropped it back to her side.

"So when he's released, you'll leave," Arlen repeated. "And then I'll have to deal with Wade, whether here or far away. You told me that yourself."

She still didn't say a word. He looked up at her for a time, and then he reached over and took the gun. He had to lean across her body to get it. When he touched the stock, his hand pressed against hers. Her skin was very cool.

He pulled the gun from her fingers and flicked open the cylinder and saw the cartridges, snapped it shut and set the weapon down on his lap.

"All right," he said.

She didn't move. He looked up at her and then got to his feet.

"That's my answer," he said. "I'll be here in the morning again. Be damned if I know why, but I'll be here in the morning."

He crossed to the bed and leaned down and placed the gun on the floor beside it. She was still standing at the window, staring out at the ocean.

"When you kissed me," she said, "I thought that's what you wanted. That you'd make me ... earn your silence."

"I understand. You weren't right, but I understand, and I shouldn't have done it. It was a mistake."

"I shouldn't have hit you."

"I think you probably should have," he said.

She turned and took a few steps toward him.

"Why did you do that, though? It didn't seem like something you would do. That's why I reacted that way. It didn't seem to fit you."

"Why did I kiss you? I think you had it right. I wanted to control you. I'm a brute, same as McGrath or Tolliver or Wade."

"That's not the truth. Why did you do it?"

He studied her for a moment and then said, "You don't need to ask a man why he'd be moved to do a thing like that. You don't need to ask that at all. You damn well know why."

She'd stepped even closer, was an arm's length away now.

Tell her to get out, he thought. *Tell her thanks for the gun, honey, but go on your way now.*

She took one more step forward and he reached up with his right hand and placed it on the back of her head and pulled her face to his and kissed her, just as he had the last time. She didn't slap him tonight. She returned the kiss but kept her body distant for a moment. Just a moment. Then she leaned in and he felt the press of her chest against his, the graze of her thigh.

He broke the kiss.

"All right," he said. "You let me have one. Thanks. It was awfully nice. Now you need to leave."

She stepped back from him and looked him in the eye and then she reached down and took hold of her gown and lifted it, brought it up over her head just as she had that night on the beach before she'd waded into the water. She held the gown in her hands for one long second and then dropped it onto the floor, and she was naked before him.

This is how far she's willing to go, he thought. *This is how far she thinks she* needs *to go. You'll get your reward for keeping your mouth shut. How do you feel about yourself now? You proud of what you've got her ready to do?*

"Go back to your room," he said, and his voice was hoarse. "I'm a rotten son of a bitch, some days, but I've never been this kind of rotten. Get out of here."

She didn't move. The moonlight lit the curve of one breast, traced the swell of her hip and the length of her leg with white light.

"All I asked for was the gun," he said. "You can go back to bed now. Go on and get to bed."

"You want me to go?" she said.

"Yes." But even as he said it he felt himself step forward. It was wrong, it was all mighty damn wrong, this moment built from everything that a moment like this should not be of—distrust, power, manipulation. A flickering thought—*Just come toward me a little, don't make me go all the way there, come toward me a little, that will make it better, so much better*—danced in his brain.

She leaned into him just before he reached her. She leaned into him and something broke free in his mind and floated clear and then his lips were on hers again and his hands were resting first on the small of her back and then on her hips. Her hair slid over his cheek and her chest pressed into his, her nipples tightening against his skin.

When he pulled her back to the bed, his foot brushed against the Smith & Wesson. He almost tripped over it just before they hit the mattress, the old bed frame creaking under their weight. She had both of her hands on his belt now and he was trying to help with one of his own. He twisted and tugged free from his pants, then ran his hands along her sides, tracing the lines of her body as he moved his lips to her ear.

"Quiet," he whispered. "Quiet. I don't want the boy hearing."

26

S HE WAS GONE when he woke, but the gun remained.
He turned away from the window to hide from the sunlight. The sheets and pillow smelled of her. He didn't remember when she'd left, but he remembered the night. Long would he remember the night.

He heard voices from downstairs then, hers first, then Paul's. The sound of the boy's voice made him squeeze his eyes shut.

Out of all the reasons you shouldn't have done it, his schoolboy's infatuation doesn't rank anywhere near the top, he told himself. *Not even close.*

Somehow it seemed to, though. Somehow it seemed mighty near the top.

They worked a full day, completing the first third of the dock, Paul in his usual high spirits. Once, Arlen went up to the house to fetch them both some water and found Rebecca with a set of ledger books. He didn't ask what she was studying on, and she didn't offer.

During dinner Paul mentioned how much he'd like to try some fishing. Rebecca left and came back with two beautiful rods and reels. "My father's," she said shortly. That evening Arlen stood on the dock and smoked a few cigarettes while the boy tried casting. He caught two black drum before the night was done, fish with high backs, steeply sloped heads, and a tangle of chin whiskers. They gave him some fun on the line, and he brought them up to the inn and made an awkward job of cleaning one before Rebecca stepped in and did the other.

"Fresh fish tomorrow," she said. "You caught it, and we can keep it cold now because you fixed the generator."

There was nothing the kid liked more than her praise.

She came back to Arlen's room that night.

"I told you," he said, "you don't have to do this. I didn't ask it of you."

"No," she said. "You didn't."

"If you don't want to be here, then go on back to your room."

"If I didn't," she said, "I would."

He sat on the edge of the bed and stared at her in the dark and said, "I need to believe that."

"You should."

He didn't answer.

"If you'd like me to go, I will," she said. "But do you really want me to?"

He did not.

The wind changed early the next afternoon. It had been blowing in hot gusts out of the west for the better part of two days, but now it swung around to the southeast and the water in the inlet rippled beneath it. The change brought a touch of cool, and they were grateful for it down on the dock, until they noticed the smell.

It was coming from farther up the inlet, somewhere back in the mangrove trees. Paul twisted his face in a grimace of disgust and said, "What *is* that?"

"Dunno," Arlen said, but he was facing into the wind and thinking that he knew very well indeed.

"You mean you don't smell that stench?"

"I can smell it."

"It's awful. You ever smelled anything so awful, Arlen?"

"A time or two."

They got back to work then, and the sun moved west and shone down on the inlet, unbroken by cloud. The smell intensified—a fetid, rotting stink. Arlen saw vultures coming and going from a spot in the marsh grass just up the creek from them, maybe three hundred yards away. They flicked through the trees as silent shadows, but there were many of them.

"Something died back there," Paul said. "Wonder what it was."

Who, Arlen thought. *You wonder* who *it was.*

Of course, it could be an animal. One of the boars they had out in these woods. Or perhaps someone's hound had gotten loose and found its way down to the inlet and ran afoul of a snake. There were any number of possibilities.

An hour passed before Paul went up to the inn and came back with a rake in his hand, a thing with a mean-looking array of wide metal tines.

"The hell you think you're doing?" Arlen said.

"We better check that out. Arlen, it smells like death."

"Could be an animal."

"Could be." Paul gave him a long, steady look, and Arlen sighed and swore under his breath and dropped his saw to the ground, gathered an ax.

"All right. We'll have a look."

It was remarkable how fast the beach gave way to forest in this part of the state. Or to jungle, rather. It was more like that than any forest Arlen had ever known, choked with thick green undergrowth and snarling vines and soil that squished under your boots. They picked their way through the mud and the brush until they were walking beneath the trees — scrub pine nearest the dock and mangroves farther inland. The woods were a litter of torn leaves and branches, and it seemed half the trees had been sheared or uprooted completely during the hurricane. The vultures ahead of them watched their approach and flapped their wings, creating an eerie background as they walked deeper into the shadows.

"Go on," Arlen shouted at the birds. "Go on!" He reached out and grabbed hold of a large banyan leaf and gave it a vigorous shake. A few of the birds took to the air then, but others stayed. Arlen could see now that the object of the scavenging was actually down in the water, which was why the vultures were perched in the trees instead of clustered around the find; they had to make quick passes and snatches with their beaks because the carcass was floating and they weren't waterbirds. Just death birds.

"Arlen," Paul said, "that looks like ..."

"Yeah," Arlen said.

The carcass was on their side of the creek but still thirty feet away and mostly underwater. Even from here, though, a stretch of fabric was visible. It was covered with mud and water, but even so you could see that it was a pale yellow.

"Give me that rake," Arlen said, and the words didn't come easily. Paul traded him the rake for the ax, and Arlen ran his tongue over dry lips and then stepped forward. The boy hung back, watching. Arlen had his eyes locked on the floating object and didn't see the snake in his path until he'd nearly stepped on it. There was a flourish of motion that froze him with one foot hanging in the air, and then the water parted almost soundlessly and the snake slid off. Arlen stared after it for a moment and then continued on.

When he got closer, he yelled again and banged the rake through the leaves and sent the remaining vultures into the air. They didn't go far, though. Only to a tree on the opposite side of the creek, where they could monitor their prize.

He knew by then what he'd suspected since the wind shifted and began to carry the smell to them. The vultures and the fish and the heat had combined to do dastardly things to this remnant of human life, and when he stood over the body he felt his stomach clench and had to take a quick glance at the treetops to steady himself. The stench was hideous, and he'd pulled his shirt up over his nose with the hand that didn't hold the rake.

She floated upside down, and he could see one hand just beneath the surface of the water, some of the flesh picked clean, bone remaining. He remembered the way she'd traced his palm with her fingers.

It's happened now, hasn't it? she'd said, watching his face after her own had gone from flesh to bone in the darkness. *He's told them. It's done.*

Arlen had let her go. He'd seen death on her and he'd let her go and now her remains floated in the marsh, picked upon by forest creatures and vultures. Yes, there'd been armed men inside, but he'd let her go, he'd let them take her.

They'll find me, she had said. *And it will end the same for me, only it will also be bad for you and the boy. And for Rebecca. I won't initiate such things.*

"Arlen," Paul called. "Is that—"

"Shut up!" Arlen shouted, and his voice nearly broke. The boy fell into a stunned silence.

You can't run from them, she'd said. *I hope you understand that.*

You're going to need to. There will be no running from what lies ahead.

Now he reached out with the rake, leaning off the bank and extending it as far as he could, and hooked one of the tines into the dead woman's dress.

It took four tries to drag her all the way over. Her flesh was so decomposed that the rake went through it like soft butter, so Arlen had to keep catching the dress as best as he could. The clothes had held up better than the body.

He dragged her back, out of the dark waters of the creek and toward the bank. He bit down, squeezing his teeth together and tightening his lips, and then he held his breath and used the rake to turn the body over. More flesh slid off the bones when he did it, and a burst of putrid gases rose. The dead woman's head rolled crookedly, turning to face Arlen. Only traces of skin remained, and they were swollen and discolored. Not even the dearest loved one would be able to look at this face and recognize it. Arlen felt his stomach clench again and his throat burn warningly, and he pulled the rake free and turned from the body, heard it slide down into the water. He walked back to Paul, cold rage in his veins.

"That's a woman," Paul said softly. "Isn't it? That's a dead woman."

"Yes."

"Where'd she come from? How'd she die?"

Arlen looked away. "She's been in the water for a time. Probably dumped in upstream and drifted down and snagged here."

"The body wouldn't have sunk? They float?"

"Yes," Arlen said. "They float."

Paul stared at him. "Who was it?"

"Too late to tell," Arlen said, and that was almost the truth.

27

A RLEN TOLD THEM they'd have to call for the sheriff, and both Rebecca and Paul stared at him as if he'd lost his mind.

"He'll likely want to arrest us for it," Paul said nervously.

"You'd let her sit there?" Arlen said. "Pretend we never found her?"

"No," Paul said, but he still looked uneasy, and Rebecca was watching Arlen with confusion and wariness, reading something in him that the boy did not. He turned from her so she could no longer stare into his eyes. There was another reason Arlen wanted Tolliver down here, all right. He wanted to watch the man face the corpse. To see her as she was now, and remember her as she had been. He wanted to see if it made any impact, if the man would feel the weight of murder or if that ability was gone from him. Arlen had an idea that it was.

They got in the truck and headed out just as they had so many days earlier, when Sorenson's body still smoldered in his twelve-cylinder Auburn and Arlen expected to be gone from the Cypress House by sundown.

Back to the same store, and this time they all went inside. The little shop was jammed with rows of shelves, and a dark-skinned, dark-haired girl stood behind a counter lined with jars of penny candy. She was an Indian, Arlen realized when she looked up at them, an absolutely beautiful girl.

"Hello, Sarah," Rebecca said. "We're going to need the phone."

Before the girl could answer, a door behind the counter opened and Thomas Barrett stepped into the room, his face flushed and damp with sweat. Behind him Arlen could see a litter of tools and the panel delivery van.

"The whole gang," Barrett said, grinning at them. "Y'all need that many cigarettes?"

"We need to call the sheriff," Rebecca said.

Barrett's smile faded. "Everything all right?"

"There's a body in the inlet. A dead woman."

Barrett looked at Arlen and then back at Rebecca, and he moved toward the girl at the counter, slipped his arm around her waist. It was a protective gesture. As if the three from the Cypress House carried danger.

"First that guy blowing up in his car," he said, "and now this? What in the hell's going on out there?"

Nobody had an answer.

Tolliver and the redheaded deputy brought a truck with an open bed out along with the sheriff's car, and they carried a wide canvas tarpaulin down to the creek with them. The deputy said something under his breath and covered his mouth and nose with his hand, but Tolliver stood on the bank with his hands hooked in his belt and looked down at the rotting remains as if he were staring at a flat tire or some such minor nuisance.

"I've seen prettier women," he said.

Arlen looked at him and found himself recalling the fields of France, the Springfield rifle bucking in his arms, plumes of blood bursting from strange men. He longed for it now, hungered for killing in a way he had not in the war.

The body's decomposition was advanced by now. Nothing accelerated that process like heat, and the water in the inlet had to be damn near eighty degrees. Rebecca and Paul remained forty feet away, covering their faces. The day's rising sun and the fact that Arlen had pulled the body most of the way out of the water had conspired to worsen an already hideous smell. Arlen could tolerate it, after the war. You grew an extra layer around yourself during something like the Belleau Wood. Or maybe growth wasn't the right way to think of it. No, it was more shrinking than growing. A part of you that was there at the start got a little smaller. The part that viewed human life as something strong and difficult to remove from this world. Yeah, that part could get mighty small over time.

Tolliver spit into the water near the dead woman's head and said, "Well, shit, we best get to it."

He and the deputy pulled on thick work gloves and wrapped scarves over their faces before attempting to retrieve the body. They'd hardly cleared it from the water before Tolliver shouted at Rebecca to bring a bottle of whiskey down. When she returned, Tolliver added a liberal splash to his scarf and the deputy's. Before he wrapped the scarf around his face again, he took a long belt of the whiskey, his Adam's apple bobbing.

They wrestled the body into the tarpaulin and wrapped it as if they were folding a sail. Halfway through, the deputy straightened up as if someone had slipped a bayonet into his side, lifted a hand to his mouth, and then lurched sideways. He fell on his knees at the edge of the creek, splashing, and tore the scarf free just before he vomited.

Tolliver gave a sigh and leaned back and waited. The deputy purged and then stayed on his hands and knees above the creek, breathing in unsteady gasps.

"Come on," Tolliver snapped, holding the scarf down from his mouth with one mud-streaked finger. "Let's get it out of here before sundown."

They finished wrapping the woman's corpse and then carried it back through the woods and dropped it into the bed of the truck. Wet stains were showing through the canvas by the time they got it there.

"Enjoy your afternoon," Tolliver said, wiping his hands on his trousers as he walked for the car, leaving the deputy to drive the truck. "You'll see me again soon enough."

He got into the car and drove away, and the three of them stood together in the yard and watched the truck with the corpse follow the sheriff through the dust and into the woods.

"Wasn't what I expected from him," Paul said. "I thought he'd have plenty of questions, like he did with Mr. Sorenson. Didn't seem to have any at all with this one, though."

"No," Arlen said. "No, he didn't."

28

THEY DIDN'T HEAR ABOUT the body again until the next afternoon, when they had their first visitor from the water.

Paul and Arlen were on the dock, had fresh planking laid twenty feet out now. Paul was chest-deep in the water, hammering braces back into place, when they heard an engine. Arlen looked up toward the house automatically, thinking it was a car, but then he realized the sound was coming across the water, and when he turned around he could see the boat.

It was a motor sailer with one forward mast, sails furled, and a raised cabin making up the back third of the boat. Maybe thirty-five or forty feet long, and wide across the beam. A good-size craft, and one that had seen some weather—its white hull was pocked with nicks and gashes and streaks. Ran steady, though, the engine hitting smoothly as it came out of the Gulf and entered the inlet.

"Who's this, I wonder?" Paul said, still in the water.

"Don't know."

The boat came up the center of the inlet with the confidence of a pilot who knew the waters—it wasn't a wide stretch of

water but evidently was plenty deep—and then the engine cut
and the man at the wheel stepped back to the stern and let a
windlass out, anchor chain hissing into the water. It was Tate
McGrath.

Once the anchor was out, he straightened and stood at the
stern and stared at them for a moment, then set to work lower-
ing the small launch mounted on the stern. Coming ashore.

He got the launch into the water and then climbed down and
rowed in. When he had the boat pulled up to shore, he walked
past them without a word and headed up the trail to the inn.

Paul stood with the hammer in his hand and his eyes on the
trail.

"One of us ought to be up there. She shouldn't be alone with
him."

"She was alone with him for a long time before we got here,"
Arlen said. "She can be alone with him now."

He didn't like it either, though. He had a memory of her
standing in his room with one side lit by moonlight, a memory
of her beneath him with her mouth close to his chest and her
breath warm on his skin...

He missed the nail head and bent it sideways instead of driving it straight. It had been years since he'd done that. Many
years.

Paul had started working again, but his eyes kept going to the
house even though he couldn't see a damn thing from here but
the top of the roof. Arlen let him glance up there a half dozen
times before he finally said, "You want to keep your head down
while you work?"

They hammered away for a while, and McGrath didn't return
and no sound came from the Cypress House. Too damn quiet.
There should be voices.

It was just while he was thinking this that another engine
came into hearing range, a car this time. Arlen finally sighed

and said, "Okay, I'll go see who it is," when he saw Paul staring into the trees with that same dark frown.

"I'll come with you."

"Like hell you will. Stay down here and keep working."

The kid didn't like that at all, but Arlen ignored the grumblings and went on up the trail. When he got back within view of the inn, he saw it was the sheriff's car. Tolliver stood on the porch with Solomon Wade, Rebecca, and Tate McGrath. Arlen came out of the trees and walked up to the porch with his head down, as if he had no interest in the gathering. When he reached the porch steps he said, "Pardon," and stepped past McGrath, who didn't move to clear out of his way, and entered the inn without so much as breaking stride. He walked back behind the bar and into the kitchen and retrieved a beer from the icebox and cracked it open. Drank about a third of it down, standing there in the shadows, and then he took the bottle and went back out onto the porch.

He was ready to do the same routine, walk past them without a blink and return to the dock, when Wade spoke.

"Mr. Wagner?"

He pronounced it Vagner, like the composer, as Tolliver had in the jail. Arlen kept walking, said, "That's not my name," without a look back.

"My mistake," Wade drawled. "Hold up. Don't hurry off."

Arlen turned to face them.

"Where is it you're from?" Wade said. He and Tolliver were standing close to Rebecca, and Tate was leaning on the porch rail.

"No place near here."

"That's not an answer."

Arlen took a drink of his beer. "West Virginia."

"Really? What town?"

"It's not someplace you've heard of."

"I've heard of some Wagners from West Virginia," Wade said. His face was damp with sweat, accentuating the glare from his glasses. "Only they pronounced it properly. Vagner. The ones I've heard of were from Fayette County, I believe. What was your father's name?"

Arlen felt the back of his neck go colder than the beer in his hand.

"You haven't heard of any of my people. We aren't a famous bunch, and it's a mighty small town."

"Maybe so," Wade said, "but you'd be surprised at all that I hear."

A tremor worked into Arlen's hand, the sort of muscle shake that white-hot anger touched off just before you swung on a man, but he willed it down.

"I'd be surprised, indeed, if you've heard anything of my people," he said. "Like I said, it's a mighty small town."

"Why'd you leave it behind?"

"The war. Never went back. Went a lot of places, but never home."

"And what did you do in the war?"

"Killed Germans," Arlen said, wondering what in the hell this was all about.

"Well, good for you." Wade seemed to amplify his southern accent when he desired. Right now he was laying it on heavy.

"What about you, Judge?" Arlen said.

"Pardon?"

"Where are you from?"

Wade's eyes flickered. "Florida, sir. Florida."

"You like the area, then. Trust the locals."

"I do. They are fine people."

"How is it you ended up with a sheriff from Cleveland, then?" Arlen said. He was doing now exactly what he'd promised himself he would not do — poking at Wade and Tolliver with a stick, riling them. He couldn't help it, though. Not after that bullshit about the Wagners of Fayette County.

Tolliver's eyes narrowed and then went to Rebecca Cady.

"Don't look at her," Arlen said. "She didn't tell me. You want people to be unaware of your roots, you ought not go on about the Cleveland Indians in front of them, Sheriff. Nobody from another city would follow such a shitty ball club."

Tolliver did not smile. He turned his gaze to Arlen and let it rest, cold and hard. Arlen winked and lifted his beer to his lips.

"That all you fellows need? Or do you want me to write a family tree?"

Tolliver turned to Wade. "It's amazing he's grown as old as he has, talking like that to men he doesn't know. Someday it'll be the wrong words to the wrong man, don't you think?"

"I surely do," Wade said.

"I believe it," Arlen said. "It's the reason I don't do much talking to strangers. You might remember that you stopped me for this chat."

"Speaking of being a stranger," Wade said, "you seem to have made yourself right at home. Interesting, with the way people keep dying out here."

"It's one of the many things I don't like about the place," Arlen said. "I'll be moving on soon enough."

He waited for more questions, waited for some sort of threat relating to the dead woman they'd found in the creek, a promise of jail time, but nothing came. Wade stared at him for a few seconds, but then his eyes shifted, and when Arlen turned he saw Paul coming up the trail and felt a surge of annoyance. Why hadn't the kid listened and stayed at the dock?

Paul walked to Arlen's side, looking at the men on the porch warily.

"Afternoon, son," Tolliver said. "Find any corpses today?"

"No."

Tolliver smiled.

"What are you doing here?" Paul said.

Tolliver turned and gave Wade wide eyes. "Nosy little bastard, ain't he? Why, we've come to provide a Corridor County resident with transportation. Mr. McGrath here was needing of a lift, and we take care of our citizens in this part of the world."

Solomon Wade looked bored with the dialogue. He stepped down off the porch and walked toward the sheriff's car. He paused when he reached Arlen and looked into his eyes.

"I'll see what I can remember about those Wagners in West Virginia," he said. "Be interesting to see what all I can recollect."

Arlen reached out and extended a hand. Wade stopped and looked down at it as if he'd never seen the gesture.

"Always a pleasure, Judge," Arlen said.

Wade gave a small cold smile and took his hand. Pressed hard against it and kept his eyes on Arlen's.

"Paul," Arlen said, "show some respect: shake the judge's hand."

Everyone looked confused at this.

"Do it, son," Arlen said.

Paul glowered, but he reached out and offered his hand. Wade watched Arlen as if he were trying to understand the game, but he took the boy's hand.

When he did it, Paul's eyes went to smoke.

"Mention the man's family," Solomon Wade said, "and of a sudden he is most polite. I find that curious."

He released Paul's hand, and the smoke disappeared instantly.

"Take care now," Arlen said.

Wade walked on to the car, with Tolliver and McGrath at his heels. The sheriff took the wheel and they went clattering away. Dust hung in the air long after they were gone.

Paul spoke to Arlen in a low voice.

"You see it again?"

Arlen nodded.

Paul seemed to blanch, but he nodded as if it were expected and said, "I'll just have to stay out of his way, then. That's all. Isn't hard to do."

Arlen didn't answer.

"What are you talking about?" Rebecca said.

"Paul," Arlen said, "go on back to the dock and get to work."

He didn't argue this time. Just walked off toward the water, moving with a quick stride that seemed uneasy.

"They say anything about the woman?" Arlen said when he was gone.

"No."

"Then why the hell did they come out here?"

"Solomon wanted to bring the boat back." Rebecca had come down off the porch and was standing close to him.

"Why?"

"To frighten me."

"You're frightened of a boat?"

She gave him cool, expressionless eyes, and after a few seconds he got it.

"That's the one? Your father went out in that boat?"

She nodded.

He took another drink and stared up the road where they'd gone.

"What's he use it for?"

"Smuggling. Mostly Tate runs it." She lowered her voice and said, "What were you talking about just then? Why'd you have Paul shake his hand?"

He turned to face her again. "Wade's going to kill him."

"What?"

"I can see it when he touches him."

She stared. "You're not joking."

"No."

"How do you . . . what do you see?"

"The boy's eyes turn to smoke every time Wade touches him."

She was looking at him with her mouth parted, eyes wide with wonder.

"I've got to get him out of here," Arlen said. "But it won't be easy."

"He believes you, though. He told me that. So he'll know that it's true."

"He still won't be willing to go."

"Why not?"

"Because he's in love with you," Arlen said.

29

It wasn't as simple as staying out of Solomon Wade's way. Arlen was sure of that. And even if it was...Paul wouldn't be able to stay out of his way. No, he'd remain with Rebecca, remain at her side, and Rebecca Cady was planted firmly in Solomon Wade's path.

Arlen had trouble working that afternoon. Made the sorts of mistakes he never made, had to tear loose boards he'd just laid and remeasure and cut them correctly and lay them again. If Paul noticed, he didn't comment. He was quiet himself, somber, but he didn't miss a nail or a measurement. He never seemed to.

The uneasiness followed them back to the inn that evening. There, though, Paul endeavored to change the tone. His idea was a boat ride. As soon as he found out it belonged to Rebecca, he wanted to take it out.

"I've never been on a boat," he said. "Not a real one. And that's a dandy."

"We aren't down here to play on a boat," Arlen said, seeing the pain in her eyes. "Quiet down about it."

"There's no reason we couldn't take it out," he said, undeterred.

"We don't know how to run it."

"Oh, there's not that much to it. I'm not saying we'll sail to China, Arlen, I'm just saying I want to go out a little ways and—"

"Damn it, Paul," Arlen began, riled now, but Rebecca cut him off.

"It's fine," she said. "Take it out."

He cast her a surprised look. She met his eyes and nodded.

"It's fine," she repeated.

"See?" Paul said. "We'll all go."

Rebecca shook her head. "No. I won't."

"Oh, come on. I want all of us to—"

"Paul!" Arlen barked, and the anger in his voice made the kid pull back and stare at him in confusion.

"She doesn't want to go," Arlen said, fighting to control his tone. "Stop pestering. Far as I'm concerned, none of us should go on the damn thing."

"I'd like you to," Rebecca said. "Really, I would. I just can't."

"You get seasick?" Paul said.

She looked away.

"I'd be very, very sick out on that boat."

There was less than an hour of sunlight left when they got aboard, and it took ten minutes to satisfy themselves with an understanding of the engine and get the anchor up. It would have taken Arlen an hour to do the same, but Paul took one look at the boat's cockpit and began addressing the various elements as if they were old friends.

"Look," Paul said as they headed out, "rifles."

There were two of them in a rack in the cockpit. Springfields.

Same rifles Arlen had used to take more than a few German lives. The sight of them made him uneasy.

"Ignorant place to store rifles," he said. "Unless you rub them down with oil constant, that salt water will work on them fast."

Paul walked up as if to inspect them, and Arlen called him off. "Leave them be, damn it. I thought you wanted to play with the boat, not the weapons."

They kept it at a crawl all the way out of the inlet and into open water, and then Paul wanted to let it run.

"We don't know what's out there," Arlen said. "Could be a reef or —"

"Rebecca said it was clear straight out from the Cypress House."

"Fine," Arlen said. "You want to drown us both, go ahead."

He turned the wheel over, and Paul opened the throttle up and got the big engine chugging away, and soon they were well out in front of the inn, chasing a setting sun across the Gulf.

It was, Arlen had to admit, a hell of a nice thing.

Behind them the rural coast extended with its stretches of beach and thickets of palms and sea grasses, and ahead the water shimmered bloodred and endless. The wind was coming up out of the southwest, warm and mild, putting just enough chop in the water that the hull of the boat spanked against the waves and sent spray over the stern and let them feel like real sailors.

When they were far enough out that the Cypress House looked like a thimble, Arlen told him to bring it around.

"Let's shut the engine off for a minute," Paul said.

"You shut that engine off, we'll likely not get it started again. Drift halfway to Cuba before somebody comes for us."

"It'll start again, Arlen. I started and stopped it three times back there before you let us take it out."

Arlen grunted and muttered but didn't lay down a firm objection, and Paul cut the engine.

"There we go," the boy said when the clattering had ceased, breathing the words out like a prayer. It was silent now, save for the wind and water, no other boat in sight. "Isn't this something?"

It was something, all right. They were alone on the ocean, rising and falling with gentle waves, nothing but warm red light and water all around them. Arlen stood up, holding on to the cockpit roof with one hand for balance, and stared out to the west, squinting against the fading sun. So much water. It just went on and on and on, a sight that squeezed the soul. He felt so damn small out here. And that felt good. Maybe that was strange, but it felt good. He was insignificant. The world was too big to care about his decisions. There was no weight here, no burden.

"I've never been on the ocean before," Paul said. "All the time we've been working there, I kept wishing she had a boat. I'd look at the water and wish I could see what it's like out here."

"You're seeing it."

"It's wonderful."

Arlen sat back down in one of the fishing chairs mounted in the stern and stretched backward and looked at the darkening sky. A pale orb of moon was rising, climbing even as the sun retreated. The boat was tinted with an ethereal red glow.

"What do you want to do, Paul?" Arlen asked.

"Sit here a little longer, if that's—"

"No. I mean with your life. What do you want to do?"

"I don't know."

"What in the hell happened? Back at Flagg, you were full of plans. Had everything all mapped out. I know we didn't make the Keys—which is a damn good thing—but what happened to the rest of your ideas?"

The boy was quiet. When he spoke again, his voice was low.

"I've got my whole life ahead of me, Arlen. Right now, I'm just worried about finishing that dock."

"Well, that's an ignorant way to think," Arlen said, enough heat in the words to raise Paul's head. "You got a damned gift, and you know it. Aren't you going to try and make something of it?"

"Of course I will."

"Get a plan in your head, then. The CCC was good for you, but it's —"

"I don't want to go back to it. Not anymore."

"That's fine. Where you ought to be is some sort of engineering or mechanical school. I don't know much about them, but I know they've got them, and that's what you should be looking for. Something that'll let you go on to designing projects instead of hauling supplies for them. You ever heard of that Carnegie school in Pittsburgh?"

He knew the boy had; it was Paul who had told him about it.

"Sure," Paul said. There was a wariness to him now.

"Well, you ought to try to get in something like that."

Paul seemed to think on his next words carefully before he said them.

"Right now, I don't want to think about leaving this place. Not without her. I know what you're saying, but I've got different priorities right now."

"Is that so?" Arlen said, voice soft.

"It is."

Arlen nodded and went silent. There wasn't much of the sun left now, and behind them the Cypress House had disappeared into darkness. The wind had stilled a bit as the light faded, the boat's rise and fall gentler now than before.

"If I were to tell you," Arlen said, "as clearly as I could, and as sincerely, that you need to get out of this place, what would you do?"

"I'd stay. I'd be careful, but I'd stay."

"All right," Arlen said. They were quiet for a time then, as the remnants of sun melted away and the moon sharpened against the night sky and the wind died down altogether until they seemed to be adrift on the world's largest pond.

"Let's go in," Arlen said.

Paul fired up the engine and brought them back. They'd stayed out too long; by the time they neared the shore it was so dark they wouldn't have been able to find the inlet. Rebecca was ready for them, though, had walked down to the dock with a lantern, and Arlen took the wheel and followed the glow through the darkness.

They'd anchored the rowboat in the center of the inlet, and he managed to position the big boat close enough so that they could climb down into it. Rebecca was waiting in silence on the dock. Just as Arlen bent to the oars, Paul said, "Thanks for that, Arlen. I wanted to be on the water. It was special, you know?"

"Yeah," he said. "Sure was."

He waited no more than ten minutes after Paul had gone to bed before he went to Rebecca's room. He paused in the hallway and looked at the two doors, set so close together. He could hear Paul still shifting in his bed when he knocked softly on Rebecca's door and stepped inside, and she looked up with surprise. She was standing by the window.

He walked over and took her face in his hands and kissed her.

"I was going to come to your room," she whispered.

"We can stay here," he said, not in a whisper, and then he kissed her again, moving her toward the bed. She went willingly, but there was confusion in her eyes.

They kissed for a while. He moved roughly on the bed, shifting, banging the old wooden headboard off the wall, springs creaking beneath him.

"Paul will hear," she whispered once.

He didn't reply.

They'd shed their clothes and he'd rolled over on top of her when she pushed him back with her hands on his chest and looked at him knowingly.

"You want him to hear."

"It's not want," he said. "It's need."

She hesitated and then nodded slowly. "I understand."

They got back to the show then. She played her part well.

30

H<small>E DIDN'T STAY LONG</small> after they were finished. She watched as he dressed but said nothing. He gave her one silent look as he stood at the door, and then he opened it and stepped out into the hallway. It was dark and empty, and there was no sound from Paul's room. He walked down the hall and opened the door to his own room and found Paul sitting in the chair by the window.

Neither of them spoke. Arlen shut the door behind him and leaned against it and waited. It was dark in the room, and he was glad.

"Of all the things to lie about," Paul said, voice trembling, "you picked the dirtiest. Lying about my *death,* Arlen? Trying to scare me away with stories like that so you can have her?"

"Wasn't a lie."

"Yes, it was!" Paul came up off the chair, his hands clenched into fists. "It was a damned lie, and you said it because you want me to leave."

Arlen didn't answer.

"You bastard," Paul said. "You lying old bastard. You knew

how I felt. Sat there and listened to me tell you all about it like we were close, like there was trust between us. You heard it all, and then you went and took her."

"She's a woman," Arlen said. "Not a boat. She can't be taken or left at the whims of other people. Don't think of her like that."

"Don't tell me how to think of her. You *know* how I think of her, and still you did this."

Arlen folded his arms over his chest and stared at a shadow just over the boy's shoulder.

"How long has it been happening?" Paul said. "Was this the first time?"

"No."

"No!" he cried, and the genuine anguish in his voice slid into Arlen like a knife between the ribs. "So it's been days of this? Days of it, and you haven't had the courage to say a word? How much older than me are you, and you couldn't be a man? You couldn't say the truth?"

Arlen was silent.

"Then you lied," Paul said, his voice softer but no less outraged. "You told me I was going to *die*, Arlen, told me I was going to be killed. That's how you handle it? Instead of the truth, you tell me *that*?"

"That wasn't a lie. It was just like on the train. You had—"

"Stop! Don't tell me more of that; I can't hear it again. None of it's true. You're crazy. You ought to be locked up somewhere." His voice broke as he said, "And she picked *you*?"

For a moment Paul stood there as if trying to gather himself to continue speaking, but then he crossed the room in a rush. There was an instant in which Arlen thought the kid was going to hit him, and wishing for it. He'd gladly take the blows. Then he realized he was going only for the door, and moved aside as Paul shoved past him and into the hall, slamming the door behind him. The wall trembled with the force of it, and his footsteps echoed through the hall, and then another door slammed and it was silent.

Arlen found his flask and climbed into bed.

Rebecca woke him in the morning. She was standing beside the bed with her hand on his forearm, and when he opened his eyes she said, "He's gone."

He sat up stiffly, the now-empty flask still on his lap, and walked down the hall. The door to Paul's room was open. Inside, no sign of the boy remained. His bags were gone. The bed was neatly made.

They went downstairs, and Arlen stepped out on the front porch and then went to the back and looked in all directions, and there was no trace of him. He went back inside. Rebecca was sitting at one of the tables.

"I wonder if there was another way," she said.

"There wasn't. He wouldn't have gone."

"I wish there'd been another way." She sounded close to tears.

He thought that he should go to her but didn't want to, not right now. He became aware of a ticking as he stood in the silent room, and when he looked up above the bar he felt something swell in his chest.

"He fixed your clock," he said.

Paul hadn't been able to get the thing back up by himself, so he'd taken the brass casing and propped it up against the wall. The hands showed the correct time, and it ticked away steadily.

"He fixed the damn clock," Arlen said, and he didn't like the sound of his voice. Rebecca looked up at him as if she were going to speak, but he walked across the room and out through the front door. He walked off the porch and down the trail and out to the unfinished dock. When he reached the end, he sat down with his feet hanging free above the water and pulled out a cigarette and lit it. He took a long drag and looked out across the inlet.

"He's better off," he said aloud. "He's safe."

He went for another drag, but this time his hand was shaking and he hardly got the cigarette to his lips. When he did, there wasn't enough breath in his lungs to draw any smoke. He took the cigarette away again and the shaking was worse and it fell from his fingers and into the water. Once it was gone, he bowed his head and wept into his hands.

Part Three

OWEN

31

HE WORKED ALONE ALL DAY, measuring and cutting and hammering as the wind died off and the sun rose high and hot, the air so humid it felt like moving through tar, searing and sticky. In the afternoon Rebecca came down and stood on the dock with him.

"You really believe he was going to be killed," she said.

"I don't believe it. I know it." He didn't turn to look at her.

"So he needed to leave. He had to."

"That's right."

"Couldn't we have talked him into it?"

"No."

"How can you be so sure?"

"Because I know him. If I'd gone to him and told him the truth about us, he would have been shattered, but he also would have stayed. I'm certain of that. I had to hurt him. Drive him away."

"I hate that," she said. "I'm not saying you're wrong, but I hate that we had to—"

"I know."

She sighed and shook her head. "It won't be the same. It's going to feel . . . empty without him."

"Yes," Arlen said.

"Why didn't you leave with him?"

He turned with a board in his hands and looked at her. "Do you really need to hear that answer?"

"I hope I don't," she said softly.

"You don't."

She waited a minute and said, "Will you go with us?"

"You and Owen?"

She nodded.

He looked away, out to the mouth of the inlet, where a pair of shrieking gulls circled, looking for a meal.

"There's no obligation to you," he said. "I'm staying, and I'll help. I will do what I can. If you want to take your brother and disappear, though . . ." He shrugged and left the rest unspoken.

"I want to disappear," she said, "from Solomon Wade. Not you."

"You say that firm," Arlen said, "yet you haven't known me long."

"I know you."

"Yeah?"

"If you don't believe it," she said, "then why are you still here?"

"Oh, I believe it. Probably more than you. We're kindred."

"Yes."

"In ways you don't even understand," he said, "we are kindred."

"What do you mean?"

"You see blood on your hands that no one else does."

She tilted her head and frowned. "And you do, too?"

He was silent.

"Tell me," she said.

He shook his head. "Another day."

"I'll wait. I've learned how to wait."

He wanted to smile, but it wasn't a day for smiling. He sat back on his heels and stared at the gulls and felt the sweat bead and glide along his skin.

"What are you thinking?" she said.

"That I showed up here looking for a ride back to the CCC. That's all I was looking for. We were supposed to be here an hour."

"My parents were supposed to be enjoying this place right now. People were supposed to be coming in with hundreds of dollars in their pockets for fishing and drinking and sunshine. I was supposed to be in Savannah." She shook her head. " 'Supposed to be' doesn't mean much to me anymore. Everyone in this country was full of plans a few years ago, and how many of them do you think even dare to make plans for the future now? They just get through each day. Times like these, it's all you can do."

He nodded and ran his fingertips along the edge of the board, wiping rough sawdust clear from the cut.

"If I'm staying," he said, "I need to know the plan. I deserve that much."

She said, "Maine."

The word shivered through him. *Edwin Main. Edwin and his wife, Joy.*

"What's wrong?" she said.

"Nothing. That's where you intend to go?"

She nodded.

"You ever been there? You know anybody there?"

"No. That's why it's perfect. We'll be strangers there, far from this place and the people from it."

She lifted a hand, rubbed at her forehead, brought it back glistening with sweat, and held it out to him as if it were evidence of something.

215

"As far from this place as possible," she said. "You don't know how often I think of Maine. How much time I spend imagining it. Right now it's moving toward autumn there. There are cold breezes during the day, and at night you pull an extra blanket over yourself and in the morning the grass is crisp and a deep breath chills your lungs instead of choking you. The leaves are going orange and red and brown. It's not trapped in green, always green. There's change. In a month or so they'll have the first snow. Just a tease of what's to come, but it will snow. There will be a white dusting of it in the morning, maybe, or a few flakes in the air. You know I've only seen snow twice in my life?"

She was staring across the inlet as she spoke, into the thick green tangle that grew there, where a few unseen birds shrilled and occasionally something splashed in the water.

"Have you seen many winters?" she said. "Real winters?"

"I've seen a few."

"I'll see one this year," she said, a blood vow in her voice. "I'll see one this year."

By nightfall the wind had returned, and Arlen was nearing completion of the dock. He figured to have the last board laid by noon the next day, and then he could start on the boathouse, though they'd need more lumber before he could make much headway there. It was a ludicrous endeavor, working so hard to rebuild a place that they'd soon abandon, but he didn't know what else to do. It kept up the pretense that they'd remain, for one thing, but it also gave him a task to handle. He needed that.

He loved work. Physical labor. It was a strange thing, maybe, but he loved the ache in his muscles at the end of a day, loved the sweat that coursed from his pores, loved the sound of a saw and the feel of a hammer, the clean crack of a well-struck nail.

So many men wandered this country now, looking for so simple a thing as *work*. It was a bizarre notion when you stopped to think about it, and Arlen figured it was a birth pang of a new world. So much had happened to cause this Depression, so many things he understood and more that he did not, but in the end they all captured a simple idea: you couldn't depend solely on yourself anymore. Not in the way men once had. You could have skill and strength and desire, but you had to find someone who needed to utilize those things. Was a time when, if you knew how to work metal, you'd set up a blacksmith shop and make enough to support your family. Now, if you knew how to work metal, you'd likely need a job in a factory where the needs of not a town but a state, a nation, a world, had to be met. It was all about size now: the big ran the world on the sweat of the small, and if the big faltered for any reason, the small were the first to go.

The funny damn thing was, Arlen had no desire to be among those in charge. That was the goal, supposedly, the ordained American Dream, to rise from the ranks of the small and become a colossus.

It wasn't in him, though. The bigger your role, the more people you impacted with your decisions. He didn't want to have to make those sorts of decisions. All he wanted to do was work. If his day ended when the last nail was driven, it had been a good day. It had been a damned good day.

Or at least it usually was. For once, the standard satisfaction stayed away from him when he gathered his tools and walked back up the trail to the Cypress House. He'd worked, yes, done the pure labor of a man who was small in the eyes of the world but content in his own heart, and even that hadn't been enough today. Today, he'd felt the weight of decision upon him.

It was the right decision, he knew. It was right.

But, oh, how he'd hated to make it.

*   *   *

The days passed with surprising speed and silence. Solomon Wade didn't come by, nor did Tolliver, nor anyone else except Thomas Barrett, the delivery man. When he arrived at the end of the week, Arlen asked if they could make a run for some more lumber.

"You're not sending the boy this time? I enjoyed him."

"He's gone."

Barrett's freckled face split into a curious frown. "For good?"

"That's right."

"Strange. He told me he intended to stay. What put him back on the road?"

"I can't speak for him," Arlen said shortly.

"Well, it's a shame. This is a tough place for a lad like that to be on the road alone. Did he have any money?"

"Let's go get that wood," Arlen said.

They went out to the paved road and then south toward High Town. It had been silent since they left, and though Arlen didn't feel much like talking, he also didn't want to seem ungracious, so he asked after the name of the town as a means of conversation.

"Where I'm from, the place would be called Flat Town," he said. "Nary a hill in sight from what I saw."

"Where are you from?"

"West Virginia."

Barrett nodded. "Well, it's plenty different terrain than that. High Town might not look much different to an outsider, but it's one of the few places around here that's always been clear of flooding. So, it's High Town—and Dry Town."

They turned east at the center of town, and Arlen twisted his head to look back at the jail as they passed. Tolliver's car was parked in front.

"Didn't you say you ran for sheriff?" Arlen asked.

"That's right. Al Tolliver beat me fair and square," Barrett said dryly.

"You had any policing experience? Or just wanted a piece of it?"

Barrett flicked his eyes over and then back to the road. "No policing. Did my time in the Army and then came back home. I like my home. I didn't like the people who were taking control of it. That ain't changed."

"There anybody around here that could actually make those boys answer for something?"

"If there is somebody," Barrett said, "I ain't found him yet."

Arlen nodded, and they were quiet again for a time, riding with the windows down and the hot air pushing into their faces. The forest had given way to swampy stump fields now, and Arlen looked out across the litter of slashed timber and felt a pang, remembering the way forests of his boyhood had fallen. He'd been at Arlington National Cemetery once after the war, and the first thought he'd had, staring over the columns of stone markers, was of the clear-cut woods that climbed the hills behind his home. They were both fields of death, filled with inadequate reminders of what had been.

"They cut a lot of timber out here," he said.

"Yes, they did. Sawmill was not far from here. I worked there for three years. Used to hear the band saw in my sleep."

"When it went under, the town went with it, is what Rebecca told me."

"That's right. There were two thousand people in this town not five years ago. Ain't but a few hundred left, and a lot of stumps. You take a canoe out through the swamps not far from here, and you'll find stumps nine, ten feet around. Some big boys, they were. The wood lasts, too. Cypress is damn strong."

"It makes the finest coffins," Arlen said.

"How in the hell do you know a thing like that?"

"My father told me," Arlen said. "He paid a lot of mind to such things."

The memory lingered. Long after he and Barrett had returned with the lumber and carried it down to the dock, Arlen was thinking of his father. He could see the dark eyes above the thick beard, hear the deep, easy voice. He could see the big hands wrapped around a plane or a piece of sandpaper, smoothing the grain of someone's final home. He spent time on coffins that few would, treated each pauper's grave as if it were a rich man's tomb. Even in the summer of the fever, when twenty-nine died in eleven days, he'd taken care with his coffins. Arlen could remember him working through the night that summer, the summer his mother had died. Arlen had been twelve at the time, and she'd gone slow and suffering and with her hand in Isaac's, who'd looked his son in the eye and told him to have no fear, the earthly being mattered not in the end.

That was twenty-five years ago.

He sorted and stacked the lumber and tried to push it all from his mind, but it would not stay at bay, and that evening when he sat on the porch with Rebecca, he said, "I reckon I'm ready to tell you the story."

She studied him for a moment and then said, "Why? What changed?"

He thought on that while he slipped a cigarette out and lit it. Nothing had changed. Everything had changed. It wasn't the sort of thing he could pin down; the world had shifted on him in a way he didn't fully understand. It had an awful lot to do with her, he knew that much.

"It's just time to tell the tale," he said. The tale he had not told anyone, ever.

She didn't answer. Sat with her hands folded in her lap and waited. He smoked the cigarette down a little bit and watched the waves, and then he told her about the day his father died.

32

IT WAS FIVE YEARS after Arlen's mother had passed. Isaac had taken to spending more time in his shop, particularly at night, when visitors were unlikely. The shop was located beneath the room where Arlen slept, and the sounds drifted up, barely muffled by the thin floor that separated them. He'd long known the sounds of the tools on the wood—his father's paying job, other than a bit of small-time farming, was as a furniture maker—and sometimes Arlen could also hear Isaac humming to himself or occasionally speaking bits of German, his mother tongue. The conversations, however, were a new twist.

At first Arlen had thought his father was talking to himself. The words were soft-spoken, and initially it was just background noise, mumbling of which he did not take much heed. It was only after it had persisted for a time that he began to pay attention, and the phrase he heard uttered again and again raised a prickle across his spine.

Tell me, Isaac Wagner would say. *Tell me.*

The more he listened, the more evident it became that his father was trying to speak to the dead. Not only that—he believed he was. The words that left his mouth were parts of an exchange.

The conversations had gone on for many weeks before Arlen chanced a trip down to the shop to see for himself. What awaited him was chilling: Isaac spoke with his hands on the corpses. Stood above them and placed his palms flat on their chests or on either side of their heads. When he'd talked himself out, he removed his hands and returned to work and fell silent. Always he was silent unless he had his hands pressed against their dead flesh.

He was a different man outside of the shop as well—both with Arlen and with the townspeople. Moody and unpredictable, given to perplexing statements and a constant tendency to dismiss the worries of the living.

It was a few months before Arlen could admit that his father was truly losing his mind.

Rumors swirled through the town but avoided a troublesome pitch until a teary-eyed man came to the shop with a child's toy in his hand, prepared to ask that it be buried with his wife, and found Isaac in his now-customary pose, standing above the body with his hands on the dead woman's head like a preacher offering a blessing. The sight had rankled the grieving husband, and while no more than a heated exchange of words took place—with Isaac taking no steps to pacify the man, simply saying that he'd talk aloud in his shop if he was so inclined, to whomever he liked—it added coal to the fires of suspicion already smoldering throughout the town.

What did you do with a father who was insane? The question haunted Arlen through his days and kept him awake through his nights. It was just the two of them now; there was no other family in the town. Isaac had led the way to this place, and Arlen's mother had been unable to conceive after giving birth to her first and only child. No confidant existed. He listened to his father speak to the dead and thought of what might happen if he sought help for him, if he told anyone in town the truth, and he decided that it would be better to keep silent. There was no harm being done. It was strange, certainly, unsettling and troubling, but it wasn't harmful. He promised himself that if it ever became so, something would have to be done.

It was a day on the fringe of winter when Joy Main died. Three nights of frost had been followed by a final gasp of Indian summer that burned out behind a cold wind, and no one in the town had passed in six weeks. Isaac was making furniture instead of coffins, and Arlen had been allowed to slip into something close to a peaceful state. At night his sleep was uninterrupted by voices from below, and the dark rings around his father's eyes had lessened, his strange remarks becoming fewer. Then they brought Joy Main's body to the shop.

The Mains were the power family in town. Edwin's father had been a surveyor — and a damn shrewd man. He asked for, and received, acreage instead of wages, and he had a fine eye for land, acquiring large parcels along the New River and through the gorges that bordered it. It was coal and timber country, beautiful land that was soon to become rich land, and by the time Edwin was grown, the mining boom was under way and the property he inherited made him a wealthy man. He stayed in Fayette County and filled his father's void. He was large and pompous, and charming when he had cause to be. At other times he was harsh and cruel, but the townspeople seemed to believe you could expect that from your leaders.

Joy Hargrove was the most beautiful girl in the county, bright and clever, a gifted piano player and blessed with a haunting, gorgeous voice that turned heads at Sunday services. The marriage was of the arranged sort — Joy's father was vying for purchase of a promising mine. The courtship was strongly encouraged despite the fact that Edwin was past forty and their daughter just seventeen, and it was only a matter of weeks before Joy Hargrove became Joy Main.

They were married for seven years before her death, and during that time she bore three children and grew increasingly quiet, seeming content to offer formalities and then retreat within herself. She was well known in Fayette County but yet not really known at all.

On that early November evening, when they brought her to the Wagner house just as the burst of warmth from earlier in the day was disappearing with darkness, Joy Main was a week past her twenty-fifth birthday and dead of a fractured skull.

Edwin came with her, tears in his eyes and the sheriff at his side. He explained that Joy came out to the stable to see him and a horse had bucked and thrown a sudden high kick and a rear hoof caught her square in the head.

He'd shot the horse, Edwin explained in a choked voice, and then sent for the sheriff. Maybe it wasn't the right thing to do, shooting that horse, but he couldn't help it. There needed to be blood for blood.

Arlen had heard it all from inside the house, the men standing on the porch with the body at their feet, wrapped in blankets. When Edwin told the story, Isaac Wagner said, "You had the mind to shoot the horse while your wife lay dying?"

The sheriff stepped in then, told Isaac that Edwin was a grieving man, damn it, and there'd be no such questions, who cared a whit about the horse at a time such as this? Isaac had said nothing else, but Edwin Main had watched him with dark eyes, and Arlen, standing at the window, felt the coldness pass through the glass just like the wind that had returned out of the northern hills.

Isaac gathered the body in his arms and prepared to carry Joy Main back to his shop. Edwin spoke up again and told him to make it the finest coffin he'd ever constructed; anything less would be a sin, and how much the box might cost mattered not, he'd pay any price.

Isaac told him that every coffin he made was a fine one.

It wasn't long after they'd left that Arlen heard the dreaded phrase from his father's shop: *Tell me.*

This time he'd crept to the door. Usually he tried to clear himself away from the sound, but there'd been such tension in the air tonight, with his father asking that question about the horse and Edwin Main staring at him ominously.

Not her, Arlen thought, *of all the ones in town for you to speak with, not his wife. We'll be run out of this place if anyone knows.*

The talking persisted, though, and it horrified. Isaac Wagner was pretending to hear an explanation of murder.

"He laid hands on the servant? That girl's no more than fifteen, is she? He intended to violate her? Did she see what happened after? What did he strike you with? Had he beaten you before? Did the children see? Did anyone see?"

Arlen stood at the door and heard it all and felt a trembling deep in his chest that intensified when Isaac said, *"I'll see that it's dealt with. I'll see that he has a reckoning. I promise you that; I swear it to you."*

Arlen opened the door and went into the room then and shouted at him to stop, and what he saw was more terrible than he'd imagined. Isaac had lifted the dead woman and placed her hands on his shoulders and was looking into her face. There was still blood in her hair, and her eyelids sagged halfway down, but the hint of blue irises remained and seemed to stare over Isaac's shoulder and into Arlen's own eyes.

"She's telling me what happened," Isaac said. "Don't be afraid, son. She's telling me the truth."

"She's not," Arlen screamed. "She can't speak, can't tell you a thing, she's dead! She's gone!"

"No," Isaac said, "the body is gone. She is not."

Arlen stood at the door and shook his head, tears brimming in his eyes. Isaac lowered the body slowly and very gently, then turned to face his son.

"I have to touch them to hear," he said. "There are those who don't, those who can conjure without needing a touch, but I'm not one of them. Maybe in time. It took me many a year to reach them at all."

"Stop," Arlen said. "Stop, stop, stop."

"You don't believe," Isaac said. "Those who don't believe can't hear. But you've got a touch of the gift yourself, boy. I'm sure of it. I see it in you."

"No more," Arlen said, backing away through the door. "Don't say any more."

"Look past your fear," Isaac said. "It's about doing what's right. This woman was murdered, beaten with an ax handle and killed, Arlen! That demands justice. I'll see that it's delivered. I've promised her that. And if there's anything I hold sacred, it's a promise to the dead."

Arlen turned and ran.

He spent close to two hours in the wooded hills, stumbling through the underbrush with hot tears in his eyes and terror in his heart. He wondered if his father was still down there with Joy Main or if he'd gone off in search of the promised reckoning. The longer Arlen walked, the more certain he became that he could not allow such a thing to take place.

You've got a touch of the gift yourself, boy. I'm sure of it. I see it in you.

It was that statement more than any of the others that drove him out of the woods and back into town. His father was insane—the dead could not speak to the living; they were gone and nothing lingered in their stead—but Arlen was not insane. He was *not* and he wouldn't ever be.

Let Isaac Wagner bear his own shame, then, and not put it on his son as well. If Isaac would show the world that he was mad, his son would show himself to be sane.

The sheriff was home, and when Arlen told him the story, he stared with astonished eyes. When it was through, he gathered himself and thanked Arlen for coming down and told him to go on home and wait.

"I'll come for him shortly," he said. "And you did the right thing, son. Know that. You did the right thing."

Arlen went home. He waited. Isaac was back in his shop, silent.

Thirty minutes passed before the sheriff came, and then he wasn't alone. Edwin Main was with him, wearing a long duster to fight the chill night wind. When Arlen saw them approaching, he felt sick. Why had the sheriff told him anything?

They came through the door without knocking and saw Arlen standing there and asked where his father was. He pointed an unsteady hand at the closed door of the shop.

They went in for him. Arlen stayed outside, heard the exchange, Edwin Main shouting and swearing and Isaac speaking in deep, measured tones. When they emerged again, Isaac was handcuffed.

Isaac looked over and locked eyes with Arlen, and his face was so gentle, so kind.

He said, "You're going to need to believe. And something you need to know, son? Love lingers."

They shoved him out the front door then and off the porch and down into the dark dusty street. Arlen trailed behind. Edwin Main was still shouting and offering threats. They'd gone a few hundred feet before Isaac spoke to him.

"You killed her," he said, "and it will be proved in time. We'll talk to your house girl and to your children and they'll tell me what Joy already did."

Edwin Main went for him then, and the sheriff stepped

between them. Edwin was a big man, but Isaac was bigger, and he stood calmly and looked down at the screaming widower and didn't seem troubled by him.

"You struck her with the ax handle," he said. "She'd run out of the house to get away from you, and you chased her into the yard and killed her there. Then you dragged her into the stable so there'd be blood in it, and you shot the horse because you believed it would add credence to your tale. That's what happened. That's the truth of it."

Edwin Main shook free of the sheriff's grasp. The sheriff stumbled and fell to his hands and knees in the road as Edwin reached under his duster and drew a pistol. Arlen cried out and ran for them, and Edwin Main cocked the pistol and pointed it at Isaac's head from no more than two feet away.

Isaac Wagner smiled. Edwin Main fired. Then Arlen was on his knees in the road and his father's blood ran into the dust and the wind blew down on them with the promise of coming snow.

33

I T TOOK HIM LONGER to tell it than he expected, and he was
strangely nervous recalling the events, went through three
cigarettes before he was done. Rebecca just listened. She didn't
interrupt, didn't even give a murmur or a shake of the head as he
spoke, never broke eye contact.

He told her about the way it had looked out there in the street,
the wind blowing dust over the blood and Edwin Main with his
coat flapping around him like some old-time gunslinger and the
sheriff with his hat in his hands, and then he finished his last
cigarette and put it out and it was quiet for a moment.

"So what happened then?" she asked eventually. "Who took
you in?"

"Nobody took me in. I left."

"Left?"

He nodded. "Worked in a mine for nearly a year, lived in a
boardinghouse. The war was on in Europe, but we hadn't
stepped in yet. I figured I'd try to enlist. I was too young, but I
lied about it and they let me in. Wasn't a hard thing to do. After
the mines, I didn't seem much like a boy anymore."

"How old were you?"

"Seventeen when I enlisted. I was almost nineteen before we started fighting, though."

"You've never been back?"

"Hell, no. What's there for me?"

She thought about it for a moment and then said, "This is what you meant when you said we were kindred."

"Yes."

"At least I didn't have to see it happen," she said. "But somehow that doesn't seem much comfort."

"I'd expect not."

Out in the darkness the waves broke over the sand and insects trilled and there was the sound of something banging in the wind down by the boathouse.

Rebecca said, "How long was it before you realized he was right?"

Arlen frowned. "Pardon?"

"Your father. What he said about you having the gift."

Arlen shook his head slowly. "He wasn't right. I can't speak with the dead, and neither could he. The man was crazy."

"But you see warnings of death. You have for years."

"That's different."

She pulled her head back. "How?"

"Nobody's talking to the dead," he said. "They can't *be* talked to. They're gone, Rebecca. Anyone who says anything else is as crazy as my father was."

"So you don't believe what he said about the dead woman."

"No."

"Then why would Edwin Main have shot him?"

Arlen felt a swelling of frustrated anger. There were a handful of reasons he'd never told the story, and this was one of them. He didn't need some outsider telling him the crazy old bastard could have been right. Because if he had been...if he had been...

"Edwin Main was enraged," Arlen said, "in the way any man might be after hearing the sort of story my father told. He reacted out of rage."

"Was he arrested for shooting your father?"

"No."

"But your father was in handcuffs! It was cold-blooded—"

"He was provoked," Arlen said. "That's what the sheriff ruled. Nobody argued."

"I can't understand how someone who's had your experiences would be unable to believe in the possibility of what your father claimed," she said.

"It's a league of difference. I've got an ability with premonition, probably resulting from all the death I've seen, far too much of it. I don't know, I can't explain that, but it's only premonition. A sense of what's about to happen. Talking to the dead, though?" He shook his head. "That's the belief of old women and children, not sane men."

"Your father's last words to you were to say you'd have to learn to believe."

Actually, his last words had been a promise that love lingered. Spoken so soft, so kind, so damned forgiving, that years later Arlen would still wake in the night almost unable to breathe from the memory of it.

"The only thing I have to believe," Arlen said, "is that I did the right thing. I've got to believe that. And you know something? I do. Always have, always will."

She paused, then said, "Arlen, if you know that you can see the dead before they're gone, why can't you speak to them after they are?"

He got up out of the chair swiftly, ready to go inside and pour a whiskey and get the hell away from this conversation. He ought never have told the story.

"Stop." She caught his arm, and her hand was soft and cool, and stilled him. "We won't speak of it anymore."

He ran a hand over his eyes and leaned against the wall, suddenly exhausted beyond measure.

"Let's go to bed," she said, rising with her hand still on his arm.

"It was wrong what was done to him," Arlen said. "That was wrong. Murder, as you said. But what he'd done was wrong as well. He was out of his mind, Rebecca. Hearing about it is one thing, I suppose. But you didn't see it. You didn't see the way he held that poor dead woman and looked into her eyes."

"I know," she said.

"He was going to be a problem. He was going to cause harm."

"Of course he was," she said in a soft voice. "Of course."

They didn't speak of it again in the days that followed. He worked on the boathouse, the walls going up quickly, and there were no visitors. Rebecca's brother was to be released on the upcoming Tuesday, and she went into Thomas Barrett's store once to make phone calls and arrange to go out and collect him. Arlen asked if she wanted him to go along, and she said that she didn't.

"You can meet him when we get back."

Arlen nodded, but he couldn't help wondering if he'd ever see her again. If she might pick up her brother and drive off in some unknown direction, and that would be the end of it. He hoped not, but he couldn't help the thought.

It turned out he didn't need to worry over it — she never had the chance to make the drive to Raiford. Owen Cady arrived on Monday, the day before his scheduled release, and he arrived in the company of Solomon Wade.

They came around noon, and Arlen and Rebecca were both out on the back porch, having just finished lunch. They heard the car and looked at each other with shared displeasure, fearing it would be Wade. When they walked through the barroom, the gray Ford coupe was visible in the yard, and Rebecca said, "He's come to make a last round of threats in case I'm thinking about running tomorrow."

Then the doors on the Ford opened and two men stepped out: Solomon Wade from the driver's seat, and a tall, rangy kid with blond hair from the passenger's. Rebecca said, *"Owen,"* in a whisper, and went onto the porch.

The two men walked toward her, Solomon Wade with a blank face, Owen Cady wearing a wide grin. He crossed to the steps and hugged his sister fiercely.

"I'm home!" he yelled. "Made it home!"

He stepped back from her and laughed, still wearing the easy grin, Rebecca standing there stunned and silent.

"Well, I thought you might be happy," he said.

"I was supposed to get you," she said. "Tomorrow. I was supposed to pick you up tomorrow. That's when they said you'd be getting out."

She was staring at Wade.

"Solomon here pulled a few strings and got me out a day early," Owen Cady said. "Figured we'd surprise you."

"You could pull strings?" she said woodenly, still looking at Wade. "You could do that to get him out a day early? A *day?*"

"You're welcome," Wade said.

"Get off my property," Rebecca said. "Get away from here. And stay away from him. You stay —"

"Rebecca, what in the hell's gotten into you?" Owen said, raising both hands in a peacemaking gesture, glancing back at Wade in apology. "Solomon hasn't done a thing but help."

Arlen thought that might snap her. Thought she might turn

and go running up the stairs and come back with a Smith & Wesson in her hand. Instead she just swiveled to stare at her brother and said, "He didn't pull strings to *keep* you out."

"That isn't his fault! It's mine. I don't know what——"

"It's fine, son," Solomon Wade said, his voice awash in generosity. "If your sister wishes this to be a family occasion, a family occasion it shall be. I just wanted to welcome you back to Corridor County myself."

He gave a little bow, said, "Y'all have a fine afternoon." Then he turned and walked back to his car and drove away, one hand lifted out the window in a neighborly wave. A dark red flush rose in Rebecca's face as she watched.

"I don't know what's gotten into you," Owen said. "I wanted to surprise you. Can't you be happy to see me?"

She looked back at him, blinked, and tried to force some cheer.

"Of course I'm happy."

Owen looked up into the doorway at Arlen and said, "Who's this?"

Arlen stepped forward and put out a hand as Rebecca said, "Arlen Wagner. He's helping me rebuild things after the hurricane. We lost the dock and boathouse and most of the back porch."

"Good to meet you," Owen said. He gave Arlen a measuring stare, though, some suspicion in his eyes.

"Likewise," Arlen said. "Your sister has been eager for your return."

"Half as eager as me, that's for sure. Raiford isn't a fun place to be. Tough fellas in there." He gave that grin again, and there was a cockiness to his eyes and bearing, as if he considered his prison days a point of pride.

Arlen said, "I'm sure it isn't fun."

"Let's go on inside," Owen said to Rebecca. "I want to pour a drink, a good one, and then I'll tell you some stories. Tell you what it was like in there."

Rebecca frowned, and Arlen understood why. The kid was talking like he'd just returned from a holiday trip. Wanting to tell stories? Shit. It reminded Arlen of men he'd known who always wanted to tell stories about what the war had been like. Inevitably, they were the ones who hadn't seen any real combat. He had yet to meet a man who'd emerged alive from the Belleau Wood with any desire to tell tales about it.

As Owen Cady swaggered into the barroom, bellowing about how beautiful the liquor bottles looked, Arlen missed Paul with a sudden, deep ache.

He told his stories. They sat around for an hour while Rebecca made him a thick sandwich and brought him a cold beer. Owen ate, and drank, and talked. And talked some more. Everything was designed to impress. He told of how tough the Raiford bulls had been, how quick with their billies and their fists, but he didn't sound chagrined about it. He told about one man the guards had beaten so badly he'd been taken out with a fractured kneecap and broken ribs, and when he finished that story he laughed and shook his head, as if recalling some moment of horseplay. He bragged about the other inmates as if they were a collection of mythical heroes instead of a cell block full of cruel bastards and swindlers.

"Thing about it is, you got to fall in with the right crowd early, or they'll eat you for lunch in that place," he said. "I found some boys who knew those I'd run with, and that was the start. You find somebody to back you when it's needed and you do the same for them and that's how you make it. If there's going to be fighting, you better not be alone."

Rebecca was listening quietly but unhappily. Owen had

turned most of his attention to Arlen, gesturing and pointing with his beer.

"There was a fella who ran with Dillinger," he said. "Did you know that Jack — that's what Dillinger was called by them that knew him — came down to Florida for a time when things got hot back in Indiana? It's the truth."

"Dillinger was killed last year," Arlen said.

"I know that. Everybody knows that."

Arlen shrugged.

"So were Pretty Boy Floyd and Baby Face Nelson," Owen said. "All in one year. And Clyde Barrow and Bonnie Parker. No, thirty-four was not a good year to be in the rackets."

"No year is," Rebecca snapped. "I wish you wouldn't say that like you think it's a sad thing. Those people were criminals. They were killers."

"I know, sister, I know." But he winked at Arlen as he drank the beer.

After a time he ran out of stories or tired of making them up, and told Rebecca he wanted to go upstairs and get some rest.

"You got no idea how sweet a real bed will feel," he said. "A beer and a bed in one day? Must be heaven. Now all I need to do is find myself a girl."

He gave Arlen another wink, and Arlen tried to plaster a grin on his face in response as the kid strutted toward the stairs. Rebecca showed him the bedroom she'd made up. Paul's old room.

When she came back down the stairs, neither of them spoke at first.

"He's a good boy," she said eventually.

"I'm sure he is."

"All this talk, the way he's going on, he's just trying to seem tough. I imagine that's a skill you learn pretty fast in a place like that."

Arlen nodded. "I'm glad he made it out, and made it out so quickly. A lot of guys who go into a place like that don't come out so cocky. Since he did, I'm guessing the months went easier on him than on some of the others."

"I hope so," she said.

He didn't say the other things he was thinking, like there were some men who jailed well because, frankly, they liked the credibility it gave them in certain circles, same as men who valued scars because of what they told the world: *I've been to rough places and seen rough things, and, buddy, I'm still standing here.*

Arlen had his share of scars. He kept them hidden the best he could.

"He's a good boy," she repeated. "Just give him a little bit of time."

"Sure. Can I ask you something, though? When do you intend to lay out your plan with him? About leaving this place and heading to Maine."

"A few days," she said. "I want him to adjust, settle down. I want Solomon to see that we haven't run yet. I want everyone to relax."

"All right."

"In the meantime...be patient with him. I know the way he sounds right now, but it's not him. It's not really him."

"Hell, he can talk however he wants," Arlen said. "It's got nothing to do with me."

"I know, it's just that I...I want you to like him."

He saw the sincerity in her eyes and said, "I like him, Rebecca."

It was one of the easiest lies he'd ever told.

34

O WEN WAS BACK AT it that night, telling more of his stories, speaking of Karpis and Barker and Dillinger, any number of other well-known gangsters he'd certainly never met but wanted Arlen to believe he had. He spoke of bank robbers and killers and hustlers, spoke of them with a voice of adoration. He was twenty years old now, a big, good-looking kid, with deep blue eyes and a smooth smile that no doubt would draw in plenty of women. Rebecca, clearly growing more frustrated by the minute, didn't wait as long as she'd suggested before explaining that they'd be leaving the Cypress House.

"Now that you're back," she said in the midst of one of his tales, "we need to find some time to talk things over. Doesn't have to be tonight, but soon."

"Talk about what?" he said, leaning back in his chair.

"Where we're going. What comes next."

He frowned. "Going? I don't need to go anywhere. Hell, I just got home."

"This isn't home," she said. "There's nothing in this place for you except trouble. The same trouble you got into last time."

He gave her a grin and a dismissive wave. "Aw, I'm fine."

"No, Owen. You're not fine. And this isn't home."

"The hell it isn't," he said, dropping the chair legs back to the floor and looking at her with a hard stare. "I'm not going to Savannah."

"Not Savannah, just…somewhere else. There's no money here, Owen. No one ever comes except the people Solomon Wade sends. You can imagine what sort of people those are."

Owen flicked his eyes over to Arlen, frowned, and said, "We don't need to be saying harsh words about Judge Wade."

Rebecca stared at him. There was a tremor in her jaw. "I'll say what I feel, and that man is a plague. He's evil."

"He's the only man who kept Daddy and me afloat in hard times."

Now it was Rebecca's turn to look at Arlen. She had a desperate quality in her eyes, and Owen followed the look.

"What's he doing down here anyhow?" he said. "Talk like this is family talk. We don't need your hired man involved."

"He's more than a hired man. He's a friend, and I trust him. He'll stay."

Arlen was expecting resistance to that, but Owen just gave him a dark, knowing look.

"We'll discuss this another time," he said. "But I've got no desire to leave. There's money to be made here, you just don't see it."

"Money to be made in the same way you were making it last time?" she snapped. "The same way you ended up at Raiford? Yes, I'm sure there is. Trust me, I'm well aware of the money. I've been asked to keep count of it while you were gone! That's what *Judge* Wade has provided in your absence."

"Well, thank Providence that he did," Owen answered curtly. "Otherwise, you'd have been busted. Ever think about that?"

Rebecca's mouth worked, and a wet shine took over her eyes.

She laid one hand on the table as if to steady herself even though she was seated, and then she stood abruptly and walked to the steps and left them. Arlen rose, but Owen Cady waved him down.

"Let the women bed down early while the men stay up and drink, that's what I've always said."

That's what you've always said? Arlen thought. *What are you, twenty years old now? Yeah, I bet you've been saying that for a mighty long time.*

But he sat down. It was her story to tell, and he would respect that. If anyone in this world understood such a burden, it was Arlen Wagner. He accepted the bottle. Owen had switched from beer to whiskey an hour or so earlier, and the change was showing, his eyes unfocused and his cheeks flushed.

"Damn, that tastes good," he said when Arlen poured a drink and passed it back. "Been a long time, let me tell you. Sure, we had hooch, but it ain't the same as real whiskey, I can promise you that. You ever been in prison?"

"No."

"Jail?"

"Yes."

Owen nodded sagely. "I knew it. You got a look about you."

"Do I?"

"Sure. You know, one that says you've seen some things. You been around, same as me."

Same as you? Arlen thought. *You took a six-month fall for running dope. You haven't seen shit, boy.*

"I didn't like jail," Arlen said. "I don't intend to return."

Owen threw his head back and laughed as if that had been a joke, but when he dropped his face again, his eyes had narrowed, gone cold.

"You sleeping with my sister?"

Arlen took a drink. "Seems to me she's sleeping alone right now. Unless she's got somebody else hid up there."

The kid stared at him, then said, "If you are, fine. Doesn't have a thing to do with me. But something you best understand—I'm the one runs the show at this place. Not her, and sure as shit not you. My father left this place to me."

He tapped his chest with an index finger, in case Arlen had any confusion.

"Fair enough," Arlen said. "I just swing a hammer."

"Better remember that."

"I've not forgotten it yet."

For a moment Owen stared at him as if those had been fighting words, but then he burst into another of his too-loud laughs.

"I like you," he said, lifting the whiskey bottle and drinking straight from it. An unnecessary flourish considering his glass was still full.

"Glad to hear it."

Owen dropped the bottle and leaned across the table. "You want to make some money? Some *real* money?"

"Depends how it's made."

Owen grinned. "Shit, don't matter how it's made, matters that it *is* made. I'll tell you something you probably don't know, old-timer—that judge who brought me down here from Raiford? He as good as runs this state. And I'm in solid with that boy. You want a piece of it, I could get it for you."

"Don't know that you could," Arlen said. "Solomon Wade isn't as sweet on me as he is on you."

"Nah, I could get you in on some cash deals, no problem." Owen leaned back, confident of his position in the hierarchy of Wade's outfit.

"Thanks," Arlen said, "but that isn't for me. I'll stick to carpentry."

"Stick to being broke, you mean."

Arlen shrugged.

"Have it your way," Owen said.

Arlen took a drink. "You know, your sister doesn't want Wade anywhere near here."

"I give a shit? Tell you this—Rebecca ought to be back in Savannah. This place isn't for her. I don't know what in the hell she thinks she's doing."

Arlen looked at him and then away. "Might be she came here for you."

"Me?"

"And your father. To help you."

"Well, Daddy's dead, and I don't need any help."

Arlen didn't answer.

"Listen," Owen said, "I'm not intending to spend my life cuttin' boards or haulin' feed sacks or pickin' oranges or whatever it is you think I ought to do. I'm going to make a mark, old-timer, and I know the right folks to help me do it."

"Solomon Wade."

"Among others." He nodded. "I know plenty of men."

"Gangsters. Hoods."

Owen grinned. "Call us what you like."

Us. It took all Arlen had just to listen to this chucklehead. He tossed the rest of the drink back and stood.

"Rebecca wants out of this place," he said. "She's done some suffering, waiting on you."

Owen gave another drunken wave of his hand, and Arlen felt his fingers start to curl up into fists at his sides. He looked at the kid for a moment, his jaw working, thinking of all the things that should be said. Wasn't his place to say them, though.

"Welcome back," he said, and then he turned and walked up the steps and went to his bedroom alone.

35

THEY'D SLEPT IN THE SAME BED since Paul left, but that night they did not, and she didn't come down to his room in the darkness the way she once had. He tried not to let her brother's presence rankle him, but it was hard not to. Her idea was that they were all going to run off to Maine together like some happy damn family? Arlen couldn't see it.

He also couldn't see leaving her, though. Ever.

When he awoke it was to the sound of loud, angry voices. He got out of bed and pulled on some clothes and went downstairs, feeling a vague, hungover sort of angry, as he often did in the mornings after sleepless nights. By the time he reached the bottom of the stairs, another voice had joined Rebecca and Owen's chorus, though, and this one pushed away the mental fog. It was Solomon Wade.

"I told you to leave him alone," Rebecca was saying. "I mean it, too. You stay away from this place!"

"I'm trying to help the lad get back on his feet," Wade said in that drawl of his, a voice carefully designed to show no reaction, to create a constant sense of control. "I shouldn't think you'd object to that."

"You stay away from him."

"Rebecca, quit hollering," Owen said as Arlen stepped into the room. "The man's trying to help, he comes here to give us a—"

"We don't need gifts from him."

"It's not a *gift,* it's a loaner," Owen said. "Something to drive, is all."

Arlen looked out the window and saw that there were two cars beside Rebecca's old truck: Solomon Wade's gray Ford coupe and a blue convertible with whitewall tires.

"To drive for *what?*" Rebecca said.

"I've found the boy some work," Wade said.

"No." She shook her head. "No, he will not work for you."

"Now, Rebecca. Times are hard, and I've found Owen an opportunity. Him fresh out of prison? I'd think you'd be more appreciative. Why, you've done some work for me yourself, have you not?"

She didn't speak.

Solomon Wade said, "I'll leave y'all to sort this out. Owen, you be in touch, hear? I need you, and there's dollars in it. Stacks of them."

He walked through the door and out to his car. Tate McGrath was waiting in the passenger seat; evidently he'd driven the convertible down.

"I don't understand you," Owen said to Rebecca. "I don't understand you a bit."

"Owen, you're not to work for him. I won't allow it."

"*You* won't?" He had a challenge to his voice, his eyebrows raised.

"That's right. That man is—"

"Is the only person in this county who sees anybody gets paid,"

Owen said. "Maybe you haven't noticed, but there's a Depression on, Rebecca. And Judge Wade sees that people get paid. What's he ever done to you?"

"What's he done?" she echoed. "What's he done?"

"That's what I asked."

Her whole body was trembling. "He's a criminal. He hurts people and he steals from them and—"

"No worse than most of the world."

"And he kills them. He's a murderer."

Owen laughed. "Oh boy. You been hearing some tall ones. Who's telling them? This guy?" He pointed at Arlen.

Rebecca stood there and stared at her brother, who gave a mocking smile in response, and she didn't say a word.

"I'm going for a drive," Owen said. He walked past Arlen and through the door, and a minute later the convertible was roaring away.

"Why won't you tell him?" Arlen said. "Damn it, he needs to know."

She wouldn't look at him. "I will. It's just…not the right time."

"Well, it better be the right time soon," Arlen said. "Because I'll tell you something—that brother of yours isn't some confused kid who got himself into trouble. He thinks he's going to be a gangster, and he likes the idea."

"That's not true!"

"No?" Arlen said, and they exchanged an unpleasant stare.

"Listen," he said after the pause had gone on awhile, "I thought you were waiting here until he got released. I thought the only reason you were staying at this place was to keep Wade happy until your brother got released."

"That's exactly why I stayed."

"Well, Rebecca, he's been released. And he says he's going to stay."

"He won't. He'll leave."

"Going to take some convincing to get him to do that. I talked to the boy last night. He thinks he's the next Al Capone."

"That's just talk."

"Hell, yes, it's just talk. What isn't talk, though, is the idea that it's what he *wants* to be. He thinks Wade is aces. So if you want him to be hitting the road with you, you're going to need to tell him the truth of it. Your father didn't drown; he had his throat cut. That kid needs to know."

She nodded. "I'm going to tell him. I don't want to do it here, though."

"What do you mean you don't want to do it here?"

"Owen is…rash," she said carefully. "Foolish at times. He's so young."

"I don't follow."

"I can't tell him the truth when he is around Solomon Wade and Tate McGrath," she said. "Don't you understand that? He won't want to leave; he'll want to settle scores. He doesn't know enough to see that you can't settle scores with men like that. I'll tell him once we're gone from this place. First, though, I need to get him away from here."

"You're trying to protect him from Wade," Arlen said, "and from himself. You might be able to do one. I can guarantee you'll never be able to do the other. The kid's going to chart his own course. Seems like he's already well under way."

"I just need to get him away from here."

"Well, why aren't we going, then? Every day we linger is another day he falls in deeper with Wade."

"I can't…I'm waiting on something."

"Waiting on something?"

She looked away.

"This is how it goes," he said bitterly. "I'm trusted only so far. You still keep your secrets, though. The ones that matter most."

"Arlen, it's not an issue of trust. It's not. And I'll talk to Owen. You'll see — as soon as he comes back, I'll talk to him."

He didn't come back that day, though. When the knock on the door came just after sunset, they both assumed it would be Owen. It wasn't.

It was Paul Brickhill.

36

He looked tired and thin, with a face streaked by road dust and sweat. His shoes were caked with mud and split on one side from miles of walking. Rebecca held the door open and stared at him and didn't move. Arlen was sitting at the bar and he could see over her shoulder to the boy, who looked back at him without a word or a change of expression.

"Maybe I could step inside?" he said at last, addressing Rebecca.

"Yes, come on, get in here."

She moved aside and let him pass, and he dropped his bags to the floor and walked over to the bar and looked at Arlen. Neither of them spoke. Arlen's first thought, the one that had cut right through him at the sight of the kid, was relief. He was glad to see him again. Then he remembered the smoke he'd seen in Paul's eyes, remembered the purpose for the whole damn terrible thing, and thought, *No. You weren't supposed to come back.*

Paul gave him that steady gaze and then went around the bar and pulled a bottle of gin off the shelf. He poured a glass of it, took a sip, and then came back and sat on a bar stool a few down from Arlen. He looked up at the clock.

"Still working," he said. There was no note of pride in his voice. Not like there had been with the generator.

"Yes," Rebecca said. "Thank you so much for that. Paul, let me get you something to eat. You look like you need it."

"I could stand to eat."

"I'll fix something right away." She'd walked over to him and laid her hand on his shoulder, and he turned his head and stared down at it and then lifted his eyes to hers, cold eyes, and she removed her hand.

"Right away," she murmured again, and then she left.

It was quiet, nothing but the sound of the kitchen door swinging slower and slower until it came to a stop, and then all that could be heard was the ticking of the clock.

Arlen said, "You all right?"

"You care?" Paul lifted the glass and drank a little more of the gin.

"Of course I do," Arlen said. "And you know that."

Paul shook his head wearily. "Sure, Arlen. Sure."

"Look, son, the way it happened—"

"I don't want to hear it. Not ever again. Just don't speak of it."

Arlen went silent. They could hear Rebecca moving around in the kitchen, laying a pan on the stove and sparking the burner.

"Where you been?" Arlen said. "Where'd you go?"

"I went to Hillsborough County. The CCC camp down there. Ones that are working on the park, where you wanted us to go after we got off the train?"

Arlen nodded. "I remember it."

"Yeah? Well, if I wanted to have a chance with the CCC again, I should've gone down earlier." He turned the gin glass in his hands, his face dark and sullen.

"They wouldn't let you re-up?"

"No. Want to know why? Because they'd heard about the

trouble I got into up here. That's what I was told. Evidently Solomon Wade called down there. Him or the sheriff."

"When did he call? Day we were jailed?"

"I'm not sure. But somebody from up here called and spoke to them and warned them we might show up looking for work. Told them we weren't wanted in Florida, so they should send us packing if we did show."

Arlen felt the squeeze of anger in the back of his neck. That was the best job the boy could have found, and Wade had shut it down.

"I thought about trying to get back to Flagg," Paul said, "but my company left in the summer anyhow. Besides, Wade called up there, too, checking on our story. I doubt they'd be any happier to see me."

Arlen didn't say anything. He would have liked to argue, say that the supervisors back at Flagg knew Paul too well to believe that sort of shit, but he knew it probably wasn't true. The only supervisor who'd really gotten to know him well was Arlen.

"I stayed around Hillsborough for a few days. Hitched a ride into St. Petersburg. There's this fancy hotel there called the Vinoy, right on the bay. Heard they were hiring porters, but I couldn't catch on. So I headed back." Paul finished the gin and added, "I don't want to be here. Hope you understand that. I don't want to be here, but I got nowhere else to go."

Right then the front door banged open and Owen Cady stood before them. He was wearing a suit and polished shoes.

"How y'all doing?" Owen said. "We got ourselves a guest, eh? I hope he's paying for that liquor."

"He's not paying for it." Rebecca had stepped back out from the kitchen at the sound of her brother returning. "He's *my* guest. Where have you been?"

"Seeing the free world again. Don't you think I deserve that?" He crossed the room and put his hand out to Paul. "I'm Owen Cady. I own the place."

"Paul Brickhill." Paul shook his hand and passed a curious glance at Rebecca. "This your brother?"

She nodded.

"You've heard of me?" Owen said, retrieving a cigar from his jacket pocket and clipping the end.

"I worked here for a time," Paul said. "Came down with Arlen."

"Yeah? Why'd you leave?"

Paul looked at Arlen and then Rebecca and said, "I was hoping to catch some work down near Tampa. It didn't go well."

"Ain't that the way anymore?" Owen lit the cigar and took a puff. "Well, welcome back to the Cypress House, Paul Brickhill. Stay as long as you'd like. We're not busy, as you've probably noticed."

"He's not staying," Arlen said.

Everyone gave him a hard look at that.

"Actually," Paul said, "I think I will be until I get things straightened out."

Arlen shook his head. "It isn't safe for you here. It—"

"I told you that I don't want to hear any more about that. It's a pack of damned lies, and I won't listen to it ever again. I'm not intending on staying here long, trust me. But I need a bed for a few days while I figure it out. You'd refuse me that?"

He stared at Arlen with challenging eyes.

Owen said, "What in the hell are you all talking about?"

Nobody answered.

"Listen here," Owen said, tapping some ash free from his cigar, "I'll not have anyone else laying out the rules for who stays here and how long. Rebecca's not the owner. I am. When our daddy died, he left it to me. And I'm damn sure"—he pointed at Arlen with the cigar—"that he didn't leave it to you."

He waited for somebody to object. When no one did, he smiled, satisfied, and said, "So, Paul Brickhill, you stay as long as you'd like."

"Thank you."

Arlen said, "You keep the hell away from Solomon Wade while you're here. Understand me? You keep the hell away from him."

"Oh shit, my sister's got you singing her song, does she?" Owen said, giving a theatrical groan as he walked around the bar in pursuit of booze.

Arlen ignored him, looking hard at Paul. The boy turned away from the stare.

That night Paul sat up with Owen Cady and listened to the latest round of gangster stories. Rebecca had gone upstairs in a cold silence, and Arlen went outside and circled back to the front porch, where he was beside an open window and could hear what they were saying. He slid down until he was sitting on the porch floor with his back against the wall, then put a cigarette in his mouth and listened.

Owen Cady was singing the praises of Solomon Wade.

"Man doesn't look like much, and doesn't sound like it either. Just a judge in a backwater town nobody's ever heard of, right? Well, I'll tell you this: you go around the country, you'll find men who know the name. New Orleans, Miami, New York. They've heard of him, and they respect him."

Arlen waited on one of two things: Paul's rebuttal, or his silence. What he heard was Paul's encouragement for Owen Cady to keep running his mouth.

"You been working with him for long?" Paul asked.

"Few years, ever since I was old enough to be worth a damn to him. See, he and my father used to run liquor through here, back in Prohibition days. Bring boats into the inlet or keep them off the coast and go out and meet with them."

"Rebecca was around for this?"

"No, she was in Georgia. She never understood my father anyhow. He was a good man, but he was also a smart one. Knew what had to be done to make it in this world. Rebecca's never gotten that. Be better for me if she left again."

"You want to stay here?"

"Hell, no, but I need to for the time being. Solomon Wade, he's holding my ticket for wherever it is I want to go, understand? I can make more money in a month of working with him than I could in two years doing anything else. I'll build my nest egg and then head out of this place."

"Where would you go?"

"New York, maybe. Chicago? Hell, I don't know. Someplace where there's always things going on. It's a big world, brother, and I intend to see it."

"I'd like to myself," Paul said. "I don't know what I'm going to do."

"Where you from?"

"Jersey. Be damned if I'll go back there, though. But I can't get back into the CCC, and I've got no money. It's why I came back."

"How'd you boys end up here anyhow?"

"Arlen's out of his mind, that's how," Paul said. "I'm not fooling either. He's crazy. We were on a train headed down to the Keys, and he pulled us off because he thought he saw dead men aboard."

"You're lying."

"Not a bit. He pulled us off that train, and we got into a car with a guy named Walter Sorenson."

"I know Walt."

On they went, Paul narrating the events that had led him to the Cypress House, cursing Arlen at every turn, and Owen Cady offering grunts of disbelief. Arlen still hadn't lit his cigarette. It dangled from his lip, going soft as he listened.

"I want to get out of here," Paul said. "Go someplace brand-new, start over. But I don't have a dime to my name."

Tell him why not, Arlen thought. *Tell him what contribution the great Solomon Wade has made to your fortune.*

But Paul said, "Any chance you could find me some work? Maybe I could help out, make a few dollars."

Arlen almost came up off the porch and went through the door. He wanted to grab the kid by the neck and slam him around, slap him in the mouth and ask him what in the hell had gotten into him, how stupid could a person be? He held his place on the porch floor, though. He knew what had gotten into the kid — Arlen and Rebecca. He was different now than he had been before, sullen and bitter, hardened. It was no mystery what had made him that way.

I thought it was the right decision. I thought it was the only way.

Inside, Owen said, "You said you run across Wade in the jail?"

"That's right, but I haven't done a thing to cause him trouble since."

He's caused you trouble, though, Arlen thought. *He put smoke in your eyes, Paul. That man will be your death.*

He jerked the cigarette out of his mouth and crushed it in his palm and flung it into the yard.

"Let me talk to him," Owen said. "I'll put in the good word. I bet he goes along with it. I'm going to need a hand with this thing we've got coming in."

"What is it?" Paul said.

Owen Cady laughed. "Not yet, Paulie. Not yet. You ain't cleared."

"Well, get me cleared," Paul said. "I'll do whatever it takes to make some money. I want to get out of this place, and I don't want to do it walking down the highway. Not again."

"You get in with Wade, and you'll leave this place in a Cadillac."

* * *

They went on for another hour at least. Arlen sat where he was the whole time, listening to them and shaking his head, thinking that Paul sounded like an entirely different kid. Like someone Arlen had never met. He was trying to act hard, for one thing, and for another he was buying into Owen Cady's bullshit. It didn't seem like the same kid who'd been so hellfire determined to repair the generator and the clock, didn't seem like the same kid who'd charged Tate McGrath in that barroom and nearly gotten killed.

That was on Arlen, though. Paul *wasn't* the same kid, damn it. He'd left the Cypress House a different person, and his time on the road had done nothing to help, just allowed him to soak in his bitterness.

All I wanted was for you to leave, Arlen thought, *because I knew what staying would mean. Why can't you see that it was the truth?*

He didn't see it, though, and now he was back and planning to partner up with whatever Owen Cady had to offer. Arlen thought of the way Paul's eyes had swirled to smoke during that handshake with Wade, the way it had vanished as soon as the man released his grip, and he knew what had to be done.

He was going to have to kill Solomon Wade.

37

OWEN ROSE EARLY and took off in the convertible, and Paul went with him. They didn't leave word of where they were going or when they'd be back.

When Tate McGrath arrived, Arlen somehow had a feeling he'd known that it would be just Arlen and Rebecca at the inn. The old truck clattered into the yard, and Arlen took one look and then went upstairs and found the pistol he'd left under the bed. He checked the load and snapped the cylinder shut and then held the gun close to his leg as he walked down the steps. He stopped halfway down when he heard Rebecca at the door.

"Solomon wanted y'all to have this" was all McGrath said. Then the door swung shut and Arlen heard his boots slap across the porch. Arlen came down the steps and looked outside in time to see him getting into the truck.

"What are you doing with that?" Rebecca said, looking at the gun. She was holding a sealed envelope.

"I don't like that son of a bitch. I'd rather have a gun in hand anytime he pays a visit." He nodded at the envelope. "What's that?"

"I don't know." She tore the envelope open and slid a folded piece of paper out. As she unfolded it, Arlen saw it was a newspaper clipping. He set the gun on the bar and came to her side, studied the picture with her. The face was familiar — it was the man who drove the black Plymouth.

The article was from the Orlando newspaper, detailing the discovery of two bodies dragged from a swamp in a desolate stretch outside the village of Cassadaga. Both bodies were male, both were homicide victims, but only one had been identified: David A. Franklin, a Tampa native and known underworld figure. The second victim's identity was unconfirmed, police said, due to the fact that both of his hands were missing. Anonymous sources suggested that the corpse was Walter H. Sorenson, also from Tampa, and a close associate of Franklin's.

"Sorenson?" Arlen said. "That's whose hands we have? That can't be."

Rebecca slid slowly away, almost soundlessly, dropped until she was sitting on the floor and her back was against the bar. Her eyes were distant.

"I didn't...I thought it was the other man," she said. "Franklin. I didn't understand what they wanted me to know."

"Those can't be Sorenson's hands. He burned..." Arlen's voice faded and he turned his head and looked out the window at the spot in the yard where Sorenson's Auburn had exploded. He thought of how quickly the body had gone up, how the flesh had already been singed beyond recognition when Arlen reached the car.

I would have seen it coming, he thought. *I would have seen smoke in his eyes, would have known before he stepped out this door.*

"That wasn't him in the Auburn," Arlen said.

Rebecca shook her head.

"I thought the man in the Plymouth killed him," Arlen said.

"That man was David Franklin, probably. But he didn't kill him. If he had, I'd have seen the signs. No, Sorenson had a chance when he left this place. He had a chance, and they tracked him down, and they took that chance away."

Rebecca didn't answer.

"Franklin drove that Plymouth down here to help him," Arlen said. "Is that it? He came down to pick him up and set fire to that car so we'd be left thinking the man was dead."

"Yes."

He stared at her. "You knew this. You've always known it."

"No. But I've wondered."

Arlen got slowly to his feet. He left her sitting there on the floor and walked around the bar and poured himself a drink, though it was not yet nine in the morning. When he spoke again, he couldn't even see her.

"I want to hear it," he said. "I want to hear it all."

For the first time since the hurricane, she drank with him. They sat at a table beside the fireplace and drank, and she told him about Walter Sorenson.

Sorenson was intrigued by Rebecca. He didn't understand why she'd stayed at the Cypress House after her father's death, and he didn't buy the drowning story that had been offered. He inquired about it often.

"He was here about twice a month," she said. "It would vary depending on whether there was money to collect. The way it worked was that he'd come by to pick up what was owed to Solomon. If you didn't have the right amount, it wouldn't be Walter who came back for you. It would be Tate McGrath and his sons."

At first she resented him in the way she did everyone else affiliated with Solomon Wade. But over time, as he confided in her, as he told her how badly he wanted out of the enterprise he'd joined, she began to trust him.

"I told him the truth in July," she said. "Told him what had really happened to my father and why I was still here, that I was waiting on Owen."

Sorenson had been sympathetic but not shocked. He'd expected as much since Rebecca first replaced her father at the inn. He inquired about her plan to leave once Owen was free, and was unimpressed.

"All I knew was that I'd take Owen and we'd go," she said. "That seemed like enough to me. He said we'd need money. That if we tried to leave without money, we'd end up seeking help from my family, and if we did that, Solomon would find us. So it was the breadline, he said. That was where we were headed. I told him that trying to steal money would only make Solomon search for us harder, and he disagreed. He said Solomon would do it anyhow, and that we couldn't hide without money."

"It won't be easy for you if you're broke," Arlen admitted.

"That's what Walter said. He told me that my father's plan was almost right, just missing a few touches: money and witnesses."

"Witnesses," Arlen echoed.

She nodded.

"That's why he picked Paul and me up," Arlen said. "We served a role. So did you. We'd all tell the story in the same way."

"I think you're right," she said. "But he also called you a good-luck charm. Apparently he stopped to speak with David Franklin's girl in Cassadaga, and she offered him some sort of advice. You even said that yourself; I remember you told it to Tolliver. That she'd told him to watch for hitchhikers."

"For travelers in need," Arlen said. He thought about that conversation, the bolita game, the way Sorenson had let Paul drive the Auburn. His mood had changed dramatically when they arrived at the Cypress House, when the next step of his attempt at escape loomed large.

"I wish he'd made it," he said, and he was surprised at the sadness in his voice for a man he'd hardly known. "I wish the son of a bitch had made it."

"Me, too."

He looked at her. "You didn't know this. You truly did not?"

"No. I'm making guesses, and that's all. But I think they're good guesses. I didn't recognize the hands, though. Wade must have thought I would."

"He also must have suspected you were involved."

"I know that he did. They confronted me about it, Solomon and Tolliver and McGrath. I think the only reason they believed me in the end was that you and Paul were telling the same story."

"So we were good-luck charms," Arlen said, "but not for Sorenson."

"They asked me a lot of questions about David Franklin," she said. "Whether he'd ever been around with Walter, things like that. I'd never seen him. Had no idea who he was. Not until the night...the night they brought him here."

"Gwen, the one from Cassadaga, she was Franklin's girl," Arlen said. "They used her to get to Franklin, and Franklin to get to Sorenson. But who in the hell burned in that car? If it wasn't Sorenson, who was it?"

"I have no idea."

"Well, they didn't just find a body. Someone was killed. Who?"

"I just said that I have no idea. But Walter...he wasn't a murderer. He wouldn't have killed anyone."

"Well, it wasn't a mannequin that burned in that car."

"He wouldn't have killed anyone," she repeated stubbornly.

Arlen lifted the newspaper article. "Why'd they bring this to you? Why today?"

"Reminder," she said. "Solomon likes me to be refreshed, time to time, on what happens to those who cross him. Now that Owen's out, he can't hold that one over me. So he's turning to other things."

She lifted her hands to her face as if shielding her eyes from a bright light. "Poor Walter. He was the best of them. Not a bad man at his core. Just a man who'd made too many concessions for money."

"If you're right, then he didn't make the concession he needed most," Arlen said. "He was a thief but not a killer. Right?"

"That's right."

"Well, to get away from Solomon Wade, he needed to be the latter."

She lowered her hands and looked at him.

"He has to die," Arlen said simply. "There's no running from him. All this is simply more proof of that. We can't afford to leave him behind."

"No," she said, shaking her head.

"Yes," he answered. "I'm going to do it, Rebecca. It's the only chance you've got. You aren't going to walk away from him."

"You can't kill him. I can't let you do that. Not for me, not for Paul, not for anyone."

"It's not a matter of what you can let me do," he said, "it's a matter of what needs to be done. What has to be done. You want out of this mess? This is the way you'll get out. I don't believe there's any other."

"We're not killing anyone. No matter how evil they are, we're not going to do murder ourselves."

"Then he'll find us," Arlen said, "and he will settle the score. I wonder who will get your hands as a reminder? Mine? Your brother's?"

They shared a long stare, and then she broke it and turned away.

"It's not just him, though," she said. "Solomon Wade is valuable to people we've never even heard of, dangerous people. He's part of a chain, and if we remove that part, don't you think those other men will want to retaliate?"

"I don't intend to leave a calling card saying it was me that killed him," Arlen said. "And if he's in as deep as you say, then they'll have plenty of other people to worry about. We're nothing to them."

"Arlen, no."

"The way to leave this place without having to look over your shoulder every day for the rest of your life," Arlen said, "is by leaving with Wade dead. You know too much about what he does. You're a danger to him. The things you could tell the law, they're things that put him at risk. He'll find a way to keep you under his control, just as he always has. Last time it was with your brother. This time he may have to give up on any such patient technique."

They were both quiet. She had tears in her eyes, but they didn't spill over.

"I wanted it to be as easy as it could be," she said. "I just wanted to take Owen and go. To run away and hide and let time pass. I thought that we could do that. But he won't let us, will he? He'll never let us."

"No," Arlen said. "He won't. And you're going to need to tell Owen the truth now. You're going to need to trust him. Because I can assure you of two things: one, he isn't going to leave of his own accord. And, two, we're going to need him."

38

I<small>T WAS NEARING SUNDOWN</small> when they finally returned. Paul walked up to the porch in stride with Owen, head high and shoulders back.

"Been a long day," Arlen said. "What were you doing, Paul?"

"He was agreeing to do the right kind of work for the right kind of money, old-timer," Owen said. "Going to carve himself a piece out of this world."

"You want this piece?" Arlen said, still looking at Paul. "This swamp county, this seems big-time to you? You bothered to ask yourself what in the hell must go on in a place like this that it's worth a damn to anybody?"

"I need your opinion like I need another hole in my head," Paul said.

Owen laughed. "Damn straight, Paulie. Why don't you mind your own, old-timer?"

"I'll mind what I like," Arlen said. "And you call me old-timer one more time, I'll have you spitting teeth, you shit-brained little bastard."

Owen's face darkened and he stepped toward Arlen, only to

be cut off by Rebecca. Arlen wished she hadn't been there, wished the little shit would step on up and get his blockhead knocked right off his shoulders.

"Owen," Rebecca said, her hand on her brother's chest, "we're going to talk."

"Isn't talking I want to do with this son of a bitch," Owen said, pointing at Arlen.

"Talking is what you're *going* to do with him, and with me," she said. "I waited in this place for six months for you, and you're going to listen to me for once! You are going to listen!"

Her voice had risen to a shout, and it seemed to surprise everyone. Owen stared down at her but didn't put forth an argument.

Rebecca said, "Paul, I'd like you to go inside. This is a family matter."

"What's he staying for, then?" Paul said, nodding at Arlen.

Rebecca put her eyes on him and said, "I'm asking you, please."

Paul wanted to object. Arlen could see that. He wanted to tell her to get lost, he'd do what he pleased, and to hell with her, the one who'd broken his heart. He didn't have it in him, though. Not when her eyes were on him like that. For everything else that had changed in him, one thing had not: he cared for her. He wanted to please her.

In the end he went inside as he'd been asked, shoved past Arlen and stomped indoors like a sullen child.

"All right," Owen said, "I've got strong patience for you, Rebecca, because you're my sister and I love you. But I don't need a mother."

No, Arlen thought, *what you need is a swift kick in the ass.*

"I'm not trying to be your mother," Rebecca said. "I'm trying to be the one who keeps you from behaving like a fool any longer."

"I don't want to hear this," Owen said, stepping toward the door.

"You're going to hear it," she said, cutting him off. "I've got some things you *better* hear. Like how your father died. My father. *Our* father."

He stopped and tilted his head and stared at her. Then he flicked his eyes over to Arlen, a suspicious look, and stepped back.

"What are you talking about?"

"He didn't drown," Rebecca said. "He was murdered. His throat was cut. And Solomon Wade did it, or had it done."

Owen gaped at her. He looked at Arlen again and forced a laugh, as if maybe Arlen could join him in appreciating this ludicrous situation.

"You are so full of shit," he said.

She was calm. Even-keeled, the way she was so often. She'd grown remarkably good at holding her emotions at arm's length. Arlen wondered if that was a healthy thing.

"He was trying to run away," she said. "To fake his own death. He owed Solomon money, lots of it, and he was tired of the way he had to pay it off. Tired of the way his life had infected yours, tired of what you were becoming. I was supposed to get him off the boat that day, and we were going to sink it, and he was going to disappear. I'd stay long enough to sell the idea that he had drowned. Then I would take you and leave, and we'd find him again."

Owen shook his head. Not believing it, not wanting to hear it.

"I saw him," she said. "I saw him lying on the deck of that boat, I saw his blood drying in the sun, I saw his eyes, Owen, *I saw it all!*"

Her voice was trembling, and he was still shaking his head.

"You don't want me working for Wade, fine, say your piece, but don't you dare tell a story like that."

"Look at me."

He shook his head and stared away.

"Look at me."

This time he met her gaze. There was a wet sheen to her eyes, but no tears fell and she stared at him and did not speak. Arlen could see the resistance dying in him. His bravado and bluster couldn't hold off the truth that was in that look.

"I want you to read something," she said. "Then you tell me I'm lying."

She took a piece of paper from the pocket of her dress. It was a sleeveless dress, and though the day was warm Arlen could see a prickle along the flesh of her arms. She unfolded the paper and passed it to her brother.

Arlen knew what it said by now. She'd shown it to him while they waited for Owen and Paul to return. It was a letter that had been mailed from Corridor County more than a year earlier, when Rebecca's father was still alive and she was still in Savannah, a two-page lament of the life Owen was falling into. *I don't believe he has a dark heart,* David Cady had written, *but I fear he has a dark mind. I fear he can rationalize so much evil away, and perhaps I've put that in him...surely I have. But if we can get away from this terrible place and these terrible people, Rebecca, I know that he is not lost.*

Owen took his time reading. He didn't say anything, but Arlen could see his jaw tightening as he read, and when he finally folded the letter and passed it back to her, his movements were very slow, controlled.

"Neither of you ever told me a thing," he said. His voice had gone huskier.

"He thought that was safest. We would tell you when we were away."

Before you could get them into trouble, Arlen thought, *and it's the same damn plan she had this time around. I'm the one who talked her into this change, who talked her into this trust. So don't let me down. Don't you let me down.*

"Was likely McGrath that did it," Owen said eventually, his eyes vacant. "Or one of his boys. I never did think they could be trusted."

"Whoever did it," Rebecca said, "did it at Solomon Wade's instructions."

He shook his head. "I've worked with Wade many a time, Rebecca. He's not what you believe."

Her eyes went wide. "Not what I believe? He's what I've *lived with* for the last six months! Don't tell me it's about what I *believe*. Do you know why I'm still here? Why I've not gone back to Savannah or somewhere, anywhere, else?"

Owen didn't answer.

"Because I'd been told he would have you killed if I did," she said. "He explained it to me very clearly, told me all of the power he had at Raiford and that he could make your stay as easy or as painful as he wanted. That was up to me. It depended on whether I continued to help him. While you were in prison, I was here. I was watching drugs and fugitives pass through my doors, I was *counting* the drugs and the money and providing the records to Solomon Wade. He won't get his hands dirty; if anyone ran into trouble with the law, it would have been me. I played our father's role for him because our father had left an unsettled debt. That's what Wade told me. So I paid his debt, and they kept me here paying it by promising me what would happen to you if I didn't. *That* is Solomon Wade."

Owen said, "He wouldn't have done that. Not to someone in my own family. Solomon respects me. Likes me and respects me. He wouldn't have —"

Rebecca turned to Arlen and said, "Go get the shovel, please. I'd like to see the box you buried."

He led them to the dead tree along the shore, walked off the paces, and began to dig. It didn't take long to find the box. Owen spoke once, asking what the hell they were looking for, and Rebecca just told him to be quiet and wait. When Arlen had found the box, she said, "Owen can open it."

Owen took the shovel. There was a vague unpleasant smell coming from the box, but it was nothing like that of the body in the creek.

"This is what Solomon Wade delivered to me," Rebecca said. "In person. This is the sort of care Solomon Wade showed me while you were away. Now open it."

Owen wet his lips and turned back to the box and used the shovel blade to pry the lid off. He gave it a final toss and flipped the lid away entirely, and what he saw made him stumble backward and lift a hand to his mouth. He kept his body turned sideways when he looked again, as if he couldn't face it directly.

"Solomon Wade brought that to me," Rebecca repeated. "Those hands belonged to Walter Sorenson. You remember Walter?"

Owen nodded, still staring at the box, still with his hand at his mouth.

"I thought you would. He was a nice man. Kind. Wrong sort of man for this sort of business, just like Daddy was. Just like *you* are."

Arlen took the shovel from Owen's hand and knocked the box and the lid back into the hole and began to cover it with sand.

"You've known this for so long," Owen said, looking at Rebecca.

"What was I supposed to do, write you a letter and say it? Tell you on one of my visits to Raiford, the ones that you ordered me to stop making?"

"You could have told me."

She shook her head. "Not while you were in that place. I couldn't tell you until you were out. And then you got out, and you wanted to go right back to the life you'd led before, Owen.

You rode in here with Solomon Wade, told me what a great man he was. Can you imagine how that made me feel?"

Owen stared out at the sea. There was a good breeze blowing, and the waves were hitting hard, pounding the beach as if angered by its existence. The sun was a smudge on the western horizon, and shadows lay all around them.

"I'm going to kill him," he said. His voice was cold. "I'm going to slit the son of a bitch's throat." He tightened his hands into fists and said, "I'm going to make him bleed, Rebecca. I'll take him slow. I'll take —"

"No, you won't," she said. "This is exactly why I was waiting to tell you the truth. I can't allow you to make the situation worse than it already is."

"So what's your idea?" Owen said. "Call the sheriff? Think Tolliver's going to arrest him?" He gave a disgusted laugh and shook his head.

This time, Arlen spoke for her.

"We're going to kill him," he said. "But we're going to do it right. You need to be a part of it, and you need to have your damn head on straight when it's done. You go off half-cocked, and you'll end up dead yourself and probably take your sister with you. Don't shake your head at me; that's the damn truth of it. You better understand that."

Owen stood and glared at him. Arlen finished tamping down the sand and then leaned on the shovel and looked him in the eye.

"You want him dead? You want to settle up?"

"Bet your ass I do. I'm going to see that it happens, too."

"Good," Arlen said. "Then let's you and I climb in that fancy car he gave you and take a ride. We got some things to discuss."

Owen looked from his sister back to Arlen and nodded. Rebecca was staring out at the ocean, her face grave. She didn't like the idea. Didn't want them to be discussing such things. She'd have to deal with it, though. The only thing in all this mess that Arlen was certain of had been told to him by the hands he'd just buried for the second time.

You couldn't run from Solomon Wade. Not successfully.

39

P AUL WAS OUT ON the back porch when they returned. He watched them with a frown, and Arlen saw he had a glass of gin in his hand again.

"Family meeting finished?" he said.

"Yes," Rebecca said. "I'm going to make us some food."

Arlen set the shovel down beside the porch and then started around the side of the house and toward the car with Owen.

"Where are you going?" Paul called after them.

"Taking a ride," Arlen said. "I want to see this silly buggy move."

"I'll go along."

"You'll stay."

"That isn't your decision to make."

"It's mine," Owen said. "We'll just be gone a bit." His voice was soft and weary. Everything about him spoke of a sudden fatigue. He kicked along through the sand with his shoulders slumped and his hands jammed in his pockets, and he never even bothered to look at Paul. Paul didn't argue, but when he sat back down his face was dark with anger.

"First thing you need to understand," Arlen said when he'd slid into the passenger seat beside Owen, "is that we're going to keep that boy out of this. Completely. You got that?"

Owen nodded. He'd put the car in gear, and now he looked at Arlen and said, "Where am I going?"

"Just take it down the road," Arlen said. "You drive, and you talk. Tell me about Wade's work. Tell me the things your sister doesn't know. Tell me how you think he should be killed. Could be killed. And one more thing: tell me how we can lighten his pockets before we kill him."

Owen stared at him, surprised.

"Make no mistake," Arlen said, "people will likely give chase. We'll need money to run. On that score, Walter Sorenson was right."

Owen pulled out of the yard and onto the rutted road, the headlights capturing ghostly shadows from the Spanish moss that dangled just above the car.

"It's going to be hard," he said. "He'll have a lot of men around for this next deal. Men like Tate McGrath."

"I figured on that," Arlen said. "Now let's hear the whole scenario."

It would be the sort of transaction that took place often at the Cypress House, but never while Wade was present. He kept his distance from the actual cargoes. The McGraths and the Cadys handled that task. Owen had started his work for Solomon Wade as a driver, taking truckloads of orange crates out of Corridor County and on to Memphis, New Orleans, and Kansas City. The crates contained heroin smuggled in from Cuba.

The money would come from Wade and be given to Owen a day before a group from Cuba was to arrive. They'd bring a boat up to the waters off the beach from the Cypress House and wait for a light signal that showed them it was safe to put in. Then they'd come all the way into the inlet, and the unloading would commence immediately. Tate McGrath and his sons would handle the unloading. The cargo would be crates and crates of oranges. Some of the crates would be marked with a single hole drilled in a side slat. Inside those marked crates were thin false bottoms, the grains of heroin packaged beneath. Owen didn't know how much of the drug would come in, but it had to be plenty—the orange crates, once unloaded, were taken in trucks. Owen was expected to drive one truck, and he'd told Wade that Paul would be riding with him. It was supposed to be a sort of test for both of them, giving Wade an opportunity to determine that nothing about the prison stay had tainted Owen's loyalty, giving him an opportunity to assess Paul's loyalty for the first time.

Arlen asked for more details about the money. Owen said he knew that Wade paid thirty dollars for an ounce, and the next person in line probably paid sixty or seventy per ounce at least.

"How much money will he give you, though?" Arlen asked. "What are you going to pay these guys who bring it in?"

Owen said he couldn't be certain because he had no way of knowing the exact size of the load, but if it held the pattern he'd seen before he was jailed, then they'd be bringing in at least three hundred ounces.

"Then he'll be giving you nine thousand dollars," Arlen said. The sum overwhelmed him. They were going to carry that much money down to a bunch of Cubans in a boat and hand it off in exchange for orange crates?

"That's probably close to it," Owen said. They were out on the paved road now, screaming along at close to seventy miles an hour, and with the wind whipping in the car it was hard to hear. Arlen didn't want to tell him to slow down, though. He figured the kid needed to be in motion right now, needed to have his foot heavy on the gas.

"He just hands you that much money? He trusts you with that?"

"Well, everybody's awful careful about their counting," Owen said. "Come up a few dollars short, and it's bad news, buddy."

They were going to come up many dollars short this time around, if Arlen had any say in it. Tough for a dead man to miss the cash, though.

"You're in charge of the cash? Not McGrath?"

Owen nodded. "Tate and his boys stay back in the inlet. They handle the unloading, but they never go out to meet the Cubans. I take our boat out and meet them before they bring it in. I give them half the money then, while they're still on open water. They get the second half after everything's been unloaded. Tate will have all his boys down there, with three or four trucks, and they go through the crates pretty quick. Time it gets finished, I hand over the rest of the money, and everybody heads in a different direction."

"How much is your cut?"

"He said I'd get a hundred dollars for this one."

A hundred dollars was a good month's work for most men, but it also didn't seem too hefty a cut when you considered the likelihood of a long prison stretch if you were caught. Arlen figured Wade had a carefully constructed alibi if anyone ever did take a bust and try to point back to him as the source of the money. He also figured the fool who tried to do such a thing would have a mighty short prison stay and wouldn't be walking out of the cell when he left.

"You'll have this money a full day ahead of time?" Arlen asked.

"That's right. He doesn't want to see me the day of the delivery. He won't see anyone the day of the delivery."

That was good, though. It gave them some hours to work with, made this thing a hell of a lot easier than it would be if

275

McGrath himself handled the money and they had to go through him and his pack of thug sons to get it. Having Owen serve as the money handler made things much simpler. They'd have the cash in hand from the start. All that remained to be done was to kill Wade.

Shadows loomed in the headlights, and Owen slowed as they approached a group of black men and women walking along the road. They were barefoot, their eyes white in the headlights. One of the women was holding a child in her arms.

Looking for work, Arlen thought. *They're out here wandering in the night, walking barefoot, looking for any form of work they can get. And Solomon Wade is waiting to put nine thousand dollars in a case and send it out to some Cubans on a boat in exchange for a drug that hides your pain—mental or physical varieties. This world.*

They roared on past the walking family, two white men in a convertible out here in the backwoods. He wondered what they thought of that. If they took one look and knew that crooked money had bought the car.

"What'll he do on that day?" Arlen asked. "Wade, I mean."

"I've got no idea. Keep his distance, like I said."

"Well, I'm going to need to find him. You know where he lives, where he works, that sort of thing?"

Owen gave a nervous nod. He looked over at Arlen, his face pale in the darkness, and said, "You're really going to kill him."

Arlen looked away. "I can't let your sister end up like your father. I can't let her stay here either."

"You ever killed anyone before?"

"Killed plenty. Were days in the war I killed quite a few in just an hour."

"What about away from the war?"

Arlen shook his head.

"Well, I expect it's awfully different."

Arlen said, "I don't."

"What?"

"It's taking a life. Any time, and any way, it is always about ending someone's life. There aren't a whole lot of degrees to it. Not that I can see at least. People who haven't done it, they can imagine all these differences. I might agree that the circumstances and defenses for the act shift around a good deal. But that act itself? It doesn't change."

"You're going to kill him," Owen repeated, as if all the rest of the words had slid past him without impact.

"Yes," Arlen said. "I'll kill him, and you'll take your sister and get the hell away from this place. With the money."

Owen was silent. They drove along for a while, and then he pulled off the road and set to turning the car around, ready to head back.

"What do you know about the men Wade's connected to?" Arlen asked.

"Not much. They're in New Orleans."

"They the sort that'll give chase over nine thousand dollars?"

"If they know who to chase."

Arlen nodded. He expected they'd be looked for, at least in the early days, but with Wade removed he didn't imagine the hoods in New Orleans would be willing to waste much time on the endeavor. They'd need to install somebody else to take his place, that was all.

"Paul's getting some of the money," Arlen said. "Before we do a damn thing, he's getting some of the money, and he's getting on a train."

Owen said, "He thinks he's going to be here for it. Helping."

"Well, he won't be."

Owen nodded. "How much you figuring on giving him?"

"Enough," Arlen said. "Enough."

"What the hell are we supposed to do with the Cubans?"

"Let them sit," Arlen said. "They never see the lights that signal them that it's all clear, then they think there's a problem, and they go on back, right?"

"That's the point of the signal, I figure."

"Exactly. So they won't know what happened, but they'll know something went wrong. And they'll be right about that."

"We'll need to be gone before nightfall, then," Owen said. "McGrath and his sons will come down about sunset. They'll be set up in the inlet, waiting to unload. They'll·be watching everything. That old bastard doesn't miss much."

"By the time he gets there, the place will be empty. So, sure, he'll know something's up, and what'll he do? Go looking for Wade. And find his body."

"Then shit'll get going fast," Owen said, taking one hand off the steering wheel and rubbing it over his chin, a nervous gesture.

"What's to get going? They'll come looking for us. We'll be gone."

"Yeah, we better be. Just where in the hell is it you think we're going?"

"Does McGrath have a boat that can handle open water?"

"No."

"All right. You and Rebecca will leave in the boat that day, then. That way if McGrath or one of his sons is keeping an eye on you, they won't be able to follow anyhow. You know a port town you can get to easy enough where I can pick you up in the car once Wade's been dealt with?"

"There's Yankeetown."

"That's what we'll do, then. You take the boat there and wait on me. We'll use this car at first, but we're going to have to switch it up fast. All that time you spent at Raiford talking to big-shot cons, you actually learn how to steal a car?"

"I can steal one, sure."

"Good," Arlen said. "You'll need to steal a couple before it's done."

Owen didn't answer.

"You having second thoughts?" Arlen said.

Silence.

"If you are," Arlen said, "you might think about that box we dug out of the sand again. And you might think about your father."

This time Owen turned to look at him, and his eyes were steady. "I'm not having any second thoughts."

"All right." Arlen turned and let the wind blow into his face and said, "You know where Solomon Wade lives?"

"Yes."

"Take me there now."

"Why?"

"I can't just drive up and kill him," Arlen said. "It's going to require the right opportunity. I expect I'll have to spend a good bit of the day following him. He live alone?"

"He's got a girl. I don't know how much she's there, though."

"We'll need to know," Arlen said. "I'm not hurting anyone else. He'll need to be alone when I come for him."

He had a sudden vision of the sheriff of Fayette County and Edwin Main approaching in the night, Arlen standing there at the window watching them come, waiting on them.

"Yes," he said, "he'll need to be alone when I come."

40

THE HOUSE WAS A sprawling plantation-style place about a mile outside of High Town, resting at the end of a long drive bordered with cypress trees. Lights glowed inside a broad expanse of glass that made up one side of the front of the home. Behind it was a carriage house, Wade's Ford coupe parked in front, along with another car. Arlen didn't see the second vehicle clearly at first, but then Owen Cady said, "Sheriff is here," and he remembered it well, remembered sitting in the back with handcuffs around his wrists and a notion that all he needed to do was weather a little bit of a knockabout and he'd be back on the road to Flagg Mountain soon enough.

It was a memory so strong and so strange it seemed the property of another man. Arlen would never see Flagg Mountain again. What had seemed reasonable once was gone now, taken from him by circumstances far from his control. He wondered if Wallace O'Connell and the other men from that train had felt similarly when they realized the hurricane was upon them. He wondered if any of them had remembered him, remembered that night at the station platform when he'd urged them to get off, assured them that danger lay ahead.

They'd all been heading toward powerful storms, he realized. His had just been longer coming, that was all.

"I don't like sitting here," Owen said. "They know this car; hell, it's *his* car. One of them sees it out here, what are they going to think?"

They were parked in the darkness a good quarter mile from the house, nobody was going to see them, but Arlen had no reason to hold him here either, so he told him to go ahead and drive away.

"Awful lot of house," he said as they cruised by for the final time, Owen keeping the headlights off.

"Was the owner of the timber company that built it. He was the richest man around for miles in his time. Now Wade is."

So it went. Legitimate work disappeared and what stepped in its place were the likes of Solomon Wade. Arlen wondered what the locals thought when they passed by the place. Probably felt broken, helpless, the way Thomas Barrett seemed to. Arlen wondered what they'd think when Wade was dead. Would any good come from it here, or would another like him simply fill the void?

"He have servants at the place?" Arlen asked.

"None that stay there. People come and go during the day, but he doesn't like anyone living on the property."

That would help. Now that he'd had a look at the house, Arlen was figuring it was the best spot he'd have, and dawn the best time. He'd done some killing in dawns of days past, had left men to bleed out as the sun showed faint in the east. He could do it again. As he'd told Owen earlier, all that changed was the circumstances, not the act. He'd never wanted a circumstance like this, but hell, he hadn't wanted a war either. A man never did get as much say in this life as he wanted to have, as he'd expected he would when he was young. No, you took what was offered and you handled it best as you could.

"How will you get the money?" he asked.

"Sheriff will bring it."

"The sheriff?" It was all he could do not to laugh. Some law they had in Corridor County.

"That's right. He'll drive it down Thursday evening."

"But the boat's not coming in till Friday night."

"They like to have their distance," Owen said. "And they have Tate McGrath watching. Tate'll be watching the whole time. Basically from the moment Tolliver delivers the money, Tate will be around, watching. Who was it you think killed my father? It was Tate, I'd just about guarantee it. And my father went out on the boat just the same as you want us to."

His voice was rising, and the speed of the car right along with it, his foot pushing harder at the gas as his nerves took hold. Arlen said, "Ease up, son," and Owen slowed the car but shook his head, still unhappy.

"It's a shit plan," he said. "You're sending us out just like my father went and somehow expecting it to go better."

Arlen didn't have an answer for that. Hell, the kid was right. All he knew was that he wanted Rebecca gone by the time he moved on Wade, just in case anything went wrong. He wanted the two of them to be under way and prepared to keep going. Tate McGrath, the damned watchdog, was going to be a problem.

"The boat's a bad idea," he admitted. "You leave in the boat any time ahead of when you should, they'll not like it. Better idea is you and Rebecca climb into her truck in the middle of the afternoon, nothing packed. Make as if you're just heading up the road to Barrett's store. Be so damn obvious about it that he won't imagine you've got any other plans."

"Doesn't leave as much time, though."

"No, it doesn't. But any time is better than none, and I think you're right—we try to get too crafty while McGrath's watching, it'll go sour fast. The way to handle it is for you and Rebecca to drive off in that truck of hers like it's just another afternoon, and I'll stick right where I always am, down at the boathouse swinging a hammer. Long as we all don't leave together, I imagine he'll give it some time at least. Won't expect something's wrong right away."

"So we take off that afternoon," Owen said, "and you wait to kill Wade until evening?"

"What time do the Cubans get in?"

"Long after dark."

"All right. Then I got a bit of time. Hell, I'll have a word with Tate before I leave. Tell him you gave me instructions to clear out, that I wasn't to be around the place. He'll believe that; it'll sound proper to him. He doesn't trust me and he wouldn't expect you to."

"So you'll talk to Tate," Owen said, "and then you'll—"

"Get in this car and drive up the road and kill Solomon Wade."

It would change the timing of things. He wouldn't be able to wait on Wade as the sun rose, the way he'd imagined. No, he'd have to venture into town in daylight and find him and follow him and take the first opportunity that was there. He'd have to do it fast, too. Rebecca and Owen would have a few hours of head start, but by the time evening settled in and they still weren't back, Tate McGrath would grow suspicious.

When Owen spoke again, it took Arlen by surprise. Things had been that quiet.

"It should be me," he said.

"What?"

"That kills him. Shouldn't be you. Ain't nothing personal

between you and him. Me and him, though? That's plenty personal. Should be me that pulls the trigger."

Arlen said, "You realize you helped cause all of this?"

Owen turned and gave him a confused look. "What?"

"You read that letter from your father. You know what you'd gotten into with Wade. Sure, your old man might've led the way, but it was you who helped put the knife to his neck. Don't forget that. You want to blame Wade, go on and blame him. Don't forget your own decisions, though."

"You got some brass, saying a thing like that. Just because I did some work for the man doesn't mean —"

"You did more than work for the man," Arlen said. "You wanted to be him. Wanted to run around in fancy cars with a gun in your belt and a pocketful of money, dirty money, blood money, just so you could feel like you got some power. Feel like you're a big shot. Came swaggering in the day you got out of Raiford and never so much as thought about your sister, what she's been through waiting on your worthless ass. No, all you wanted to do was tell tales about the thugs and hoods you knew. Except you don't even know them. You got any idea how sad that is, boy? You're *pretending* to be Solomon Wade. That's what you want out of this life. To be just like the man who had your daddy's throat cut."

Owen's jaw had gone rigid, and his hands were tight on the steering wheel.

"I've been places where words like that would get a man killed," he said.

"Son," Arlen said, "you ain't been anywhere. You don't have so much as a rumor of what this world's really like. You're getting a taste now, and it's your first. All that tough-boy bullshit aside, this is your first taste, and you know it."

Owen didn't answer.

"Look me in the eye and tell me if I'm wrong," Arlen said.

Silence.

"There's only one thing that you *need* to do now," Arlen said, "and that's take care of your sister. Try to make up for the mistakes you made and your father made that got you all into this fix. I'll do your bloody work. You just be a man for a change."

That night he sat awake with Rebecca on the back porch, and they listened to the waves break and roll back and break again, and neither of them spoke much for a long time. Owen had climbed the stairs as soon as they got back and shut the door to his room, never appearing again. There was a lot going on in his mind. Let him have his time, so long as he didn't set the fool's temper to work again.

Paul had been in the barroom until Arlen entered, and then he stood and walked past him without a word and went up the steps as well. Arlen let him go. How he wished Paul had never come back. He had to make sure that he'd be gone soon, long before anything went into motion with Solomon Wade. That would require waiting on the money, though, and that would give Arlen only about twenty-four hours to convince Paul to hit the road... and only about twenty-four hours of distance between the boy and Corridor County. Arlen didn't figure they'd pursue him, but there was a chance. Paul would need to travel smart, travel with a plan, and that would require a conversation between the two of them. Right now, the boy wouldn't even speak to him.

Rebecca laid her hand out in the darkness and put it on his arm, and the mere touch of her skin on his own broke some of the blackness loose inside him. He closed his eyes and felt the points of warmth where her fingertips lay, tried to focus on that and nothing else for just a few seconds.

"You shouldn't have to do this," she said softly. "Shouldn't have to be any part of it."

"Stop," he said.

"Well, it's true." She squeezed his arm once and then removed her hand and said, "I told Paul about your father."

He opened his eyes again. "What?"

"He holds such anger toward you, Arlen, and I can't stand to see it. I tried to talk with him about it, tried to apologize for what happened and the way that it happened and explain what you were trying to do. That you believed so deeply he was in danger that you would drive him away from this place at any cost."

"Let me guess," Arlen said, "he wasn't buying it."

"No. I told him that *I* believed you. He didn't care for that either. He wanted to know how I could possibly believe you."

"So you told him."

"Yes. I hope you're not angry. I knew it wasn't a story you shared, but, Arlen...I wanted him to know."

He supposed he should be angry. He wasn't, though. Just couldn't muster it, not with her, and not over this.

"I won't see that boy die," he said. "I won't let it happen. It isn't this place that threatens him, it's Wade. I'll put an end to Wade."

"We could just leave," she said. "I still think we could just—"

"No," he said. "You will leave. You and your brother and Paul. And I expect to catch up with you at some point. I fully intend on doing that. But not while Solomon Wade remains to follow."

41

TIME WAS SHORT, and moving fast. Tolliver was to bring the money down that evening, and on the next the Cubans would arrive with their boat packed with orange crates. They would, if everything went without a hitch, sit out on the Gulf and wait for lights that never came and then they'd turn around and return to their own country, still with the orange crates on board. Paul would be on a train, perhaps, and Rebecca and Owen driving north, and Solomon Wade would be dead.

All of this had to be done in less than forty-eight hours.

Arlen went down to the boathouse that morning and cut boards and sanded them down same as he would on any other day, thinking that if McGrath or Wade happened by it would be best for them to see things as they always were, no indication of a change in plans.

He spent most of the morning considering what he'd say to Paul. He wanted to prepare him for what was to come but didn't think the boy would hear him out. He would have to wait until Owen had the money, break off a portion of it for Paul, and drive him to a train station. If Paul wouldn't listen to Arlen, he'd listen to the money. He was looking for a way out. They'd give it to him.

That was what was in Arlen's mind when he walked back up from the boathouse shortly before noon and discovered that Paul was gone.

"Said he was walking into town," Rebecca told Arlen. "Owen offered him a ride, but he said no, he wanted to be alone and wanted to walk."

Arlen didn't care for that.

"What in the hell does he want in town? He doesn't have a dime to his name. What's he going to do?"

Rebecca spread her hands. "I don't know, Arlen. He wasn't holding discussions over it. He just left."

He thought about borrowing Rebecca's truck and going after him but decided against it. He was probably the reason Paul had wanted to get out of here; it would serve no purpose to chase him down.

The day dragged by, and Paul didn't return. The heat had gone unbroken for a full week, but there were thin, swift-moving clouds skidding over the sun today, and Arlen thought there was the promise of rain in the air. The sea was riding stronger swells than normal, the Gulf carrying a green tint, the gulls shrieking and fighting the wind currents above him. All the things that had become standard to Arlen now, the smell of the salt breeze and the feel of that intense, near-tropical sun on his neck and arms, the rustle of palm fronds. It should have been a beautiful place. *Was* a beautiful place, were it not for the men who'd invaded it. Reminded Arlen of the Belleau Wood, once he got to thinking about it. That had been a pretty parcel of land in its own right, field and forest. Damned gorgeous spot until the wrong men came across it, and then it was tangled with bodies and barbwire and the cries of the wounded.

By four Paul had still not returned, and the clouds had thickened and begun to move slower, like troops massing for an advance. When the first fat drops began to fall and the woods around the inlet took to swaying and rattling in the wind, Arlen gathered his tools and retreated to the house. It was really starting to come down by the time he got inside, and he joined Rebecca and Owen at the back window and watched the rain lash down and pelt a gray, tossing sea.

The rain fell different here than in other places Arlen had been, thicker and faster, turning the yard into an ankle-deep pond in a matter of minutes. The beach drank it in easier for a time, but then it began to form puddles even on the sand, and the waves raced up and chased the rain as if they intended to work together and turn the whole world to water.

It had been raining this way, Arlen recalled, the day they'd returned from the jail. He remembered how he and Paul had broken into a run on their way up to the porch, laughing like children, bursting through the door feeling like they'd just stepped out of the worst of it in more ways than one.

That seemed a mighty long time ago.

He was lost in that memory when he realized Rebecca and Owen had turned and gone to the front windows, were looking out at a car parked at the top of the hill, its headlights glowing against the gray gloom of the storm. The sheriff's car. Tolliver was parked up there in the exact place where he'd let Arlen and Paul out that day before the hurricane.

He's come with bad news, Arlen thought, a sudden certain clench going through his gut, images of Paul stretched out in the back of that car with a white sheet over his body. *He's come to tell us —*

But right then Owen said, "He's here for me. He's here with the money."

They all turned and looked at one another as a gust of wind shook the inn and lightning sparked almost on top of them, filling the dim barroom with one blinding flash. Thunder crackled, an angry, aggressive sound.

Arlen said, "You best go get it, then."

There was another silent pause, all of them realizing this was it, the starting point. The moment that money passed from Tolliver's palm into Owen's, the plan was under way, no longer about ideas and possibilities and only about execution. They'd need to do it as they'd planned, and do it right. Most of that burden rested with Arlen and the Smith & Wesson upstairs under his bed.

Owen blew out a breath and started for the door. Arlen called, "Hey," and brought him up short, his hand on the doorknob.

"You got to look relaxed," he said. "Same as any other day. You ain't doing anything but helping. The sheriff up there, he's your buddy, and so is Wade. Don't show them anything else."

Owen nodded.

"The rain'll help," Arlen said. "Sheriff will be in a hurry. He doesn't like driving in the storm."

Owen gave another nod and then pulled open the door. The wind was blowing hard out of the south, and it caught the door and wrenched it from his grasp and banged it off the wall. A spray of rain showered in and soaked the floorboards before he got his hand on the door again and slammed it, and then both Arlen and Rebecca moved closer to the bar so they could watch him.

He ran across the yard with his shoulders hunched. Watching him go, Arlen had the bad feeling again, dark images flickering through his mind — gunfire opening up from inside the car and dropping Owen out there in the mud and the rain; the window sliding down as Owen approached and a knife blade glinting ever so swiftly as it snaked toward his throat.

I wish I'd checked his eyes closer, Arlen thought. *I didn't see anything, he was looking me full in the face and I didn't see anything, but maybe I didn't look hard enough ...*

Nothing happened, though. The door to the sheriff's car swung open and then Owen had a black case in his hand, same sort of case that Walter Sorenson had carried. He stood beside the car, head ducked against the rain, and said a few words. Arlen couldn't see Tolliver from behind the door, but Owen looked relaxed enough. The rain was a help. Made any tension on his part easier to explain, as if he just wanted to get the hell back inside and out of the downpour.

It wasn't but thirty seconds before Tolliver slammed the door and Owen turned and began running back toward the house. Rebecca let out a breath, and Arlen looked over his shoulder at her and realized she'd been sharing his dark thoughts. He managed to get a grin on his face.

"We're good," he said. "All right? Wade thinks your brother is in league with him, and he thinks he's got you owned by fear. They aren't waiting on trouble. Not from us."

She nodded, but her face was pale and she couldn't match his smile.

The door swung open, and then Owen was back inside and dripping rain all over the place, his blond hair turned dark with water and plastered over his forehead and down into his eyes. He gave them a stare and lifted the case high.

"Here we go," he said.

Arlen nodded. "Here we go."

They counted the money back in the kitchen, hidden from windows. Arlen saw the stacks of bills inside and thought of the money he'd worked so hard and saved so long to gather, those 367 stolen dollars. He wondered if they were included in this pile.

Rebecca did the counting. She fingered the bills swiftly and familiarly and didn't say a word as she riffled through the stacks, kept a silent count in her head until the last bill had touched the edge of her thumb. Then she turned to them and said, "Ten thousand."

"Ten thousand dollars?" Arlen echoed. He'd been watching her count it, had seen the bills with his own eyes, but he still wasn't sure he believed the number. The CCC paid thirty dollars a month. There were more than twenty-five years of work sitting in that simple black case.

"Yes," she said, and then, for the first time, she smiled. "He's not going to like losing it."

"Hell," Arlen said, "he's going to lose something else he'll like even less."

Somehow that got them all to laughing. It wasn't a healthy kind of laughter. More the sort born out of fear, jangling through nerves strung tight as bowstrings, but it felt good all the same. They had their laugh together, and then a particularly strong racket of thunder struck and shook the walls of the inn and they all fell silent again.

"Paul gets his cut," Arlen said. "I'll give it to him, and I'll take him to a train station and see that he gets on one headed far from here."

"How much are you intending to give him?" Owen said.

"Half." He said it flatly. Owen rocked his head back and stared with wide eyes.

"Bullshit, he gets half. He'll be gone 'fore anything even starts to happen! He ain't playing a role in this, ain't helping, ain't —"

"He gets half," Arlen said, and there was a challenge in his voice that shut Owen's mouth for once. He went tight-lipped and angry and stared at Arlen with distaste, but when he spoke again his tone was softer.

"There's four of us here," he said. "Fair split would be twenty-five hundred. That's more than fair."

"That boy's got a mother was counting on CCC checks,"

Arlen said. "He's got to look after her and himself. He gets half."

Owen started to shake his head again, but Rebecca cut in.

"That's fine," she said. "That's right."

She counted out half the money and placed it in a burlap bag and handed it to Arlen. He put it on a high shelf behind a sack of flour and then he and Owen both watched as Rebecca replaced the rest of the money in the black case and fastened the latches and set it beneath the table.

"One day left," she said.

42

Paul returned at the height of the storm. The rain had
lessened just a touch, but the lightning and thunder were
gathering energy, the walls and windows of the inn trembling
consistently, wind howling in off the Gulf. It wasn't yet sundown
but might as well have been; no sun would shine on this day
again. The three of them had returned to the barroom, ostensi-
bly to discuss the plan, break down each movement and time it
out to the last second. Nobody had much to say, though. It was as
if the delivery of the money, that first squeeze on a trigger nobody
else even saw, had somehow silenced them.

Instead they sat and listened to the storm and drank. Arlen
and Owen passed a bottle of whiskey back and forth, and even
Rebecca had a short one. Her eyes moved from the beach to the
fireplace to the clock, flicking from place to place as if taking
inventory.

"What's on your mind?" Arlen said.

"I was thinking that it really isn't such a bad place."

It was the same notion he'd had that morning, working on
the boathouse.

"I came to hate it, you know," she said. "To almost blame the physical location for everything that was happening here, for everything that had happened. But you know what? My parents were right. It's a gorgeous spot. It will be special someday. Someone will probably make a nice living doing just what my father always hoped to do here. They will be different people, though, and it will be a different time. Right now, it's as if this place is infected. The sickness will pass. But no time soon. No time soon."

Arlen nodded. She wasn't alone in those thoughts, and they weren't limited to this place. It was an infected world right now. He remembered reading newspaper pieces about the black dust that had risen in the plains and driven farmers to take shelter in the ground, dust clouds so mighty that they'd drifted all the way across the country and darkened the skies above New York. It was a hell of a thing. Grasshoppers had descended over the same farms like a biblical plague, picking crops to shreds and ruining any hope of a cash harvest. At the same time banks were going under and women and children standing in breadlines, and young men like Owen Cady and Paul Brickhill were willing to throw in their lots with the Solomon Wades of the world because they saw no other way to climb out of the trenches in which they lay.

It would pass, though. Arlen believed that, had to believe it. You kept your head down and you weathered what this life brought you and believed it would pass. He looked at Rebecca now and thought, *You are all that I need.* She was, too. Through all the hell that might come to pass in a few short hours, he had no qualms about staying around to endure it. Just the chance to be with her, it was enough. It was something the likes of which he'd never hoped to find.

A memory caught him then, Paul in the darkness on the dock while Tolliver and Tate McGrath prepared to kill in this very room. Paul saying, *I feel like I've been traveling through time to get here, Arlen, just to find her.*

Damn it, why did it have to afflict them both? Why couldn't love be parceled out evenly and easily?

It was then that a sheet of white light filled the room, and for a moment nobody reacted because they'd grown so used to the steady, brilliant flashes of lightning. This one held, though, and Arlen turned and looked through the window, and, as a snarling, raging clatter of thunder shook the sky, he saw Thomas Barrett's delivery van parked at the top of the hill, its headlight beams cutting across the yard. The passenger door swung open, and Paul burst out and ran through the rain. Barrett gave the horn a little double tap and turned the van around and headed back up the road.

When Paul broke through the door and stood before them in a sopping mess, everyone stared at him in silence. He had a paper sack clutched to his chest.

"Some storm," he said.

"Where in the hell you been?" Arlen said.

"Went up to the store, if it's any of your business. Which it isn't."

"That store's every bit of five miles away."

"Felt about like that," Paul said, flip and indifferent. "Once it commenced to storming, Mr. Barrett said he'd give me a ride back or I'd be waiting till morning. He thinks this one isn't blowing off quick."

"Come on over here and get dried off," Rebecca said, rising and pulling a towel off the bar. "Maybe we should start a fire. It's warm, but on a night like this it just might be —"

Paul had been crossing to her, and everyone stopped short when Arlen reached out and grabbed the paper sack from his hands.

"Hey!" Paul cried, and reached for it, but Arlen turned his

shoulder and blocked the grab long enough to open the sack and see the contents. There were some penny candies and a few packs of cigarettes.

"Give me that," Paul said, and this time Arlen let him take it. "What's the matter with you? Got to steal everything from me, is that it?"

"I haven't stolen a thing from you in the past," Arlen said. "Never took a damn thing that was yours."

Paul gave him cold eyes and didn't answer.

"You don't smoke cigarettes," Arlen said.

"What?"

"You got cigarettes in that sack, smart guy. Why?"

"Because I wanted a few, that's why."

"I'll say it again," Arlen said, "you don't smoke."

Paul drew his shoulders back and looked Arlen in the eye. "They're for Owen. I figured he'd appreciate them. You probably would have, too, but I'm not of a mind to give you anything."

"Hey, thanks," Owen said, and Arlen wanted to backhand the fool right through the window.

"So all you got is candy," Arlen said. "You walked five miles up the road to fetch yourself some candy?"

"That's right."

"Arlen, what does it matter?" Rebecca asked softly, passing Paul the towel. He took to drying his face and neck, and Arlen looked at Rebecca in silence. He didn't have an answer, really. All he knew was that he didn't like this. It didn't feel right, Paul taking a walk that long in this kind of heat just to get some damn candy.

"You happen across Solomon Wade in your travels?" he said.

"No. Didn't happen across a soul but Mr. Barrett and his wife. What it matters to you, I have no idea. It's none of your concern what I do."

"How'd you pay for it?"

Paul stopped with the towel over one side of his face. "What?"

"This shit you went hiking for. Cigarettes and candy. How'd you pay for it? I was under the impression you were busted-ass broke."

Paul switched the towel to the other side of his face and dried it slowly. He seemed to be thinking.

"Mr. Barrett let me have it on credit," he said.

"Credit," Arlen echoed. "Son, this is a Depression. That man don't know you from Adam. Why in the hell's he giving you anything on credit?"

"I told him I'd be coming into some money shortly," Paul said. "Owen here set me up with a bit of work."

"Let me fix us something to eat," Rebecca said, nervous, bothered by the tension in the air. "We'll all sit in here where it's dry and have some food."

Arlen and Paul held a long stare, and then Paul turned away and tossed the cigarettes to Owen.

"There."

"Thanks."

"Sure. We still got our job tomorrow night?"

Owen looked at Arlen, uneasy, but nodded. "Yeah. We got our job."

"Good," Paul said. "I could use the money. No offense to you, Owen, but I've had my fill of this place."

Arlen went to the bar and poured a drink but didn't take a sip of it. He was watching Paul and remembering him the way he'd looked that day when he corrected Arlen's mistake on the pitch of the roof at Flagg Mountain, the good-natured, deep-rooted interest he took in every joint and every hinge. The way he'd taken that generator apart and scattered its pieces over the porch and set to work putting it back together again without a doubt in his head, sure it could be done. He remembered those times, and the night they'd taken the boat out, and he looked at this thin young man with the permanent scowl who stood before him now and thought, *I did this. I was only trying to help, but I did this.*

"What are you staring at?" Paul said.

"Nothing," Arlen said, voice soft. "Nothing at all."

He took a drink, but he had no taste for it, and then he slid the glass away from him and went through the swinging door into the kitchen.

Rebecca had a slice of ham frying in a skillet on the stove, and she turned to him as if to speak but instead she just stepped forward and wrapped her arms around him and put her face to his neck. He wrapped his own around her, and they held each other in silence for a long time. Her face was warm on his neck, and he could feel her breathing and for some reason he had to close his eyes and hold that moment in darkness.

"I'm sorry," she said.

"Sorry?"

"For it all. This isn't something you should be a part of. I wish I could—"

"Stop," he said, voice gentle. "We're going to handle this. All right? It's not but a day left, Rebecca. By the time the sun goes down out there on the water tomorrow, you'll be gone from this place. Going north, to Maine, just the way you hoped. I'll see that it happens."

He pushed her back and lifted her chin and kissed her. Soft and slow. When he broke the kiss, he said, "Is there a train that could be taken yet tonight?"

She frowned. "One more before the end of the night, but it's an hour's drive. What are you asking for?"

"I'd like to give Paul his share and put him on it."

She stepped back and looked at him in surprise. "Already?"

He nodded. "I want him clear of this, Rebecca. Make no

mistake—I intend to see it through just as we've planned, but I want him clear of it. He's ready to leave this place. We've soured him on it, on us, on damn near everything. I can't change that. But I can put money in his pocket and get him aboard a train and hope for the best for him."

She put her hands on his shoulders and said, "I love you."

All he could get out was "Yeah." They both laughed then, and he took her close and said, "I love you, too. And I don't give a damn what's happened since I got here, or what's left to come—I found my way to you. Any price that must be paid in exchange for that is a small one."

She kissed him again, and this time he could feel a tear gliding off her skin and onto his own, and then she took the burlap sack with the five thousand dollars down from the shelf and handed it to him. He left her there in the kitchen and went for Paul.

43

PAUL WAS DRINKING WITH OWEN. Trying to engage him in some of the usual tales, asking about Dillinger and Handsome Harry Pierpont, the one they electrocuted up in Ohio, inquiring about them as if he thought Owen had ridden at their sides. Even Owen wasn't having it tonight, though. He looked worn, and all he said was "Ah, those boys didn't hardly spend any time in Florida at all. A few months when they was hiding out once, but that was all."

Arlen said, "Paul?"

He turned and looked at Arlen with that usual expression of distaste, a glass of liquor in his hand. "What?"

"Give me a minute, would you? Step out on the porch."

"I'm having a conversation."

Arlen said, "Paul," one more time, no change of tone at all. He got a sigh of annoyance and the slap of the glass smacking down hard on the table before the boy rose and followed him out onto the back porch. It was still raining, but the wind had shifted direction and lessened enough so that it didn't spray under the porch roof and soak them. They stood out there in the dark, and Paul folded his arms across his chest and stared at Arlen.

"Whatever you got to say, it's probably not worth the time. I don't need to go through it again. I don't need to hear your stories or your warnings or your —"

"Open that up and take a look inside," Arlen said, passing him the sack. He watched as Paul took it warily, opened it, and went slack-jawed. He reached inside gingerly, as if he were going to frighten the money right out of the bag by moving sudden, and fanned his thumb over the edges of the bills.

"Where'd you get all this?"

"The same man you were hoping to earn it from."

Paul looked up. "Wade?"

"That's right. There's five thousand dollars in that bag."

"Five *thousand* —"

"And it's yours," Arlen said. "Provided you get your gear together right now and ride with me to the train station. You go wherever you like from there. I'm not going to tell you another thing, not going to give you another bit of advice. You don't want to hear it, and I don't deserve to say it. Not anymore. But regardless of what you think or what you believe, I want you to know this: you better get your ass out of this state, and fast."

Paul was still staring at the bag.

"We got an agreement?" Arlen said.

"How'd you get this?"

"Don't worry about that. It's my concern. The money, though, is yours. And it's enough to take you far from here and put you up for a time. Be smart with it, though. Use it to get yourself set in a way…" He stopped then and shook his head. "Hell, I just said I was done telling you what you ought to do, and here I go again. I'll shut my mouth now. But you take that money and tuck it down in your bags and let's go. You ready to do that?"

Paul nodded. He seemed to have gone pale at the sight of the money. When he swallowed, it looked like it took some effort.

"Okay," he said. "Yeah, I'm ready."

Arlen hung back and sat with Owen while Paul got his bags together, moving slowly, as if his limbs had gone numb. Rebecca came back out of the kitchen and watched him ready his gear.

"You can't even stay for a meal?" she said. She was speaking to Arlen.

He shook his head. "Faster we move, the better. Aren't going to be trains going through if we let it get much later."

"Long drive to the station, too," she murmured. She'd already given him instructions on how to get there. With no train station left in Corridor County, it would take some time. Might be longer than an hour, with rain like this.

Paul straightened and looked around as if he had no idea what to say or do next. He knew there was something playing out in the room that he wasn't privy to, but in the end he decided not to ask. He just said, "You all take care."

Rebecca crossed the room and hugged him. He bristled for an instant, as if he wanted to resist, but then he returned the embrace, and Arlen saw him, for just an instant, close his eyes exactly as Arlen had done back in the kitchen.

"Take care," Paul repeated, and then he stepped away.

They went outside and splashed through the yard and climbed into the truck. There was another band of storms passing over now, and the thunder was so loud and close that for a moment Arlen didn't even realize the truck's motor had caught. Once he had it in gear, he cast a backward glance at the Cypress House, the top half dark, the bottom lit, Rebecca's silhouette in the window, watching them. He saw her lift a hand, and he lifted his own, though he knew she could not see it.

The road was a washout of gleaming silver rainwater, and the truck's tires spun once in the wet mud and threatened to bog down before finding enough purchase to push ahead. It was the hardest rain Arlen had seen since the hurricane they'd come in with. Seemed fitting to take Paul out in the same weather.

Paul was quiet until they got to the paved road. Then he said, "You going to steal that money or earn it by working for him on some crooked thing?"

Arlen didn't look at him, didn't answer.

Paul said, "Arlen, if I'm traveling with those dollars in my pocket, I ought to know how they were gained."

"You know damn well. They belong to Wade. You think they came to him honest?"

"But how did *you* get them?"

"Don't trouble yourself none over that. Just take them and go on. You have an idea of where you might go?"

"Not really."

"Could try that Carnegie school you've talked of," Arlen said. "Don't know how much money would be needed for such a thing, but I imagine that's a hell of a start."

"It is." Paul's tone had changed, the sharp edge dulling as they drove farther into the swamp woods. "Arlen, what are you going to do?"

He stayed silent, wondering whether any harm could come from the boy knowing the plan. If they caught up with him, Tate McGrath or somebody else entirely, would ignorance help? Arlen didn't figure it would. Not at that point.

"I'm going to kill him," he said finally. They'd just passed their first car, the road fading back to darkness as soon as its headlights went by.

"Wade?"

Arlen nodded.

"Are you crazy? What do you mean, you're going to kill him?"

Rebecca had said it was an hour's drive to the train station. That was time to tell it. Arlen figured it might as well be told.

"You remember the day McGrath came at you with that chair leg?"

"Of course."

"You remember the box Wade brought with them that day?"

"Yes."

"Good," Arlen said. "Let me tell you what was inside. It's as good a place to start as any I know."

They drove along through the darkness and the rain and Arlen explained it all, starting with the night he'd retrieved the box containing Walter Sorenson's hands from the sea. He explained about Rebecca and Owen's father and the threats that had been made to Rebecca while her brother was in prison.

"There's plenty of evidence as to what happens when a man tries to run from Solomon Wade," Arlen said. "More than enough evidence for me. I'm not going to leave him behind to chase her. I can't."

"When are you going to do it?"

"Tomorrow."

"*Tomorrow?*"

"That's when the Cubans are coming in," Arlen said. "It'll have to be done then or he'll miss his money. We'll need that money to have a chance."

Paul dropped his eyes to the bag on his lap. "How much is there? Total."

"Ten."

"You gave me half?"

"That's right."

"Why? I'm not doing a thing. You're giving me half that money and setting me out a day before anything's to happen?"

"Hell, yes, I am," Arlen said. "I don't give a damn what you care to believe, because I know that it is true: you'll die at that man's hand if you stay in this place. All your words of argument aren't going to change the truth of it."

But Paul didn't offer any words of argument. Instead he said, "Rebecca told me about your father," in a soft voice.

"I heard that."

Paul looked up. "Is it true?"

"It's true."

"She told me about France, too," he said. "The things you claimed you saw..."

"Claimed" you saw. Still not believing.

"Tell you something about that," Arlen said. "The worst things I saw there were the real ones. A man with smoke-eyes, he could still be saved, time to time. The others, though? The fields I walked through stacked with corpses? Those men's chances had passed, Paul."

Paul didn't say anything. Arlen knew he didn't believe it, and that was fine. He'd long ago lost the hope of convincing people to believe him. Some might for a time — Paul had once, Rebecca seemed to now — but most wouldn't or couldn't, and he'd made peace with the realization that all he could do was provide help. Tonight was more of that.

You're going to need to believe.

His father's words floated across the years to him now, the sight of his bearded face and those eyes that had looked so soft, so gentle in the moment that he'd uttered his final sentences to his son.

He told you that, Arlen thought, *and you've spent the rest of your days trying to convince others to believe you, but you still won't believe him. That's what Rebecca doesn't understand. How come you can't believe him?*

It was a question with an easy answer, but Arlen had avoided facing that answer head-on for years and would continue to do so. If his father had been telling the truth, then his death out there in the cold wind and the dust, well, it had been at Arlen's hand every bit as much as Edwin Main's. Arlen had gone and brought that death home, had sought it out and betrayed his own family and...

He was crazy, Arlen thought with so much vehemence that he nearly said it aloud. *What he believed, no man should. You can't speak to the dead. Those who try are fools, and those who claim to... well, they're a shade darker.*

They came to a crossroads unmarked by signs, but Rebecca had described it and he knew to turn left, north. They were probably twenty minutes from the next town now, from the train station. The rain was slackening, but the lightning had picked back up, illuminating the countryside in ghoulish flashes.

"You might put some of those dollars in an envelope and send them to your mother," Arlen said. "If you need it all, fine. But she was used to your CCC checks. Don't forget your family, no matter how they seem to you."

Paul didn't answer. Arlen knew his days of influence with the young man were past, but he couldn't help himself, not now that more cars were passing and the woods were broken here and there by clusters of homes, making it clear that they were nearing the town. This would be the last he'd see of him, and he couldn't hold back from offering advice even when he knew he should not.

"You keep a sharp eye out for a time to come," he said. "I expect you'll never be looked for, never be connected to what we do. But there's a chance, and you better be ready for it. Get far from this place and live quiet for a time. Keep your head up and your eyes open. If they send somebody, you'll need help, and you'll need it fast. I hope they don't send anybody."

His voice went a little unsteady at that, and he cleared his throat loudly and blinked at another flash of lightning.

"I want you to know," he said, "I didn't plan on her."

Paul turned and looked at him, didn't say a word.

"It wasn't a decision I made," Arlen said. "What I did to get you to leave was, and maybe it was the wrong one. She always thought it was. I just thought...I needed you to leave. But I didn't plan on her. All right?"

Silence.

Arlen nodded as if Paul had offered some response, and drove on through the dark.

"We've got the money," Paul said eventually. "Maybe you left half of it back there, but I've got five thousand in this bag. We could get on a train together. Isn't any reason you'd have to kill him. We could head out together, same as we came in."

All the bristle that he'd carried since his return was gone. He sounded, once again, like the boy Arlen had met at Flagg Mountain, the boy who'd conceived of the concrete chute that saved them who knew how much money and time. It made something in Arlen loosen and sag a little, knowing that the old Paul was still in there. It was a hell of a thing, the way a simple change in tone of voice could hit you. The idea that he'd be willing to leave this place at Arlen's side, after everything that had happened, stilled the words in Arlen's throat.

"I appreciate that," he said finally. It was an odd thing to say. Awkward, formal.

"But you won't do it."

"When I leave here," Arlen said softly, "it's going to be with her. It'll have to be with her. I can't go any other way."

Paul went silent. Arlen thought again of the night they'd spent sleeping on the broken boards of the boathouse, the way the boy had told him he couldn't leave her behind, and he felt hot shame spread throughout his body.

I can't help it, he wanted to say. *You'd think we're supposed to be matched up one by one, and the matching would be easy. You'd know her for certain when you saw her, and she'd know you. That's how easy it should be. It isn't, though. It isn't, and I'm sorry.*

They'd crossed into the outskirts of the town now, and train tracks had appeared parallel to the road. Up ahead the lights of the station were visible. There was a locomotive spitting easy, gentle smoke from its stack. Warming, ready to take to the rails and head north. Last train for the night.

Paul said, "You can't kill Solomon Wade tomorrow."

"Don't you worry on it," Arlen said. "I'll do what needs to be done. You just look out for yourself. I'm sorry for the way it's come to pass, sorry for a hell of a lot of things, but—"

"No," Paul said, shaking his head. "You *can't* kill him tomorrow, Arlen. You'll be jailed if you try. You'll likely be jailed anyhow."

"The least of my concerns is the law," Arlen said. He was bringing the truck in close to the station, slowing. "The good sheriff of Corridor County is a threat, but not the jailing kind of threat."

"It won't be the sheriff," Paul said. "It'll be a team of treasury agents from Miami and Tampa."

Arlen brought the truck to a stop as the train whistle blew. He turned and looked at Paul and didn't speak. The boy's face was pale.

"There will be two boats on the water and more than a dozen men on land, watching every step you take," Paul said.

"What are you talking about?"

Paul lifted his head and met Arlen's eyes. "I wanted to hurt you," he said. "And her. How I wanted to hurt her."

"What in the hell are you—"

"I didn't come back because I had nowhere else to go," Paul said. "I came back because I thought I could see you put in jail."

44

T HE TRAIN LEFT while he told it. They both watched it pull
away and chug north, and neither of them commented.

He'd made it to Hillsborough County's CCC camp. That part
was true enough. The rest of it had been a lie — had he desired to
stay on at the camp, he could have. And would have. At least until
his third day there, when a pair of unfamiliar men in suits showed
up with a visitor from Corridor County: Thomas Barrett.

"The shopkeep?" Arlen said.

"Yes. He's been working with them for nearly a year."

"Working with *who*?"

"Federal Bureau of Narcotics," Paul said. "That's what they
told me at least. I guess they approached him because he was at
odds with Tolliver."

He surely was — had run against him for sheriff. Arlen
thought back on the drive he'd made to the lumberyard with
Barrett, and he could see it easy enough. If they'd wanted to
enlist a local to help, Barrett made plenty of sense.

"At first all they wanted to do was talk to me," Paul said. "Find out what I'd seen and heard. But I kept asking questions, said I wouldn't tell them a thing unless I knew the situation, and once they told me . . ."

"You saw it was a chance to hurt us. Just like we'd hurt you."

Paul didn't say anything, but he nodded.

"Why in the hell haven't they gone to Rebecca?" Arlen said. "She'd have helped."

"Barrett doesn't trust her. Said her father was close with Wade, and her brother was, too, and that she'd just come on down and fallen right in with them."

She had done that. At least from an outsider's view.

"It was her brother," Arlen said. "Damn it, they were as good as holding him hostage even though he was in prison."

"That's not how the agents saw it," Paul said. "What Barrett and the others told me was she's as bad as any of them."

"You actually believed it?"

Paul looked away. "Wanted to at least."

"So what's about to come down on us?" Arlen said. "What have you done?"

Paul winced at that, then said, "They'll be watching tomorrow night for the boat coming in. Barrett already told them Wade wouldn't be there himself. That he keeps his distance. So they'll arrest everyone else and lock them up and push the charges hard, hoping they can get more information, more evidence."

"You were to have been there," Arlen said.

Paul nodded.

"You'd have watched us go off in handcuffs."

Paul couldn't look at him now, and Arlen gave a slow shake of his head and then cranked the window down and lit a cigarette. The rain was still falling but without the wind to push it, and the air was cooler now.

"I guess we had you pretty well soured if you could do a thing like that."

"It's why I told you," Paul said softly, head down.

"You were mighty close to letting us run right into that hornet's nest," Arlen said. "Why didn't you?"

Paul looked up at him. "Because you said you couldn't leave her behind. Not even with all this. That made it...I don't know. It meant something, that's all. It meant something."

Arlen nodded and smoked and thought. After a time he said, "When you hiked up the road today, you went to report in with Barrett."

"Yes."

"So they know exactly what the plan is. They know, and they'll be watching."

"Yes."

"If we were to leave," Arlen said, "all of us, leave tonight, there wouldn't be anybody left for them to arrest but McGrath and the Cubans."

"I suppose not."

"But that wouldn't give them much. Because the Cubans won't come in without the light signal, and McGrath and his boys won't be holding a damn thing that's of value — no money, no dope."

Paul didn't answer.

"And then they'd all be looking for us," Arlen said. "These government agents who are counting on you, for one. Solomon Wade, for another. By then he'll know exactly what was set up, and he'll know who did it."

"So what do we do?" Paul said.

Arlen raised his eyebrows and blew smoke and held his hands up, palms raised. "That's the question, Brickhill. And I'll be damned if I have a good answer. We go ahead with what we had planned, we'll all end the day in jail. We could go to Barrett and tell him we want to help. Or we could warn Wade of what's about to commence, gain his trust, and hold the fight till another day."

"They think Owen and Wade are awful close," Paul said. "That's why they held me off coming back as long as they did. They wanted Owen to be there. Wanted me to try and get in good with him."

"They were close," Arlen said, "until Owen found out Wade had been using him against Rebecca. Until he found out the son of a bitch had his father killed."

"So what do we do?" Paul repeated.

Arlen smashed the cigarette out on the door frame and tossed it into the street and started the truck again.

"We go back," he said. "And let everyone have their say."

It was more a case of letting everyone have their silence than their say, though. When he showed up with Paul still in tow, Rebecca and Owen were surprised, to say the least. When he let the kid tell what he'd been helping to arrange, they went from surprised to stunned. Even Owen didn't mouth off much. Just shook his head like he didn't believe it and poured himself a glass of whiskey, which he let sit untouched.

"I swear," he said, "it was an easier fix I had at Raiford."

"From the sound of it," Arlen said, "your return there can be arranged easily enough."

Rebecca gave him a sharp look, and he shrugged. She got up from her chair and went to the window and stared out into the darkness as if the agents were already circling through the woods, watching. Hell, maybe they were.

"We can leave now," she said. "We've got the money. We can leave now, and then they can all tangle together tomorrow and forget we ever existed."

"I don't reckon they'll forget," Arlen said. "Not a one of them, on either side. They'll be at our heels by sundown. And when it comes to that, we'd best hope for the law to catch us first."

"You go, then. You and Paul. You've done nothing wrong. This trouble belongs to no one but Cadys."

Arlen said, "No." Quiet but firm. She turned to look at him, and Owen did the same, and he looked from one to the other and shook his head.

"All right," Owen said, "then what in the hell do you propose?"

He'd been thinking on that for the whole hour's silent drive back from the train station. None of the options was appealing, but only one made any real sense to him.

"We've got to go to Barrett," he said, "and offer to help."

"According to Paul, we're the ones he's intending to arrest," she said.

"That might be the case right now. But he's not entirely ignorant—it's Wade he's really after. He thinks removing the two of you might help him get to Wade. We'll have to convince him you don't need to be jailed to do that. In fact, you're a hell of a lot more help to him out of jail than in it."

Rebecca looked at Owen, uncertain.

"I've helped them," she said. "I've handled his money and allowed my property to be used for any number of horrible things, and I've not said a word."

"Because you feared for your brother," Arlen said.

"You understand that," she said. "Will they?"

"I expect they might."

"So then we end up working for them against him."

"That's right."

She didn't answer.

"You don't think they're good enough, do you?" Arlen said.

"They're not," Owen said. He'd been listening with a distant stare and that untouched glass of whiskey near his hand.

"You can't say that for sure."

"The hell I can't. You know how long Solomon's been running this part of the state? You don't think the law's taken some shots at him before this? Taken some shots at the Italians he's in with down in Tampa, and at the boys in New Orleans? Shit, that's all they do, take shots at men like that. And year after year some of them go under. Wade, though? Wade gets stronger."

"Well, maybe," Arlen said, "this is his year."

They were all quiet again. The rain had finally ceased altogether, and the wind was flat and all that could be heard was the ticking of the mantelpiece clock and, very soft, the breakers out on the beach.

"He'll listen," Paul said.

They all turned to look at him.

"Barrett," he said. "He'll listen to you. He'll understand."

"You haven't been around long enough to guess at who can be trusted and who can't," Owen said.

"I think I have. And I can tell you this: Arlen was right. Barrett and those that he's working for, they want Solomon Wade. All you and Rebecca are to them is a chance to work toward him. They'd do most anything to arrest him, I think. The way Barrett told it to me, Wade's near impossible to get at because of the way he isolates himself. Both by living in a place like this and by having people like…" He hesitated, then finished, "…people like you do his dirty work."

"You *know* that's true," Arlen said. "That's the way he runs his show, sure enough. And if they understand that much, then they ought to be able to believe what we have to say. Hell, they may have seen it before."

Owen blew out a held breath and leaned over and picked up the whiskey glass for the first time, drank until it was half gone.

"All right," he said. "Let's give it hell, then."

Arlen nodded. "We'll go in the morning. First thing."

"To Barrett?"

He nodded again.

Rebecca said, "Owen should wait. I'll go alone."

Arlen cocked his head and frowned. "I expect they're going to want to talk with him, too. You can't do his bidding for him."

"I don't intend to. But by tomorrow, the police might not be the only ones watching. The two of us go into Barrett's store and stay there long enough, or go off to wherever he'll take us next, we'll be seen. And on a day like tomorrow, that's not something we want. Not all of us. Wade's placed his trust in Owen, and he knows that I won't do anything to jeopardize my brother. So as long as Owen stays here, we'll keep them at ease."

Owen said, "She's right," but Arlen was already nodding.

"Okay," he said. "But I'll go with you. We'll see Barrett together. First thing in the morning."

"First thing in the morning," she echoed, and with that Owen raised his glass and drained the rest of the whiskey. He didn't say a word, but his face was the color of the stones that lined the fireplace behind him.

45

DAWN BROKE WITH A gorgeous crimson sunrise. No trace of the night's rains remained, but all that red in the east was a warning sky. They ate a quiet breakfast as the sun cleared the treetops and filled the yard with warm light, and then Arlen said, "Well, we best be to it, don't you think?"

Rebecca nodded. "You'll both stay here?" she said to Owen and Paul.

"Sure," Owen said. "Just another day." But then he cleared his throat and said, without looking at her, "How are we fixed in the way of guns?"

Everyone was quiet for a moment. Then she said, "Why on earth—"

"It's a good question," Arlen interrupted, "and a good idea. Leave him one of the pistols. We'll take the other. There are rifles on the boat."

She didn't seem to like it, but she went upstairs and returned with the Smith & Wesson revolvers. Owen accepted one, and Arlen took the other.

"All right," Arlen said. "Y'all keep a weather eye out till we're back. Could be we're coming back alone, could be with a few police."

Owen said, "Best not do that."

Arlen frowned. "I expect they'll see it the other way."

"Maybe so," Owen said, "but anybody who sets foot on this property today will be seen. You make them aware of that."

Rebecca said, "We should take the money with us."

"Why?" Arlen asked.

"Show of good faith to Barrett. He's not going to just believe us out of the good nature of his heart. We have to have something that backs up our story."

"What if someone comes looking for the money?" Owen said. "What if Solomon sends Tolliver or Tate to check on me? What in the hell am I supposed to tell them?"

It wasn't a bad point. Arlen thought about it, then said, "Okay, we leave half here, in that case Tolliver brought it down in. It doesn't seem likely that they'll actually count it. They trust you."

He hoped.

There was nothing else to be said then, nothing else to be done except for Arlen and Rebecca to drive down the road and put this day in motion. Arlen turned to Paul, who looked up and met his eyes. He felt as if he should say something, offer some word of caution or advice, but none came to mind, so he settled for another nod, which Paul returned. Then he and Rebecca went out into the yard — Arlen tucking the pistol into his belt and guarding it with his arm, conscious of what Owen had said about watchers — and got into the truck. The golden light of the morning sun picked up Rebecca's hair and made it shimmer as she sat behind the wheel and cast him an exhausted gaze.

"This will help?" she said. "Won't it?"

"Yes," he said. Then she started the truck and they were off.

They didn't say much as they rode, but once, she reached out for his hand across the cab. Her jaw was set and her face calm.

She had firm bracings within her, he knew. After watching her deal with the hurricane and Wade and the delivery of that damned cigar box, he knew that awfully well. They'd hold today, just as they'd held before. He wasn't worried about her.

Owen was more of a question. He didn't seem enamored with the plan, no doubt had a con's natural disfavor of anything that involved cooperation with the law. So long as he stayed put at the inn and nobody came looking for him, though, there shouldn't be trouble. Arlen wished Paul had left already, boarded that final train of the night, but after the revelation he'd shared just before its departure, that had hardly been an option.

The roads were empty. Arlen watched the mirrors for a following car but saw none. He tended to agree with Owen, though; McGrath and his sons were keeping an eye on the activity at the Cypress House.

The garage doors were up at Barrett's service station, his day already begun. Rebecca parked in front, and they opened the door and saw the pretty Indian girl behind the counter again. The inside of the shop smelled of tobacco and molasses, already thick with humidity.

Barrett's wife nodded a hello to them, but before Rebecca could say a word the door from the garage opened and Barrett stepped inside. He'd seen them come in, Arlen could tell that from the way he entered, and for just a second something flickered in his face, a quick look of unease. Then he folded it beneath one of those grins of his and said, "Mornin'. What has y'all up so early?"

"Is there someplace we could talk in private?" Rebecca said.

He frowned. "Something the matter?"

"Should anyone else happen by," she said, "I doubt you'll want this conversation overheard."

He gave up the game right then. Arlen expected he'd drag it out a bit, but instead he just nodded like he'd been expecting this and said, "The boy talked."

"Because he needed to," Arlen said. "He might've saved some lives, Barrett. You got no idea what sort of operation you're putting into action tonight."

"No?" Barrett's jaw worked, anger showing in his eyes, and then he said, "Okay, follow me."

He walked across the warped floorboards and back through the door into the garage. His wife didn't say a word as they passed, but she looked noticeably tense, her eyes on the road as if she expected to see someone at their heels already. Arlen cast a look back at her as he went through the door and saw that there was a small revolver on a shelf beneath the cash register.

Barrett tugged the overhead garage doors down, sealing them in the dank, musty room. He put a stool in front of Rebecca and then sat on a stack of tires by the far wall. Arlen stood.

"I could have y'all arrested right now," Barrett said. "And maybe I still will. But I'll hear it first."

"It's her story," Arlen said, "so I'll let her do the telling. But let's make something clear at the start—you want Wade. Not Rebecca, not Owen, not McGrath. You're after Wade and Tolliver."

"I want to clean the trash out of this county, and I'll do that one at a time if I need to."

Arlen said, "Really?"

Barrett held his eyes for a long time and then said, "I want Wade."

"Okay," Arlen said. "Well, we're the best chance you've got of getting him. And a damn sight less useful in jail than out."

"I could reach a different conclusion."

"You won't," Arlen said, and then he nodded to Rebecca. "Tell it."

She told it. Started with her father and wound through the past six months and the threats that had been levied at her brother.

When she got to the part about Wade delivering Sorenson's hands, Barrett's face darkened, and he said, "You let that pass? You took evidence and tossed it into the sea? That's the level of cooperation you care to show?"

"Cooperation with whom?" she shot back. "Was I supposed to call Tolliver? All you were to me was another local. And, I thought, a friend. Back then I didn't know you were waiting to lock me up."

He scowled and put a cigarette in his mouth but didn't light it. "Go on."

She went on. Up through Owen's return and Paul's last-minute disclosure. Then she showed him the bag with the five thousand dollars. Barrett accepted the money in the way Paul had—as if too harsh a touch would cause it to vanish. He studied the bills, and then he put them back into the bag and returned them to her.

"Stealing from Wade isn't a real bright idea," he said. "You been around here long enough to know that."

"Well," Arlen said, "you see, I intended to kill him. Today."

Barrett stared at him.

"Yes," Arlen said. "Believe it. We didn't see any other way to get out of this. Now we're hoping you're the way."

Barrett took the unlit cigarette out of his mouth and blew out a long breath, then rubbed a hand over his face.

"There are fifteen agents coming in tonight," he said. "Two boats on the water, five cars on the roads. We had it set."

"What you'd have gotten," Arlen said, "was Owen for money-handling, and the McGraths for dope-handling. Maybe you could have thrown something at Rebecca. I'm sure you would have. And, if your boys had been paying enough attention, you'd have had me for murder."

Barrett looked at him in silence.

"You could run the operation tonight," Arlen said, "and get

the same things. Except don't count on me to kill Wade now. It wouldn't seem prudent."

That actually raised a smile, however faint.

"We could still get the McGraths," Barrett said. "If I can convince the boys from Tampa to trust you, then we'll still come away with the McGraths."

"Is that enough?" Arlen said.

"They're damned dangerous men. And important to Wade."

"But will they help you? Will they tell you anything that can help? I don't see Tate McGrath rolling on Wade."

Barrett's silence confirmed that he didn't see it either.

"You can help, though," he said eventually. "Rebecca can help. You've got plenty to tell. And are Sorenson's hands still around?"

"They are," Rebecca said.

"Well, that's something."

"Is it?" Arlen said. "Seems to me he could lawyer his way out. You got two witnesses who say he brought them in. He'll find at least one, McGrath, who will say that box was filled with chocolates when he dropped it off for Rebecca."

"Yeah," Barrett said softly.

"You've got to get him with something solid," Arlen said. "Get him with his hand actually in the jar. And it doesn't sound like he reaches in too often. Not with his own hand."

"You're saying we let it go off without a hitch?" Barrett said. "Let them bring in their dope and take it out in trucks, without saying a word? It ain't going to happen. Trust me on that. The badges in Tampa aren't going to let it happen."

"Look," Arlen said, "what it boils down to is this: without us, nothing happens tonight. You don't get a damned thing, except for maybe the Cubans. Maybe. You don't get anybody in Corridor County, that's for sure. With us, you can get the McGraths. That leaves Wade, though, and it also leaves him knowing damn well who set him up. So what do we do then? Shake your hand and go on our way and wait for him to cut our throats?"

Barrett sighed and got to his feet, setting the cigarette down carefully on the edge of the tire.

"Let me call Tampa," he said. "I'm not authorized to decide such a thing."

He went back inside the shop, and they could hear him speaking in low tones to his wife. Then it went quiet. Arlen put his hand on Rebecca's shoulder. She touched it briefly with her own but didn't look at him.

They'd been in the garage with Barrett for maybe an hour, and already the morning sun had faded beneath gray clouds. It would rain again today. Barrett was gone for about twenty minutes before he stepped back inside. He closed the door and leaned against it and studied them.

"Tampa's ready to grant you immunity," he said, "provided you keep the exchange in motion tonight. If you derail it—if *anything* derails it—they'll come at you with charges."

"That's a hell of a fair thing," Arlen said. "More of tonight is out of our control than is in it."

Barrett shrugged. "They aren't impressed with your story."

"Aren't *impressed* with it?" Rebecca said. "They aren't *impressed* with the idea that this man, this *judge,* murdered my father, murdered Walter Sorenson, threatened my brother, threatened me? They aren't—"

Arlen put his hand on her shoulder again, and she stopped and shook her head, her mouth tight with anger.

"Look," Barrett said, "I think it's a square deal. All you've got to do is make sure things get off as they're supposed to. That's on your brother more than you. He's the one running the show, right?"

Rebecca nodded.

"Well, make sure he runs it right," Barrett said, "and then you're good. You can watch in shock and surprise when the McGraths are arrested."

"That'll be awfully convincing," Arlen said, "when they're arrested and we're not."

"Oh, you will be."

Rebecca said, *"What?"* but Arlen finally began to get it, and he nodded.

"This is how you remove us from Wade," he said. "Anything else, and he smells the truth. If we all go down, he can't be sure who the leak is."

"That's right. And you'll be jailed out of county. You and the McGraths."

"We'll be jailed?" Rebecca said.

"Only on paper," Barrett said. "It all works right, we'll get you out of here and to someplace safe. But you've got to testify against him when it comes time."

She looked at Arlen, and he turned his palms up. "I don't like it either," he said. "But I don't see another way."

Barrett nodded. "Your man's right. There ain't no other way. Not at this point."

There'd been another way, and it was the way Arlen had been planning on until Paul's disclosure. He wasn't convinced yet that it hadn't been a better plan either. A man like Wade was easier to kill than he was to convict.

"So we just go home now?" Rebecca said. "That's the plan?"

"Not just yet," Barrett said. "First we wait on Tampa. There are a few men coming up who'd like to meet you. I think they'll have some paperwork."

"And what will that say?"

"That you're protected," Barrett said, "provided tonight's little game plays out like it was supposed to."

46

THEY SAT AROUND THE GARAGE as the heat seared in and choked the air and Barrett continued to ask questions. The longer he went at it, the more Arlen thought that he would probably make a damned fine lawman. He played all the right notes. The harder his edge, the more he was bluffing you; the more casual he got, the more focused his interest. Rebecca answered everything he had for her. Told him details of her time at the Cypress House down to the last ounce of morphine. She hid nothing.

"Let me ask you something, Barrett," Arlen said after nearly an hour had passed. "You didn't so much as blink when Rebecca told you that she had Walt Sorenson's hands in a cigar box."

"Didn't surprise me at all. Wade's men have done worse than that."

"Surely they have. But it doesn't seem like you believed Sorenson died in that Auburn of his."

Barrett didn't answer.

"There was a body inside that car," Arlen said. "Whose was it?"

325

Barrett studied him for a long moment, then said, "George McGrath. Tate's oldest son."

Arlen looked at Rebecca and saw dim recognition on her face.

"You knew him?" he said to her.

"I've seen him. He used to come around with Tate. Most of the time, in fact. Lately, it was just Tate. Except for the night…"

"When he brought the whole family," Arlen said, thinking of the girl from Cassadaga who'd waited in Tolliver's car with handcuffs around her wrists. "That's why they all came, even the young ones. It was a family matter."

He turned to Barrett. "Who killed George McGrath? Sorenson or David Franklin?"

"I couldn't say, Wagner."

"Bullshit."

Barrett sighed. "Look, I don't know. George McGrath was, like his daddy, muscle for Solomon Wade. A thug, a killer. When someone steals from Wade, the McGraths make them accountable. Walt Sorenson had been stealing from Wade. Skimming. We *know* that. The rest… we're fairly certain of the rest."

"Wade sent the McGrath boy," Arlen said, "and Sorenson got the best of him. That's how you see it."

"That's how I'm guessing it, yes. George McGrath disappeared a full day ahead of Sorenson. A body burned in Sorenson's car, but it wasn't Sorenson's."

"So Franklin hauled the body down there," Arlen said. "And Rebecca, Paul, and I were all supposed to tell them it was Sorenson inside. That was his escape plan. Make them think he was dead, and make them uncertain of what had happened to the McGrath boy."

"That's how we figure it, yes. Problem was, they knew who they'd sent George to kill. That kept them from believing it was

Sorenson inside the car. And Sorenson..." Barrett's face went grim. "He needed them to believe that was him inside the car."

Arlen sat in silence for a minute, trying to piece it together.

"He was out driving the countryside after he'd killed the boy?" he said. "Why in the hell would he have done that? Why'd he keep making his rounds?"

"Cash," Barrett said simply. "When they went for him, he knew he'd have to run mighty far. He needed the money to do it. That last round of collections was to go right into his pockets. His, and Franklin's."

"You know all of this," Arlen said, "and yet nobody's been arrested. Nobody's been—"

"There's a powerful difference between what we know happened and what we can prove happened!" Barrett snapped. "Corridor County's full of whispers and bare of witnesses."

"That's what you're supposed to fix," Rebecca said. "Isn't it? They need a local man's help."

Barrett nodded. "They came to me almost a year ago. I was more than happy to help. Somebody round here has to."

"Many people would," Rebecca said, "if they weren't so scared of the results. And I don't know if they picked the right man for the job—you told them I was working with Wade, doing it happily. Some judge of character."

"I didn't know much about you," he said evenly, "but I knew plenty about your daddy, Rebecca, and every bone in that man's body ran crooked."

She stared at him in furious silence. Arlen watched her eyes and thought, *He's right, and she knows it. It was her old man got them into this, and he did it with a grin on his face until he saw his son arrested. By then it was too late.*

"It is not," she said, "an inherent family trait."

"I hope you're right," Barrett said.

The phone rang then, and a moment later Barrett's wife called for him. He rose and went inside to take the call. He wasn't gone long.

"That was Tampa," he said. "It's been decided that you're to go back."

"Go back?" Rebecca echoed. "I thought they wanted to see us."

"That's what they said. But the man in charge is down in Miami, a fella named Cooper, and he says it's not worth the risk of having strangers up here until the show starts. He figures the longer you're gone from your place, the more likely Wade gets edgy and calls it off. He doesn't want it called off."

It made a bit of sense, but it also left the group at the Cypress House operating on the promise of immunity granted by a shop-keep turned undercover agent. Barrett seemed to be a good man and a sharp operator, but his clout with the agency that had brought him in was minimal at best. Arlen said, "What about the papers, Barrett? The immunity?"

"You'll have to take my word."

Arlen shook his head. "I'd like some writing with that. No offense."

Barrett said, "Ain't going to be any writing, Wagner. So you'll have to make a decision. Take my word, or don't."

Arlen looked at Rebecca, who gave him a nod, deferring to him. He didn't like the situation, but he also didn't know what else he could say.

"It better be worth something," he said. "Your word."

"It always has been, and always will be."

Arlen nodded and got to his feet, and Rebecca followed. They stepped outside the store and into a thick breeze fragrant with the smell of coming rain.

"Just see that it goes off as planned," Barrett said. "All you got to do is see that..."

His voice trailed off, and when Arlen looked up, he saw that

Barrett was staring up the road. Tolliver's sheriff's car was approaching from the north. It went by slow, and Barrett lifted a hand, gave a friendly wave that wasn't returned. The car carried on down the road and then turned left. Away from the jail. Toward Solomon Wade's house.

"Just see that it goes off as planned," Barrett said again, but his voice was softer now. "And watch your asses, hear?"

He went back inside without waiting for a response.

47

I DON'T LIKE IT," Rebecca said as soon as they were in the truck again. "I don't feel good about this, Arlen. Owen and Paul out on that boat...what if there's trouble? What if people start shooting?"

"The way it was told, they're going to wait until the orange crates have been unloaded before they move," he said. "Owen and Paul should be back inside the inn by then, and we'll all stick together and out of the way until whatever trouble there is dies down."

She shook her head, unconvinced. The bagful of money was on the seat between them. Five thousand damn dollars, just sitting there. Arlen wondered how much it really meant to those nameless, faceless men in New Orleans who ran this whole show. He knew how much it would mean to most people in the world, but men like those? He really couldn't figure.

"Look," he said, "I don't like it either. But what else can we do?"

She was quiet for a mile or two, then said, "He was right, you know."

"Barrett? About what?"

"My father," she said. "I don't blame Barrett for looking at Owen and me the way he does. My father would have done anything for the right amount of money. He would have done just about anything."

"Well, you've kept your brother from being the same," Arlen said. "You see that, don't you? You've shown him the truth, and he's changed."

"I hope so," she said.

They drove west under a strange sky, dark clouds massed to the south and then split on an almost perfectly even line with clearer skies showing to the north. It was the way fronts often developed here, blowing in fast and shifting in ways that were tough for a native of the mountains like Arlen to follow. A few stray raindrops speckled the windshield, but the wind was puffing in unenthusiastic gusts, the storm front sliding away to the south this time, leaving them clear.

It seemed that way until they were a mile from the inn at least, and then the wind swung around fast and sudden and drove the clouds up over them, and the sun was hidden again and the path to the Cypress House was bathed in shadow. An armadillo waddled along the dirt road, indifferent to the truck that nearly ended its life. They broke out of the trees and the inn came into view, the sea beyond it caught between light and dark beneath the shifting cloud front. Owen's convertible was parked where it had been when they left, and there was no sign of visitors. Everything looked calm.

"What time is it?" Rebecca asked.

"Nearly noon."

"And the boat's supposed to come in after dark. Around nine is what Owen said."

"Right."

"So we've got one afternoon left," she said as they stepped out of the truck and faced the inn. "That may be it. That may truly be the last time I spend here."

She stood on the hill and looked down at the inn as the sky continued to darken and the wind pushed the Cypress House sign back and forth on creaking hinges. A pair of gulls shrieked as they flew over the roof and then vanished down toward the beach, where a large wave blew in with a cloud of spray and an angry snarl.

"I won't miss it," she said. "Not one bit."

"We'll get you to Maine," Arlen said. "I promise."

She smiled faintly and took his hand and squeezed it, and then they walked down to the inn together. Up the front steps as the sign continued its rhythmic creaking, like a porch swing on a hazy summer afternoon in some sleepy, happy town, and then they were through the door and into the barroom. Arlen was carrying the money bag. The lights were off and it was dark with the sudden cloud cover, and Rebecca called, "Owen? Paul?" as they came in. Arlen closed the door behind them. The latch had just clicked when she screamed.

He'd had his eyes down, but now he raised them. Looked across the room and through the windows to the back porch. Saw Owen Cady's body dangling in the wind, upside down, a wide dark gash torn through the center of his throat.

48

THERE WAS A ROPE knotted around his ankles, holding his feet together, secured to someplace on the roof. Probably the widow's walk. His hair hung straight down, matted here and there with blood. There were also streaks of blood tracing his jaw and lining his face. Either the wound had been very fresh when they'd hung him up or they'd cut his throat with him in that position.

Rebecca screamed again, calling out his name this time in an anguished howl, and then she ran for the porch. Arlen grabbed at her arm and missed, and then he dropped the bag of cash and followed as she burst through the back door. The wind pushed her brother's corpse closer to her before his weight swung it away again, a gentle pendulum motion. She said *Owen,* this time so soft it could scarcely be heard, and then dropped to her knees on the porch.

Arlen knelt and held her in silence, thinking, *Paul, where is Paul?* as the body swung back and forth and Owen Cady's blood dried in his hair, an occasional drip still plinking off the floor-boards, where a pool of it had gathered.

"Get inside," he said, looking away from the corpse and out to the open beach and realizing for the first time how exposed they were. "Come on."

She was unresponsive but didn't fight him. He tugged her inside and let her go again, and she slumped back to the floor. He let her drop, looking around the room and seeing now what he hadn't at first, when the body occupied all of his focus—a single chair turned over, a broken glass, two gashes in the front wall surely left by bullets.

The gun was still in the truck. He said, "Wait here, Rebecca, please wait," and then ran across the room and through the door and out to the truck. When he had the gun in his hand, he closed the door and straightened slowly, took a long, panning gaze around him. It was a different sort of look than he'd given in many years, a battlefield survey, everything significant now and everything potentially threatening. All around the Cypress House, it was quiet but for the wind and the gulls and the creaking of the sign.

He shouted, "Paul!"

Silence.

"Paul!"

Silence.

"Damn them," he said, and his voice shook a little now. "Damn them."

He went back through the yard and inside the house. Rebecca was still on the floor, but now she'd lifted her hands to cover her face. When she spoke, her voice was muffled.

"What?" Arlen said.

"Get him down," she said, and this time he heard it through the sobs. "Please get him down."

He laid his hand on her back. "Rebecca, we've got to get out of—"

"Get him down!"

He straightened. "All right." Logic screamed at him to get her the hell away from here immediately, back to Barrett before the bastards who'd done this showed up again, but instinct told him they were gone now and wouldn't be coming back. Where was Paul, though?

"We can't leave him like that," Rebecca said, not looking up, her voice heavy with tears. "We can't."

"I'm going for him," Arlen said.

He stepped out onto the porch and gave the beach another one of those slow, panning stares, saw nothing but sand and shells and water. Just as it always had been. There were no indentations in the beach where a boat had been put in. Anyone coming from the water would have used the inlet.

He stepped over to the dangling corpse, taking care to avoid the blood, and dragged a porch chair behind him. Then he climbed onto it and took hold of Owen's legs, making sure to keep his eyes on the shoes and not look down into the poor dead kid's face.

I didn't see it in you, he thought. *I'm sorry. It wasn't there this morning. Something changed after we left. I couldn't have warned you. I wish I could have, but I couldn't. I'm sorry.*

He was thinking this as he took a firm hold of Owen's legs and drew his pocketknife out. At the touch of the dead body, he thought of Paul Brickhill and said, in a whisper, "I'm coming for you, Paul. I don't know if there's time left, but I'm coming for you."

He lifted the knife to the rope as he said the words, and when the response came he nearly sawed through his own finger.

There's time.

Two words, spoken right in his ear, right inside his damned head. He stumbled and fell from the chair, upending it. The gun was on the porch rail, and he snatched it up.

Nothing but silence now. Those two words only a memory.

He turned and pointed the gun in first one direction and then the other, still backing away from the body, and saw nothing, heard nothing.

It had been Owen's voice.

"No," Arlen said softly. "No, it wasn't."

But it was.

For a moment he was frozen there, but then the sound of Rebecca's sobbing from inside shook him loose, and he stepped up to the body again. This time he didn't touch Owen's legs but reached higher on the rope. He grasped the lower portion of the cord with his left hand and sawed away above it with his right, and eventually the rope parted and the body was deadweight tugging his arm down. He let him go as gently as he could, laid him on the porch in his own blood. Then he picked up the gun again and went back inside.

"He's down," he said gently, kneeling beside Rebecca and lifting her face so he could see her eyes. He regretted it as soon as he got a glimpse of the terrible pain trapped in them. "He's resting easy now, okay? But I've got to go have a look around. I've got to see..."

"Paul," she said.

"Yeah." He got to his feet again and flicked open the cylinder on the gun, checked the load, then spun it shut and walked to the stairs. It was very dark inside now, lights off and the clouds thickening, and he went up the steps in the gloom with the gun held out in front of him. Five rooms upstairs, five checks, five views of undisturbed furniture.

Back downstairs, he saw Rebecca crawling out onto the porch. He frowned, not wanting her to see that sight again. It was her brother, though, and if she was going to insist on seeing him, he wouldn't stop her. He followed her onto the porch and pressed the gun into her hand and said, "Here. Use it if anyone comes. I'm going down to check the boathouse for Paul. Then we have to leave."

She didn't answer. He dropped her hand and she held on to the gun and stared out at the ocean. He watched for a few seconds and then told himself that there was nothing to be done for her right now, left the porch and jogged down to the boathouse.

It was incomplete, no roof on it yet, the smell of sawdust mingling with the brine of the sea and decaying fish. He checked the boathouse and walked the length of the dock and stared into the water and saw nothing. The boat was where it had been. He looked at it for a minute, hesitating. He didn't want to take the time to go out to it, but he remembered that it was where Rebecca's father had been left six months earlier, and maybe the act had been repeated with Paul.

He dragged the rowboat into the water, splashing out in a hurry, thinking that they'd been here for far too long already, and then he rowed out to the fishing boat and climbed aboard. Empty. Before he left he took the two rifles from the gun rack and tossed them down into the boat. They were loaded, but he didn't see any additional shells and couldn't take the time for a thorough search. When he reached the beach again, he carried a rifle in each hand as he jogged up the path to the Cypress House. Even the gulls were gone now; nothing could be heard but the waves. Any trace of that clear sky had vanished.

When he got back to the porch, he saw she was standing and was glad of that until she turned to him and said, "Why didn't you know?"

"What?"

"You're supposed to know!" she shouted, her face streaked with tears but her blue eyes alight with anger. "You're supposed to see it coming! To be able to warn, to be able to stop it, why couldn't you stop it!"

She'd rushed toward him with her hands raised as if she were going to strike him but fell into him instead and began to sob.

"Why couldn't you stop it?"

"I didn't see anything," he said. "I'm so sorry, Rebecca. There was nothing there this morning. Something changed. Whatever happened...whoever came for him...they weren't coming when we left this morning. Death wasn't close to him then."

The truth of that caught him, and he realized what it meant.

Someone had told Wade recently. Had they been coming to kill this morning, he should have been able to look into Owen's eyes and see the promise of death there. But he hadn't, and he thought now of the long delay Barrett's federal contact had put them through, all of them sitting around the garage waiting for an arrival that never came, and understood the source of the leak. It wasn't Barrett; it was someone in Tampa or Miami. The man who'd sent them back. What was his name? Cooper.

Rebecca was still crying against his chest and he wanted to hold her, but he had a rifle in each hand.

"Find out who did it," she said.

For a moment he didn't respond, just stood there numbly. Then he dropped the rifles and wrapped his arms around her and said, "I will. I promise. But right now we need to—"

"No," she said, her lips moving against his neck, which was now wet with her tears, "find out now. Talk to him."

"Rebecca...what are you—"

"You can speak to him," she cried, pushing away from Arlen to look into his eyes. "You know you can, you can do it just like your father did."

He shook his head, reaching for her again, but she stepped away.

"That's not real," he said. "I'm sorry, but that isn't real, it can't be done."

"Yes, it can!" she shouted.

He wanted to argue, but those two words — *There's time* — were trapped in his brain and with them the certainty that it was true, always had been true, his father's gift was real and it was also his own.

"Owen's dead," he said in an unsteady voice. "He's gone."

"I know that. But you can hear him."

She began to cry again then, and he held her for a while. He did not let her go on long, though. There wasn't time. He pushed her back from him and said, "Come on."

"What about Owen?"

"There's nothing to be done."

"We can't just leave him here. We can't —"

"I'll see to him," he said. "But you're leaving."

She shook her head, and he said, "Yes. You're leaving. You have to."

He took her unresponsive fingers and tugged her down off the porch and into the inn, retrieved the bag of money from where it lay on the floor, and then led her all the way up to the truck. She wore a face he'd seen often during the war after the shells had stopped, and he knew that her mind was not entirely her own anymore. That would pass, and when it did the real agony would sink its teeth into her. For now, though, it was better that she be this way.

He opened the door to the truck and helped her inside. She didn't say a word, just followed his guidance, and then, when she was behind the wheel, turned and looked at him with questioning eyes, as if she didn't understand.

"I've got to go for him," Arlen said. "For Paul. I can't leave him behind."

"Don't make me go on alone," she said, and for a moment his resolve nearly evaporated. He looked back at the house and the dark clouds blowing in off the sea and thought of Paul Brickhill and shook his head.

"I can't leave him."

"I'll stay with you."

"No." He leaned into the truck and put the bag in her lap. Then he took her face gently in his hands and forced her to meet his eyes. "You've got five thousand dollars. You can get to Maine easy. But drive fast and drive steady. You need to get far from here."

"What? I can't—"

"What's left here?" he said. "They've killed him, Rebecca. Your brother is gone. They'll come for you next."

She was silent, her lips parted, eyes hazy.

"Was there a town in Maine?" he said.

"What?"

"Where you wanted to go. Was there a specific town?"

She blinked at him, as if she no longer recognized his face, and then said, "Camden. I wanted to go to Camden."

"Then go," he said. "Find your way there. Drive careful and keep the pistol at hand. If anyone tries to stop you, use it."

"I can't. Don't send me on my own. I can't go alone."

"It's not done yet," he said. "When it is, I'll join you. But I'm not running out on that boy, Rebecca. He's with them. With the same men who murdered Owen."

At the sound of her brother's name, she winced.

"I'll go to Barrett," she said.

"It was going to Barrett," Arlen said, "that led to this. Maybe it wasn't him directly, but it was damn sure the men he's working with. You can't go to him. You need to leave, and you need to leave now."

She didn't answer.

"Drive north," Arlen said, and then he stepped back from her. "I'll find you. I'll catch up soon enough."

"Arlen, no."

But he'd closed the door, and now he held it shut and looked through the window and into her eyes and said, "Rebecca, you have to go."

She was silent, staring at him through the glass. He said, "I'll settle up for him. Believe that. I'll put an end to it. To them. Then I will find you."

She started the engine. He let go of the door and stepped back and lifted his hand in a parting wave. Then he turned and walked down to the house and her brother's body to make good on his promise.

49

By the time the sound of the truck's engine was gone, he stood above the corpse as a freshening sea breeze pushed the salt smell toward him and rustled the portions of Owen's blond hair that were not held down by dried blood.

"All right," Arlen said in a whisper, his throat thick with tension. "Let's give it a try."

He'd merely had to touch Owen's legs the first time. He could try that much again.

He knelt on the porch beside the body and reached out and laid his right hand against Owen Cady's calf. He felt no warmth through the pant leg. Just stiff, unresponsive flesh.

Let me hear you again, he thought. *Speak again. Let's see if I can hear it.*

He heard nothing, felt nothing.

All right, speak aloud, then. He wet his lips and said, very softly, "Owen?"

Nothing. This was the height of insanity, so damned foolish it was—

You're going to need to try harder.

It was Owen's voice again, reaching Arlen like a piece of ice laid gently on the back of his neck. He sat there on the porch with his hand on the boy's leg and didn't move, didn't speak.

"What do you mean, try harder?" he said finally. His voice was a whisper.

I'm farther from you now.

Arlen took his hand away and sat back on his heels and wiped his hand over his forehead. It came back slick with cold sweat. He had an idea. Or a memory, really. He moved forward, laid a hand on each of Owen's shoulders, and looked down into his face. The gray, blood-streaked flesh showed nothing. He hesitated for a moment and then reached out and, very gently, used his thumbs to lift Owen's eyelids. They rose just a touch, a trace of blue showing, and at the sight Arlen's chest tightened, making the simple act of breathing difficult. He forced himself to look into the eyes, his hands still on Owen's shoulders, and then he spoke again. A little louder this time, a little more forceful. As if he believed.

"All right," he said. "I'm trying. Come back to me, damn it. Come back."

I'm here.

It was beyond eerie, that voice. Beyond anything Arlen had ever heard or even imagined. It floated up from within his own brain, but it was so clear, the voice so recognizable. His mouth was dry and his words croaked. He cleared his throat and tried again.

"Tell me," he said, and the familiar old phrase sent an electric shiver over his skin. "Tell me what happened."

They knew.

"Knew what?" he said. "That we were setting them up?"

Yes.

The wind gusted hard and with a strange touch of cool to it as a loud wave broke on the beach, and Arlen wanted nothing more than to remove his hands and get the hell off this porch, join

343

Rebecca and drive and drive until they were far from this terrible place. He took a moment to will the urge down, and then he asked his next question.

"Who did it? Who came for you?"

He didn't get a response this time. It felt as if a whisper slid through his brain, but it came too quick and too soft, and then he saw that Owen's eyelids had fallen shut again, and he reached out and opened them. Peeled them back farther this time, saw more of the blue, felt something cold and sickly melt through his stomach at the sight.

"Who came for you?" he asked again.

McGraths. Tate and one of his sons. They came up the inlet by boat, and Tolliver came in by car. I went out to talk to Tolliver. While I was doing that, the McGraths snuck around from the inlet. I heard Paul shout.

The voice stopped then, and Arlen squeezed the boy's shoulders and said, "Tell me. Keep telling me."

I pulled the gun and ran back. Tolliver drew his, but he didn't shoot, he just chased me, and I came back inside and they had Paul and I fired twice. I didn't hit anything. I had a bead on Tate, I was ready to kill him, but Tolliver got to me first. Tackled me. Then Tate was on me. I think Tolliver intended to take me alive, but I'd fired at Tate, and so when he came, he came with the knife.

The voice was fading, like a radio signal going steadily weaker, and Arlen leaned closer to the dead boy's face and squeezed his shoulders.

"What happened to Paul?" he said. "Please tell me."

They took him.

"Is he dead?" Arlen's voice was louder now, but he couldn't help it. The moment had taken on the feel of a fever dream. A sudden, terrible headache had sprung to life in his skull, and his face was bathed in cold sweat. The world was unsteady around him. It was hard, holding the line open. It was damn hard.

Not yet.

"Where is he?"

With the McGraths.

"Why haven't they killed him?"

They need to find out who he talked to. Who's involved. They'll wait for Wade. He'll want to be there for the questioning.

"Who told them?" Arlen said. "Was it Barrett?"

Don't know.

The voice was so damn faint, so hard to hear. He squeezed Owen's shoulders and realized he was now hanging directly over the body. A drop of sweat fell from his chin and onto the dead boy's face.

"Tell me what to do," he said. "Can he be saved?"

I don't know. You have to get my sister away. They'll come for her next. For you, and for her. They'll come for you all. He won't let anyone stand now. Not after this.

"She's gone. I've sent her away. She's driving north."

Arlen's breath was coming fast and ragged now. The physical toll was something he didn't understand, but it was fierce, his body responding as if he were pushing through a long, arduous march. His muscles ached and his head throbbed and that chilled sweat ran from every pore.

Good, Owen said. *She can't stay here. Neither can you.*

"But Paul..."

I don't know. Maybe. There's still time. But there's also more death to come. More than mine. If you stay, death stays with you. I'm certain of it. Follow my sister. Go with her now, and go fast.

Arlen thought about that as the waves broke and the wind pushed off the Gulf in puffs and put a crisp skim over the pool of blood beneath him.

"Paul is with the McGraths?" he said.

Yes.

"And he is alive?"

Right now. But there's so much death around him.

"Can you get me to them?" Arlen said. "Can you guide me?" He was speaking with his lips almost at the boy's ear now, could smell the coppery scent of blood. Each time Owen spoke, the voice was fainter.

I can.

The headache flared with a sudden, unbearable agony, and he had to release his hold and lean away from the body. The pain relented then, but he was awash in perspiration and felt a trembling exhaustion through every muscle, an odd dizzy sensation on top of it all, as if he'd gone too long with too little air.

"I'm sorry," he said, leaning forward and grasping the boy's shoulders one more time. "I'm so sorry."

I know. A whisper now, scarcely audible.

"I'll set it right," Arlen said. The wind rose in another sweeping gust and sprinkled a few raindrops across the porch, and suddenly he felt alone and was aware, for the first time in several minutes, that he was staring into a dead man's eyes. The reality of that had just vanished for a time; he hadn't been seeing much at all, really, just hearing it. It was like entering a trance, but now something had pushed him away from it, back into reality.

"You're slipping from me," he said.

I can't hold here long, Owen Cady's voice whispered from somewhere outside of time and place. *You don't know how to keep me here.*

"I'm trying."

Yes. But you can't do it yet.

So soft. Almost gone. Arlen said, "You take care. Wherever it is you're bound, ride easy."

That was all. Arlen could feel it when he left. The sweating stopped, dried quickly on his skin, and the sounds of the real world returned, the calls of the gulls and the rustle of the palm fronds and the creak of the shifting house.

His father could hold the dead with him longer. Could find them easier. How had he done it?

You could have asked him, Arlen thought, *but you didn't. You refused to believe a word of his tales, and now what guidance you might have had is gone. You've got his parting words — an instruction that you have to believe, and a promise that love lingers. That's all. You'd best make it enough.*

Paul was still alive. Temporarily at least. They'd taken him, but they'd taken him alive. He might still die today. But if Paul went, Arlen would see that he didn't go alone.

He straightened up from the body. He didn't want to leave Owen here untended but saw no other choice. He went inside the inn, thinking he'd fetch a blanket and cover him with it. The smallest of token gestures, but it was something. He had taken maybe ten steps through the dark room before he glanced at his own reflection in the mirror behind the bar and came to a stop.

The man looking back at him from the glass was a skeleton. He stared at it, motionless, and then he slowly lifted his hand to test the image. The man in the mirror moved with him, bone fingers fluttering in the glass. Arlen wet lips that had suddenly gone dry, and when he did it, the man in the mirror flicked a black tongue out and ran it over bare, unprotected teeth.

If you stay, death stays with you, Owen had said. *I'm certain of it.*

He turned from the mirror and looked out the window, to the drive from where Rebecca had left not long ago.

Follow my sister, Owen had told him.

But he'd also said that Paul was still alive.

Arlen kept his eyes away from the mirrors as he crossed the room and found the keys for the convertible. Kept his eyes away from the mirrors as he went upstairs and retrieved a blanket. Kept his eyes away from the mirrors when he came back down and went outside. He knelt at Owen's side and closed his eyelids one final time, then draped the blanket over him and wrapped it so that the wind would not tug it free. When he was finished, he rose and gathered both rifles and looked them over. Springfield M1903 model. Twin guns. Rebecca and Owen's father had probably purchased a pair of them at the same time he'd bought the two pistols. They were good weapons. They'd ended plenty of lives over the years. Such was the standard of good weapons.

He tugged open the bolts and made sure each rifle was already loaded with five .30-caliber shells. The guns could bury those bullets a foot deep into the trunk of a pine tree from six hundred yards away. The last time Arlen had held one, it had a bayonet fixed to the barrel.

He slammed the bolts closed and hefted a rifle in each hand and gave a final look down at the covered corpse near his feet. Then he walked off the porch and around the house and out to the convertible. The clouds were dark and ponderous overhead, but no rain fell. He laid the guns in the backseat and got behind the wheel and started the engine. It was a powerful motor, would be a fast car. He didn't know where he was going, but Owen had said he could guide him, and he believed that. He saw no reason for a dead man to lie.

Before he put the car into gear, he moved his eyes to the rearview mirror. The light was strange and shifting under the clouds, but his eyes looked like they had a skim of frost over them. He took a matchbook from his pocket and lit a match and held it up to his face, leaned closer to the mirror.

His eyes were filled with white smoke. It drifted out of the sockets and mingled with the smoke from the match and swirled up into the sky and the storm clouds above. He took a long look at his own eyes, and then he blew out the match and dropped the car into gear and pressed firmly on the gas.

Part Four

DEAD MAN'S ERRANDS

50

THE CLOUDS THICKENED and continued to hide the sun, but the rain held off. It was as if the storm were being kept at bay, and angry about it. The skies contained menace that hadn't been able to break through, just bathed the world below in shadow and trapped the heat and humidity close to the ground. Arlen took the dirt road all the way to the end, came out at the T-intersection with the paved road and thought, *What now?*

He turned left. There was no conscious decision, no reason for going left instead of right, he just looked in each direction and felt his foot leave the brake and return to the gas when his eyes locked on the windswept gray moss that dangled from cypress trees ahead to the north.

He's guiding me, he thought. *Owen's guiding me.*

He didn't know how, but he felt confident in it, had a strange assurance that this was the right route, that it would lead him to Paul.

The wind picked up as he drove under the cypress grove, and a piece of Spanish moss drifted down in a lazy arc and landed in the passenger seat beside him. It was just past one now but so dark it felt like dusk. The arrival of the Cuban boat was still eight hours away. If it showed up at all. He had a feeling it would not, that word would have been passed somehow, and everything Barrett and the others waited for would not transpire.

Rebecca was on this same road, somewhere well ahead of him. She would have a few hours at least before they began to look for the truck.

And then I'll catch up with her, he tried to think, but a single glance in the rearview mirror revealed the smoke in his eyes.

He would not see her again.

It was an agonizing thought. He'd never feared death. Had, at times in his life, longed for it. But those were in days past, days before her.

It was right for him to bear such a loss, though. It was needed. He thought of how he'd laid his hands on Owen Cady's shoulders and looked into his dead eyes and heard his voice so clearly, heard the truth from him, and he remembered his boyhood trip down to the Fayette County sheriff and the way his father's blood had pooled in the dust, and he knew that all things circled back in time. You paid for your sins, and he would pay for his today.

As he drove down the road, he reached into the backseat and moved one of the rifles up front with him, braced it against his leg with the barrel pointed down and the stock and trigger close at hand.

The car drove beautifully; Solomon Wade had a fine taste in machines. Arlen was holding it close to seventy. Twice he passed other cars moving at half that speed, saw drivers lift hands in annoyance and surprise, and blew by them and continued on. He'd gone at least five miles headed due north, passing two intersections without much pause, certain somehow that they held no significance, before he reached a four-way and again found himself turning left without thought or reason. The pavement soon disappeared and he banged onto a dirt road. The water from the previous night's rains had not drained well here, and he splashed through deep puddles and spun the tires through soft mud. Thunder rippled to the south, but there was no lightning and the wind was still. He tried to keep the speed up, but the road was deeply pocked and rutted, and he was afraid he'd rattle the wheels right off the car. He felt one solitary raindrop find his forehead as the road narrowed into what looked like a thin green tunnel. The strange bird-of-paradise plants pressed close, their wide green fronds stretching toward the sky in search of sunlight.

"Where am I going?" he said aloud, hoping for an answer, hoping that Owen's voice might reach him even here. There was nothing but silence, though. The road wound on and on, and no sign of humanity existed, just that green jungle.

He'd believed in each move he'd made in the car, believed that the dead man was guiding him, but what if that was all a foolish trick of the mind and he was driving away from Paul? His doubt grew as the road led him farther into the woods and farther from anyplace he knew, and he dropped the speed off again so the car was moving at a crawl and began to consider turning around. The road was so damn narrow that such a feat would be difficult. There were tire tracks in the mud and hoofprints from horses, but what did that prove? Only that someone had come this way; it didn't have to be the McGraths.

A stretch of muddy water showed through the trees then, a creek winding into the woods. Arlen studied it, saw that while it was narrow it was also deep, and remembered the boat from the inlet the day he'd been up repairing the roof just after the hurricane. Tate McGrath. And Owen had said the McGraths emerged from the inlet today.

"It's the right place," he said. "You're getting me there, aren't you?"

Again, no answer. He wished he could hear him, or at least feel him, know that he wasn't making this ride alone, but there was nothing. He had to take it on faith, had to believe, and the sight of the water made that easier.

He drove on, and a rickety wooden bridge appeared ahead. It was many years old. Arlen wasn't sure it could even support the weight of the car, but then his eyes drifted ahead and what he saw made that concern vanish.

There was a car coming his way. It had just rounded a bend well ahead of him and was approaching the bridge, driving at a slow speed. Arlen pushed the brake all the way down and stayed where he was, watching it come on. When it passed out of the shadows and took on enough clarity, he recognized it—the county sheriff's car. Tolliver.

He felt his breathing slow, felt his muscles go liquid and soft, the way they once had in fields far from this country, and he wrapped his hand around the walnut stock of the Springfield and waited.

The sheriff's car had slowed when the driver spotted Arlen, but it kept coming on, up to the edge of the wooden bridge, which was maybe a hundred yards ahead, and then stopped. Arlen could see Tolliver clearly now, the big man riding behind the wheel with one hand out of sight. Surely resting on a gun, the same as Arlen's was. Only Tolliver's gun was a pistol, and it didn't have the range to do damage until he crossed that bridge. The Springfield had plenty.

They'll hear the shot, Arlen thought. *He's come from a good ways off, but not so far that they won't hear the shot.*

Tolliver's car lurched forward again, out of the mud and toward the old bridge, and Arlen knew that the sound of the shot was going to be the least of his concerns if he let him drive on.

He engaged the parking brake and rose up as the sheriff's car spun mud and neared the bridge. Put one knee on the seat to support himself and then cleared the Springfield and rested it across the frame of the windshield. The engine of the sheriff's car howled with a sudden increase in gas as Tolliver saw the weapon and realized what was coming. Arlen dropped his face and pressed his cheek against the smooth stock of the rifle and gazed down the barrel. The car was driving fast but still centered; until it cleared the bridge, Tolliver couldn't maneuver to the right or to the left. Arlen let the front wheels find the boards of the bridge and then he exhaled a slow, patient breath and focused right-center on the windshield and squeezed the trigger. The gun gave a gentle buck in his arms, an old but unforgotten sensation, and then he ejected the shell and closed the bolt and fired again. There were three shots left in the Springfield, but he didn't need to use them. The car gave a last lurch forward and then the growl of the engine dropped off, and the car rolled slowly down from the bridge and came to a stop in the mud. The engine was still running, but no foot remained on the gas pedal. Tolliver was out of sight. He'd fallen sideways, down onto the passenger seat.

Arlen left the convertible running, climbed out and jogged toward the sheriff's car with the gun held out in front of him and the mud sucking at his boots. When he got close enough, he dropped to a knee and pointed the rifle at the passenger door and waited. Tolliver could be baiting him, could rise up with the pistol in his hand the moment Arlen reached for the door handle.

He didn't rise, though. The two .30-caliber bullets from the Springfield had landed true; there were twin holes cracked through the windshield, inches apart, fractured glass surrounding them just above the steering wheel. Arlen gave it a few more seconds, listening to the engine run, and then he saw something drip out of the car near the base of the door frame. Blood.

At the sight of it, he rose and walked to the passenger door and pulled it open, holding the Springfield against his side with a finger on the trigger. Tolliver's wide body was jammed between the dashboard and the passenger seat, shoulders wedged tight. Blood pooled on the floor beneath him, and a thin stream of it ran out onto Arlen's boots when the door was opened. Arlen could see the big man's back shudder. Trying to breathe. Not gone yet.

There was a pistol on the driver's seat, the weapon Tolliver had held when the bullets found him. Arlen reached over and picked it up and slid the barrel through his belt. Then he took a handful of the sheriff's shirt and hauled him out of the car and down into the mud.

Not a sound had come from anywhere up the road. The shots from the Springfield had been loud, though, and Arlen suspected the McGraths could move as silently as they chose through these woods. He kept his back against the car, protected, as he rolled Tolliver over. He had to set the rifle down to do it; the sheriff must have gone every bit of two fifty. When Arlen got him over, he saw the holes punched through him, one high on the right side, blown through the collarbone, and another lower and centered. Tolliver gave a long blink, smoke billowing out from under his eyelids, moved his lips like a fish searching for water, and then he died. Arlen knew the moment that he went; he'd watched enough men find that moment in the past.

Arlen said, "Bad news, buddy: you can't hide from me that easy."

He left the rifle leaning against the car, and then he reached down and cupped each side of Tolliver's head with his hands, lifted the dead man's face and looked into his eyes.

"Come on back now," he said, "and tell me how many they are."

You'll never cross this bridge again.

This voice was nothing like Owen's had been. Recognizable as Tolliver's, yes, but changed, gone dark and twisted. As Arlen held the dead sheriff's head in his hands, the man's flesh drained of color, went white as sand under moonlight, as if every ounce of blood had been pulled away. Arlen felt a shiver ride through him and nearly dropped Tolliver and stepped back. He held his position, though, swallowed, and said, "I didn't ask about crossing the bridge. I asked how many they are."

Don't understand this game, do you? Tolliver's ghost whispered. *We ain't all here to help you, friend. Just because you can reach us doesn't mean we're required to help.*

Arlen didn't say anything. Tolliver's blood was running with the slope of his torso, dripping down his throat in warm rivulets and caressing the sides of Arlen's hands.

You're a good shot, Tolliver said. *Tate's better.*

"We're about to find out," Arlen said.

Hell, yes, you will. That man's as natural a killer as I've ever seen. More natural than a rattlesnake, more natural than a shark. You ain't never seen his like. And there isn't a life that old boy values but his sons. You? You're partnered up with them that killed one of his sons. I'd call that a death warrant.

The world had begun to spin around Arlen. He was holding his focus on Tolliver's eyes, but outside of that center everything was in motion, a whirl of trees and sky and colors. This wasn't like talking to Owen at all. It felt like being lost in a terrible fever.

"Is Wade with them?"

Not yet. But he'll be riding close soon enough. He'll see you before the end of your time, and then you'll wish you'd not come this way.

A high, harsh hum was in Arlen's ears now, coming in waves, like a pulse, and he squeezed his eyes shut and grimaced. When he opened them again, the hum was louder and the world seemed draped with fog. He could see nothing beyond Tolliver's face, could hear nothing but that hum, and ...

Let him go.

It wasn't Tolliver speaking. A familiar voice, but not Tolliver. Was it Owen Cady? No, it seemed to come from a time much longer ago than that. So familiar, though. So damn familiar. Whose voice was it? How could he—

Let him go.

forget a voice like that, so deep and strong and full of command? He knew its source, knew it well, but here in the fog and the hum everything was lost. If he could only remember the—

Let him go, son.

Isaac? No. It couldn't be. How could a man so long dead reach and find Arlen now and tell him...

The instruction finally registered. He had to let Tolliver go. He dropped his hands from the sheriff's head and fell back against the car with a gasp as a searing rod of pain drilled through his chest.

A bullet, he thought. *I've just been shot.*

But there was no bullet, and the pain passed. He closed his eyes and opened them again and drew in a deep breath, and now the world was steady except for a tingle on his hands where Tolliver's blood stained his skin. He wiped them on his pants, looking down at the dead man and realizing what had nearly happened—Tolliver had been holding him here. Arlen had opened the contact, maybe, but Tolliver had nearly closed it, and that trancelike state that Arlen had entered with Owen could have turned deadly this time. He'd been unable to see anything around him, unable to hear, would have been utterly unable to defend himself if he hadn't released the body and stepped back. The longer he'd held on to Tolliver, the longer he'd tried to keep that corridor open, the deeper he'd sunk into the trance. He might have stayed there in the road for a long time.

That was his father's voice. He was damn near certain of it, and somehow it chilled him more than any of the others.

This was a dangerous game. Wasn't as simple as talking. There was more to it than that, and what Tolliver had said had been the truth — the dead weren't required to help him. The ability to reach them wasn't necessarily a good thing.

He stood up now and stepped over the body with the rifle in his hands, scanned the road ahead and the woods and the creek, watching and listening and holding his finger tight against the trigger.

There was no one in sight, no sound that wasn't natural. He stepped back to the front of the car and put his hand on the hood. The engine was still running, and it was running hot. Tolliver might have come a longer way than Arlen had initially suspected. It could be that the McGraths remained unaware of his presence here. Or it could be that the engine always idled hot, and Arlen's time was running dangerously short already.

He went through the inside of the car quickly, searching for weapons. There were none except the pistol he'd already taken from the sheriff, but he did find two pairs of handcuffs. There was also a length of tow chain in the back, outfitted with a lock. Arlen hung the handcuffs off the other side of his belt, opposite the pistol, and then stepped back and looked down at the body, saw Tolliver's big hands stretched open in the dirt and remembered the beating the sheriff had given him in the jail while Solomon Wade leaned against the bars and watched wordlessly.

He'll be riding close soon enough, Tolliver had said. Wade was on his way.

Arlen thought about that and then turned and studied the trees that grew thick alongside the road on either side of the bridge. There was one limb that was low enough and stout enough for his purposes. He'd have to hurry, though. He reckoned if the McGraths had held Paul alive for this long, they'd continue to do so until Wade arrived, but he couldn't afford to be caught on the road like this.

He backed the sheriff's car off the bridge and pulled it far enough away that the road was clear for the convertible, which he drove over the bridge and parked behind the sheriff's car before climbing out again. It took him only two tries to toss one end of the tow chain over the limb, and then he lowered it until both ends were on the road. It was just long enough. He took one set of handcuffs and wrapped them around Tolliver's ankles, then fastened them together. Dragged the body over and fastened the chain to the cuffs, then pushed Tolliver's body into the ditch and went back to the convertible and fastened the free end of the chain to the back bumper. When he climbed in this time, he drove very slowly, pulling forward inch by inch. The chain tightened and began to slide over the tree limb, and then Tolliver's feet were tugged into the air. There was a short hitch as the chain hung up on something, and Arlen pushed harder on the gas pedal, driving the car into the weedy, rutted ditch. The chain slid free again, and Tolliver's bulk was hoisted into the air.

He kept the car moving until the sheriff was dangling about four feet over the road, upside down, his body swinging just as Owen Cady's had. Blood dripped off the corpse and found the muddy road below. It would be the first thing visible for a driver who rounded the bend.

"Come on down, Wade," Arlen said softly as he got out of the convertible and went back to the sheriff's car, positioning himself behind the wheel with the rifle across his lap. "Come on down."

He cast one look in the rearview mirror before he drove on, saw the dark sky and the body swinging in the wind, and the smoke — thicker now, darker — in his own eyes.

He was close.

51

THE ROAD RAN DOWNHILL over the bridge, and the ground on either side grew marshy, black puddles lining the ditches and tangled mangrove roots visible farther out, where the creek curled around and followed the road. He went at least another mile without seeing a thing, and the distance reassured him — it was unlikely that the McGraths had heard anything of the gunfire at the bridge.

Finally the road hooked to the right and narrowed even more, and there he shut off the engine and got out of the car. He couldn't see a house yet but felt he must be close. For a moment he knelt beside the car and listened and watched. The trees gave him nothing but wind rustle and birdcalls. Water lapped against the shore just through the woods, the creek riding high after the previous day's downpour. The way the sky looked, another was due soon enough. He wished the rain would begin to fall; it would offer sound cover that he needed. So far, though, the clouds had just continued to build and darken without letting loose. There was occasional thunder, but it was well to the south.

He started forward on foot. It was awkward moving with a rifle in each hand and the pistol and handcuffs on his belt, but he'd rather have all the weapons if it came to that sort of fire-fight. Empty one Springfield, drop it and pick up the second, empty that and roll on to the pistol. If he ran that dry, too, he probably wouldn't have much need to reload one way or another.

Here the road was so deeply wooded that it was almost dark. The trees pressed close on every side and the wind roused them to a constant rasping sound that unsettled him because the noise was so damn close. It was one of the things he didn't like about this part of the country; the leaves were right at your side, not well overhead. A rustle in the leaves fifty feet above you was less disturbing than one ten inches to your left.

He didn't even consider leaving the road and venturing into the woods. It would slow him down and make him noisier. Even though they likely hadn't heard the gunfire, the McGraths would be ready for trouble. It was a day of trouble, and they were well aware of that by now.

To his right the woods opened up, and he could see the creek merging with the mangroves, creating a knee-deep swamp of tangled roots that looked like hundreds of frozen snakes. He came to the bottom of the gentle slope, and then the dirt road rose again and he could see the first building just ahead.

It was a shed or barn of some sort, with a hide stretched over the wall. A dark gray skin, probably a boar. There was the smell of smoke from that building, but he couldn't see any. Whatever fire had burned there was extinguished now. Farther on he could see the roof of another building, this one a cabin, long and low. He pushed down into the weeds and dropped to his knees, felt moisture soak through his trousers. He laid one Springfield in the weeds and brought the other up and held it against his thigh.

There were voices coming from up ahead but not from inside the cabin. He thought they might be at first, but then his sense of the place corrected and he realized they were coming from below the cabin, out of sight to him but close to the creek. He heard the thump of boots on boards and the sound of a splash and realized there must be a dock of some sort down there.

How many sons did Tate McGrath have? There'd been three with him the night they'd come to the Cypress House. If all of them were with him now, that meant four enemies to contend with. Unless there were others. Neighbors, cousins, collaborators of some sort. Hell, maybe even men from New Orleans by now, maybe the Cubans themselves. Could be a dozen down there.

He pushed farther down from the road, water bubbling up and soaking his boots and pants. Pointed the rifle at the cabin and squinted down the barrel and liked what he saw. He could pick men off quickly if they'd just walk out there and stand around. It hadn't been so long since he'd fired a Springfield rapidly that he'd forgotten how it was done.

First he had to bring them out, though.

He waited a few more minutes, heard those muffled voices but saw nothing, and then he slid back out of the wet ditch and returned up the edge of the road, walking backward and holding the gun high. He left the second Springfield tucked down in the weeds. He could find it again if he needed it.

His focus coming up the road was on the sheriff's car. Particularly the windshield. He wanted to see how close you had to be before the bullet holes were obvious. Here in the shadows, he found it was better than he'd expected. Even knowing they were there, he had to close to within about a hundred feet before they became obvious.

The sheriff's car was the only bit of cover he had, the only touch of confusion. He figured there were two ways to approach this: One was to slip right up into the homestead and start shooting. The other was with a bit of a ruse. He knew he could take some bodies down with the first approach, but taking bodies down wasn't enough. He had to get to Paul, and doing that required finding out where the boy was. Once the shooting started, nobody would be volunteering that information.

The only time he'd seen the sons at all had been the day they arrived at the Cypress House to avenge their brother's death, and then it had been Tate who did all the talking. Likewise, it had been Tate who dealt with Wade, Tate who traveled with Wade. He was the decision maker, the leader. He would also, Arlen assumed, be the one who came out to see why Tolliver had returned.

Maybe not. Maybe they'd all come slinking through the woods with guns. If that were the result, the second of Arlen's options would blend quickly into the first, and he'd have to open up with the Springfields and hope the old instincts weren't far gone. But if Tate McGrath came out alone…

"Love lingers," Arlen said quietly as he opened the door of the Corridor County sheriff's car and slipped behind the wheel. They'd been his father's last words, and he hoped like hell they'd been accurate. What was it Tolliver had said of Tate McGrath? The only human lives he valued were those of his sons. Arlen intended to test the truth of that. If he could bring old Tate out to this car alone, he intended to do something that had probably never been attempted anywhere in this world before — hold hostage the living to gain the help of the dead.

52

A FEW DROPS OF RAIN splattered off the windshield as he drove, and he was momentarily hopeful that the sheltering storm would finally appear, but then the sprinkle ceased entirely. The Springfield was in his lap and the pistol on the passenger seat. He could feel warm moisture under his thighs. Tolliver's blood. The inside of the car reeked of it, a wet copper scent baked by the heat.

He drove down just short of the point where he'd left the second rifle. Just out of sight of the buildings. Nothing moved around him, but the sound of the approaching car had surely been heard, and his throat felt tight. The moment was here now. Preparations had ceased; battle would begin.

I've come out of worse places, he thought. *I was in the Belleau Wood. Will come a time when that doesn't mean anything to a soul in this country, but for those who were there, it did one of two things: killed you, or changed your perception of fear. This place doesn't scare me. Not after the Wood.*

He cast a look in the mirror, watched the smoke swirl in his eyes, and thought, *I won't be coming out of this one, though. So I should fear it even less.*

The end was here. There was a certain measure of peace in that. All that remained was a bit of unsettled work.

It was a good spot, close to the mangroves and where the creek had flooded well over its banks and turned the marshy ground into a shallow pond of shadowed water. Reeds and grasses grew tall and thick in the ditch, offering prime cover. The clouds were a roiling mass, some layers as black as fresh-laid tar, others the color of wine. Beneath them the mangrove trees stretched endlessly and cast shadows on an already dark day, the gloom so deep it seemed to be dusk.

He turned the headlights on, and their beams cut farther down the road than should have been possible during the day, harsh and white and, he hoped, distracting from the bullet holes in the windshield. They'd also draw focus away from the water and make the area just beside the car seem darker still.

As soon as the lights were on, Arlen popped open the driver's door and pushed the Springfield into the driest weeds he could find. When he glanced back up the road, he saw nothing. Tate McGrath had no doubt selected this location for his homestead because of the near impossibility of sneaking up on it, but that worked against him as well; it would be damn hard to sneak away from the cabin. Arlen would hear them when they came.

When the rifle was hidden, he put Tolliver's pistol in one hand and took out his pocketknife and opened it with the other. It wasn't a large knife, but it was a good one. Had a strong handle with a textured grip and a four-inch stainless steel blade that he worked over a whetstone regularly. He held it tight in his left hand as he leaned out of the door, then reached back inside and hit the horn with the butt of the pistol. Two short taps, then one long bleat. He hoped it sounded like a signal. He flashed the lights three times, and then he was out of the car.

He slipped down into the ditch, moving carefully into a gap between the reeds so that they wouldn't be trampled and broken down. The water soaked through his clothes and chilled him. He dipped his hand into the soil, took a palmful of thick black mud, and coated his face and neck with it. Insects buzzed over him and one mosquito drank from his forearm, but he didn't swat it away. Instead he kept his eyes on the road and on the trees.

He was quickly hidden behind the tall grass as he slid away from the gap and deeper into the water, taking care to avoid crushing the reeds in a way that would be easily spotted. He remembered the paces he'd carefully measured toward the car before he'd seen the bullet holes in the windshield and tried to match that distance. The best place he saw looked to be about eighty feet ahead of the car. He was moving as quickly as possible, keeping to a crouch so that his shoulders were submerged in the water, holding only the pistol up to keep it dry.

He was now neck-deep in the water, the same water where just a few miles downstream the girl from Cassadaga, Gwen, had been left by these very men. He positioned himself behind a thatch of reeds close to the edge of the road. He laid the pistol in the reeds, then lowered himself until his chin touched the top of the water. He was able to see up the road with his left eye only; the reeds blocked any other field of vision. The glow of the headlights cast long, empty beams into the gloom. No one appeared inside them.

He was counting on the sheriff's car, counting on it to a critical level. Tolliver was a friend, not a foe, and he'd left in this same car less than an hour earlier. His return, while unusual, should not necessarily be an indication of true trouble. Arlen's hope was that Tate would hear the horn and see the flash of the lights and perceive it to be a signal, Tolliver calling for him because something had changed. Perhaps he'd encountered Wade and had new instructions; perhaps he'd seen something he didn't like or thought of something he should have said. It might be odd for the sheriff to sit outside the homestead, but on the day he'd driven down to the Cypress House to drop off the money with Owen, he'd parked at the top of the hill and leaned on the horn. It had been pouring rain then, but rain was threatening now as well.

When he finally heard the first footstep, it crunched on brush, which meant the approaching man was walking on the side of the road and not up the middle of it. The car's horn and lights had drawn him out, but he didn't trust them yet either. Not completely.

This was good. This was as planned.

He was advancing along Arlen's side of the road. Also good, also as planned. Whoever was coming now was approaching the driver's-side door. The footsteps came on and on, and still Arlen could see nothing. He had sunk so low in the ditch that even his chin touched the water, his head buried in the thicket of reeds and painted black with mud. The footsteps were very close when they stopped entirely, and at the cessation of the sound, Arlen felt his heart go cold.

Seen? Have I been —

Crunch, crunch, crunch. The feet were on the move again, and no more than twenty paces away. Down in the water, Arlen tightened his fingers around the handle of his knife. He could see the pistol resting in the reeds and knew that he could grab it quickly, but would it be quickly enough?

You're a good shot, Tolliver's ghost had whispered. *Tate's better.*

We're about to find out, Arlen had said. Yes, they would.

He didn't want to shoot. Wanted this — *needed* this — to be a silent killing.

There was another step, and another. They seemed to be coming quicker now, with more confidence, as if the sight of the sheriff's car had proved reassuring to whoever was approaching. Arlen hadn't so much as glimpsed the man yet, but he was almost sure it would be Tate. There was only one man on the way, and he wouldn't have sent one of his sons to talk to Tolliver alone. He'd have come himself.

Right then a shadow flicked into the edge of the headlight beam, and Arlen saw a heavy canvas boot and mud-streaked trousers above. Another step forward, and now he could make out the man completely — Tate McGrath. He was walking at a fast clip, but his head was on a swivel, looking everywhere but at the sheriff's car. Guarding himself against attack, which was a wise play, but the longer he spent staring into the swamp woods, the longer it would be before he noticed the pair of bullet holes just above the steering wheel.

Tate had a knife in the sheath at his belt and a long-barreled revolver in his right hand, held down against his thigh.

Tate's better . . .

He'd certainly have the fastest draw. Arlen was going to need to move quickly, quicker than his body had in years, quicker maybe than his body was still capable of. And right now, Tate's attention was beginning to drift toward the sheriff's car.

Wait till he sees the holes, Arlen thought suddenly, an abrupt reversal of his original plan. He'd wanted to move before Tate realized someone had fired a rifle into the sheriff's car, but now he had the instinctive thought that in that one sharp second of realization, Tate's focus would narrow. For an instant at least, he'd be more aware of that car than anything else.

Tate's boots hammered into the mud and the reeds not five feet from Arlen now and came on. Down in the water, Arlen wriggled his fingers on the knife handle. The soil was soft, would make it damned difficult to push off quickly, and he gave up on the thought of trying to clear the ditch completely. No, he'd need to take Tate's legs out first and drag him down here and finish it fast. He'd need to —

McGrath's foot hitched in midair, paused and fluttered as if he were searching for a step in the dark, and as it finally descended again Arlen realized what had just happened—he'd seen the bullet holes.

Arlen blew out of the water and the reeds as the soft mud clung to his boots and tried to suck him back down, as if the land itself were Tate McGrath's ally. Had he been attempting to reach the man at full height, he'd have surely been killed, but that last decision, to go for the legs first, saved him. He got his left hand around McGrath's calf and gave a powerful yank as Tate spun with the lithe grace of a young man on a ball field, bringing the revolver around as he did it.

Don't shoot, Arlen thought, *don't shoot, I need silence, I need silence!*

Tate fired. He was falling as he pulled the trigger, and the bullet sailed well clear of Arlen, tearing into the mangroves behind them, but the damage had been done: this time there was no doubt that the gunfire had been heard.

Tate McGrath landed on his back on the dirt road and seemed to hardly feel the impact at all, was swinging the gun barrel right back toward Arlen's face when Arlen swept it aside with his left hand and lunged with his right.

Another shot rang out as Arlen sank the pocketknife into Tate's chest, buried it all the way up to the handle. He was scrambling out of the ditch now and had Tate's gun hand pinned down against the road as he pulled the knife free, a warm geyser of blood splashing his neck, and then slammed it down again, aiming higher this time, finding the heart. He leaned into this second thrust, felt the blade push in until the handle caught, and then he put his weight behind it and the handle itself pushed through the wound with the terrible sound of tearing flesh. Tate McGrath opened his mouth to let loose a howl of pain that never came.

He might be the better shot, Tolliver, Arlen thought, *but it doesn't always come down to shooting.*

He knew they'd be coming now, after the sounds of those two gunshots, and so he didn't pause at all before beginning his retreat, sliding back into the reeds with a hand around each of Tate's ankles, dragging the dead man into the water with him.

53

THE FASTEST WAY TO MOVE would be without the body, of course, but Arlen needed the body. He took Tate's revolver, dug Tolliver's out of the weeds, and pushed them both into the dead man's belt. Then he laid the Springfield across Tate's chest and backpedaled into the water, towing the corpse behind him.

Thunder crackled again, a low rumble that went on and on, as if the storm were stretching out before beginning its real work. Still to the south but closer now. Down here in the mangroves it was nearly dark, and he was grateful for that.

He couldn't see anyone approaching yet, but he also couldn't hear anyone, and that concerned him. Silence meant they were treating this with caution. If they'd all come running down the road at the sounds of the shots, he could have reduced their numbers quickly and easily.

Now, though, he knew there'd be no rash mistakes made by those who lingered up at the cabin. And that meant the dead man in his arms was going to become awfully important.

Love lingers.

He would see if it did.

Back into the mangroves he went, keeping low, floating the corpse and towing it through the water. The mud at his feet was very soft and difficult to move through, but the tangled root systems of these strange, hurricane-proof trees provided cover. He pushed back until he found a snarl of roots that twisted well out of the water, three feet at least, and then he nestled into them so that his back was to the road and Tate McGrath floated in front of him. From this position, he couldn't see a damn thing, but that was fine; no one would be able to take a shot unless they were directly in front of him, and to accomplish that they'd have to come through a hell of a lot of water. He had a little time at least, and that was what he needed. Time to talk.

He looked down at McGrath's body. The mouth was parted and showing yellowed teeth, several of them missing, and long gray hair fanned out into the swamp water. Arlen took it all in and felt awash with astonishment over the plan he'd conceived. The idea was insane, and yet he believed it could work.

Love lingers, his father had promised. If indeed it did, then Arlen was about to have a dead man's assistance.

He took the Springfield off McGrath's chest and leaned it against the tree, then kept his left hand wrapped around one of the mangrove roots, as if seeking anchor in reality, before he reached with the right and pushed Tate McGrath's eyelids up. Then he moved the hand under the dead man's back, in such a way that he could keep him upright and facing toward himself, and spoke softly but clearly.

"I'm going to kill them all. Understand that? I know you can hear it. I've reached the dead all day, and I'm reaching you now. Here's a promise, old man: I'll wipe all your sons from the earth unless you help me. Your sons, and whoever else waits up there. A wife, a daughter. Makes no difference. I'll kill them all."

There was no answer, but he felt himself begin to slip through that unseen door again. It was so strange, simultaneous sensations of falling and walls closing in, like taking a tumble into a long, narrow well. His peripheral vision went first, trembling at the edges and then going to gray, and the swamp faded until all that was left was McGrath's face. He had sullen brown eyes, and even in death they carried a feral quality. Arlen squeezed his left hand tighter against the mangrove root, not wanting a repeat of the situation that he'd fallen into with Tolliver.

"You got to speak fast, Tate," he said, his voice less steady than before. "I won't give you much chance, old boy. I'll leave you here and then I'll kill them. I'll send them to join you, if that's as you'd like it."

Nothing. Arlen's head ached and his throat was dry and now everything in the world seemed gray and wrapped in mist except for those brown eyes. He felt the bark of the mangrove root rough under his palm and tried to focus on that but couldn't, and abruptly he moved his right hand away from McGrath and let the dead man float free into the water. He drifted away slowly, and his legs sank and his torso rotated until his face had turned away. Arlen caught him and dragged him back and shoved him into the mangrove roots so that he couldn't drift far. Then he took the Springfield and lifted it, his finger on the trigger.

"All right," Arlen said, feeling weak. "I gave you a chance, you son of a bitch. Now I'm going to send your boys to join you."

He leaned around the tree, slid the barrel of the Springfield between two of the roots, and looked back up at the road. The mangroves were some of the best battle cover he'd ever encountered. He didn't like standing so deep in the water, but the root coverage was dense enough that he knew he was nearly impossible to see, and he had a decent view of the road. To his left he could make out the roof of the shed and part of the cabin beyond, but nothing else. The sheriff's car was still running where he'd left it. They'd have to head up there soon enough. They'd have to go in search of their father when he didn't return. Sort of boys the McGraths were, they might have even been able to recognize the gunshots as Tate's. Could be they figured he'd dispatched with whatever trouble had come their way. But time ticked on, and when he didn't make his way back up that road, they'd know that it hadn't been so easy, and they'd come for him.

Arlen's fatigue drained away as he waited, the physical effects of the attempt to connect with McGrath's ghost easing. Damn it, he'd thought it might work. A wild idea, to be sure, but on a day such as this, when all he'd known to be true had blown apart beneath the mortar shells of firsthand experience, wild ideas had seemed possible. *Just because you can reach us doesn't mean we're required to help,* Tolliver had whispered from the beyond, and it had been the truth. But Arlen had thought, had hoped, that perhaps he could coerce such help.

McGrath hadn't answered him, though, hadn't heeded his request or even allowed proof that whatever form of him remained could hear Arlen at all.

Come on, he thought, searching the road for McGrath's sons. *Come on, damn it, let's get on with this.*

The mosquitoes buzzed around him and drank of his blood and he forced himself not to react. The boys were out there somewhere, and they knew this swamp far better than he did.

He finally saw them. Saw one at least. And when he did, he couldn't help but feel a sense of true admiration. This man, this *boy,* he moved through the woods as quiet as a snake. He was coming up through the water just outside the reeds, and even though he was moving steadily, he'd somehow avoided Arlen's eyes until just now, when he was halfway down the length of the road. He held a shotgun in his hands, just above the waterline, and he shifted sideways here and there to avoid obstructions that Arlen couldn't even see. He was nearing the place where Arlen had once hidden in the reeds. He'd detected it somehow, had looked from a great distance away and spotted some small disturbance there that told him it was an area of danger. Unlike his father, he no longer trusted the sheriff's car, not after the gunfire.

The water eddied around Arlen, and Tate McGrath's corpse shifted in it slightly, his legs bobbing against Arlen's back, trying to sink but prevented by the roots below. As his father's body floated in the water, the boy moved on, moved like a creature of the swamp, and that, of course, was exactly what he was. Arlen watched him and thought that in his own way this boy was very much like Paul — gifted, truly and deeply gifted, at a very particular craft.

It was almost a shame that he had to die.

Arlen lowered his cheek to the stock of the Springfield, sighted, and trained the muzzle on the boy's chest. He was close enough that a headshot was possible, and Arlen thought maybe that's what he would take, even if conventional wisdom ruled against it. He'd end things quicker that way.

No.

He wasn't sure he heard the word. A whisper in his brain but so faint, so weak, that at first it seemed like a figment. Then he heard it again, and this time it was clearer and seemed pained, as if the delivery of the word came at a terrible strain. *No!*

Arlen pulled his head away from the stock of the Springfield and looked back at Tate McGrath's body. The legs were banging against Arlen, the only form of contact he had with the corpse, and the eyelids had slipped nearly closed. But he was calling to Arlen. He was calling out for a second chance.

Arlen reached out and laid a hand on McGrath's chest, close to the knife wounds, and whispered, "Come around, did you?"

Don't take that shot. Don't.

Arlen slid soundlessly back around the tree, so that he was hidden completely, and, with his hand pressed firmly on the corpse, watched the edges of the world shudder and go gray again.

"I told you I'll kill them all," he whispered, his face close to the dead man's. "I wasn't lying. You don't want me to take that shot, you best be prepared to guide me to Paul. It's the only thing that saves them."

I will.

"How many are there?"

Three. Only my boys. That's all. They're my sons. They're my —

"Owen Cady was a son," Arlen whispered.

You've settled that. Was me that killed him, and you've settled that.

"Do you have Paul? Is he here?"

Yes. Yes, he is here.

"Where? That cabin?"

No.

"Where?" He was talking in the softest whisper he could, but even that was a risk. The trance was intensifying, pulling him in deeper and pushing the real world farther away, and he couldn't afford to let it go on for long. A few more seconds, at most. If Tate wouldn't help him in that time, or couldn't, he'd let him go and kill the first of the sons. He'd have to.

Not the cabin. Other side. The creek. Under the dock.

"Under?" Arlen echoed, his voice barely audible. "He's dead? You killed him, too, you —"

Alive. In chains. We was waiting on Solomon. He'll be here soon enough.

Just as Tolliver had promised. He'd also promised that Arlen wouldn't make it back across that bridge, and the smoke in Arlen's eyes hadn't shown him to be a liar. But Paul was alive. That was all he needed to know.

The thought of Rebecca entered his mind then. For a long

time it had been held at bay by the action of battle, but now he thought of her driving north, alone, the image of her dead brother lingering in her eyes, and he felt a sense of loss more acute than any he'd felt in his life. It unsteadied him for a moment, but then he squeezed his eyes shut and made himself say, *Paul*. Had to stay focused. Had to stay at this task. It was the only one left for him, and he'd better do it well.

"You guide me," Arlen whispered to Tate McGrath. "I know that you can do it; was a dead man who guided me here. You get me to him, and those boys won't die today."

Yes. I can guide you.

"Well," Arlen said, "let's get to it."

He released the body then. Leaned back into the trunk of the mangrove and took a few deep breaths as the gray mists that had built around the edges of his eyes drifted free and the world took on clarity again. When he cautiously swung his head out around the trunk and looked for McGrath's son, he found him now almost to the place where Arlen had killed Tate. He was moving much slower now, taking inventory of the signs ahead of him and shooting occasional glances up at the car. He'd be seeing the blood by now, certainly, the blood and the bullet holes in the windshield, and trying to determine what had happened.

If Tate led Arlen in the way that Owen Cady had, Arlen wouldn't hear a voice, would operate more through an instinct that wasn't his at all, moving with confidence but without reasoning. Without known reasoning at least.

He didn't trust such a technique here. There was a whisper in the back of his mind that said a man like Tate McGrath was not to be trusted dead or alive, and that while he surely wanted to see his sons survive, he'd rather achieve that by watching Arlen perish.

So he reached back to Tate, laid his palm flat on the still-bleeding chest wound, and said, "Where?"

Walk backward. Have to put more distance between Davey and you. He knows these woods better than you, better than anyone. He'll hear you soon enough, but that shotgun in his hand don't have much range. If you don't make much of a sound you'll be able to circle down and come up behind the cabin. Need to get into the creek on the other side to get to the boy. That'll take time.

Deeper into the swamp. Some of what the dead man had said made sense, but when Arlen looked up and surveyed the brackish water extending through the trees and into the marsh beyond, he wasn't sure he liked this plan.

Could just shoot him, then. Say the hell with trying to negotiate with a dead man and kill his son right now, kill this one he'd called Davey and then keep moving and try to take the rest of them. So far he was doing just fine — two for two with Tate and Tolliver.

What Tate had said was true enough, though — his sons knew these woods, and eventually Arlen was bound to run into trouble because of it.

He hesitated only briefly and then began to backpedal, walking deeper into the marsh, moving slowly enough so that his passage was nearly soundless, even with the corpse that floated behind him. He moved in a straight line, so that the large mangrove would continue to shield him from view.

It was foolish, maybe; the awkward extra weight made every maneuver more difficult, but he also had the notion that as soon as the sons located their father's body, they'd have but one thing on their minds: killing. So long as Tate was missing, they might take a different tack. The idea that there were still two of them out there, unseen, was bothersome. After watching the first of McGrath's sons move through the water silent as an eel, he felt no degree of confidence in his ability to detect the others before they were upon him.

He was cautious with each step, the Springfield grasped in his right hand and Tate McGrath's belt in his left as he moved backward. Every now and then he turned to glance over his shoulder at what lay ahead. There was an empty stretch of water, maybe thirty feet across, and then more trees. Looked like the water grew shallow over there, which was tempting because he'd love to be out of it, but that would also make his movements noisier and his ability to tow McGrath's body nearly impossible. Again he wondered if he was making a fool's play by trusting Tate's guidance.

It was just as this thought slid through his mind that Tate's voice returned, a whisper that came from nowhere but that rang clear in Arlen's head.

Move left. He'll be seeing you soon enough otherwise. See the base of that tree what has the split in the trunk? Walk toward it. Get right down in there by the roots and wait a piece. See what he does.

Arlen pulled up short, the corpse floating against his belt, Tate's mouth open and slack, and then turned to look over his shoulder. He found the tree Tate was indicating but couldn't imagine how it would prevent his being seen. If anything, it might put him in the son's sight line.

Get moving, Tate McGrath whispered, *and you best do it quick.*

There was urgency to his voice, and Arlen decided he had to listen. This was the bargain he'd made, and the time had come to put it to the test. He walked on toward the base of the tree, and as he walked he turned so he was moving sideways, tugging Tate alongside him. He could no longer see Davey in the reeds, but he could make out the top of the sheriff's car.

Go on, Tate said, *close in now.*

Each time he spoke the world tightened on Arlen, the edges going gray, the hum coming back to his ears. He didn't like it much, wished the old bastard would stop trying to communicate. Arlen was headed exactly where he needed to be, only a few steps from the tangled roots of yet another mangrove...

He was one stride away when one of those roots moved. For an instant he froze, and then he saw another shift, the roots sliding among one another, and he realized that they weren't roots at all.

They were snakes.

Four of them at least, maybe more, a nest of water moccasins coiled at the base of this tree, the tree to which Tate McGrath had urged him. He tried to take a step back, but he was too close, the evil little creatures felt threatened now, and the first snake slid down out of the roots and struck.

It caught Tate McGrath's neck. Arlen didn't know what sort of senses snakes had beyond vision, but it was as if this one had smelled human flesh and assumed it was the enemy, had been unable to tell the dead from the living. Its fangs sunk into the side of McGrath's neck, just below his dead eyes and just inches above Arlen's hand.

The first miss was enough.

Arlen twisted the dead man in the water so that the body was between him and the snakes and watched as two more moccasins came down out of the roots and struck with stunning speed. One caught the corpse's shoulder and one the arm as the first of them pulled back and struck a second time in the neck.

Arlen snatched Tolliver's pistol from McGrath's belt, praying that the water hadn't left it useless, and then he took aim and fired.

It was mighty close range. He blew off the head of the closest snake, the one on McGrath's arm, then turned and fired at the one floating just off McGrath's shoulder as it struck forward again, this time coming at Arlen. The shot caught the fleshy body solid and dropped it into the water no more than a foot from Arlen, but still the jaws snapped, so he fired again, blowing the snake clean in half this time. By the time he turned to the one that had struck first, it was gone. He felt a cold, horrible fear — *It's under the water, it's coming right at me, I'll feel those fangs any second* — but then he saw the ripple ten feet away, watched as the snake glided into the swamp. The roots were empty now, all others gone as well, and Arlen's flesh prickled as he pictured them in the water that surrounded him.

He waded clear of the mangroves so he could see the road. Tate McGrath's son was standing in the reeds just where his father had died, and he'd turned and lifted the shotgun. When he saw Arlen, he fired. Tate had been telling the truth about one thing: the shotgun didn't have much range. It blew bark off the trees well ahead of them, but nothing touched Arlen as he lifted the Springfield and took aim.

Tate's whisper came again, urgent, clear: *No!*

"You had your chance," Arlen said aloud, and then he put his cheek to the gunstock, sighted, and pulled the trigger.

The sound was shatteringly loud in the still swamp, and McGrath's boy let out a cry as he fell. He was able to let out a cry because Arlen had sighted low instead of high and blown out the boy's legs. He was down now, down in the water and the reeds, but he was alive. He moaned and thrashed, but he did not scream again. As Arlen watched, the boy pulled himself deeper into the reeds, seeking cover. Then he put a hand out and grasped for the shotgun.

That, Arlen thought, again with some measure of admiration, *is a damn soldier right there. That's a warrior.*

And then Arlen fired again, one round into the reeds. He didn't hit anything, but the hand jerked away and the gun sank, leaving the boy unarmed.

Behind Arlen, Tate McGrath's body floated free, the flesh on the side of his neck already puffed with venom. Arlen reached out and grabbed his foot and pulled him closer. The minute he touched him, his brain was racked with the single most terrible sound he'd ever heard — a dead man's howl.

It came at him from the unknown just as Tate's whisper had before, but this was a cry, a shout of anguished pain, and Arlen jerked his hand free as if McGrath's foot had seared it. For a moment he stood where he was, waist-deep in the water, holding the Springfield and searching the rest of the swamp. When he saw nothing, he reached out again, tentatively this time. When his hand touched McGrath's calf, he said, "I told you, you bastard. It was up to you. Still is. I can see him now, and I can kill him. You know how easy I can kill him."

The boy was trying to push out of sight into the reeds but couldn't, and Arlen watched him twist and moan and said, "I was told that love lingers. I suppose you didn't have enough of it."

Don't, McGrath's ghost said. *Don't kill him. Don't you kill my boy.*

"You walked me into a nest of snakes. I'll kill them all now. I'll kill every son you have left."

No. I've told you where he is. You can find him. I'll guide you —

"You won't guide me to shit," Arlen said. He'd ducked low because as McGrath talked his vision faded again, and though the wounded boy couldn't do him harm, the others well could. He had no time for this.

I'll tell you how, McGrath whispered. *You got to use Davey. It's the only chance you have. You'll never leave this swamp without him. They'll kill you.*

"Use him?"

Get to him quick, and keep him alive. His brothers won't kill you if it means his life. That's the only —

Arlen released him and shoved him free, because the world was going too gray and the hum in his ears too loud. McGrath bobbed in the water, twisting and sinking, the side of his neck and face already grotesquely bloated with venom. Arlen watched him drift away, then looked back at the road and realized that in the last moment Tate McGrath had told him the truth.

Having that wounded boy as a hostage was his best chance.

Love lingered, all right. Tate McGrath had just needed a bit of convincing.

54

T HE BOY MCGRATH had called Davey was not making a
sound as he lay in the reeds. Arlen was certain he wasn't
dead; Arlen had probably cost him the use of a leg, maybe the leg
itself if this water was as filthy as it looked, but he hadn't shot to
kill. Anybody else, he'd have thought perhaps the silence was
due to a blackout from pain, but with this young man he imagined otherwise. He was faking death, probably, holding silent
and willing the pain aside as he hid there like an animal caught
in a trap and tried to think of a way out. His way out was in his
brothers. He knew that, and so did Arlen. The only difference
was the boy knew where they were, too. Arlen had not the faint-
est damn idea, and because of that he knew he had to move fast.

He splashed through the mangroves, heedless of the noise
because it was long past the time when noise mattered. With
every step he thought he saw snakes. If there were any, though,
they didn't strike. He was twenty feet from the reeds when the
first shot came.

A rifle, and not a large one. Maybe a .22, some old varmint
gun. It had a dry, sharp crack, not a powerful sound like the

Springfield. The bullet it fired, though, was plenty hot and plenty painful when it found Arlen's shoulder.

It burned a furrow between his left shoulder and his neck, and the pain sent him stumbling face-first into the water, and that was probably all that saved him from the next shot. He'd been looking left as he ran, up toward the houses, and had seen no one. Whoever had taken that shot was mighty fine with a rifle. Fine and cocky — they'd been looking to take a headshot and had damn near succeeded. Matter of inches.

When he hit the water, he kept moving his legs, driving forward through the mud and into the nearest cluster of mangrove roots. Two more shots came in quick succession, but they caught only the roots.

He came up spitting water and gasping with pain. He could feel hot blood on his neck and chest but didn't look at the wound, turned quickly and fired the Springfield twice in the direction of the shots. It was blind shooting, useless shooting, painful shooting, and he stopped himself before pulling the trigger a third time, finally realizing that it was the last cartridge he had in this Springfield. The second, the one he'd used to kill Tolliver, was up in the weeds with three rounds left in it, but he had to get there first.

The tree sheltering him was one of the closest to the road. He pushed deep into the roots, and the absence of gunfire told him that the tree screened him for now, and whoever was taking those shots knew better than to waste bullets.

He looked into the reeds and found Davey McGrath, hunkered in the ditch with his right leg bent sideways, a painfully bright and clean bone showing amid all the red. The Springfield had been built to do damage, and built well. It was a gory wound, to be sure, but there was no smoke in his eyes — just rage.

This was the oldest of the remaining sons. Probably twenty years old. Arlen remembered him from the night they'd come to the Cypress House. He lay on his side now with his cheek in the mud and took fast, shallow breaths and kept his eyes on Arlen. He never looked at the wounded leg.

Arlen turned and pointed the rifle at him and said, "Call out to your brothers, boy. Call out and tell them to cease fire."

He didn't answer. The shotgun was gone, down in the water that separated them. Arlen saw for the first time that he had a knife in his right hand. He was trying to hide it in the reeds.

"That knife might kill me if I get over there," Arlen said, "but this rifle will kill you without the trip. And you know what? It's not going to stop with you."

Still no answer. Just that rapid breathing and the flat eyes. Arlen glanced down and saw the blood coursing over his own chest, then shook his head.

"It bleeds bad," he said, "but not fast enough. You ain't going to outlast me. And all I want, all I've come for, is that boy you all have chained up under the dock. It's a simple thing."

He gave him another moment even though by now he knew there would be no answer, and then he let out a holler. The pain made his voice even louder than intended. It echoed through the swamp woods.

"Listen here — your brother, this boy Davey, he is alive. I'm facing him right now with a Springfield rifle in my hands and a finger on the trigger. I don't want to kill him. But if you don't start down that road, I surely will."

There was no answer but a crackle of thunder. The wound on the top of Arlen's shoulder was throbbing now, and the rifle felt heavy in his hands. This thing needed to end, and soon.

"Y'all have thirty seconds," he bellowed. "And if you don't think he's alive, I'm plenty ready to make him scream to prove it."

The wind picked up and put a tremble over the surface of the water.

"Twenty seconds," Arlen called. His dilemma was made worse by the fact that this damned boy wouldn't speak, wouldn't cry out to his brothers. They had no proof that he was alive. Arlen expected they'd need such proof to lay down their weapons, if indeed they did.

"Son," he said, looking the wounded boy in the eye and speaking low, "your father's last wish was that I let you live. I told him I'd keep it if I could. You're going to hinder that? You want your brothers to die, too?"

Davey McGrath lifted his head and spat at Arlen.

Arlen nodded. "Fair enough," he said, and then he drew Tolliver's pistol from his belt, aimed, and fired.

He'd wanted to put the bullet in the boy's thigh, same leg but higher, but it worked out even better than he'd planned. He missed by a touch, and the bullet scorched over the edge of the leg. Didn't do much damage, but it did some hurting, enough that even this tough little bastard couldn't bite down on the scream that rose. He cried out and then tried to twist as if to cover the wound with his palm. When he did it, his mangled lower leg shifted and caused even greater pain, and this time the scream was louder.

The shots came then, two guns involved this time. Arlen expected they would. Even if they didn't have an angle on him, the sound of their brother's scream would make them waste some bullets. He pushed as far down into the roots as he could and listened as bullets cracked into the tree behind him and drilled into the water in front of him, some coming far closer than he'd thought possible. They were awfully good shots.

They didn't push it long, though. Knew that they couldn't hit him, and knew a lot of useless fire wasn't going to help their brother. If anything, he stood a greater chance of being hit by a wild shot than Arlen.

"You heard him!" Arlen bellowed as more thunder rolled and

a few drops of rain began to fall. "He's still alive, and I'm still shooting. The next one I fire will be the last in his direction! Now put your weapons down and come up the center of the road. If you want Davey here alive, you do it *now!*"

This time they came. Didn't seem like they spent much time conferring on it either. When they stepped into view they had their hands lifted, no weapons in them. Arlen rose up out of the roots of the mangrove, dripping with water and mud and blood, and pointed the Springfield at them.

"Stop walking," he called. They stopped. From here they looked so much alike it was as if he had double vision. Same height, same frame, same stance. It was a bloodthirsty family, Arlen thought, but a close-knit one all the same. They'd do what was needed for their brother.

"I'm here for one reason," Arlen said. "Paul Brickhill, the boy you've got chained under the dock."

If they wondered how he knew Paul's location, they didn't show it. Neither of them spoke or moved, just waited.

"Here's what's going to happen," Arlen said. "One of you is going down to get him and bring him to me. The other is going to stand right where he is. I'll wait five minutes before I set to killing."

There was a hesitation as they looked at each other, holding some silent conference.

"Something you'd better keep in mind," Arlen said. "Paul Brickhill doesn't mean a damn thing to either of you. I expect the three of you mean plenty to each other. So ask yourself if any of this is worth dying over."

Neither answered, but the one on the left broke off and went back down the road. These were the younger brothers, Arlen knew—they'd looked no more than fifteen when they'd come up to the Cypress House. Looked like the many boys he'd worked with at Flagg Mountain, in fact.

It took the boy a long time. Too long. The wound in Arlen's shoulder was becoming more painful with every passing moment, and he was having trouble keeping the Springfield up. How in the world could eight pounds possibly feel so heavy? He shifted his gaze from the boy in the road to the one in the reeds, but neither moved. The wounded one had closed his eyes, his face drained of color. Suffering. Arlen thought about their father, floating dead back there in the swamp, and felt a sudden, savage hate. Who raised boys like this? Put guns in their hands and knives on their belts and sent them out into the world as killers? He was glad he'd dispatched with Tate. Had probably been far too late to save his sons from the life he'd set them on, but he was glad all the same.

When the boy finally reappeared, with Paul Brickhill walking at his side, Arlen almost dropped the rifle. He'd been struggling with it anyhow, but the sight of Paul took strength from him that the bullet had not. He felt his breath slide out of his lungs, and the Springfield almost went with it.

"Bring him here," Arlen said, and then he waded through the water and fought his way past the reeds, staying well clear of Davey McGrath and the knife in his hand, and up to the road.

Paul Brickhill was pale and covered with dirt. His nose had been broken and there was dried blood on his face, and he was taking halting steps, as if his legs and maybe his ribs were hurting him, but he was alive. He was alive.

Arlen said, "Paul, come here and take these handcuffs."

He shuffled past, looking at Arlen with a face caught between amazement and horror. Arlen had a sense that anyone who saw him would be horrified. Covered in mud and water and with blood flowing freely along his neck and down his chest, a rifle in his hands and a pistol tucked into his belt. Arlen kept the rifle pointed at the McGrath boys as Paul took the handcuffs. The McGraths watched with sullen hatred.

"You'll want to tend to your brother," Arlen said. "But I don't mean to leave one of you to do that and the other to follow us. Paul, you fasten that one's right hand to the other's left. That'll leave them moving well enough, but it won't make things easy on them."

He held the Springfield on them as Paul did as instructed.

"Get in the sheriff's car now," he told Paul.

Paul said, "All right," the first words he'd spoken, and then he was out of sight and it was just Arlen on the road facing the McGraths.

"Davey isn't going to die," Arlen said. "But he's bad hurt. Do what you can for him. There will be men headed this way soon. The law. They'll see to your brother, but I expect they'll have some reckoning to do with you as well."

Neither of them answered. They looked every bit as mean as the water moccasins that had sunk fangs into their father's corpse.

"You want to know who's responsible for it all," Arlen said, "you need look no farther than Solomon Wade. Your daddy thought of him as a friend, I'm sure. But he's the one who dug your daddy's grave. Remember that."

He backed up, keeping the gun on them, and fumbled the door open. Fell in beside Paul and said, "Time to drive the hell out of here, wouldn't you say?"

He put the sheriff's car into gear, backed it up, and then turned it and drove away. The McGrath brothers were paying no mind to the car, busy instead with climbing down into the ditch to find their eldest. Once he was cared for, they'd go after their father, Arlen knew. They wouldn't like what they found.

"There's blood all over this car," Paul said.

"Yes," Arlen said. "The sheriff didn't want to let me borrow it."

The rain had begun to fall now, steady but quiet, and Arlen

got the wipers going, then removed a waterlogged handkerchief and pressed it to the wound on his shoulder. Paul looked over at him.

"Owen is —"

"I know," Arlen said. "We found him. They'd hung him upside down from the roof."

Paul shuddered.

"How bad did it go?" Arlen asked. "You've taken a beating, clearly."

"Went fast, that's all. One minute it was only Tolliver out in the yard and the next they were on us." His voice was close to breaking when he said, "It's all on me, Arlen. It's on —"

"Stop," Arlen said. "There'll be no more of that. It's on Wade and these bastards who work for him. None other."

"Where's Rebecca?"

"Driving north," Arlen said. "I sent her alone. Then I came for you."

"How?" Paul said. "How did you do this?"

"Wasn't easy" was all Arlen could answer. He thought of those gray trances and the harsh whispers of dead men and the snakes coming at him through the water, and he shook his head. The idea that he was in this car now with the boy at his side was incredible. Because he'd known from the start that he was going to die out there, and yet...

He looked up then. Raised his eyes and shifted his face to the mirror. What he saw chilled even the searing pain of the bullet wound in his shoulder.

There was still smoke in his eyes.

How? He dropped back into his seat, lips parted and mind spinning. How in the hell could it still be there? He'd survived every challenge, taken every comer, was driving toward safety. The wound in his shoulder throbbed, but it wasn't a killing wound.

"What?" Paul said. "What's wrong?"

"Nothing," Arlen said. He was remembering the battlefields of France, though, remembering the Belleau Wood and what he'd discovered there. The dead couldn't save themselves. He could help those men with smoke in their eyes, but they couldn't ever help themselves.

He said, "Hey — look at me."

Paul turned to face him. He was a wreck, all right, covered with dirt and dried blood, but his eyes were clear. Nothing but deep brown. Not even a hint of those gray wisps.

"All right," Arlen said softly. "Let's keep driving, son. Let's not stop."

It was no more than a minute later that they rounded a bend and the bridge came into view and they saw the roadblock. The convertible was parked where Arlen had left it, and Tolliver's body still dangled from the trees, but another car had been pulled in sideways on the other side of the bridge, blocking any attempt at exit. It was a steel-gray Ford coupe.

55

For a moment they sat in silence and stared ahead. Arlen was squinting to see through the fractured windshield, and finally the bullet holes rang a bell in his mind and he said, "Get down, Paul. Get real low, out of sight."

The shots Arlen had taken at Tolliver had been clean and simple. He didn't want to leave Paul exposed to the same.

"Pass me that rifle," he said.

Paul handed him the Springfield. It felt good to have it in his hands again, but hard in his mind was the knowledge that he had one cartridge left. The other rifle was still in the weeds down there with the McGraths. In the moment he'd seen Paul, he'd forgotten it. All he'd wanted to do then was move, get the hell away from this place and do it fast. Now he was wishing for those extra rounds.

No one was in sight, though. The rain fell gently and pattered off the hood of the sheriff's car. Paul was crouched low, keeping his head below the dash.

"That's Solomon Wade's car," he whispered.

"Yes, it is."

"And that body in the trees, that was the sheriff."

Indeed it was. Tolliver's body was swinging more vigorously now.

Paul said, "Did you—"

"Yes," Arlen said. He was still staring at the Ford. It didn't look as if there were anyone inside. The headlights were on, pointing down at the swollen, swift-running creek, but inside there was nothing but shadow. The rain was falling harder, making visibility difficult. Arlen's left side was wet and warm. Blood.

He was feeling a touch dizzy and nauseated, the pain working at him, and when he thought of the three McGrath boys back there, with vengeance in their hearts, he knew that he didn't want to wait this game out. Wade had come down and parked his car in a way that blocked the bridge, but he didn't appear to be in it. Perhaps he'd gone ahead on foot, or maybe he'd had a boat in the creek. Maybe he'd been accompanied by someone in another car and they'd taken that one and headed back up the road. Arlen wasn't short on maybes. Just on time.

The smell of blood was heavy in the car, his own blending with Tolliver's. He wiped a hand across his mouth and then looked in the mirror again. The smoke was storm-cloud gray now, dark and dense.

"I may need your help," he said to Paul, watching the smoke waft from his own eye sockets. "I may not be able to do this alone."

"Okay. Just tell me what to do."

That was the question. And when he looked back at Paul and saw his clear eyes, he found himself shaking his head.

"No," he said. "Actually, you just sit here, all right? You sit low. Even lower than now. I don't think they know you're here. My guess is, anything happens out there, they'll drive on by you."

He hadn't been sure of this until he said the words. Now that they were out of his mouth, though, he could almost see it, was so certain that he found himself nodding slightly. If Wade thought Arlen was alone in this car, he'd drive on by and head toward McGrath's. There was nothing about a bullet-riddled car that was worth his time. Not with the situation he was trying to handle today.

"I think he'll drive on past," Arlen said, "and if he does, you let him go. You don't move, hear? If any car comes toward you, do not move."

"Arlen, what are you saying? Don't go out there and—"

"Just sit low and watch your ass," Arlen said. "Anything goes sour, use this pistol."

He passed him Tolliver's pistol. There would be at least a shot in it yet. McGrath's gun was still tucked in his belt, floating out there amid the mangroves and the snakes. If gunplay lay ahead, Arlen and Paul didn't have much left for it.

"I'm going to go move that car," Arlen said.

"What? He might be back there, Arlen. He might be just on the other—"

"Well, if he is," Arlen said, "he doesn't seem to be inclined to move the car for us. So we'll have to do it ourselves."

For a moment Arlen just sat there in silence in the pounding rain, and then he checked the mirror one last time, as if something might have magically changed. This time he didn't stare at the smoke for long.

"If Wade drives this way," he said, "you let him go, and you count to one hundred, all right? Count nice and slow. When you hit one hundred, you get behind this wheel and drive. Drive as fast as you can, and as far."

He popped open the door before Paul had a chance to answer and stepped out into the mud. The Springfield banged against his thigh as he swung the door shut, taking care not to look back inside, not to give any indication that he hadn't come this way alone. He held the rifle in his good hand and walked up to the center of the road and on toward the bridge in the rain.

Still no one was visible, and now he thought he could make out the interior of the Ford pretty well. If Wade was here, he must be out of the car and on the other side, using it for cover.

He paused when he reached Tolliver's body. For a moment he was tempted to reach out and take hold of it and try to get the dead man to speak. There was nothing to be gained, though. Tolliver would offer no more aid out of this life than he had in it. Ahead the rain pounded off the Ford, and the headlights glowed through the trees to where the creek continued to rise on its banks.

His right foot came down on the first plank of the bridge with a hollow clapping sound. He paused again and now he swung the rifle up and pointed it at the Ford. What he wouldn't give for a boxful of cartridges. He'd pound shots through that car until it was more holes than metal, shred Wade if he was back there waiting. But he had just the one round left.

He crossed the bridge with the Springfield up, doing his best to support most of its weight with his right arm because his left was no longer working particularly well. There seemed to be a numbness spreading down from the shoulder. The Ford was no more than twenty feet away, and now Arlen was certain there was no one inside. He could see through the windows to the trees on the other side. He could also see his own reflection back here in the shadows—a skeleton with a rifle in hand.

He stopped while he was still on the bridge, ten paces from the car. He'd studied the shadows underneath, searching for signs of a man hidden there, and couldn't see any. Now he steadied the rifle as much as he could and called out, "Wade? It's done. Let us pass."

For a long moment he could hear nothing but the rain. He

thought, *Maybe he's actually gone, maybe it's as simple as pushing that car to the side of the road,* and then the shot came.

There was no time for recognition or understanding—the bullet entered his back and blew through his chest and drove him forward. He pulled the trigger on the Springfield as he fell, an instinctive move, and his final bullet merely blew out the window of the Ford, taking Arlen's skeleton image with it. Then the rifle was out of his hands and he was down on the boards of the bridge.

He tried to move, tried to hide, just as any animal in its last moments will. He made it as far as the rail on the north side, thinking he could slip off the bridge and into the creek, and then he knew it was hopeless and he stopped moving and turned back to see Solomon Wade standing before him.

Under the bridge, he thought. *He hid under the bridge, but on the opposite side of his car. Just where he should have been. Just where you should have thought to look.*

It didn't matter now. Arlen's blood was running freely across the boards, and Wade was walking toward him with a pistol in his hand. He wore that white Panama hat, rain shedding off its brim. He smiled when his eyes met Arlen's.

"You liked that trick with my sheriff, did you?" he said. "Hanging him up to greet me. You'll wish you hadn't done that."

Arlen didn't answer. The pain was radiant right now, and his blood looked very bright on the worn planks of the bridge.

"Don't you go so easy," Wade said. "Wanted to drop you, not kill you easy. You're going to beg me for another shot. Beg."

Wade had never so much as turned to glance back at the sheriff's car. The last lobe of Arlen's numb brain that retained capacity for thought registered that and whispered, *Good. He doesn't know. He'll drive right past Paul without a look.*

Wade stepped over Arlen and picked up the Springfield. He

hefted it, gave it one curious glance, and then tossed it over the bridge and into the creek.

"Your mistake," he said, "was in doubting my reach. You're not the first man to have schemed against Solomon Wade. Won't be the last, I'm certain. But you know what? I'm still standing now, and you're down there choking on your own blood. That's how it goes. That's always how it will go."

Wade shoved his pistol into his coat pocket and then withdrew a knife. It had a six-inch blade with a hook at the end, the sort you used for gutting deer. When Arlen saw it, he closed his eyes.

Picture Paul, he told himself, *picture him driving fast and far. Driving north. Chasing the coast as far as he can go, all the way to Maine. Rebecca's waiting there. He can find her.*

Wade knelt beside him, said, "No, no, no. You stay awake, tough boy. You stay awake for this."

You should have told Paul the town, Arlen thought sadly. *The place where she's going. Camden. You should have told him, so they could find each other.*

Wade registered the sound of the engine before Arlen did. One second he was kneeling over Arlen's body with the knife in his hand, and the next he was gone, on his feet. The sound was clear in Arlen's ears, but it had no meaning, not right away. Then he got it. A car. Coming this way, and coming fast.

No, he thought, anguished, and tried to lift his head. *No, Paul, damn it, all you had to do was wait...*

The sheriff's car barreled on toward them, the engine howling and the tires spraying mud as it neared the bridge. Solomon Wade took one step back, into the center of the bridge, cleared the pistol from his belt, and began to pull the trigger.

Arlen opened his mouth to scream, but all that came out was blood.

Wade looked entirely calm as he worked the trigger. Looked calm for his first shot, and his second, and his third, and only then, when the front wheels of the sheriff's car hit the bridge with a bang, did his face show any concern. He fired once more, and then the trigger clicked on empty, and he turned to run. The edge of the bridge, and the safety on either side of it, was three steps away.

He made two of them.

The car missed Arlen, stretched on his side beneath the rail, by maybe a foot. It might have been less. It did not miss Solomon Wade.

He was diving to his left when the hood caught him. The impact threw him into the air as the sheriff's car came to a squealing stop with its front wheels on the road and its back still on the bridge. The side of Wade's head smacked the top of the windshield and spun him sideways, and he landed on the bridge near Arlen.

The door opened and Paul ran out of the car with the pistol in his hand. He went to Arlen first, but Arlen called him off. There was blood in his mouth when he spoke, but he got the words out.

"Shoot him."

Paul turned and looked down at the man he'd just hit. Solomon Wade's neck seemed to point in two directions at once, and the side of his face was a fractured, bleeding mess.

"He's dead," Paul said.

"Shoot him," Arlen said again, and blood dripped from his lips.

Paul shot him. Once in the head. The body jolted and then was still. Paul came back to Arlen and dropped to his knees on the bridge. He looked at the wound and then pulled his shirt off and pressed it against Arlen's ribs. His face was very pale.

"You'll make it," Paul said, but his voice was shaking. "It went in below the ribs. That's good, isn't it? You'll be fine. You're going to be—"

He was talking too much and hearing too little. Arlen was trying to speak, trying so hard to get the words out, but it had become a terrible strain. Finally the boy heard him trying. He leaned closer.

"What?"

"Camden," Arlen said.

"Camden?" Paul echoed, his face registering nothing, and then he looked away from Arlen again and back down at the wound, and his lips pressed into a grimace as he began to work with his fingers. He was no longer paying any attention to Arlen, but that was fine.

He'd heard the name.

Camden.

He had heard it. Arlen was sure of that. They would find each other.

Part Five

FAYETTE COUNTY

56

Barrett was in his garage with five federal agents from Tampa, counting the hours until they moved on the Cypress House, altogether unaware of the bloody swath that had already been cut through the county, when Paul Brickhill arrived in Solomon Wade's Ford with Arlen unconscious in the backseat.

One of those narcotics agents, a tough old-timer named Miller, had been a field medic in France. He took one look at Arlen and told Barrett and the others to shut the hell up and let him focus.

They did.

He was still alive when they got him to Tampa, which surprised everyone but Miller, who was confident in his work. Last thing he'd said before they'd started along the road was "We're good. Just need blood."

It was an accurate diagnosis. The internal damage was minimal; the blood loss tremendous. It was a day before he was conscious again. In Tampa, then, in a hospital with guards outside his room.

By then they thought they had the leak figured out. It hadn't been Cooper, the man in charge of the planned bust in Corridor

County, but one of his agents, who'd taken off as soon as word of the disaster came, leaving behind a bank account that was surprisingly well stocked. The manhunt for him ended five days later, when his body turned up in a Louisiana bayou, missing its hands.

All three of the McGrath boys had been arrested at their home. They didn't put up any struggle. By the time the police got there, the oldest had his leg wrapped with blood-soaked blankets, and Tate McGrath's body, bloated with venom, was resting on the front porch.

They told Arlen all of this amid their endless questions, and he didn't care about any of it. What he cared about was missing. They asked about her hundreds of times, with techniques ranging from gentle prodding to outraged shouting, and he gave them nothing. What held him through it was one word, a word that became a talisman for him, a prayer: Camden.

It was Barrett who seemed most dubious of Arlen's account of the fight in the swamp. He never questioned it in front of the others, but once, he stood at the foot of the bed and asked if Arlen was willing to tell him the truth of what had happened out there.

Arlen looked at him for a long time and then said, "It was a mighty strange journey, Barrett. And I don't think you'd like to hear the details. Or that you'd believe them if you did."

Barrett seemed unhappy, but he nodded. "I'll give you this much," he said. "I believe they are questions that don't need answers."

"You're right about that," Arlen said, and then he asked for his reward. Barrett told him he was crazy. Arlen said he didn't believe that was the case. A lot of blood had been spilled in Corridor County because of the ineptitude of a federal police agency. Arlen could do some talking on that to the press, or he could not. He wasn't sure yet. A certain reward, a bounty, could impact his decision.

*   *   *

It was only two days later that Paul came in to tell him the incredible news. They were sending him to Pennsylvania once all this was done. To the Carnegie engineering school. Someone had arranged it as a token of gratitude. Arlen did his damnedest to act surprised.

Arlen had been ten days in the hospital when Thomas Barrett returned to Tampa with an envelope in his hand. He tossed it onto Arlen's bed.

"That was mailed to me direct. Inside another envelope. The one for me came with a note that said she'd trusted me once and saw what had come of it, but she was going to try it again. She asked that I deliver this to you unopened."

It was unopened. Arlen's throat felt tight, but he kept his eyes on Barrett.

"I should open it," Barrett said. "You know that. There's plenty of people who'd like to talk with her and are probably entitled."

"I'm sure there are."

Barrett nodded. "When you talk to her," he said, "you tell her that I'm sorry."

He turned on his heel and walked out of the room. Arlen waited until his footsteps were no longer audible, and then he opened the envelope. Inside there was nothing but a sheet of stationery with a telephone number.

Rebecca didn't answer his call. It was a boardinghouse, evidently, and the woman who took the call went wary as soon as Arlen asked for her.

"Tell her it's Arlen Wagner," he said, and something changed in the strange woman's voice, and she went away for a time, and then Rebecca was on the line. At the sound of her voice, Arlen closed his eyes.

"You're okay," she said.

"Yeah."

"It made the papers at first, but then it went away. I wanted to come back, but you'd told me not to, and so—"

"You did the right thing. You should never come back here. Barrett didn't open the envelope either. Nobody saw it but me."

He was talking low because there were people passing nearby, but no one was interested.

"Paul's safe?" she said.

"He's safe, and Solomon Wade's dead. Tolliver, too. And Tate McGrath." The weight of it was settling on him now as he put it into words for her in a way it never had when he'd explained it over and over to the police. The memory of the Springfield bucking in his arms and the feel of the mud on his face and the damp heat of the marsh and the whispers of dead men in his head...

"Will you come?" she said.

He laughed. It was all he could think to do. Then he said, "Yes. You better believe I'm on my way. Soon as they let me out of this place, I am on my way."

The smile left his face then, the first smile he'd worn in many a day, and he added, "I've got to make a stop first. Shouldn't take long, though."

"A stop where?" she said.

"A place I used to call home. There's something I've left unsettled too long. Then I'll move on. Did you make it all the way?"

"Yes," she said. "I'm in Camden."

"How is it?"

"Lonely," she said. "But when you get here, that will change."

"Seen any snow yet?"

"Not yet. But the wind's already cold. At night, it's quite cold. You have no idea how much I love the way it feels."

"I'm glad," he said. "And I'll see you soon. Just a few days. Like I said, there's just the one stop."

He and Paul left Tampa together. Arlen's legs were steady beneath him, but they didn't last long. He tired quickly, and figured he would for a time to come. Barrett drove them to the train station and shook their hands and said they were welcome in Corridor County anytime.

"It'll be different," he said. "I can promise you it will soon be a very different place."

"I'm certain it will be," Arlen said. "All the same, don't look to see me again."

Barrett nodded, tipped his fingers in a salute, and drove on.

They could take the same train as far as Nashville, and then they'd have to part ways. Paul was excited about the Carnegie school, had plenty to say. More talk than they had miles. Arlen sat back and listened to him and thought of another day and another train and at one point he had to make as if he'd fallen asleep because he didn't want to respond any longer, didn't want Paul to hear the thickness that had come up sudden and firm in his throat.

They had time to kill in Nashville between trains, Paul headed on to Pennsylvania and Arlen bound for West Virginia for the first time in almost twenty years. On to Maine, then, on to the town called Camden.

They were sitting there in the station sipping Coca-Colas when Paul turned to him and said, "I know it's always been true, Arlen."

Arlen looked at him and frowned, and Paul talked on, hurrying now, the words tripping over one another.

"What you can see," Paul said. "I believed it from the first because I trusted you, but then I didn't want to believe you anymore, I was scared to, and I didn't know what to think of the world if something like that *could* be true, and —"

Arlen said, "I know."

"But I'm so sorry. You were trying to keep me from harm, and I just —"

"Stop," Arlen said. He was watching people wave good-bye from the platform as a train departed the station, and the sight allowed a memory to slide in and bite him. A picture of the train he'd ridden to join the war, all the other boys, older boys than he, hugging their parents long and hard on the platform while he sat alone at the cold window and watched.

"Listen," he said, looking Paul in the eye, "it's mighty hard to believe in a thing you can't see with your own eyes. I've had my struggles with it. I don't fault you for a thing. And I don't know what to make of this world either, most times. Been a long while trying to figure it out. You just take the days as they come and keep your mind open, hear? That's all you have to do. All you can. Don't always try to be the smartest fella in the room, all right? Because in the end, even the smartest of us don't know much at all. If there's anything I'm sure of, it's that."

Paul nodded. They finished the Coca-Colas and then Paul's train was boarding, and they got to their feet. Arlen wanted to help him with his bags but didn't yet have the strength.

"You're going to her, aren't you?" Paul said. It was the first either of them had spoken directly of Rebecca.

"Yes," Arlen said.

Paul looked away, managed a faint smile, and said, "You tell her I said hello. Please?"

"I will. You know that. And I love her, Paul. I hope you understand that."

Paul nodded. "Yeah. Didn't make me glad at first, doesn't really now, but maybe there'll come a day ... anyhow, I know you do. I know it, and it matters."

"Good."

"You know where to find me," Paul said. "So when you land somewhere, let me know."

"You'll hear first thing," Arlen said. "And you'll come see us."

Paul nodded again, and now people were shoving past them toward the train. Paul put out his hand. Arlen ignored it, reached out and wrapped his arms around the boy's lanky frame and hugged him long and hard.

He remained on the platform long after the train was out of sight.

57

H E RETURNED TO FAYETTE COUNTY to put smoke in an old man's eyes.

He had never wanted to set foot on this soil again, never wanted to see this place again, beautiful though it was. All he wanted to do today was head north, on toward Camden, but there were duties in this life, balances to be kept, and Arlen Wagner owed a large marker in Fayette County.

So did Edwin Main.

The town looked different, almost unbelievably so, but Arlen supposed it might say the same of him if it could.

His first stop after getting off the train was at the site of his boyhood home. It wasn't there. A woman was out across the street, and she was a young woman, unlikely to remember, so Arlen walked by and inquired.

"You mean the devil house?" she said.

"Devil house?" He tried to keep his voice steady.

"That's what the children and the old women called it," she said, and she laughed. A light sound, carefree. "Man who used to live there, he was the craziest this place has ever seen, and then some. Thought he could talk to the dead."

Arlen kept his eyes away from her as he said, "What happened to the house, though?"

"Fire took it. Has to be fifteen years ago now. I was a girl."

He nodded and thanked her and told her to have a fine day. She smiled brightly, looking up at the overgrown yard where the devil house had once stood.

On into town then, his stride weakening the longer he walked. From time to time he reached under his jacket and touched the butt of the pistol in his belt.

Anything goes wrong, he thought, *and your stay here will keep you from ever seeing Camden. You'll see the bars of a jail cell for the rest of your days, or, if you're lucky, a noose.*

It had to be done, though.

The house that had once belonged to Edwin Main was now the property of another family. A young boy was playing in the yard, and when Arlen asked his name, he said Lichman, Ben Lichman, and nice to meet you. He had heard of no one named Edwin Main.

Arlen allowed that it was nice to meet him, too, and then he spent a time staring up at the house before he moved on down the road.

A man near the town square was unloading bricks from the bed of a truck, and Arlen stopped and tipped his hat and said beg pardon, but I have a question.

The man straightened, nodded, waited. It was a simple question, but Arlen was having trouble getting it out. The pistol was heavy on his belt.

"I'm looking," he said, "for a man named Edwin Main. I was hoping you could tell me where to find him. I have some business with him."

The man looked at Arlen, frowned, and said, "I can tell you where to find him, but I don't know what sort of business you'll be conducting at the graveyard."

Arlen stood in the street and stared at him. The pistol felt much lighter on his belt now.

"Edwin's passed?"

"Nine year ago at least. Horse threw him."

"A horse," Arlen echoed, and suddenly he wanted to laugh, wanted to fall down in the middle of this street where once his father's blood ran into the dust and laugh until tears streamed down his face.

"That's right. Was a powerful loss to folks around here. Edwin Main, he was the best we had."

Arlen said, "Was he, though?" and then he tipped his hat again and walked on toward the cemetery.

It wasn't hard to find Edwin Main's grave. He had the largest monument in the place, a ponderous marble slab bearing the dates of his life and the phrase "missed and loved by all." Joy Main's grave, older, smaller, sat beside it. Arlen dropped to his knees and brushed aside the grass and leaves that had gathered on the stone's face. When it was clean, he stepped back and looked at Edwin's marker and drew his pistol. He thought about putting a few rounds off its shining marble, driving some nicks into that pretty stone, but then he slid the gun back into his belt.

"Thrown by a horse," he said. Yes, there were balances to be kept, and markers owed. He'd come here to see to them, but the world, this wonderful, terrible world, had beaten him to it.

He remembered the location of his mother's stone, so it was easy enough to find his father's. They were together at the base of a hill, overgrown and untended, but there was one feature that made his father's stand out: someone had drawn a pentagram over it with charcoal.

Arlen knelt in front of it and took off his jacket and used the sleeve to wipe clean every trace of the charcoal. When it was clear again, he sat back on his heels, laid his palm flat on the stone, and said, "I think I can hear you now. If you care to be heard."

Nothing answered but the wind.

"I heard you already," Arlen said. "Down south, when Tolliver drew me in and nearly had me, I heard you. And I thank you."

He sat there for a while and looked at the stone. No words of sorrow or love marked Isaac's stay in this place. Just those dates, and too short a time between them.

That was all right, though. It wouldn't have troubled Isaac, Arlen knew that. This life was nothing but a sojourn anyhow. A temporary stay, that of a stranger in a strange land.

"Love lingers," Arlen said, and then he straightened, put his jacket back on so that it covered his pistol, and left the graveyard.

There was another northbound train today. If he hurried, he could catch it.

ACKNOWLEDGMENTS

I've utilized—and misappropriated—some history in *The Cypress House,* and I would be remiss not to point readers to two excellent accounts of the 1935 Labor Day hurricane that took such a tragic toll on the Florida Keys: Willie Drye's *Storm of the Century* and Les Standiford's *Last Train to Paradise.*

Stefanie Pintoff took time away from her own fine writing to explain the science behind the decomposition of a body in a swamp and the means of identifying such a body in 1935, and no sooner did she invest her energies than I decided to cut most of that thread from the book. To Stefanie, my thanks for your time and apologies for wasting it!

The Little, Brown team—Michael Pietsch, David Young, Heather Rizzo, Heather Fain, Geoff Shandler, Terry Adams, Tracy Williams, Nancy Wiese, Eve Rabinovits, Vanessa Kehren, Miriam Parker, Laura Keefe, Karen Landry, and many others—make it happen. Echo that for David Hale Smith and Shauyi Tai of DHS Literary.

Sabrina Callahan, also of Little, Brown, deserves special recognition for bearing the brunt of my undoubtedly annoying day-to-day existence, and for promoting my books with a passion and enthusiasm that is truly humbling.

Tom Bernardo offered insight and support and listened patiently through a lot of late nights, and even though he never lets me win at darts, his friendship is much appreciated.

The rest of the usual suspects—Christine, Ben, Ryan, Michael, Dennis, my family, and the many others who continue to provide support, answers, and patience—should hopefully know my eternal gratitude by now.

If you were gripped by THE CYPRESS HOUSE, don't miss Michael Koryta's new supernatural thriller, THE RIDGE, available to purchase in hardcover and as an eBook in September.

There is a lighthouse in Blade Ridge, Kentucky, a lighthouse that illuminates nothing but the desolate, wooded hills around it. The handiwork of a well-known local eccentric, for many years the lighthouse was a source of amusement only – until its builder is found dead at its summit and his belongings reveal a bizarre and macabre local history.

Audrey Clark is in the midst of moving her big-cat rescue centre onto land adjacent to the lighthouse. Sixty-seven tigers, lions, leopards, ocelots, and one legendary black panther are about to have new homes. Her husband, the shelter's founder, died recently and Audrey is determined to continue his legacy, despite the troubling developments that surround her new home.

For Kevin Kimble, the deputy sheriff, and Roy Darmus, a veteran newspaper reporter, the odd beacon contains disturbingly personal elements – and, for Kimble, proof that a long-held secret was somehow known to others. The death of the lighthouse builder and the strange occurrences at the big-cat shelter convince Kimble that his secret is connected to the ridge, and that a terrifying evil might be on the other side of the divide between dark and light.

THE RIDGE is without question Michael Koryta's fastest, scariest, and most deeply compelling novel yet. Turn the page to read the first chapter now.

ZELLER'S HILL LANE CAME into Blade Ridge at a harsh angle and began to climb immediately. Roy made the turn, some loose gravel sliding under the tires, and heard the pitch of the Pilot's engine turn harsh as it strained up the incline. For about half a mile it was like driving through a tunnel because the trees hung so dense and so close to the road. Then it broke to a crest, and there were a few gaps that allowed you to see between the mountains and out to the Marshall River and an ancient railroad trestle.

There was a long fence protecting the lighthouse property from the road. The gate was padlocked; Wyatt French didn't care for visitors. Built at the base of the lighthouse was a structure that looked no bigger than an average shed. It was there that the old man lived.

Roy pulled the Pilot off the road and onto the shoulder, nestled it up to the fence as close as he could. The weeds were tall around the gate.

"Crazy old bastard," he muttered, staring at the lighthouse. Who in their right mind would have built such a thing? French had been a carpenter for years, had built his share of houses around the area, but even so the lighthouse must have been a challenge.

Roy hit the horn, three taps.

Nothing. He gave it a minute and laid on the horn again, longer this time, figuring the blaring noise would raise old Wyatt's ire and call him forth.

It didn't, though. Roy shut the car off and climbed out into the rain. The fence was there, but fences could be climbed. Wyatt French hadn't added razor wire and guard towers to the property, though they were probably on his list.

There was not a sound except for the rain, but the light was flashing steadily against the steel-gray sky.

I'm getting scared of what I could do in the dark.

Roy wet his lips and looked back at his car, thinking that he had no business being here, thinking that he should get back behind the wheel and drive to Roman's Tavern and sit out the rest of this shitty afternoon on a bar stool.

"Just go knock on the damn door," he muttered to himself, and then he went forward. The fence was simple, six-foot chain-link, and Roy was still in decent shape, cleared it easily. There was only one door, and it was on the little housing portion built onto the side of the tower. Roy went up and knocked. Nothing.

He cupped his hands and shouted Wyatt's name. The rain was streaming down his neck and under his shirt collar to his spine. Phrases from Wyatt's letter — *Sleep with one eye open* — were dancing through his mind now, and he didn't want to try the knob, but he did and then swore at himself when it turned.

Unlocked. Shit. Why couldn't it have been locked? Why were the doors you knew you shouldn't open always the ones that were unlocked?

He pushed the door open and peered into the darkness. The living quarters seemed larger than they should have, but they still weren't much to speak of. There was a small bed in one corner, a desk beside it, some shelves, a kitchen table in the middle of the room. Refrigerator and range and sink. A bathroom blocked off by an old-fashioned accordion-style door.

"Wyatt? Mr. French? It's Roy Darmus."

By now he'd given up on getting an answer. He stepped into the room, and in the nickel-colored light of the rainy afternoon he could see that the walls were lined with maps. Topographic maps of Meade Township, the sparsely populated territory where Wyatt French had built his lighthouse. As he walked farther in, he saw that each map had a different year written on it in bold black marker: 1965, 1940, 1952, 1977…there were dozens of them.

Across the room was another door, also closed. This would lead to the lighthouse steps. Maybe this one would be locked. That would be nice. If this one was locked, he could get back into his car and drive the hell out of here.

It wasn't. Opened outward and revealed the base of the spiral stairs that curled up and away. There was a large spiderweb across the third step. Roy used his shoe to knock it aside and then began to climb, one hand on the railing.

"Wyatt?" he called. "Mr. French? People are starting to worry about you."

There were more steps than he'd have thought. He climbed for a long time, into progressive darkness, and then finally the top showed itself in a gray glare of daylight.

By then, Roy didn't need to go any farther. The smell assured him of that.

He lifted his shirt collar and dragged it over his mouth and nose, steadied himself, and climbed on anyhow. At the top step, his head finally broke the surface and he found himself staring at the light itself. The control was beside it, a simple master lever, on-and-off, nothing to it. The lever was pushed to *on.*

Electrocuted himself, Roy thought. *He was doing something to the light, trying to repair it, and he electrocuted himself.*

That thought lasted only until he pushed all the way up onto the lighthouse platform, turned his head to the right, and looked directly into Wyatt French's dead face.

He'd shot himself in the mouth, and if Roy had made a full circle around the lighthouse he would have been able to see the blood and brain tissue that had dried onto the glass. There were flies buzzing near the gaping, grotesque hole in the center of his face, and his gray hair was clotted with blood. There was a gun on his lap, one hand folded beside it.

All of this Roy saw in a half-second flash, and then he turned away, turned too fast. His feet were still on the top step, and one of them slid off and his balance was gone. He fell sideways and put out a hand to steady himself. When it landed, he heard a pop and felt immediate, scorching pain just before the blood began to flow.

He'd put his hand on one of the oversize lightbulbs. This one had been on the floor, discarded, and he'd landed on it with his palm out and his weight driving down, and that was all it took for the glass to shatter and bite.

"Son of a bitch," he said, lifting his hand free, blood dripping onto the floor and splattering his jeans.

When he'd stumbled, his shirt had fallen away from his face, and now the smell of Wyatt French's corpse enveloped him and he felt his stomach clench, and then the blood and the pain were momentarily forgotten as he turned and stumbled down the stairs, grabbing at the railing with his good hand.

Suicide note, he thought as he ran, *it was a damned suicide note. But why did he send it to me? Why in the hell did he send it to me?*

ABOUT THE AUTHOR

Michael Koryta is the author of six previous novels, including *Envy the Night,* which won the Los Angeles Times Book Prize for best mystery/thriller, and the Lincoln Perry series, which has earned nominations for the Edgar, Shamus, and Quill awards and won the Great Lakes Book Award. His work has been translated into twenty languages. A former private investigator and newspaper reporter, Koryta lives in Bloomington, Indiana, and St. Petersburg, Florida.